GILDED ROSE

THE CELESTIALS

EMMA HAMM

None of this would have been possible without the incredible support of the reading community. Thank you to EVERYONE who reached out to help make this book happen.

I adore you.

CHAPTER 1

*C*laws scraped along the stone floor overhead. Amicia squeezed her hands against her mouth, holding in her screams. The sounds dug into her tongue like needles.

The earthen scent of herbs and dirt emanated from underneath her nails. She'd been gardening, her hands buried in the ground from where she planted lettuce in the garden. Then *they* had attacked Little Marsh.

One of the creatures, perhaps more, was above her head at this very moment. The talon-like claws on its feet clicked upon the stone floor above her head. The long slithering rasp of its tail followed the footsteps as it descended the spiral stairwell into the root cellar where she hid.

Her hands shook against her mouth as the metal handle turned. Her father was a tinker. He'd created a complicated locking system that kept out thieves. But would it also keep out something as monstrous as one of the Dread?

The handle turned again, then shook, and jerked out of the door with ease. A glimpse of gray, leathery skin filled the small hole where the handle had once been.

Amicia shrank back. She pressed her spine against a wine

barrel, trying to tuck herself far into the corner. It couldn't see her if she made herself small enough. She could hide just a little longer, as her father had made her promise.

Make yourself scarce, he had whispered before leaving to help defend their home. *Stay where you are. I will find you.*

But he hadn't returned. She reached forward and yanked her worn brown skirts tight against her leg as the door opened.

She might be hidden in the darkness, but the creature was not. It stood next to one of the wall sconces with fire playing across its strong features. Red light highlighted the long length of its horns, the harsh angles of its face, and the broad muscles of its gray form. Little more than a loincloth covered its lower body, revealing more skin than she had ever seen before. It looked as though it were made of stone. Considering how difficult the soldiers claimed these creatures were to wound, perhaps they were.

The beast tilted its head back, inhaling through its flattened nose. She was certain her scent would be impossible to isolate, even for hunting hounds. Herbs hung from the ceiling of the root cellar, drying next to this season's meat. Barrels of wine and mead hid her from its view, and her scent wouldn't overpower all that.

The male, for it had to be male with shoulders like that, took a few more steps into the cellar. Grunting huffs of air chuffed from his nose, followed by the strange reverberation of a growl deep in his chest.

Had he found her? Did he know she was hiding here?

Be brave. That's what her father would have said.

Amicia glanced around one last time, hoping there was some hidden door in the root cellar she hadn't ever known about. Hoping there was something that might help her.

But all she could do was wait. No weapon rested nearby, and she was not a strong woman to begin with. She had not worked in the fields with the other peasants; she had helped her father in his endeavors, fixing locks, clocks, and any mechanical bits in the kingdom. Calluses had never settled into the fine lines of her hands, muscles had never formed in her arms. She couldn't fight one of the Dread and hope to win.

A clawed foot stomped the dirt-packed floor beside her. Another chuffing sound echoed, and its exhale brushed against her head.

It must be able to hear her heart. The stubborn organ beat hard against her ribs, trying to convince her to bolt and run as far away from this place as she could. But running wouldn't save her. It would only give the creature a better chance at catching her. Still, her heart wanted to flee this place. The fear turned her muscles to twitching fibers, ready to lunge at any moment.

She squeezed her legs closer and stared at the pool of her dark hair tangled on her knees. *Don't make a sound*, she told herself. *Don't even breathe.*

The Dread beside her gave one last huff and turned to leave. Amicia squeezed her eyes shut as the sounds retreated, her breath catching at the sight of the great, leathery wings attached to the creature's back.

The membranes stretched and flared open for a moment, the claws at the high joints brushing the ceiling and knocking a few of the herbs to the ground. Then, he started his way back up the stairs, his long tail lashing as it disappeared.

Amicia counted her heartbeats, all the way to one hundred and then back down to zero. One of the Dread had already checked this cellar; she could stay here, wait it out.

But her father was out there. Somewhere. Maybe he'd already been grabbed by one of the creatures and she would never see him again.

Tears built in her eyes, and then terrified droplets fled her body as her heart had wished to. She might never see him again, and then what would she do? He was her only family. The only person who cared if she was alive or happy. The one who had bandaged her scraped knees and listened to her rambling stories of fairies in the garden.

No, she couldn't stay here. But if she left, then she'd be out in the open, and they could grab her, drag her back to their castle, and turn her into one of their own kind. But she couldn't remain frozen in the same corner she'd hidden in as a little girl, while all the people she loved faced the monsters of their nightmares.

Amicia rolled onto her hands and knees, then crawled out of her hidden spot between barrels. Every movement sounded as though she were banging pots and pans together. *Here I am, Dread! Come and find me.*

She ground her teeth. *Be braver.* Her father hadn't raised a daughter frightened of the world. He'd raised her to think through issues, to solve problems and to fix them. Not to remain frozen in fear.

Standing, she dusted off her long skirts and righted the white apron that had twisted around her hips. She'd lost the kerchief which should have held her hair away from her face.

Amicia rubbed her hands down her arms and surveyed the root cellar for anything she might take with her. Something that would give her some kind of protection. The only thing that might work was a frying pan hanging on the side wall. Her mother's trusted pan that had cooked many a meal before she'd fallen ill.

With the frying pan securely in her hand, she felt a little better. Almost as though her mother's spirit was guiding her. The weight pulled her arm down, but that didn't matter. She could swing a frying pan and perhaps knock one creature out. At least she'd get one before they changed her into a monster.

She made her way to the spiral stone staircase, peering around the corner before stepping up. So there would be no sound, she carefully placed each step. Her soft slippers whispered against the floor, the hushed sound barely audible to her own ears.

When she reached the door leading upstairs into her home, she took a deep breath and pressed her hand against the caramel-colored wood.

"Careful now," she whispered to herself. "Quiet."

Amicia leaned into her hand, easing the door open. The small sliver revealed the room beyond had been torn apart.

The table where she and her father ate breakfast every morning was split in half and laid on its side. Chair legs were scattered across the floor, haphazardly tossed aside. The fire in the hearth was long dead, leaving the entire room gray and cold.

How long had she been hiding? The sun had already gone down, but it felt as though she had only been hiding for moments. Or perhaps forever.

Swallowing hard, she nudged the door open the rest of the way. Her home was empty and ruined. The small bed in the corner where she slept was nothing more than feathers and torn scraps of fabric. The tapestry of her mother rested in shreds beside her bed. Broken plates and cups decorated the floor like pieces of her history all smashed at her feet.

Her home was gone.

She stood in the wreckage and let her eyes drift shut. She remembered the room as it used to be. A warm, crackling fire in the corner, beside it her father working on his newest invention. The soft clinking of gears and his chuckle when something worked the way he had planned it to. The savoriness of soup on the stove and bread in the oven. No monster could take those memories from her.

Shifting her grip on the frying pan, she picked her way to the window and pulled aside a tattered curtain. The stone streets were empty and eerily silent outside her small home. No people. No laughter floating down the cobblestone steps. Just murky silence.

There were so many people in this city; the Dread couldn't have taken everyone in the span of a single day.

Could they have?

Amicia opened the door and eased out onto the narrow street, shaded by four-story buildings pressed tightly together.

She kept her back against the wall of her house for a moment. The Dread had a sound, the soft hush of wings and heartbeat of leathery pounds. She would hear them if they came for her.

The sky above her deepened in color as the night took over. Dim, silver-fletched light cast dark shadows over the laundry stretched above her head. The fabric snapped in the slight wind, the only sound that echoed through the deserted street.

Amicia stared down the labyrinthine alleyways leading into homes and saw only more pain and heartbreak. The Dread had destroyed not only people and homes, but their livelihoods as well. She climbed over a wagon that had been rendered to pieces. On the side of the street, a fruit stall had its end ripped off, the precious lemons and grapes spilling over the edge and onto the ground. Broken glass littered the street from windows and storefronts.

She didn't know where to go other than the center of Little Marsh. Surely, that was where most people would hide? The fortress at the center was for the marquis, but he wouldn't turn people away in their hour of need. Her father would be there, likely waiting for her to arrive. He'd know what to do once she found him.

Air beat above her head, the whoosh of wings making her heart stutter. Amicia stepped into a doorway, hiding herself from anything that might see her from above. She was getting close to the center of the city and found her hypothesis was correct.

Long after the Dread flew past, she kept her back pressed against the door. Sweat pooled at the base of her spine. Her clothing stuck to her, brown skirts helping her blend into the wood. She was safe, for now. But that didn't mean she would stay safe for long.

If the monsters were here, then the townsfolk were hiding within the fortress. And the beasts would tear it apart to get to her people.

Her breathing ragged, she tried to think like her father. He wouldn't risk himself in finding her, because he was too smart for that. How could she find him without revealing herself to the Dread?

She couldn't go to the fortress on the main roads. The Dread would see her, which meant she had to find another way. A hidden way.

She reached behind her and opened the door into the house. The Duchamps lived here and the door was always unlocked. Madame Duchamps sewed most of the plain clothing in the city, and her prices were affordable. Amicia had only been inside a few times, but she knew her way to the garden, where she could slip out into the back alley. These alleys had covered walkways between the apartments on the second and third floors. It would be difficult for the Dread to see her.

The wet earth in the garden seeped through her soft slippers. Cold and wet, she curled her toes and kept on.

She clambered over the fence at the far end. Her skirts caught between the slats, and she yanked on them. She dropped her mother's skillet to pull with both hands.

The fabric ripped loudly.

A howl answered from somewhere else in the city. A chilling bray of hunting animals.

"Cursed thing," she whispered under her breath.

A gurgled response made her freeze. Had one of the Dread found her? Had she already foolishly ruined a chance to save her people?

She turned around to see a fallen walkway trapping a man

beneath its weight. His silver flecked beard gleamed in the thin moonlight. A curling mustache drooped to his chin. But it was his eyes she would have known anywhere. Those vivid blue eyes had rocked her to sleep every night.

"Father?" she whispered in horror.

The boards pressed against his chest, pinning him to earth that had turned to mud in his attempts to escape. Deep furrows surrounded his hips and shoulders. He must have been digging for gods know how long.

Her frozen body burst into movement. She sprinted to his side, then fell to her knees in the muck. She plunged her hand into the dirt, not caring that stones bit at her sensitive fingers.

"Father, help me," she cried out. "We can get you out. Please."

He reached for her, his hand smeared with dirt and blood. "Stop, my girl."

"No, there's a way. We can do this."

"Amicia—"

"*Please*," she cried out. The word was ragged and raw, tearing out of her chest with more emotion than she'd ever felt in her life.

She couldn't look at him without an ache spreading through her chest. His strong form was crushed, and his face so pale. She paused in her digging and then let her hands fall to her sides. She knew the look in his eyes. He'd already decided.

Amicia laced her fingers in her lap, took a deep breath, and exhaled. "What would you have me do, Father? Leave you here?"

"The city has fallen." He pulled her hand to his own, holding it so much weaker than he had in the past. Slick blood coated her palm, mixed with soil and mud. "Sacrifices must be made. In our home, there is a lever behind the bookshelf in my room. Pull it."

She hadn't ever seen a lever in his room, and she'd read every book on that bookcase. "Father?"

"Move the bookcase. You're strong enough to do that. Pull the lever and save the city from this fate."

"How? How will it save the city?"

"All I ask is that you run once it's done. Run as far as you can, through the hidden door I showed you when you were a child." He tugged her hand, forcing her to bend down so he could press his cheek against hers. "I am a selfish man, for I will not know you suffered the same fate as the rest of us. I love you, *mon ange*."

Tears filled her eyes, dripping down her cheeks to land on her father's forehead. "What are you asking me to do?"

"Save all of us from the darkest of fate, dear one."

She could not deny him this. Not now. "I love you, Father."

"And I you, my daughter."

There was nothing she could do for him. The planks were too heavy for her to lift, and she could see the blood pooling around his body, far too much blood.

Time was ticking. She could feel every second passing like a sledgehammer against her back. Hundreds of people needed her to help, and she had to weigh her father's life against theirs. The longer she stayed with him, the more people died.

A single heartbeat thudded against her ribs.

She remembered him tucking her into bed every night. He never gave her a kiss on the forehead like other parents. Instead, he reached out and touched their pointer fingers together. A tinker's promise, he called it. That they would always solve each other's problems.

Another heartbeat, this one weaker and quiet.

She used to sneak out of her bedroom when her mother was still alive, just to watch them dancing. They would twirl until her mother's skirts were nothing more than a blur and she had to press her laughter against her father's shoulder. They never knew Amicia was awake, watching them from the stairwell.

A final heartbeat, thudding against her ears like a great bang. Chiming that her time was up.

Her father, staring up at her with blood splattered on his cheek and pooling around his torso. He couldn't survive this. Even if she could lift the boards. Though they could solve any mystery together, it appeared this was the one that would best them.

She couldn't leave him here to die alone.

Black spots danced in her vision.

She was his *daughter*. He deserved more than the cold and mud.

Should she put him out of his misery? Could she...?

A rock would do it, but she wasn't strong enough to hit him just once and...

No. She couldn't do it, and that would become the greatest regret of her life. Amicia stumbled to her feet. "I'm sorry," she whimpered.

He breathed out a long, pitying sigh. "I never asked. Now *go*."

Casting one last look back to her father, Amicia ran through the streets once more.

She traced her journey back to the house through eyes blurred with tears. She hated the monsters. Every last one of them could burn in Hell for all she cared after what they had done to her city and all the people she loved.

The beating whoosh of wings in the air heralded another Dread who wanted to snatch her off the street. Amicia ducked underneath an overhang outside one of the houses, narrowly missing the clawed hands that reached for her.

Chest heaving, she stared at the Dread as it landed on hands and knees just down the street. Like the other, this one was monstrous. The creature stood, granite skin rippling, then turned to stare back at her.

Slitted yellow eyes bore into her soul. It flared its leathery wings wide and let out a low hiss as it stepped toward her on legs that were *wrong*. Its feet were elongated, creating the illusion of knees that bent backward.

Rage burned her chest. She would not be afraid of this one.

Baring her teeth, she hissed, "You must be faster than that, monster."

Amicia reached behind her, twisted the doorknob, and disappeared through the home. She didn't look to see if the inhabitants were still there. She knew this place like the back of her hand.

Their garden connected with hers. She could run through this house, out the door, over the fence, and already be inside her father's... her... her quaint home before the creature thought to fly up and over.

A great banging knocked the front door off its hinges. It fell with a crash, dust buffeting up from the ground.

Amicia's breath sawed out of her chest as she burst into movement. Ten steps and she was at the back door, frantically shoving it open and racing out through the mud. The creature, however, was stuck within the house. She heard the flipping crash of the family's wooden table and the blast of plates shattering on the floor.

Just a little farther now.

Amicia placed a hand on the fence and rolled over the top, falling onto her behind hard enough to knock the wind from her lungs. Wheezing, she got back to her feet and ran to the back door of her home.

Plunging into the darkness, she slammed the door behind her and turned the lock. That would take the creature a few minutes to figure out if the door could hold.

Amicia spun, skirts whirling in a wide arc around her, and raced up the spiral staircase to her father's room.

She ran down the hall, past her own bedroom where there were items she would love to grab. Her mother's hairbrush. Her first kit of tools that her father had given to her on her sixth birthday. Things that had become dear to her heart.

The door downstairs cracked. When wood splinters hit the ground like rain, there was less time than she'd imagined. The solid wood held, but the creature would soon render it to pieces.

"Think, Amicia," she scolded herself. Legends said the creatures could hear better than they could see. Which meant the bat-like Dread would search for her by listening. Perhaps the sound of her breathing was too light, so she would need to stay quieter than a mouse.

She slowed her thundering steps and tiptoed to her father's room. Though the banging on the door made her wish to sprint away, she knew better.

The door creaked under her hand. She winced, but pushed it open and slipped through once there was enough room. Then she turned to the beloved chamber where her father had always been.

His tinkering table was in the corner, taking up most of the space. The window above it revealed the night sky beyond. Moonlight highlighted a wooden desk that had seen better days, chipped by countless hammers and metal. A bookshelf stood beside it, filled to the brim with diagrams and books on the human body. Her father liked to learn whatever he could, even if that meant his cot was shoved in the back corner.

She hadn't known "heartbreak" wasn't just a dramatic term. It felt as though the organ was splitting in two within her. Every inhale was an agony when she didn't know if this was the moment when her father died.

Would she feel it? She had left him alone in the street, but would she *know* when he passed?

Hands shaking, she walked to the desk and scooped up her father's greatest possession. The locket had once been her mother's. The portrait within it had faded greatly in the years since her passing. Her father and herself, the two people her mother had loved more than anything else.

Amicia secured the necklace around her throat. Now, she would have them both with her forever.

Move the bookshelf, she heard her father's voice in her head. All she could wish was that she'd asked him how.

Downstairs, a crashing roar made the walls shake. The door had fallen, and the Dread had entered her home.

Amicia was running out of time. She placed her shoulder against the side of the bookshelf and shoved. The great screeching of metal feet hurt her ears, and worse, let the Dread know where she was.

"Come on," she muttered as the clacking of claws started up the stairwell. "Come on."

Finally, it shifted enough to create a gap in the stone wall. A small one, perhaps, but enough for her father to have placed a lever.

Another door hit the stone, nearer this time. Perhaps her smell was stronger there. Whatever the reason, the creature had unknowingly given her enough time to do what her father had wanted.

"Please help them," she whispered, then grasped the lever and pulled hard.

At first, nothing happened. She lost all the breath in her lungs. Had she not done it right? Had she failed her father?

Then a creaking noise that rocked through the city and filtered through the windows.

She rushed to her father's desk, clutched the edge, and stared out the glass at the braziers surrounding her home. The fires that were supposed to keep out the Dread.

The braziers, which lit Little Marsh as the beacon of the North, all fell as one. The oil that filled the great cauldrons spilled out onto the streets in rivers of fire. The fortress at the center of the city was engulfed in the distance.

Thus, the city of Little Marsh burned.

Wind blew through the window and screams rode upon it. Screams of the dying. Screeches begging for help that would not come. Wails of her people damning her for eternity.

The Dread rose in a great wave of darkness from the fortress. Hundreds of them, lifting as one into the air. She hadn't even seen them attached to the silhouette but now could see how many had been attacking her home.

So many monsters, each turning away from the fortress and instead gliding over the streets. As she watched, one dipped low and then rose, a struggling person clutched within its claws.

The flames blurred as her eyes filled with tears. The creature in her house screamed as smoke seeped into the building.

She had to run. Flee from the fires like her father had said. But how could she?

She had just destroyed her home. She had killed all those people who'd sought haven in the fortress, and her father would die alone in the street, burning to death.

"No," she whispered. "Anything but this."

There were no other endings, and her father had been right. This was the only choice to make. But her heart didn't want to acknowledge the truth. Her heart wanted to punish her hands for the blood now on them.

She curled her hands into fists, digging her nails into her palms until they sliced through flesh. Blood dripped between her fingers. The simple pain wasn't enough.

Run, her father's voice echoed in her mind. *Whatever it takes, run* mon ange.

She had to be numb. Amicia turned and sprinted through her smoke-filled house. At the door, her boots awaited for gardening, but they'd do best in the forest. She ran until she was on the streets and could dodge the burning buildings. She ran until she reached the wall, where a small door would let her out into the wilds beyond.

Her mother's door. The door where she would sneak out and run wild in the forests, before she got sick. She would always bring Amicia back a single wildflower for her hair.

Even this door would burn. Heat burned her spine, the fires chasing her even now. "I'm sorry," she whispered.

Then she slipped out into the unknown.

CHAPTER 2

"*M*aster, it is done."

The shadows on the walls stretched and warped as one of the Dread made its way up the stone stairwell leading to the top of the chateau. Hunched and misshapen, the creature tried to make itself small and unnoticeable.

The King of the Dread wondered which one it was. They all looked the same to him these days. Hundreds of people turned into monsters living in the towering rookeries behind the chateau.

This highest tower was his haven, and the only place he traveled to when he needed space to think. All their voices echoed in his head. The torment a thousand souls, each one screaming within the body of a monster they had never wanted to become.

Up here in the fresh, chilly air, he could stand above all the sounds. Their thoughts couldn't pierce through the clouds, stars, and the moon casting silvery strands of light down upon him. Here, he wasn't the King of the Dread.

Here, he wasn't a monster.

He slowly turned toward the single Dread who stood behind

him. The crumbling walls that used to surround this tower in carved arches silhouetted the beast. One of the Dread's wings hung at its side, and there was a chip in its right horn.

Each detail should have been enough for him to know which one this was. A name. Perhaps even an occupation. And yet, he remembered nothing. Not even his own.

The King let out a low grumble. "And so, the last bastion falls."

"Indeed, it has, Master."

He waited for a moment. For the release of tension in his chest telling him to conquer every city and make it bend to his ways. This was the last hope. The last kingdom to remain untouched by the Dread.

The dark desire in his chest remained unsatisfied. He never understood the desire to conquer, only knew it was part of his being. The King of the Dread was made to force the world onto its knees, and he'd done so time and time again.

Why did this one feel as though it should have been different?

He lifted a clawed hand and waved it in the air. "Good. You may go."

The Dread hesitated. It took a step forward, a dangerous move when it walked toward the largest of their kind, and the only being who could destroy it. Its broken wing slithered along the stone, the rasp making his ears ache.

The creature hissed, "The others are wondering, what is next?"

He didn't know. There were a thousand other countries he could conquer. So many more he could force onto their knees and yet... he grew weary. He'd spent so long fighting and battling, and what had it done?

Perhaps he was merely dreaming, thinking he could do something more than just fight. Perhaps he'd thought after all this was done, once Little Marsh was his, that he could rest.

"The humans have fallen," he replied with a low growl. "There will be time for decisions such as that."

"Not all the humans," the Dread replied. Moonlight caught on the chipped horn and cast a jagged shadow behind the creature. "One got away."

"One?" He huffed out a low breath, rage consuming him. "Who?"

"We don't know, Master. A woman burned the city to the ground and escaped us. The others... did not survive."

So many lives. So many people he could have added into his ranks, and a single woman had destroyed it all?

He closed his hands into fists, claws digging into his palms and slicing through leather skin. Drops of blood struck the ground like rain. He stalked toward the arches and lashed out.

His fist collided with stone that pulverized underneath the power of his strike. The bones in his hands rattled. But even granite didn't cut through his skin. Nothing but the claws of the Dread could.

The arch gave one last groan before its final support snapped. Wind whistled through the stones that plummeted toward the earth, then struck the ground with enough force to shake the chateau.

This woman was the reason his soul hadn't found its peace. She was the reason he hadn't felt the ease of tension in his chest and continued to harbor the horrid desire to hurt more and more people.

Glancing over his shoulder, he snarled, "Find her."

CHAPTER 3

*A*micia stumbled through the forest. Twigs yanked at her hair, tugging her backward like claws caught in the dark strands. She tried to go slow. Noise would only bring them to her faster, and fear convinced her they would hunt her down. But she couldn't stop the thundering of her heart or the way her muscles twitched to sprint.

The forest was far more terrifying than she imagined. Dark trunks surrounded her and she swore faces peered around their bark. Rustling leaves and breaking twigs threatened there was more in this forest than just monsters. But animals as well.

She'd only been outside the city limits a few times with her father and never close enough to touch one of the trees. He'd always said this was the land of the Dread, and she was never to go in

Now, there was nowhere else for her to go. She couldn't follow the road leading to the other cities. The Dread could *fly*. They would see her, swoop down, and pluck her off the road as easily as a hawk snagging a chicken.

Night had fallen, and somehow that made it more terrifying than before. The forest came alive at night. What little moonlight remained, served only to spear beams which made the darkness all the more deep and mysterious.

Her thoughts drifted back to her home. Back to Little Marsh and what she had done.

The screams still echoed in her head. She could hear them, the people who needed help and all she had done was destroy. Why had her father wanted her to do that? Why would he rather see the kingdom burn than the Dread capture them?

Father. He'd been so certain and she had done nothing. Was he still alive? He couldn't be, the streets had ran red with fire and blood. But she hadn't felt him go. It was like he was still here with her, in her heart.

Every fiber of her soul was tainted now. She had destroyed an entire city, saving them from becoming the Dread, but still taking their lives.

A choked sound escaped between her clenched teeth. There wasn't time for this, she told herself. She had to remain strong and keep going through this forest of tangled briars and shadows that seemed to move on their own. She couldn't bog herself down with guilt and thoughts of dying people, screaming and trapped within the fortress of Little Marsh.

Amicia tripped at the thought, falling hard on her hands and knees in the dirt. Mud oozed between her fingers and, for a second, it looked like blood in the glistening light of the moon.

"What have I done?" she whispered, sinking her hands deeper into the muck. "What did you ask me to do, Father?"

Would she ever be able to ease the torment in her soul? Would she ever be able to look anyone in the eye again once they knew she was the killer of Little Marsh?

Her city had been a haven for all of the Empire of Ember. A safe place for all those who needed to seek asylum. And now, there was nowhere else for anyone to go.

Sniffing hard, she reached up and dashed away the tears on

her face. Mud slicked across her cheeks, but maybe that would help her hide if need be.

Her father used to talk about the days when they could go out into the forest. The days when humans hunted creatures in the woods for meat.

She wracked her brain for any memories of what they had done. He said they tracked the creatures, but that wouldn't help her. Though her stomach rumbled with the desire for food, she had no tools other than a small set of lock picks in her pocket. It seemed unlikely she'd kill a deer with those.

Twigs snapped to her left, followed by a heavy thud of feet. Amicia's breath caught in her chest, and she slowly tilted her head. She couldn't see much in the shadows, but she doubted creatures existed in this forest who were large enough to make that sound.

The darkness warped between a copse of trees, at least seven feet high and with horns as thick as her forearms. The shape of a Dread.

Moving inch by inch, she flattened herself into the mud, arms bent underneath her head.

The creature lifted its head, snuffled, and then moved away. For a moment, a horn snagged on a branch above it before the beast gave a quick toss of its head and snapped the limb clear off.

She couldn't stay here. Not in the forest when they were still searching for her.

Although... it made little sense why they were still looking. Certainly, they didn't care if they only missed one person to add to their army of monsters? They should have been focusing on trying to put out the fires in the city and stealing whatever humans they could from the veritable cauldron of souls within those walls.

Instead, they had come into the forest for *her*. A single

woman. Nothing more than a mere scrap compared to all the strong men in Little Marsh.

Perhaps her father had been right. The Dread in her home had stepped into the torchlight. They might truly be averse to fire, but they weren't averse to light. The others had left when the city burned, though. That was enough to give her hope.

Amicia dashed the guilt and fear from her mind. There would be time for mourning, but that time was not now. The creatures were in the forest with her, and that made this place infinitely more frightening.

What had her father used to say?

The Dread cannot stand fire. It is their greatest weakness. If you are ever lost in the forest, or if you are ever hunted by their kind, then you need to know how to start a fire, my dear girl.

But Father, she had asked. *Won't a fire bring them to me?*

If you are in the forest, little one, then they already know where you are.

She remained flat in the mud for long heartbeats, straining her eyes to find what she would need. Dry twigs, enough kindling and logs so the fire would sustain itself for a long time. She just had to get through the night, and then she had bested them.

One night. She could get through a single night.

Amicia crawled through the mud and the slush to a small incline that led deeper into the forest. She had to get out of the wet, bog-like area and to somewhere it would hopefully be drier. Then she could gather all the materials needed for her plan.

Though her progress was slow, she crawled her way across the forest floor. Bugs bit at her skin, leaving itching welts that stung whenever she touched them. A few times she heard breaking tree limbs and had to freeze for long heartbeats before the sounds died back down.

But, by the time she found what she needed, none of the

Dread had found her. Moving quickly, she gathered armfuls of bark and broken twigs from the undergrowth. She scooped handfuls of leaves into a ring around herself and buried logs underneath the leaves. The Dread would not attack her if she had protection through the night.

Amicia had one chance at this. Everything had to be perfect.

Finally, she had set up her own personal ring of tinder that would keep her safe. As a precaution, she also gathered a small bundle of thick logs and stacked them in the center.

She bent down and set to work. Her father had taught her how to light a fire with just two sticks. All it took was friction, enough movement to cause the smallest of sparks. Then, she would catch it in the dry leaves she had found and transport it to the ring.

Easy enough.

Except when she rubbed the sticks together, nothing happened. No spark. Just the bark coming off the twigs from her movement.

Come on, she thought, pressing them together harder. *We've done this before, Amicia. Come on.*

Twigs snapped in the forest beyond. It wasn't the sound from an animal passing by. This was made by a large creature who had somehow, impossibly, found her.

Letting out a low hiss, Amicia pressed the sticks together frantically. She thought she might have a little more time than this, and yet, now they had found her. The twigs shifted, moving with a speed she hadn't known possible even as her palms grew slick with sweat.

A small plume of smoke grew from the movement. She squeaked in excitement, then dove to the small embers. Cupping them in her hands, she blew on them until the flame grew to life.

Sounds of movement grew louder and louder, but she couldn't be distracted. If she lost this tiny flame, then there would be nothing else for her. She would be captured, and the rest of her life would be spent as a winged monster.

Amicia wouldn't abide by that future. She couldn't.

Blowing hard on the fire that began to burn through the leaves to her palms, she made her way to the ring she'd set up around herself. Carefully, she placed it down and gave it one last lungful of air.

The fire burst to life. It filled the ring of twigs and leaves she'd set up with a great gust The sound seemed to echo through the forest.

The sudden flames illuminated a monstrous face.

A Dread who stood close enough it might have reached for her.

She stumbled back and landed on her bottom, hands pressed into the earth as she stared up at the creature. In response to the flames, it lifted an arm to cast a shadow across its strange eyes.

For a heartbeat, she thought it would come through the fire. It stared at her with a single-minded intent that made her think her father had been wrong. That these creatures didn't care at all if there was fire. That it would come for her as it had her entire kingdom.

The creature took a step back. Its strange, elongated legs bent, and it moved away from the light. Arm still lifted to cover its face, the beast unfurled leathery wings and burst into the air through the canopy of leaves. The fire sputtered, but remained glowing strong.

Amicia shuddered. Fear and relief made her entire body shake until she could hardly hold herself together. She felt as though she might shatter.

She'd survived. Her father had been right.

She curled her arms around her knees, drawing them tight against her chest and tried to stop shivering. She should sleep. The night was young and the fire would keep going for a little while longer, but she didn't know when it would stop. What if the creatures were just waiting for the right moment?

A cold breeze blasted by her. The flames shuddered along with a cold chill that danced down her spine. She would not get any sleep, not when the bitter winds of autumn tried their best to take away her safety.

Curling into a tighter ball, she tried to ignore the mud drying on her face and sticking her clothes to her sides. She would survive this. She had to.

Amicia stared into the forest, watching the reflection of the fire bouncing upon eyes that saw better in the dark. She didn't know if those were the eyes of the Dread watching its prey or some other animal in the forest that stalked her now.

Either way, she wouldn't sleep this night.

CHAPTER 4

*S*omething cold touched the tip of Amicia's nose. Once, twice, three times. She wanted to continue sleeping on her side and go back into happy dreams. The tiniest of brushes made her snort, then open her eyes.

The fire was nothing more than a weak smolder. Her father must not be working on a project this morning. If he had remembered the fire, then maybe he had remembered breakfast as well. Her stomach growled.

She pushed herself up onto her elbows and stared down between her hands. The ground was crystalized with frost.

The ground?

All the memories rushed back through her, striking over and over like a sledgehammer breaking through precious stone. *The Dread*. They had attacked her home; she had been the one to destroy everything, and then...

"Father," she whispered, tears welling in her eyes once more. "Father, what have I done? What did you make me do?"

She pushed herself up, stumbling onto her feet and staring at the forest now flooded with light. A faint dusting of snow-covered everything but the circle of flame as far as her eye could see. The first snow had always been her favorite; the way it danced down from the sky made her laugh with glee.

Her father used to place her on his knee when she was little and it snowed. He'd point at every single snowflake and say each one was unique. Special.

Amicia lifted a hand and caught a few of them on her palm. They melted, but they were coming down thicker and thicker. This wasn't just the first snow, but a storm that threatened to cover the entire forest in a blanket she wouldn't be able to survive.

She had to find shelter. The trees wouldn't keep her safe from the snow, but she also didn't want to leave her circle of safety just yet.

This land was foreign. Amicia hadn't even seen maps of this area before. There never had been a reason for her to leave the safety of Little Marsh. What had her father been thinking? Sending her out into the wilds on her own with no training on how to stay safe didn't seem the smartest task he'd ever given her.

But that wasn't fair. He'd wanted her to live. He'd had faith that if something like this were to happen, she would know how to take care of herself. That she would continue to survive because he and all the people of Little Marsh hadn't.

"You can't stay here forever," she muttered. "Find a way."

She decided the only way to find a shelter was to continue forward. She couldn't go back to Little Marsh. The Dread were probably still swarming the place, looking for survivors.

Which meant she had to continue through the forest. The mere thought made her knees weak. The Dread were already here, she'd seen them last night, and somehow she was certain they would attack once her fire was out.

So, she would have to take the fire with her. Amicia bent down and grabbed a large branch. She tore a small strip of fabric off the bottom of her skirts and wrapped it around the end. That would burn for longer than just a plain stick. She'd have to keep ruining her apron, but the damned thing was already mud-splattered.

She trudged through the forest, brandishing her makeshift torch high above her head. Let the Dread come to her if they dared. She would fight them as she had before. The creatures were not as nimble as she.

The snow continued to fall, blanketing the earth in a thin layer of shimmering ice. Her books kept her feet warm, and she was grateful for the socks preventing frostbite from eating her toes.

She shivered, wrapping her arms around herself. She would have given anything for a shawl. Even just a scrap of fabric to wrap around her arms and shoulders.

The pine trees grew laden with snow, their branches bowing down and touching the ground. The snow deepened. Soon, Amicia was trudging through snow halfway up to her knees.

I will endure this, the words echoed in her mind, forcing her to move forward. She could survive. She *would* survive, for what other choice did she have?

The cold bit through her clothing. Her breath fogged in front of her face, and she couldn't quite feel her fingers any longer. She tried very hard not to think about what that meant, but it wasn't good. People died very fast in the cold.

She peered through the snow and the icy storm. A hut, that's all she wanted to find. Something, anything, to give her a little shelter. She couldn't even build a fire with all the twigs and branches, wet and cold. A thin layer of ice covered everything, warmth disappearing from the world.

As if by magic, the storm stilled for a heartbeat of time. Amicia stared forward at a chateau stretching as far as her eye could see. A great monolith of a building, stunning and splendorous in sudden clarity.

This place must have once been a sight to behold. She could

hardly fathom the sheer size of it, as it seemed to go on for miles. A lake surrounded the chateau, though the waters were now frozen. Great pillars stretched up from the corners of the building, high up to the many stories. From the windows, she counted at least three levels where people might have lived.

Gold and silver gilded the entire building. Gardens stretched in a maze around the sides, and she wondered if they went all the way behind the chateau.

"What is this place?" She whispered the words, and the wind took them from her lips. Pulling them away and dashing them toward the chateau as though the castle might answer her question itself.

If someone so grand had lived near Little Marsh, wouldn't she have heard of it? Surely, the villagers would have spoken of the great lord, or prince, who lived far away in the woods.

She didn't have time to ponder what strange anomaly had brought her to this place. It was serendipity, and she was saved. The servants wouldn't turn her away from a warm fire and perhaps a few bites of bread before they sent her on her way.

The storm picked up again, but she knew where to walk now. Putting one foot in front of the other, she forced her body to continue moving. Her knees shook, wanting to collapse with the weight of exhaustion and cold. Her shoulders ached from keeping her body straight, and her heart thundered in her chest.

Amicia touched a foot to the ice and paused when the entire lake heaved a gurgle of protest. The ice was only recently frozen. Though it had been a cold fall, she still wasn't certain the lake was solid.

But, she was so *close* to warmth. She could almost feel a fire crackling at her side and her toes finding feeling once more.

There hadn't been a road to the chateau. Only the great lake circling it. The mere idea of having to trek around the entire chateau to double check was enough to make her body tremble. She couldn't manage that. It wasn't possible for her to continue on much longer. If she risked walking around the chateau, then she would find herself face down in a snowbank and that would be the end of her.

She placed her other foot on the ice and tried to disperse her weight. Amicia had once seen a man fall through a pond in Little Marsh. He'd been playing with his friends, jokingly trying to run across the not quite frozen water.

The man had fallen in four steps away from the land, but it was still too far for him to find his way back easily. He'd laid across the ice and crawled his way back once he'd pulled himself out of the frigid water.

Of course, the pond had been much smaller than the lake she now struggled to cross. If she fell through in the middle of this lake, then she wasn't getting back out. Her skirts weighed enough to drag her to the bottom.

Amicia shifted the torch lower, staring down at the ice to guess its thickness. White bubbles had lifted and frozen in place, giving the entire lake a spotted texture. She wasn't sure why the snow wasn't sticking to the surface. The white flakes blew across the ice until it resembled a mirror.

Every step felt as though it would be her last. Every time she moved, the lake seemed to as well. Amicia paused each time, exhaled long and slow, then continued forward.

It might have been hours to cross the lake, or only a few moments. However long it took, she found herself with her feet touching land.

The muscles in her legs loosened in relief, sending her down onto one knee for a moment. She pressed her fist into the cold ground. Would she ever catch her breath again? She heaved gulp after gulp of the frigid air until her lungs ached.

You made it, she thought. *Now get back on your feet and continue.*

She shoved herself to standing and shuffled forward. This

close, the chateau appeared even larger. It loomed over her like the peak of a mountain, dark and ominous.

From across the lake, it had seemed only a forgotten lord with a handful of servants might inhabit such a place. Now, staring up at the broken windows and aging pillars, Amicia wasn't so certain there would be anyone within the walls at all. Perhaps the Dread had already done their work here.

Some inner voice whispered she was in danger, and she hesitated. Shards of broken glass littered the ground, not ice. Vines and branches poked through windows where plants were growing within the walls.

No one had been in this chateau for years, it appeared. This place had long been abandoned.

The question was why? Who would leave such an opulent home to rot? Or had they?

A bitter wind blasted through her clothing, sending goosebumps across her flesh. But this time, she didn't feel the cold. Not at all. Instead, all she felt was a numbness that frightened her more than the Dread.

There was no choice. She had to go inside this forgotten chateau.

Amicia circled the building, looking for a side entrance that servants might have used. That seemed far safer than waltzing in through the front door. Although it looked abandoned, she didn't know what creatures had made this place their home.

A small door on the side of the building had been left open. Perhaps in their attempts to escape? Amicia imagined the Dread attacking a building like this. How they would have destroyed the windows, torn up the beautiful artwork within the walls of this place. They would have turned something so lovely and beautiful into nothing more than rubble.

She placed a hand on the open door. Three deep grooves marred the mahogany wood, nearly from top to bottom. Her fingers didn't even reach between the expanse of them. Whatever had made such a mark was a great beast indeed.

Her stomach twisted. She should go. She should leave this haunted place, but there was nowhere else to go.

"Strength," she muttered to herself. "What would Father say? Be strong, because there is no one else to be strong for you."

Repeating the words and hearing them in her own voice, not her father's, only made her remember just how alone she was.

Tears pricked her eyes, but she dashed them away. She had little time for emotions like this. First, she needed to find herself a safe place to rest her head.

Holding the torch higher, she stepped into the abandoned chateau.

This was the servants' quarters, and the door led into the largest kitchen she had ever seen in her life, although it had been a hollow shell for many years. The blackened remains of food littered a large table that could have seated twenty people in the center of the room. One wall was lined with so many stoves she couldn't imagine how much they might have cooked at once. The other wall was lined with pots and pans, each with a thick layer of grime.

Despite the clear neglect and age, this place was still beautiful. The table's gilded legs might have shone if she polished well enough. Each stove was carved with a story, although she was too tired to figure out what they were. A fairytale, perhaps? She couldn't hazard a guess. None of the depictions were familiar.

The kitchens were a fine place to sleep for the night. She could even check to see if there was charcoal or wood left in the stoves. But she wanted to know what this chateau was. If the floors of the *kitchen* were made of the finest marble, what did the rest look like?

Curiosity sang in her ears like the ringing of bells. Her father used to tell her stories about chateaux such as this place. He'd claimed they were a haven for tinkers. Secret doors. Hidden switches. Passages that led all throughout the castles so servants would never be seen by nobility.

She wondered if any such secrets were hidden within these walls.

She made her way through the kitchen, then pressed a hand against the door leading out. Her own curiosity was getting the better of her, but she still closed a hand on the doorknob. Anyone could live in this chateau. Even the Dread might have taken it over, although she couldn't imagine the creatures living in such a beautiful place.

Amicia turned the doorknob and opened the door. She stepped out of the servants' quarters and into a long hallway that took her breath away.

The ceiling was hand painted with scenes of knights on noble steeds, their hunting dogs racing away ahead of them after a white hart. Each painting was more detailed than the last, stretching so far down the hallway that she couldn't even see the end of the murals.

Chandeliers larger than she was tall hung from the ceiling. Delicate pieces of glass shifted in the wind coming through the broken windows, creating a clinking music that danced through the hall. On the walls, gold braziers hung just above white marble statues of the most beautiful people she'd ever seen in her life. The closest was a woman wrapped in a robe, one breast bare. Her face looked as though she had been frozen in a moment of time, for no artist could carve a face that perfect.

Holding up her torch, Amicia stepped down the hall. Her boots crunched broken glass shards everywhere she went, but she ignored the danger. Instead, she allowed her eyes to feast on the sights before her. She couldn't get enough, drunk on the artwork, the beauty, and the splendor she would likely never see again in her lifetime.

What family had lived here? Were the statues a likeness of

the people who had called this place their home? Surely not. No one was so handsome in real life.

Amicia stopped in front of a knight. His armor had been carved with such detail she could see the scratch marks from battles long before. Staring up into his cold, vacant eyes, she lifted the torch higher just so she could see more of the details.

"Who are you?" she whispered.

The carved figure was so lifelike, she would have sworn the marble eyes turned to look at her and his lips pursed as though he would answer her.

Something shattered down the hall, glass or perhaps some kind of pottery against the floor. Amicia ducked into the small alcove behind the knight.

What was it her father always said? *Where there is one Dread, there are many.*

As if in slow motion, the back of the knight shifted. A large slab of marble had propped it against the wall, holding it up for all eternity. But when she moved behind it, the statue shifted.

Amicia put her back against the stone and wedged her feet against the wall. Another shard cracked. She caught it just before it hit the ground, but also dropped her torch as well.

The fabric at the end hit the floor while the wooden handle thankfully landed on her foot. All the sounds were muffled.

Please don't be loud enough for something to hear, she thought.

Amicia remained frozen in the shadows, hidden behind the blocky form of the knight, holding it in place. Her fire flickered, then guttered out. Something approached down the hall. She knew the sound all too well, and it made her breath catch in her chest.

Strange tapping, followed by the slow slithering of a tail.

The Dread had found her. How? She had been so careful, and none of them had seen her cross the lake or she would have heard the flapping of their wings. Her footprints wouldn't be left in the snow, not with the wind covering them.

She held herself still. The Dread was nearly upon her, but this time there was another sound attached to its movement. The sound of something heavy being dragged.

Holding her breath, she shifted position and peered around the knight's shoulder. The Dread walking toward her pulled a body behind itself. A man, unconscious and limp. The creature held the man's collar and pulled him down the long hall. It didn't seem inconvenienced by the additional weight.

As she watched, time seemed to slow. The Dread pulled the man past her and she stared down into a familiar face. Remy. He'd survived Little Marsh--perhaps others had, too. A bloom of hope grew in her chest.

An unkempt beard covered his chin, and Amicia had told him many times to cut it. Remy wasn't old enough to grow a beard, even though he was a man now. He wanted people to think of him as older, so he didn't mind if his beard was patchy. At least he looked like he was trying.

The Dread stomped down the hall but did not enter the kitchens as she feared. Instead, it went through a different door on the left she hadn't noticed, then disappeared from sight with her townsman in tow.

Amicia's fingers had yet to find feeling in them. She was cold, tired, and scared out of her wits. This place was infested with the Dread. It seemed there was nowhere she could hide from them.

Her knees shook and her palms slicked with sweat. She was frozen in place, incapable of moving even the slightest. She was stuck. Where could she go when she had wandered into the den of beasts?

Her father's voice whispered in her ear, *Rational thinking, dear one. Think.*

A chateau this large must have some kind of cottage nearby where the huntsmen might have lived. That would be safer than staying in this building teeming with the very creatures who had hunted her people down.

A single woman couldn't save anyone from the clutches of hundreds of beasts. They were stronger. It didn't matter her gut told her to help. She couldn't save Remy. She shouldn't even try, else she lose her own life.

Amicia searched the hall for any of the other Dread. No one stepped forward, and the only sound was the whistling of the wind. A gust of air brushed snow onto the marble floors through the nearest broken window.

Carefully, she let the statue lean back against the wall, propped once more. She hopped down from the alcove and took one step toward the window. Though the shards of glass made it more dangerous, she could step out onto the grounds and be gone in a moment's notice.

From the door on the left, came a shout of fear.

"No!" Remy's voice echoed through the hall. "No, please don't!"

She winced. The window was so close. Her freedom was right there, and there was nothing she could do to stop Remy from whatever fate he now faced.

Don't, she warned herself. *Amicia, don't.*

But her feet turned on their own accord. She reached down and pulled off her boots. And though her toes ached with the cold, she was still silent in each step closer to the door.

The Dread were just beyond.

Amicia pressed her hand against the closed entrance. She could almost feel the panic in the room beyond where Remy continued to shout for mercy. There would only be one chance, and if they saw her...

She didn't want to think about that.

Slowly, she eased her shoulder against the door and let it swing open just enough for her to poke her head through.

Arches outlined the long hallway that led to a throne. A

second level above the arches made it look like a monastery, or perhaps a courtroom where prisoners awaited judgement. Each arch was carved out of white marble, lilies of the valley and English ivy decorating every inch. The floor was white and black checkered, seeming to draw the eye to the throne at the end of the hallway.

Amicia's eyes found *him*. The largest Dread she had ever seen, and the others were much larger than a human. But this one? This one could only be their king.

He lounged on the throne, so tall his crimson wings draped over the back and their tips folded onto the floor. His legs were as large as tree trunks, his tail coiled around an ankle and tipped with a wicked barb. The other Dread were gray skinned, but his skin was like charcoal. Twin horns rose from his head, larger than life and twisted back toward his skull. Matted dark hair hung between the horns and rested atop his arms, his hair nearly longer than hers.

She'd seen nothing like him before.

The Dread dragged Remy to the throne where it tossed him like a child dropping a doll. Remy turned onto hands and knees, begging the large Dread to release him.

"Please," he whimpered, his words echoing in the hall. "I am but a poor servant. I've done nothing. I beg you for mercy."

She'd never heard the Dread speak. And this creature was no different. When he lifted a hand, the sound of a hundred wings beat through the air.

Amicia looked up at the second level of arches. Twin walls of the Dread stepped forward to stare down at Remy. There were more than she could count, all standing at attention, their wings folded back, their gray faces grim.

There would be no mercy here. And there was no way for her to save Remy, not with so many of the Dread who would kill her on sight.

Her fingers clenched on the door. She stared at the largest of the Dread, who had his hand raised. Slowly, his fingers curled into his palm, his thumb remaining up. Then, he tilted his hand down until the clawed thumb pointed at the ground.

"What does that mean?" Remy asked, his voice frantic. "What does that mean?"

The Dread behind him stepped forward, lifted a clawed hand, and brought it down upon Remy's back. Three ragged tears sliced through Remy's shirt. Three bloody lines appeared, blood oozing from them and dripping down his back.

He let out a scream that made the hairs on her arms rise. It wasn't the scream of a man, but a monster. His voice warped from the warm tones she had known into something howling with rage.

Even from her distance, she could see his body changing. His spine arched, bulges appearing that shouldn't be there. Something moved underneath the skin of his back. Snakes underneath the long columns of back muscles, writhing with every movement. Then, two wings split open the skin of his back. They flared out of his body, even as he leaned forward and dug his now clawed hands at the floor.

Tears slid down her cheeks, and she pressed a hand to her mouth to silence her own cries. The howling rage of his voice filled the air, but that was no longer Remy. Her father had been right. They weren't trying to kill her people. They were building an army, and all they needed was to bring everyone back to this chateau to turn them into slathering beasts like the rest of them.

Amicia stepped away from the door, unable to watch what happened next. She couldn't bear to see him as anything other than the miller's boy who used to throw apples at her when she got too close to him.

Why had she thought she could save him? *She?* She was just the tinker's daughter who had gotten too close to the monsters underneath the bed.

She grabbed onto her skirts to still the shaking of her hands.

The huntsmen's cottage was her only chance at a small bit of safety. They wouldn't search there, not right under their noses. They couldn't.

In her haste to leave, Amicia didn't notice the stand with a candlestick beside it. Her hip caught the table at the right angle to rattle the candlestick.

She snagged it, stilling the sound.

All fell silent.

She would have heard a hairpin drop onto the floor, and that was somehow worse than the howls of pain from Remy who had also paused to listen.

A voice in her head whispered, *Run.*

Amicia bolted toward the kitchen even as the first call resounded from within the strange room beyond. The braying of hunting hounds chased her down the hall.

CHAPTER 5

*H*er heart thundered in her chest, and her lungs heaved for air even as her vision swam with dark spots. They were coming for her. Hunting her like nothing more than prey they could catch in their claws.

The pattering sound of her footsteps was too loud, even to her own ears. They would find her if she didn't hide. Tuck herself into another nook or cranny and hopefully find a few moments of peace. Moments to figure out how she would get out of this chateau and out into the forest once more.

Fire. If only she hadn't lost her torch.

Amicia raced into the kitchen, catching herself on the door just before she slammed into the wall. She turned and closed the door behind her. The loud click of the door handle was the pound of a nail in her coffin.

They heard the sound. The hungry growls followed, the clicks of their nails on the floor, and the soft hush of their wings beating at the air.

She spun on her heel and pressed her back against the solid wood. There was no lock. She only had a few heartbeats to save herself.

She could run out the back door and into the snow once more, but the chateau had little cover from the sky, and they would find her if she bolted. They would hunt from above as they had in her own village.

Remy... He might be with them, perhaps, and she wouldn't even be able to recognize him.

Did it mean her people were still alive? Surely not. She had burned the city to the ground like her father had requested. No one could have survived that. They must have caught him before she'd spilled the braziers and taken away their chances of turning her people into monsters.

The knot of guilt that had churned her stomach for so long now eased. She understood why her father had been so set this must happen.. Her people would have died a horrible death either way. At least with the fire, their souls had burned away, clean and pure.

She shook her head and stepped away from the door. Her father had not raised a daughter who would freeze in fear. The back door wasn't an option, but old chateaux such as this hid many secrets. Perhaps passages allowing the servants to move easier.

All she had to do was find one before the creatures found her. If she was right, then she would live a few more moments as a human. If she wasn't...

A shiver trailed down her spine like one of the Dread had run their nail down her back. If she was wrong, then life as she knew it would cease, but her body would continue on.

She ran to the wall where all the pots and pans hung, then swept her fingers over the stones. There had to be something. Some hidden latch she could pull or a button she could push to reveal the chateau's mysteries.

The pounding feet of creatures passed the door. Their claws scraped the ground as they moved, but it was the thud and slide of a wing hitting the kitchen door that made her flinch. They had passed by the servants' quarters for now, a small blessing that wouldn't last for very long.

Her shoulder hit a pan.

It swung on its hook, and each swing was a clock ticking down to her last breath until it fell and struck the stone floor.

The clang was enough to warn the Dread where she was. She froze but already knew she had limited her time even more. A call resounded through the hallway beyond, and the hunt changed directions.

The door bulged forward as something strong hit it from the other side. Amicia dropped onto her hands and knees, then crawled underneath the table below the pots and pans. She pulled herself as tight as she could, wishing there was more than just a few baskets full of rotten vegetables to hide behind.

Please. If there is anyone listening, please help me.

The door rocked forward again, this time the wood splintering. A clawed hand reached through the gap, and a yellow eye stared through the warped wood. It rotated wildly in the socket until it settled on her, their gazes locked. The eye disappeared as more of the creatures clustered around the opening.

She had only moments of control remaining over her own body, of knowing she was still herself.

Amicia shifted backward again, pushing with her heels until her back hit the wall. A small click echoed in her ear, and a tiny panel in the wall opened underneath the table.

She held her breath. Surely, this wasn't something the servants had used. It was only large enough for a child to fit through, or a small woman who was thin enough to slide through.

The time to think had already passed. Amicia jolted forward and shoved at the panel. The stone gave way beneath her hand, allowing her to push it open and slide through on her belly. She pulled herself into the narrow tunnel beyond.

She could just barely remain crouched once she slid through

the narrow opening. Stone on either side pressed against her sides and stone from above touched her head and back. But it was enough room to slither through the walls.

She kicked out with her foot behind her and touched the loose stone that had opened the panel. The rock slid back into place as the door shattered and the creatures burst into the room.

Amicia moved. A heavy net of spiderwebs filled the strange tunnel. Their gossamer threads clung to her hair, stuck to her lips and face, and tangled in the long length of skirts trailing behind her. The many legs of spiders skittered along her arms and back, angry she had so carelessly destroyed their hard work.

She choked the whimpers in her throat, swallowing whimpers until they lodged in her chest like peach pits.

Hand over hand, she dragged herself through the small tunnel in the wall until it opened into a space between rooms. The hidden area where servants might have brought food, drink, or messages between nobility who had gorged themselves on fine dining and solitude.

Amicia straightened, her bones aching as though she had aged years in just a few moments. The fear had drained from her body, leaving behind nothing but an empty husk who didn't know what to do.

Her father.

Remy.

Little Marsh.

What did she have left now? Just herself, the breath in her lungs, and the knowledge her father would never have wanted her to give up.

Keep on living, he had once told her. *When the darkness closes in on you, that is the only way you can defeat it. Continue to live in defiance of all the shadows want to take from you. Keep the light inside your chest burning.*

And so, that was all she had. All she could continue doing.

Amicia blew out a breath. The space wasn't large, but there was enough room to breathe without feeling like the stone was closing in on her. Beams crossed above her head, disappearing into the shadows and weighed down with so many cobwebs she could hardly imagine how many spiders called this place their home.

Dim, silver light filtered through small holes in the walls where the servants might have watched the nobles in the days when this chateau had been more splendorous than haunting. A few square stones were missing from their places, so she'd have to duck under them or the Dread might see her.

She brushed the cobwebs from her shoulders and moved forward. Gingerly. Each step she chose with careful precision, as she'd already made enough mistakes for the night.

Amicia reached up and brushed aside a thick blanket of web, only to find herself at a crossroads. There were three different tunnels, each leading in opposite directions.

She couldn't make her way out of the chateau now. They would search for her outside as well as within. Which meant she needed to find some kind of safe nest and give herself a few moments of peace. .

She didn't know what kind of safe place she could make with the spiders crawling through their homes, long legs scratching along the ceiling and floor. A few other skitters suggested there were rats. Amicia swallowed hard. Rats were among the few creatures she feared. The tiny beasts always found themselves in the storerooms at her father's home. She'd always refused to kill them, no matter what project her father was working on.

It doesn't matter, she told herself. *Pick a tunnel and continue on, Amicia.*

Turning right, she made her way down a hallway, identical

to the one she had just left. This place was a labyrinth, and she could find herself lost if she wasn't careful.

She caught her foot on a loose stone and nearly tumbled forward. Biting her lip against the sudden, jarring pain, she leaned against the wall. Amicia reached down to rub her toes, only to realize her hand braced against the stones was touching not just a textured rock but a pattern.

Stooping low, she stared at the small marker. It was a bunch of grapes. Crudely done, yes, but it was grapes with a small arrow pointing to the left, back down the hall from which she'd came.

Clever. The grapes must be a direction for the kitchens. Which meant she could look for another clue to see where she was going.

Wind whistled down the tunnels, ending in a low moan. The hairs on her arms rose. She could see through the faint moonlight the spiderwebs hadn't been disturbed in years. But that didn't mean she still wasn't afraid of the spirits that walked these halls.

Amicia straightened and continued down the tunnel to distract herself. She didn't know where she was going, or why she had chosen this route, but she could find out where it went. The small nugget of information would satisfy the curiosity that still sat in her chest.

Even now, she could feel the dim light of her soul glow brighter with direction and purpose.

Father's curiosity, she thought as she walked through the walls. *Mother's bravery. Auntie's dreams of the future. Uncle's kindness.* She listed all the things that made her the person she was, the things she could never forget. All the traits she had taken from her family, and thus had turned her into the woman she was.

All the things that made her stronger. Not just the lost woman in the walls.

The next four way meeting of tunnels held three new symbols. A book, a diamond ring, and a crescent moon.

Amicia pondered for a time. The book must be a marker for a library, which she would greatly enjoy seeing if the circumstances were different. But she knew if she went, she would give up. It was better to die doing something she loved, such as reading a book, than hiding in the walls like a mouse. She simply wasn't ready to die yet.

The diamond ring stumped her, although she supposed it could be a symbol for one of the nobles who had lived here. She didn't want to find a room to sleep in, for that could only end the same way as the library. They would sniff her out.

Which meant the only other option was the moon. The strangest symbol of them all.

Breathing out a low breath, she picked webs out of her hair as she traveled straight forward and followed the markers of the moon. Strangely, she came to a set of stairs.

The spiral staircase had seen better days. There were small grooves in each step where thousands of footsteps had worn the stone into a different shape. Somehow, that was the most reassuring thing she'd seen in this place yet.

This chateau was not cursed. It had once been a place for the living, a home where people had walked through these walls to serve those they worked for. This was a place she could live if the Dread hadn't destroyed the world.

Amicia reached out a hand and pressed it against the wall where it had been smoothed by thousands of hands steadying themselves. Her fingers caught on the smallest of carvings, unlike the others. *E + S.* A love letter, perhaps? Smiling, she made her way up the dark staircase.

The light faded behind her until she couldn't even see her hand where it rested. But she continued, picking her way in the blackness and focusing on her breathing.

Finally, she turned a corner, and light assaulted her eyes. She blinked against the haze of brightness, lifting a hand to shield herself from the gleaming moonlight.

She looked down at her dust and web-covered skirts, only to see a rainbow of colors cast upon the worn fabric.

"What?" she whispered, stepping into the most beautiful room she had ever seen in her life.

White marble pillars stood at attention, one after the other against the wall where they had been carved into tree trunks. Where leaves might have been, stained glass stretched toward the ceiling. Intricately placed glass shards made it look like a hundred colors decorated each individual tree.

It was a forest of glass and stone. Man made, and yet so beautiful that it rivaled nature itself.

Jaw agape, she stepped into the room and pressed her hands against her mouth. But her body wanted to gasp. Somehow, not acknowledging the artistic achievement of the room felt sacrilegious.

The room was empty. No furniture. No paintings. Nothing more than glass, stone, and the moonlight filtering through the false leaves. And yet, this room was the first she had seen that did not appear to have fallen into disrepair.

Exhaustion nearly swallowed her whole. She was so tired, her limbs aching. Perhaps, for a few moments, she could rest her head here.

Amicia made her way to the farthest corner, close to where the servants' stairs began, and curled up into a ball on the cold marble floor. Tomorrow, she would investigate this place further. Tomorrow she would find out why these creatures were in this chateau, and perhaps if they had more of her people hidden away.

Tomorrow. But no sooner.

CHAPTER 6

*T*he King of the Dread braced his hands on the remains of the table, a crack down the center long forgotten. Had he done that in one of his rages? He couldn't remember. He couldn't remember much these days.

The sound of the Dread hunting filled the halls of the chateau. Hours upon hours of the same noise. Howls, brays, the calls of animals, even though they were not.

Something in his head reminded him they weren't beasts. They weren't meant to lose their minds and thirst for the thrill of the chase, for blood on their tongues and for meat in their bellies.

Once, they hadn't been like this.

But he couldn't remember why he thought such things. Some memory in his mind was always just out of reach.

He stared down at his clawed hands. They hadn't been like that always, had they? Thoughts like this were dangerous. They could drag him down into a tunnel he would lose himself in. It would be months before he surfaced, finding his people wandering about the kingdom with no direction.

No. He wouldn't allow his mind to wander once again.

Pushing away from the table, he stared around the ruined remains of his room. There was little here for him. A bed once graced the corner. Four posts had been carved with images of the hunt, hounds chasing rabbits up each lovingly created piece. Now, the bed and its crimson sheets were little more than scraps. The rug had long been tainted by earth and dust. His clawed feet had marked even the stones.

He didn't know why that disappointed him so much. He didn't care about the state of the chateau. This place wasn't his home. It was a means to an end, that was all.

And yet, sometimes it felt as though it were more. As though he remembered it in a different light. Once golden and shining with beauty, instead of ruin and rust.

The braying of his people broke through his concentration once again. Just when his mind might have offered a tidbit of a memory, something that might give him answers for why he was the way he was. Why his people were—

Something crashed, breaking against the floor like a hundred glasses all striking the ground at once.

"Enough!" he roared. His guttural voice echoed through the halls.

The King of the Dread crashed out the door of his private quarters, thundering into the hall with animalistic screams of rage. No more sound. He couldn't suffer through any more sound.

The first of the Dread he found was a smaller creature, with thin legs and hungry eyes darting from side to side. He snatched it from the ground, holding it aloft with his hand around its throat. Shaking the creature hard, he tossed it aside.

Its head struck the wall, and the creature stopped moving. He didn't stop to see if it was still breathing. He didn't care. They were making noise and damned if he could handle it anymore. A little blood wouldn't hurt the cursed beasts. They were nearly impossible to kill.

Over and over, he stalked through the castle, shaking the creatures so hard he was certain their teeth must have rattled in their skulls. He hadn't been so brutal to his own people in a long time. He couldn't remember the last time he had wanted to tear them all limb from limb.

When he finished, he stood in the center of the Great Hall with all the marble statues staring at him. A cold wind blew through the broken windows and chilled the sweat slicking his chest. The chandeliers dripping ice above him clicked, their music not enough to calm the anger in his chest.

What was different? He had completed changing all the humans in this kingdom, other than a single one who had escaped his horde. Just one more little human, and he would be cured. His curse lifted.

But he couldn't remember what the curse even was. He felt as though he'd always been this monster. He'd always had claws and wings, always had these horns that could tear through bodies if he wished.

Was it turning the man? Surely not. He had turned a thousand men into the Dread before and felt no remorse or guilt. They would live a happier life with him, anyway. Their needs cared for. Their inner demons allowed to break free and run loose as they wished.

A flash of memory lanced through his mind with blistering pain. A pale face peering through the doorway at him as he gave the signal to turn the man into one of his own.

He didn't remember this. If a small human had found her way into the chateau, he would have known it, would have sent his creatures to hunt her even as they hunted one of the humans who had escaped the dungeons below.

But this human he hadn't recognized. He had walked through the dungeons himself, counted every human and remembered their faces before he turned them into the Dread. As he always did.

This one wasn't from the dungeons. Her heart-shaped face was one he couldn't forget. The red bow of her lips, the high cheekbones, and dark arched brows, perhaps too thick for her face. He would have remembered the tumbling chestnut curls, and the dirt smudged on her cheek.

He would have remembered.

So this was what his mind had been trying to tell him. Why his body wanted to break things and rage coursed through his veins.

The one human they were missing had come to find her brethren and perhaps release them. But she was here, and she was the one his Dread were trying to find.

A sudden burst of energy had him spinning, wings spread wide and a wicked grin on his face. He reached for the first Dread he came upon. Clawed hands speared through the fabric of its tattered shirt, and he lifted it up to his face.

A memory bloomed, another precious and rare gift. Of a place high in the towers of the chateau where he had once found solace. A forest indoors, glowing with the light of the sun.

"She's in the sanctuary," he snarled. "And she's the last one."

"Master?"

"She's in the sanctuary!" He dropped the Dread and joined the hunt himself. "Go. Now!"

CHAPTER 7

*A*micia only managed a few hours of sleep before the haunting calls of the Dread woke her. The trilling hoots and guttural howls could only mean they were still searching for her. She huddled into a ball at the corner of the room, staring at the door that led out of the beautiful, glass forest.

Wind howled outside and rattled the delicate glass panes. The storm surrounded the chateau in full force now. She couldn't imagine how much snow it had dumped upon the world, but it didn't seem to be letting up anytime soon.

The Dread could burst through at any moment, having caught her unique scent. Eventually, they would find her.

In the hazy fog of exhaustion, she wondered if there was any reason to be running. They would capture her no matter what she did. They would hunt her down, find her in a heartbeat, and then she would be just like them.

The creatures didn't appear all that... well, sad. In fact, all the creatures appeared to remember nothing of what they were. If they did, they wouldn't hunt humans down. The thought only served to create more questions in her mind, namely, what did the Dread eat?

She pushed herself up onto her feet, holding onto the wall for a bit of balance, and then took a single step to the wooden door.

Her father's voice whispered in her ear. She wasn't this kind of person. She couldn't give up this easily. Life was worth living, even if it was only for a few more days.

There were secrets here. Things she could discover to distract herself. And perhaps, she would be the only human alive to know the secrets. That was enough to keep herself awake and going.

Knowledge was the meaning of life, her father always had said. Humans were meant to discover, and that meant she needed to find answers for herself.

Who were the Dread? Why were they here of all places? What were they doing with her people?

She already had one answer. They were turning the humans into their own kind, but the answer wasn't complete. Perhaps they couldn't have children of their own, although she had yet to see a female Dread.

Questions like this were a start. She could breathe a little easier knowing she had a purpose more than running away from the monsters and waiting until the storm had passed.

Instead of taking another step toward the door, she turned back to the alcove that led back down into the hidden area where the servants had traveled. Carefully, with her back curved, she slunk back down into the realm of spiders and webs, wary of the peepholes.

The light had dimmed to complete blackness as the storm blotted out even the thin moonlight lighting the room before. Soon, she found herself in nothing more than a tomb. Sounds whispered through the walls. Only her ragged breath kept her company, and the rough walls beneath her fingertips. The tips ached with cold and were gritty with dirt.

She smoothed her hand over the first marker on the wall, the grapes, which meant there was a crossroad around her. Her eyes saw only darkness. Her heart beat faster as fear tinged her bravery.

Could the Dread see in the dark? Their eyes were strange, inhuman, yellow, and slitted like a cat's. She would never forget the way one of the creatures had stared at her through the broken door of the kitchen. There had been only hunger in its gaze, no kindness, no thought, just rage that its prey had eluded it.

Shivering, she ran her fingers over the next symbol. A small open book with an arrow leading forward.

Libraries were always a safe place to start. There might be books about the Dread, and if there was the slightest of chances, then she had to try.

They will not stop hunting you, Amicia. So you must be brave.

She put one foot in front of the other, continuing onward and forward. Just as her father would have wished.

The passage of time seemed to slow. Or perhaps speed up as she made her way through the walls of the chateau. She couldn't tell how long she shambled onward, only that her legs were tired and her back ached. The chateau had been massive from her view outside, but this felt like a long journey through a building that must eventually end.

When she reached the library, she was ready to fall over. If only she had a few hours to lay her head down and sleep. She wanted to dream of a time when she hadn't been frightened and there had been people surrounding her with love and support. Not monsters who hunted her, listening to the plaster walls as if she were a rat they needed to catch.

Finally, her fingers bumped against a loose stone. Just like the one that had opened the small hatch in the kitchens.

Now, she thought, staring down at the rock even though she could see nothing in the inky darkness. *Do it now, or you will rot in these walls forever.*

She pushed the stone in and watched as a person-sized stone shifted to the side. The light burned her eyes, but she kept them open wide. She didn't want to be caught unaware if one of the Dread was waiting for her.

When nothing growled or raced forward at her, she took a deep breath and stepped into the library.

The chateau itself had glimmered with grandeur, therefore she had assumed the library would be splendid. Something that was meant to be admired but never used. Such was not the case of the library of this haunted place.

Gothic windows made up an entire wall, their arched peaks looking as though they were taken out of a church. The storm blustered outside. Hail and snow slapped against the windows and made the view nothing more than a blanket of undulating white.

Bookcases surrounded the rest of the room. Warm wooden bookcases, lovingly crafted with no carvings or exaggerated beauty. They were nothing more than sturdy and made to last. Leather-bound books filled their shelves, but only a few feet higher than a person, so everyone could reach a book.

She had expected everything to be covered in a fine layer of dust. Or at the very least, the books to be shredded like the rest of the chateau. But this place was like stepping back in time. Everything was pristine, old perhaps, but still clean.

The smell of old parchment paper filled her nose. How long had it been since she'd smelled parchment? All the books her father had were written on vellum to preserve them longer. Parchment was rare, and only the churches had those delicate pages in their grasp.

She took a few more steps into the library, listening for any sounds other than her own. She heard nothing, not even claws scraping the floors outside the impressive mahogany door leading out into the chateau beyond.

Perhaps, for a few moments, she was safe. They might not have thought she would come here. What peasant woman would? Only the daughter of a tinker who had taught his beloved child how to read.

The desire to touch and feel the leather bindings under her fingers got the better of her. She threw caution to the wind and stepped forward to the nearest bookcase. Reverently, she drew her fingertip down the first embellished spine.

History of the Seven Kingdoms. The gold letters seemed to glimmer underneath her gentle touch. But that wasn't possible. It was simply embellished, in gold, yes, but it didn't have its own light.

Books were just books.

Moving away from the strange bookcase, she followed the shelves and read as many of the spines as she could. Most were books she had never heard of, and a large amount of them were written in a language she couldn't decipher. The few that were written in her own language seemed to be historical.

Amicia's gaze ate up whatever words she could find. All the stories that languished here were far more important than she could have guessed. One held the accountings of Little Marsh, another told a story of a neighboring kingdom's crop records. These were far too important to be in a chateau lost in the middle of the forest.

But why were they here? Her questions were piling up higher and higher.

Perhaps the most frustrating thing was no one could explain things to her. She was locked in here by herself. Somehow, she didn't think the Dread would tell her which books were the best ones to devour.

Sighing, she pulled one of the heavier books down from the

shelf. *A History of Little Marsh*. She stroked a hand over the cover and tried hard to not let the squeezing in her chest distract her.

She missed everything about her home. Every little detail, from the laundry hanging from the windows and the mouthwatering scent of pies wafting through the street to the sound of people shouting for attention from a neighbor who had been ignoring them. She missed waking her father up in the morning with fresh bread and cheese.

It had only been a couple nights, but it felt like a lifetime. And worst of all, she could never go back. She would never experience these memories again. Someday, she might even forget the beloved tiny details.

Sniffing, she carried the book over to a small desk at the wall of windows on the other side of the room. She placed it down onto the glossy surface and opened the pages with the utmost care.

The first thing was a giant sketch of her town. It was done from outside the city walls, but that was Little Marsh in all its glory. The walls with their braziers and ever-burning fires. The Light of Ember they had kept burning for hundreds of years. The words blurred.

Dashing the tears from her eyes, she then swept her dirtied skirts to the side and sat down on the cushioned stool.

Her eyes devoured the words within the book. *Little Marsh, the capital of Ember was long known for its eternal light. But perhaps first to be forgotten was its original intent. Little Marsh was first created as the watchtower for Château Doré.*

She paused. The Gilded Chateau? She'd never heard of such a place, although this must be it. The chateau was beautiful, certainly, but it had never appeared in any of the history books she'd read.

Amicia leaned forward. She licked her finger clean of dirt and smudge, then pressed it against the lines to follow the words.

Surrounded by walls no army could ever conquer, Little Marsh was the first defense against any attack. Their history books were wiped of this information when the Great Fall occurred.

Then, the book continued on to talk about Little Marsh's ability to grow crops within the walls and therefore had no need for outside farmland.

That's well and good, she thought, *but what about the Great Fall? What about Chateau Doré?*

Amicia flipped a few pages, scanning to see if there was any more information about what the author had stated. Nothing at all. Instead, there were more pages filled with details of what made Little Marsh unique.

Slumping, she closed the book and stared down at the cover. *Andre Bernard, you have been useless. Now I must find another book to explain what you were talking about.*

What was the Great Fall? It sounded like something she should have known about. Such a title wasn't given unless it had affected the kingdom remarkably. And yet, she'd never even heard the words uttered.

The author had said the information was wiped from the history books of Little Marsh. But why? Why would anyone want to take away the history of an entire kingdom?

Hope burned a hole in her chest, far worse than guilt or fear. Within these books may be a way to save her people. To change them back from the Dread and to the men and women they once were. And this hope was infinitely worse because she had to stay alive now. *For them.*

She spun around and stared at the bookcases. There had to be some more information about that in this place. Somewhere between the covers were the answers she sought; all she had to do was find the right book.

Claws scraped the ground outside.

Amicia froze for a few moments until the doorknob turned.

She bolted from her seat and ran to the other side of the room just as the door opened.

Ducking into the secret passageway, she thought to run, but there were no sounds of destruction. The Dread were always trying to destroy everything in their path when they chased her.

Heart thundering in her chest, she turned to stare back at the small opening in the wall. No eye stared back at her. No sounds of the hunt echoed through the room. Instead, there was only the quiet sound of tapping.

What was it doing?

She should run. She should slip back through the walls and not tempt fate. This was just exhaustion telling her that curiosity was worth being satisfied, even if it put her in danger.

Her mind couldn't convince her body to run. Instead, she turned back to the opening, placed a hand on the edge of the wall, and leaned around it to glimpse the creature beyond.

It stood at the back corner of the library. No, not it. *He.*

The largest of the Dread, the one who had been seated on the throne and who was to blame for losing poor Remy. He stood staring out into the storm with his back to her. He clasped his hands behind his back, a feat she hadn't thought possible considering the breadth of his leathery wings. Feet spread wide, talons digging into the stone floor with those strange legs bent at the wrong angle.

Amicia might have been more afraid if he had seemed to be searching for her, like the others. Instead, he stood there. There was something almost sad in the way his shoulders curved forward, the way he stood frozen. But his gaze remained locked on the storm that raged outside the windows.

Who was this Dread? The question popped up in her mind like a scream. She needed to know the answer to this.

He released his hands at his back and reached for the book she'd left on the table. The Dread lifted it in his hands, turned it back and forth, then smiled. The wicked points of his fangs gleamed.

When he traced a claw over the letters, she had the strangest impression he wasn't like the others. This creature could read, or at least knew these were words on a page. Which only made her wonder just how much she didn't know about them.

Were they all like him? Were they all capable of learning?

A deep growl rumbled through his chest, the sound like thunder and a reminder she shouldn't linger in the corridors where he could see her. She needed to hide again, because the creatures weren't people who needed help.

She turned deeper into the passages and fled from the monster in the library.

These were the Dread. Monsters in the middle of the night who, though they may have thoughts of their own, were still beasts hunting her. Whether the change would take the human parts away from her or not, she wanted to remain the woman she was.

Her adventure had only given her more questions.

Who were these creatures? Why were they here? She could find the answer to these questions if only she looked a little harder.

At least she had a reason to continue hiding. A reason to keep fighting.

CHAPTER 8

*A*micia tucked her newfound blanket tight around her shoulders. She'd come across the ragged fabric in the tunnels, an old cloak that had seen better days. Rats had chewed through much of it, using the bits and pieces to build their nests. But once she'd shaken the dust and droppings out, it had made a good blanket.

She'd survived another night. One more sunrise and sunset, although it was hard to tell through the raging snow outside. When had a storm ever lasted this long? They usually passed quickly. And yet, the strange chateau always seemed to be blanketed in powdery white.

As she watched the snow fall outside the windows of her now home, a rat ran across the sill. It's fat fluffy body nearly rolled to the hole in the wall. Her stomach growled and pinched in on itself, reminding her she hadn't eaten for two days now. What little water she gathered from the snow at broken windows could keep her going for a while, but not long enough to survive.

She had to find food. Something more than just snow.

Jerking the edges of the blanket underneath her armpits, she left the stained glass room and descended back into the secret passageway where she might find the kitchens once more. She'd already seen them. There was no food she could eat other than ancient smudges of rot. But she had to try.

The Dread had to eat something. The townsfolk had always claimed they devoured human flesh, ripping it from the bone, raw. If they'd changed Remy into a monster like them, and they'd once been humans themselves, would they really consume human flesh?

The Dread were not mythical creatures living off of air and fear. They had to eat something, which meant there had to be some kind of storeroom. She'd take anything, even rat meat.

She was too weak to keep up with the dastardly beasts. Her father had taught her how to make a rat trap once, but she hadn't paid attention at the time. When would she ever have needed to know how to make a trap! She'd believed she'd always have Father to get rid of vermin.

She touched a hand to the wall, steadying herself as a wave of nausea and dizziness made her sway. Perhaps she should have listened to her father a little more.

Such trinkets were her father's favorite projects. He liked to make things other people might not have found useful until they realized he was right.

She remembered watching him at his desk, glasses on his face that made his eyes overly large. Her father would glance over his shoulder and laugh at her, blinking his eyes so she would burst into laughter.

Now, her stomach rolled for something other than hunger. Her heart clenched and she desperately wanted her father.

Dashing away the tears, she continued forward. As he would have wished.

It seemed like hours she wandered through the walls of the chateau. Hours she couldn't get back because she couldn't focus on direction or time.

Her feet carried her when her mind could not, however, and soon she stood in front of a small hole from where the most wondrous of smells wafted. It was another small place for the servants to watch what was going on, although she couldn't imagine why they would spy on other servants.

Such trivial things didn't matter. She could hardly focus over the scent making both her mouth water and her stomach clench.

Meat pies, she thought. She'd know the smell anywhere because so many people in Little Marsh had made them regularly. They would be seated on windowsills throughout the city in the early morning.

Amicia pressed a hand against her belly and then peered through the small hole. She had thought to find some kind of human servant, although that felt silly to imagine. Instead, a very thin, tiny Dread bustled around the kitchen with an apron around its waist. There were pots and pans all set atop stoves that stretched across the back wall. Ovens were at full blast, and dough had been rolled out over the tables in the center of the room.

A Dread. One of the monsters that terrified her, haunted her waking nightmares, was in the middle of a rather beautiful kitchen while cooking meat pies. This wasn't the same kitchen as before. It was too golden, too clean, and there was fresh food on the table.

Most likely the kitchens she'd entered the chateau through had been the servants quarters, nothing more and nothing less. This kitchen was far more glamorous and clearly had been maintained, even though the Dread had taken over the chateau.

Amicia's mind went blank. She didn't have any idea how to process this information. They were afraid of fire, and little more than mindless beasts. The vision in front of her didn't fit the Dread she knew.

They could cook?

The Dread in the kitchen picked up a small knife and started chopping what looked like carrots. Its claws made holding the knife awkward, but it still managed to chop the carrots into even slices. Then, it swiped the knife across the table, caught the carrot pieces in its large hand, and carried them over to a boiling pot.

The creature paused in the middle of the kitchen. In her surprise, had she made some kind of sound? Or perhaps when she'd shifted closer to the wall, had her weight made it creak?

Its shoulders tensed. It closed its fist tighter, and the wings on its back spread wider.

She was caught. If the beast made any kind of sound or called for its friends, then she would need to run through the walls. And then they could hear her sprinting.

That meant whatever escape plan she had would have to be done quietly. If she took enough corners, then maybe they wouldn't be able to punch through the plaster and wallpapered walls to grasp her.

Just as tense as the creature, she held her breath and sent a prayer to whatever deity might listen to her. She needed one thing to go right. One moment when she didn't make a foolish mistake and forget all the things her father had taught her.

Instead of sounding an alarm, the creature put down the knife in its hand. It moved away from the boiling pots of water and made its way toward the back of the kitchen.

What was it doing? Perhaps there was something in the back that would help it catch her. She should sneak away, like a mouse who knew the cat had found its hiding hole. And yet, she couldn't convince her feet to move when there was so much food here just waiting for her to eat it.

The Dread picked up a small basket in the corner and made its way closer to the wall where she hid. It was out of her sight now, although maybe it was setting a trap.

A banging echoed through the secret passage, a fist striking the wall. Amicia flinched, drawing her arms closer and her body away from the small hole where she could have seen what the beast did.

She had to run. Food be damned, she could survive a few more moments without.

Light flooded through a hole in the wall from the direction she'd come. Not at head height like she would have expected, but the puncture was as close to the ground as possible. And within the hole, the Dread had placed a basket full of food.

Bread rolls, a few apples, and a steaming meat pie taunted her. She watched the coils of heat rising into the air with so much pain she almost couldn't handle it. Her stomach seemed to chew on itself and her hands shook at the possibility of something more than the dust and cobwebs that had gathered at her lips.

This had to be a trick. Hadn't the king of the beasts been in the library, tracing words with his fingertips? They weren't the mindless beasts all the townsfolk had thought them to be. That meant this one was likely laying a trap for her, just like one would trap a mouse with a bit of cheese.

Going toward the food would be dangerous. She could wait until the beast left the room, then she could sneak out and grab a few rolls…

Another wave of nausea had her gagging. Nothing would come up but a thin thread of water and bile if she let herself vomit, but she refused to allow even that to happen. She couldn't.

She moved toward the hole in the wall again, then peered through it, expecting to see the creature waiting with outstretched claws. Instead, the Dread appeared to have gone back to its work. It was back at the table, now chopping what looked like potatoes, and not even looking at the basket it had laid in the wall.

What was the creature's plan?

She had to walk by the basket to get back to the tunnels she knew. Spending another day wandering through the walls on an empty stomach, weak and exhausted, would be fatal.

Carefully, she took a few steps toward the basket. If the creature was waiting for the sound of her footsteps, then it would have to listen hard. She'd already taken off her shoes, so every movement was silent. At least to her human ears.

The savory scent of food was divine, far better than anything she'd ever inhaled before. She wanted to drop to her knees and shove the food into her mouth like an animal. She didn't think she would even chew if she was given the chance to eat this.

One more step, and the basket was within her reach. She could lean forward and grab it. If only this weren't a trap and the creature wouldn't reach through the hole and drag her out into the light where it would turn her into one of its own...

A pang of hunger doubled her over, shooting bolts of agony through her abdomen. And bread--gods, *food*--was just within reach...

She snatched a loaf out of the basket.

She danced backward, hoping to escape an attack of the creature's claws. But it never came.

The loaf of bread in her hands was warm and soft. It split apart easily in her fingers, and when she pulled the two halves away from each other, steam rose from the center. The smell was divine. Certainly this was the scent the gods would pick if they could choose one smell.

She didn't care what the creature's game was. She stuffed her mouth and stared through the hole, trying to chew quietly while knowing she couldn't stay here forever. The beast could succumb to its desires.

Or would it?

At the moment, neither option mattered. Amicia crammed her mouth full of bread and tried not to moan at the instant pleasure. It tasted like the food of gods. Warm. Soft. Mouthwatering until she nearly drooled over every rushed bite.

She checked to make sure the creature hadn't moved closer. But she was surprised to see the creature's back was to her. It continued to stir the pot of boiling soup as if it hadn't heard her snatch something to eat.

What was this game? She hadn't seen a single Dread who didn't hunt her, all humans, to change into monsters like themselves.

And yet, this one remained cooking without a care in the world. It didn't look in her direction, although she could see its head was still tilted toward the wall.

Could this be some game where the monster was trying to fatten her up before it lunged?

The Dread picked up the pot of boiling soup. Both hands on either side of the metal handles, and no covering to protect it from the heat. It brought the large container over to the table nearest to her. If there hadn't been a wall between them, she could have reached out and touched the monster's back.

"Not all of us want to be monsters." The guttural voice that rumbled out of the creature was like that of stone grinding upon stone. She'd only heard such a sound once, when a rockslide had nearly overtaken Little Marsh.

All the hairs on her arms rose in fear. Slowly, the words processed.

What could the beast mean? Of course, they didn't want to be monsters. Who would choose to be one of the Dread?

But Remy... When they'd changed him, it hadn't appeared that he'd recognized who he was. That was why she'd theorized all the Dread were mindless beasts, enslaved to the ideas and desires all the others had.

If this creature claimed otherwise... Well, her theory wasn't correct.

She pressed herself closer to the wall until she could see the entire room. The Dread was alone, unarmed other than a pot of boiling soup. Of course, the beast could also kill her without having to worry about a weapon. It could pick up boiling pots with its bare hands.

Clearing her throat, she whispered against the wall, "Can you understand me?"

"I can. It's not safe for you to wander around the chateau, *mon chat.*" It never turned around. Not once.

"I have no food," she replied.

"And I have given you food so you might not need to endanger yourself further. Tuck yourself into a small corner of the chateau and wait for them to grow bored. Then run."

She desired nothing more than to run. She would have fled from this place if she could have, but the storm raging outside made that impossible. Had this creature not seen the storm blowing snow against every window in the chateau?

"I am not so hardy as your kind," she admitted, her tone begrudging and her teeth grinding. "The snow will kill me."

"Then find another way," the creature urged.

"If there was another way, I would have found it by now."

The Dread picked up a knife and began to chop an onion on the table before it. "Leave, little human. This is not the place for you."

"Why are they hunting me?" The question blurted from between her lips before she could even give it permission to flee her body. She pressed so close to the wall that every breath squeezed her ribs against the stone. "What could be so interesting about a single loose human?"

The Dread froze in place. Its hands closed more firmly around the knife. The movement seemed involuntary.

The Dread cleared its throat. "Return later on tonight, *mon chat.* It is too dangerous to answer questions when so many are still hunting."

She wanted to push. She wanted to know what the creature

did, but something had spooked this Dread. She didn't want to linger when the nightmare of monsters arrived.

She picked up the basket of food and made her way back through the walls until she could find the small stained glass nook where she would await the darkness of night, and her answers.

CHAPTER 9

"*M*aster." The growled tones didn't speak well of the report he was about to receive. "We cannot find the woman."

"She's in the walls," he snarled. "How hard can it be to find a single woman, still within the chateau?"

"We've searched everywhere, even torn into the walls. But she slips past us every time. We're too big to fit where she hides."

"Search harder!" His shout echoed through the rafters of his private quarters. Perhaps he was being too harsh on the creature who wanted nothing more than to please him. And yet, he couldn't stop the rage that coursed through his veins.

This was a human woman. Not a human general who had studied the tactics of war and secrecy. This was just a woman, a small one who had tucked herself into some nook in his home where they could not sniff her out.

He had never been bested by another creature before. That part of his memory, although hazy, remained. The righteous indignation that someone like *her* could survive this long without his army finding her?

The Dread were the most terrifying beasts in the land. Humans trembled at the mere mention of his forces, and yet this woman had managed to not only evade him, but send a wave of uncertainty throughout the ranks.

He hunched over the remains of what might have been a desk in his chambers. His wings opened and closed, flaring rhythmically behind him. He didn't know what to do in this moment. Punish the messenger?

He curled his claws into his fists. The need for blood and screams swelled in his body, lifting his chest and opening his wings wider than ever before. He could crush this minion who cowered before him, and yet it wouldn't be a worthy fight.

The creature would die screaming. And then all this frustration and need would remain built up in him until he couldn't think. Couldn't function.

"Get out," he snarled. The King of the Dread did not admit defeat. He couldn't. "Bring in the newest of our ranks."

"As you wish, Master."

The Dread commander left the room, closing the door behind him.

For once in his life, he wanted someone to not tiptoe around him. The Dread knew they were required to do so or he would rip their throats out of their bodies. But perhaps someday he would find someone who wasn't afraid. Someone who could treat him less like a god and more like….

A man?

No that wasn't the right word. He didn't want to be human, nor did he believe he had ever been human. That wasn't the correct word, and yet there was something dancing out of his reach. Something in his mind that hovered at the brink of existence, taunting him with a memory that could change everything.

He wouldn't let the past get the better of him. He'd never remember the things hidden in his mind. The curse prevented any of such secrecy being revealed to him. Which meant spending time thinking about such things would only make him angrier.

The door cracked open and a pale gray wing inched through. "Master?"

The new recruit had learned the appropriate way to address him. The King leaned back in the ruined chair he sat upon and waved a hand, though the newest of the Dread couldn't see his gesture. "Come forward."

The Dread that stepped through the door was... scrawny to say the least. His people were strong in form and mind. They were an army that functioned without the need of a Master most of the time. They knew how to move and what he desired without him having to ask such things.

This boy had a long way to go before he would ever be like that. The wiry muscles on his form were, perhaps, satisfactory, although they were that of a man who hadn't worked in the fields just yet. Most of the ones from Little Marsh were the same as he.

They had few farmers in this kingdom. They were more likely to be artisans, or have a small garden in the back. Those who lived safely within the walls were little more than pretty baubles, or carried the others on their backs.

He heaved a great sigh and leaned his chin on a fist. "Do you know who I am?"

"The King of the Dread." The boy held his wings snapped shut so tight to his back they might suction onto his shoulder blades if he wasn't careful. "I have heard of you."

"From whom?"

"The others." The boy gestured back to the door. "They say you are the greatest of our kind."

"Our kind?" he repeated, shifting a little. His wings began to open and close behind him once more. "Rather early for you to already be claiming to be one of us."

"Am I not? Where else would I go like this?"

The boy had a point. As the King of the Dread, he had never had a moment where he could leave them. This chateau and his people were a prison and a responsibility. A deadly combination creating more resentment than he wished to admit.

Such a memory stung in his mind's eye. He'd never resented the Dread. They were his pride and joy. He knew where they came from, what had created them, and he knew their value. Why then could he remember the vague taste of disappointment? Of entrapment?

Of fear?

The King of the Dread shook himself and stood, his great height towering over the boy that had only just begun to grow into his wings. He strode toward the child and tucked a finger under his chin.

"You are one of us now," he drawled. "But you still have to prove yourself."

What he saw in the child's eye was the same as so many of the others. Hope, that his new king wasn't really a monster. Dedication, for he didn't want to enrage the beast with claws grazing his throat. And the lingering edge of sadness, at the loss of a life he hadn't chosen to lose.

"Anything, Master," the boy replied. "I wish to serve you."

Dangerous words.

The King of the Dread lowered his hand from the boy's chin and patted his shoulder. "You knew the girl once. You should know how to hunt her down, even if you don't remember why. Can you do that for me?"

The boy's wings drew even tighter, if such a thing was possible. But he nodded and replied, "Yes, Master. Anything."

CHAPTER 10

*A*micia waited until nightfall to slip back through the secret passageways toward the kitchens. She wished her father was here with her. He would have appreciated the mystery around this place. He would have gone through these servants' quarters with her, a mischievous grin on his face and a twinkle in his eye. She would have giggled even though they were supposed to be silent.

Amicia followed the grape carvings in the wall and could almost see the ghost of her father ahead. He slipped through the corridors and told her to continue forward, to find out the mystery of this place and satisfy the burning need inside her to *know*.

He'd always wanted her to do that. No matter what question she had, he let her know it was valued. A woman shouldn't be kept away from schooling, he'd always said. They were just as important as the men, and they should know the answers to their questions.

The shadows had lengthened in the corridors. Candles might have lit them from the small holes in the walls, but the chateau appeared to have fallen asleep. Barefoot still, making certain she was almost impossible to hear, Amicia made her way back to the strange kitchens.

Her father had always had a way with words. She, not at all. Amicia had always listened to the stories with rapt attention, but she had never replicated the fervor of words. Painting pictures with her voice wasn't a talent she'd ever acquired.

The story was burned in her mind as she rounded the last corner and pressed her eye to the hole. The kitchen on the other side of the wall had fallen into darkness like the rest of the chateau. No candles were lit, nor was there anyone else in the space.

The creature had told her to meet it in the kitchens, when the sun fell. So why wasn't it here?

Amicia pressed closer to the hole, peering through and hoping she hadn't been wrong. Surely, this wasn't a trap. Surely, there was someone in this god forsaken place that she could trust.

Or was it just her heart had wished to not be so lonely?

On the table where the creature had been preparing the food was a small sliver of paper. It gleamed in the moonlight, folded until the edge was sharp as a knife.

A message? Had the King of these beasts, the one who looked like a mountain, somehow caught the Dread who had given her some food? She hated to think anyone could be so cruel, and yet she was certain that creature would have punished any of his people who had not joined the hunt. Let alone one who had helped her evade them for even longer.

Glancing around, she tried to find a way to enter the formal kitchen. There didn't appear to be any hidden secret doors to this room. The servants weren't permitted to leave this place without exiting the proper way.

Strange.

She had always thought hidden corridors behind the walls

were for servants. Now, she wondered if this one was less for the servants and more for their masters.

The only way she could get into the kitchen beyond had been made by the creature itself. The hole in which it had slid the food to her was large enough to fit through. She sank onto her hands and knees, then crawled through the opening.

Plaster scraped against her skin, catching on her ragged and dirty clothes, only to crumble into white dust. She wished there was a way to save her clothes. Or at least to wash them free from the grime that covered her from head to toe.

A waste, she thought as she made her way to the table. *This used to be a decent enough dress. Perhaps not for royalty, but it would do.*

It had been her favorite dress, but complaining about that seemed rather spoiled. She was alive. That was enough.

Quiet as a mouse. She reached above her head, slid her hand over the surface, and snatched the note off the table.

Amicia didn't waste time reading it. Not yet at least. She scrambled back toward the hole in the wall and slipped back into the safety of the corridors beyond. All without a single problem nor noise.

Finally, she had found her way in the chateau without giving herself away to the hordes of Dread looking for her. All but one, at least.

Once she was back in the safety of her wall, she unraveled the note, and her lips quirked into a half smile, the first since this ordeal had started. No words graced the paper, only scribbles of symbols. Someone else might not have understood what the message was. A grape, a moon, and the symbol of a cross. But Amicia was already using these passages as if she'd been born within the chateau walls.

This wasn't a message or a note. It was directions.

Oh you are clever, aren't you?

She crumpled the paper and shoved it into the deep pocket of her frock. *An adventure then. How lovely.*

If the Dread wanted her to see something within the chateau, then so be it. The night had fallen, but she was awake and ready to find whatever it wanted her to see.

The directions took her farther into the chateau than she had tried to go thus far. Deep into the center of the building, where she had first seen the Dread change Remy. She peered through the holes in the walls, watching for moving shadows or Dread who might still hunt her.

Instead, she found the chateau had more hidden secrets and wonders than she might have imagined. She passed by a room filled to the brim with paintings. They were stacked ten, fifteen high atop each other. Some were leaned against the wall, others still hanging by a single nail.

Another room had once been a great lady's room. Immaculate brocade in great swaths of blue hung from the ceiling to bracket a bed made of gold. The four poster bed was carved with flowers and leaves so delicate the beauty of nature itself had been captured forever.

She hadn't known such splendor was still alive in this world. Still there for people to see and experience. She'd always thought… Well, she'd always thought it was gone.

On and on she went, looking at whatever rooms she could find until the precarious map led her to a stairwell once more. Except this stairwell led down.

She had seen nothing that went *down* yet. All the other stairwells had gone up into the second and third floors of the chateau, but she hadn't any reason to think there was a basement.

Or worse, a dungeon.

The hairs on her arms raised. Was this an elaborate ruse after all? Was the Dread making her travel to the dungeon on her own where they would capture her and lock her away with all the others?

Be brave, Amicia, she thought. The words bounced back at her in the small chamber between the walls. *You have to be brave.*

The adventure was in not knowing what might happen, that's what her father always said. Small adventures could be taken every day, and it didn't matter how little they were. Each time she stepped forward and did something that frightened her, she was making herself braver.

So she lifted her feet one by one and descended into the darkness of the stairs. Very quickly she had to place her hands against the wall to balance herself. She took her time, feeling out the next step so she didn't tumble down the stone stairs and break her neck.

The bottom of the stairs did not open into a dungeon where a hundred Dread awaited her. Instead, she could just make out a luminous glow where moonlight peeked through a crack in the wall. The beam of weak light hit a small portion of the wall where a torch lay beside a tinderbox.

"Oh!" Her gasp might have been a little too loud, but the possibility of a fire, of warmth, burst forth in a sound of appreciation she couldn't have held back if she tried.

Amicia bolted forward and snatched the tinderbox from the ground. This could change everything. She would have light; she would have some kind of heat. She could stay alive longer because now she had the means to make a fire. Although, she would have to be careful as the Dread would see the beacon. A risk and a reward.

Amicia turned to leave. She could make her way back up the stairs, all the way to her hidden nest surrounded by stained glass. Once there, she could build a fire that would heat her cold bones and maybe save the freezing toes on her feet. Such things were a blessing, and she should leave while there was still a chance.

But something in her said to stay. Something deep inside her breast told her to look down at the torch on the floor, lean down, and pick it up.

It was of old make. The filigree on the handle held a pattern from years ago. But there was still enough fabric at the top that it might light. She brought the end to her face and inhaled.

Still soaked in oil somehow.

Taking a deep breath, she drew one match out of the tinder-box, struck it against the side, and placed the flame against the torch. It burst with light, so bright it burned her eyes.

Amicia lifted it high above her head and illuminated the room in which the Dread had sent her. The sight beyond stole her breath. Not in beauty. Not in awe.

In fear.

She was in a tomb. Hand carved with the faces of those who had died, stretching higher than she could have reached. The faces on the walls stared down at her with clear disapproval, and their gazes burned her skin.

They didn't want her here. They didn't want some peasant woman marring their sacred place with her dirty feet, blood-stained clothes, and cobweb-covered hair. Amicia couldn't blame them for that, but their ghosts touched her with cold fingers. Shivers shook her shoulders at each impossible touch.

The cold white marble floors chilled; she was surrounded by the dead who had lived in this chateau. Her voice disappeared, sticking in her throat like a gorge trying to rise out of her belly.

She should apologize for disturbing their rest, but she couldn't when her gaze fell upon a stone sarcophagus in the center of the large tomb. Dust covered it in a fine blanket, but she could see it had been immaculately created. Meticulously carved, there was something magnetic about it. Something that drew her closer to the stone, holding her breath.

Amicia held the torch higher. The flickering light cast shadows that seemed to move more than they should. Imps made of darkness that followed her movements, each of them chattering. Wondering if she would touch it.

Would she? Would she lay her hands upon the stone that was so clearly cursed?

She circled the sarcophagus. Each side was carved with omens of death. Plague, famine, war, all the terrible things that might bring about the end of humanity. And yet the flat top was carved with something else.

Entranced, she leaned down and blew hard against the dust covering the top. Her breath stirred the dust. Sliding off the top like a blanket, it revealed carvings of a place she'd never seen before. A castle in the clouds with winged beings in flight all around it. Not the Dread, for their wings were leathery like demons. These creatures had feathered wings.

She'd never heard of such creatures. She'd never even seen something like this before.

What could it mean?

"Open it and see," a voice whispered in her ear.

Amicia flinched, ducking as if someone were about to attack her. She held a hand up to catch whatever limb might be thrown in her direction. But nothing happened.

Slowly, she dropped her hand and stood. No one stood in the crypt with her. She turned in a slow circle, searching the shadows. There was nothing but dust motes and the dead.

A chill danced over her arms, lifting the hairs. She stared down at her forearm and swore she could see the perfect imprint of an icy hand.

"Open it," the voice repeated.

"I shouldn't," Amicia whispered, her voice so low she barely heard it herself. The chills spread down her legs. "The dead should stay dead."

"But what secrets might it hold?" The cold voice wavered, as if it were struggling to speak through the veil of the living. "What answers might it provide?"

She might have argued if her breath hadn't frosted the moment it left her lips. Puffs of icy air floated in front of her. As if the ghost or spirit stood before her and she was breathing through it.

Ghosts were inevitable in a place like this. Amicia was frozen in place, fear pinning her floors to the ground as if someone had driven a spike through them. A spirit spoke to her. Impossible and yet... she could hear him.

And it was a him. The honeyed tones were familiar in a way. As if she had heard the voice her entire life.

As if she'd heard it here, in the walls of the chateau.

Warmth bubbled to life deep in her chest. She had imagined the voice, just as she had imagined her father's voice before. She knew the tones of her father.

Of course she would imagine him speaking to her now. She was tired. Dehydrated. And though she had eaten some food, it wasn't enough to keep her going. Her mind played tricks and tried to satisfy her need for someone to be with her.

Thus, she imagined the voice of her father telling her to touch the dead.

Amicia couldn't imagine there was much the corpse of a royal could answer for her, and yet the argument festered. The logical part of her wondered why she would even consider opening what was a sealed tomb.

There could be nothing more than a rotting corpse within. She'd never seen a dead body before, and the mere idea made her stomach churn.

Logically, she knew this place hadn't been inhabited by anything but the Dread for a very long time. It meant the body in the sarcophagus was no longer looking like a body. It was nothing more than a skeleton, and the grisly bits were gone.

But that somehow didn't make it any easier. The body within was still a person. They had still walked this earth, spoken with family and friends, made children and lived a life that she didn't know about. Although, her mind could wander enough to fill in the potential blanks.

The cold voice whispered in her ear again, "What if it's not a body? What if there is something far more valuable locked within the tomb?"

Her hand moved on its own accord. An icy touch lingered beneath her wrist, lifting it without her permission. But ghosts weren't real. The dead remained dead. Wasn't that what she had said?

And yet, it felt very much as though the spirits who haunted this place were picking up her arm and placing it atop the tomb. Her palm fell flat against it. The carvings dug at her palms, scraping against them as she swept her hand from the top of the sarcophagus to the bottom.

"Push," the voice whispered in her ear. "Push and see all that you desire."

I desire nothing but the truth, Amicia replied.

"Then reveal it."

She furrowed her brows, took a deep breath, and then closed her eyes. She didn't want to do this. And yet her body was pushing against the stone top. Her biceps shook with the strain, and then the stone gave way.

The thick cover shifted then fell off the sarcophagus and struck the ground with a sound that made her very bones shiver. It was too loud. The Dread would know she was here. They would come running to find the human they hunted.

Her eyes snapped open in fear only to stare down into the sarcophagus and what lay within its four walls.

It wasn't a dead body. Or at least, not one that she had ever heard of before. The body before her was perfectly preserved and handsome.

The man lay in a bed of white feathers. His face was carved from marble, a dream more than a man. Surely it was impossible to have such arched cheekbones, such a sharp jaw, and full lips, sinful on a man. Golden curls had been laid around his head, framing the angelic face that was almost painful to look at.

His broad shoulders touched either side of his tomb. His hands lay crossed on his chest. But they were not the hands of a noble. They were calloused.

He was beautiful and intense, a strange combination she didn't know how to process. Her hands shook as she reached for him. Touching his cheek felt too forward. He was a man she didn't know, and he wouldn't appreciate someone touching his cheeks. His lips were too sensual, and she wasn't certain she would survive that. But his hands... His hands were perfect to touch.

"Touch him," the ghostly voice whispered once more. "Touch him and awaken the Celestial."

"The what?" Amicia froze, holding her hand over his. "What is a Celestial?"

"You already know."

"I don't."

Weight pressed against her hand, forcing it lower and lower until she couldn't stop herself. She touched a single finger to his folded fist.

A great rumble rocked through the chateau. Amicia stumbled to the side, catching herself on the lip of the sarcophagus with both hands. Her eardrums popped following the earthquake, and she knew in that moment that something horrible had happened.

Something she couldn't stop.

"Now I've found you, little girl," the snarl echoed throughout the entire chateau, shaking through the tomb and into her soul. "Run, like the mouse you are! I am coming."

CHAPTER 11

*S*he ran through the walls, her breath heaving in her chest but never catching up. She couldn't think. The beasts were after her, and the hunt had begun once more.

Their screams echoed throughout the halls. Where once there had been hundreds, now she swore there were thousands of creatures chasing after her. Over and over, the sounds reverberated around her.

There was very little time.

If she had thought they hunted her before, now they had caught her scent. They were a wild pack of dogs, howling at the winds, knowing this time they would capture their prey.

The pads of her feet struck the floor hard. It didn't matter anymore if they knew where she was. They had already caught the scent.

She didn't know what she had done. The body in the tomb… The beauty of the man's face was seared into her memory. Touching him couldn't possibly be enough to set the beasts off like this? How would they even know?

But it wasn't the whooping calls of the Dread that made her head ache. It was the ever present roar, the sound of thunder cracking through the air and shaking the chateau's very foundation. The king had awakened, and now he wanted her blood on his claws.

Faster, Amicia. She pressed her hands against her ears, trying to block out the noises. She could make it to her secret place with the stained glass windows that cast colored shadows onto the floor and onto her hands.

No logic supported that place would be safe. She had to make it up to the highest part of the chateau, and even then, she would be trapped if they found her. And they would. These would be her last few seconds as a human.

And if they were her last, then she would experience them in whatever way she wanted. It would be a lovely death to stare up at the stained glass windows and remember what beauty looked like.

A fist broke through the plaster just above her shoulder. Shards rained down upon her back and caught in her hair. She didn't care about that, though, because claws raked through the strands, just missing her scalp as she twisted out of the way.

She ran faster, pushing her thigh muscles until she could feel them screaming. More clawed hands broke through the walls, spectral figures with gray skin and grasping hands.

Hands of demons, reaching through the walls to drag her into their personal hell.

Amicia sprinted through the walls, not caring if she hit the sides or what noise she might make. They had found her, so all she had to do was run. She had to reach the stairs. Just the stairs, and then she could hide from them.

Somehow.

One of the Dread caught her dress with a hooked claw. The sharp point dug into her bicep before she yanked it free. Blood sprayed from the wound, and the sleeve of her dress dipped down to her elbow.

Keep running, she told herself. It didn't matter that her blood soaked the fabric. That she could smell the metallic scent in the air and so could they. It didn't matter she was still human, although their claws had turned Remy into a monster.

The raucous calls that howled through the air made her blood freeze in her veins. They had scented her. They knew she was wounded.

Her world narrowed to the sound of her heart beating like a drum in her ears. The pounding echoed each step she took as she rounded the corner and caught herself against the wall where the stairs began.

She took a single moment to press a hand against the wound on her arm. Blood gushed between her fingers. The Dread had cut her down to the bone, flesh splayed open, muscle and fat sliced through like a butcher's knife. She should have felt the pain, but instead, she was numb.

Another fist pounded through the plaster across from the stairs. This one, instead of the frenzied bluster the others exhibited, stared through the hole it had made. She made eye contact with the beast who lifted its hand and pointed a claw at her.

She understood what it meant. This was the one who would take her. This was the one who would catch her, no matter how fast she tried to run.

Teeth chattering, she forced herself to break through the fear and snarl back at the beast who thought he had bested her. She wasn't giving up yet.

She turned and raced up the stairs. Faster than she'd ever traveled before, circling up and up until she burst out of the servants' quarters and into the hidden alcove of glass trees. This was a sanctuary. She could feel it in her soul. They wouldn't dare touch her here.

And yet, now that she stood in the center of the room, she understood her own folly. She would die here.

"I'm sorry, Papa," she whispered, tilting her head back to let the moonlight dance across her face in muted pastels. "I tried."

The Dread burst through the door behind her. The blood on her body summoned them, like the animals they were. She had known this from the first moment she'd stepped into the chateau.

They might read books and cook in the kitchens. Perhaps there were a few who still clung to the limited memories of their humanity. But the rest were nothing more than slavering monsters, and they would destroy her.

An arm wrapped around her waist. But instead of carrying her backward as she had expected, she was propelled forward. She let out a shriek of surprise and lifted her arms just in time to protect her face as she was flung through the glass windows and out onto the roof beyond.

She hit the ground hard enough to knock the wind from her lungs. Coughing, she rolled away from the Dread who had tackled her through the stained glass. A shard stuck in her side, digging into her ribs.

A whimper escaped her lips as she stopped in the snow. Was this what death was supposed to feel like? Cold, lonely, and so damn tiring. She'd been running and fighting for so long, and they still made her fight more?

She could hear the Dread behind her shifting. It would stand, wings spread wide and face twisted in anger. Soon, it would reach her prone form and it would grab her again. This time, maybe it would drag her back to its king. Maybe it would bring her to the throne room where she would receive the same treatment as Remy.

Poor Remy, he never stood a chance. She swallowed. *Poor Amicia. She tried and failed.*

Footsteps approached, each crunching thud in the hard-packed snow was one step closer to her demise. She kept her gaze fixed on the powder in front of her. It had once been pristine, untouched. Now, shards of glass littered its surface and blood splatter ruined the spotless white. The nearest droplets burned through the snow, still hot with life.

Her face crumpled for a single second, just long enough for her to indulge the feelings of fear. Her lips twisted, her eyes squeezed shut, and her heart skipped a beat. But then she pulled herself together. She would go to her death with bravery and nothing else.

A shadow fell over the snow. Clawed fingers became enlarged, stretching farther and farther away from her.

The shadow paused, and then a roar split through the air. The same roar that sounded like thunder, like the crack of lightning and the grumble of stone deep in the mountains.

The shadow retreated. The sound of footsteps left her side.

Were they going to let her run away? She couldn't. She was on the rooftop that was little more than a balcony without railings. Where would she go?

She used her good arm to leverage herself up in the snow, balancing on one hand while she caught her breath. She stared out into the dark night. It was clear skies, although she had thought the storm would continue. Instead, it seemed they were in the storm's eye and that she would be spared a few moments to stare out at the grounds.

The moon stared down at her, a few stars twinkling. They showed her a frozen wonderland of forgotten grounds. A magnificent garden that might have seen better days. A maze to the left, with glorious fountains sparkling, their water held suspended in time.

She was three stories up, but it was still everything she had ever wanted. Finally, she could see the beauty of this place surrounded by a lake. Finally, she could see how lovely the chateau could be.

The snow cracked behind her, not crunched like the last Dread. This time, even the roof shook under the weight of the beast who approached her.

She would not greet a king on her knees. She shifted, pulling her legs closer and then wobbling as she stood up. Her future awaited her, and yet she allowed herself to stare at the beauty of the land for just a few more moments before she turned around.

Like a demon summoned out of the pits, the King of the Dread stared at her. His wings spread at least fifteen feet around him, yet they were still folded. The leathery lengths weren't gray like all the others, but tinged with red.

The horns stretching back from his head curled as they struck up at the sky, their wicked ends sharpened into deadly points. His yellow eyes gleamed underneath a heavy brow furrowed in a snarl as he stared back at her.

She met his gaze, knowing she was less than impressive in this moment. She was covered in dirt, blood, and cobwebs. One sleeve of her dress was down at her elbow and her bare toes curled in the snow.

Blood slid down her arm, pooling between her fingers, and dripping down onto the snow. The wet plops were the only sound on the rooftop.

Some Dread were pressed against the glass behind him, watching the proceedings with wicked grins on their stone faces.

The King of the Dread took one more step forward. Aggressive, monolithic, he approached her, like a man trying to tame a wild horse, but she knew he wasn't interested in taming her.

She answered by taking a step backward. The lip of the roof was a few feet behind her, so she could afford to give him back the ground he took. And maybe it was prolonging the inevitable, but she had to fight somehow.

"I don't want to die," she said, taking another step backward. "This is not my choice."

She knew he could speak. She'd heard him talk before, although it had been a grave tone that had sounded more painful than possible. This time, the King of the Dread did not speak to her. He tilted his head and took another lumbering step forward.

"I want to stay human." Amicia couldn't let him do this without knowing she didn't want it.

He took another step forward. She took one more step back, the last one she could give him without tumbling over the edge of the roof.

She glanced over her shoulder and stared down at the ground. So far below her. She wouldn't survive a fall; there was no chance of that. Which meant she had to stop here, and he finally had her.

Could she throw herself over the edge? That would prevent him from doing what she didn't want him to do. Her father had taken his own life. Or... he'd had her do it. He'd prevented them from changing him because he'd known it was a fate worse than death.

And yet the Dread in the kitchen had been kind. It had fed her, and it hadn't told the others where she was. At least, she didn't think it had. Perhaps the tomb *had* been a trap.

She screwed up her face at the thoughts and shook her head. "I have too many questions that have yet to be answered!" Her shout fell onto the snow, limp and tired. "I want to know what is happening here. I want to know what happened to you, who that man in the tomb is, why some of you can speak and others cannot! You cannot take away my mind when there are so many questions left unanswered."

That seemed to elicit some kind of response from the monster before her. Something flickered in his gaze. A recognition, perhaps. A thought or a memory that drifted before his eyes, only to be swallowed once more by rage and hatred.

The King of the Dread lunged forward and grasped her by the throat. She held her breath, kicking her legs and holding onto the thick wrists that lifted her higher and higher into the air.

She dangled over the edge and sent a single prayer to the heavens. Whatever god was listening, please, save her.

The King drew her closer to his face. Close enough to see that his eyes weren't completely yellow. There was a ring of red around the outside. And fangs poked out from his bottom jaw and overlapped his lips just a little.

"You should never have come here," he snarled. His voice boomed through her mind, quietly as it was said, until she could think of nothing else.

She dug her nails into his wrists and croaked back, "On that, we agree."

He lifted a brow, and the same strange expression crossed his face. An expression she couldn't put her finger on. For a second, she thought he might let her go.

And let her go, he did.

Her fingers slipped off his wrist as he opened his hand and dropped her off the roof of the chateau.

CHAPTER 12

*P*ain consumed her body in licks of great flames. She couldn't think past the sharp burn stretching from the top of her head to the bottom of her toes. She tried to recount the injuries, to focus on just one pain, but found she couldn't pick just one.

Something had scraped her cheek; the entire left side of her face felt raw, like she'd fallen onto a grater the cheesemongers used. She lifted a hand to touch the heat plaguing her face, only to drop her hand at the sizzling ache.

In particular, her right arm felt... wrong. She could tell her fingers were swollen. She attempted to open the fingers, but they wouldn't budge no matter how hard she focused.

A soft sound, a whimper, escaped, a breath of agony reminding her she was still alive.

Recounting all the pieces of her injured body, she moved her attention to her left leg. Burning, inflamed, so harmed that she wanted to forget it was attached to her body.

The thick bone of her thigh shot spikes of hot pain straight up her spine to the base of her skull where it throbbed and screamed. She couldn't feel her foot, knee, anything below that point.

Had she lost the leg? *No.* She couldn't remember how she had gotten herself in this situation. But she was still herself, and that must mean she was no longer with the Dread.

She let out another soft sound, hoping someone would notice she was awake and needed help. Even taking a deep breath was too much. When she inhaled, needles jabbed into her chest.

Broken ribs, must be. She'd seen someone get kicked in the chest by a donkey once, and that's how the little boy had described the feeling in his ribs. Like someone was squeezing him in a hug that was too tight. Every movement poked his lungs, and that's how she felt.

"Please," she croaked, "water."

She blinked her eyes open. Herbs hung from the ceiling. Basil, parsley, lavender, all preserved for the winter that would be here soon. Or was it already winter? Her thoughts were all scattered.

The scraping of a chair against the stone floor meant she wasn't alone. Thank gods. She could feel a splint on her leg now that the fog of pain had passed. And someone was watching her, which meant the bed cushioning her was in a medic's home... But why would a medic have herbs hanging from their ceiling?

The second scraping sound wasn't from a chair. Some memory flickered in her mind. The grind of wings against the floor, fists pounding through walls, and yellow eyes staring at her through the holes.

Hunted.

Her heart pounded in her chest, and she couldn't control the shallow breaths that turned into hesitant gasps. Her ribs protested, but she now remembered everything.

The roof. She'd been thrown off the roof like trash, and no one had cared. None of the beasts had tried to stop their king.

And the king. He had been a true monster. Those eyes that had stared back at her were pulled straight from the skull of a demon and set into a face much worse than the bowels of Hell could create.

There had been no mercy in those eyes. The strong set of his jaw, the frown that furrowed his brow, the rage that had set his teeth, these emotions spoke of a soul who wanted nothing more than to destroy her. And he had. He'd thrown her three stories into a blizzard.

Her hair had tangled in front of her face, but she had still seen him as she'd fallen. A dark silhouette against the storm that had opened up once more to pour snow down upon them like sharp shards of glass. He'd spread his red and black wings wide and roared to the clouds.

She didn't remember hitting the ground. Only flight before nothing at all.

How had she survived?

A grotesque face appeared in her line of vision as a Dread bent over her. The one from the kitchen, she thought, although it was hard to tell any of them apart. Its slate gray skin was a little different from the ones she'd seen up close, however. This one was a little darker than the others, a little chalkier perhaps, but certainly darker.

"Are you awake?" it asked, the words slurring as it tried to speak around the fangs poking up from its bottom jaw.

She didn't want to respond to one of the Dread. She wanted to shrink back into the darkness of pain and anguish.

But her throat needed water and her tongue had dried to the top of her mouth. Working through the dryness, she managed a, "Water," before her ability to speak disappeared once more.

The frown on the Dread's face deepened. "Stay where you are, mademoiselle."

She couldn't even move her hand. If they wanted to keep her where she was, that would be easy enough. Amicia couldn't protest, however, not yet. Once she got water, she would give this Dread a piece of her mind.

She'd assumed they wanted to turn her. They'd done that to Remy, after all. Why was she any different?

The Dread appeared once more with a tankard in its hand. The beast held out the water to her and said, "Your water."

Amicia stared at it with desire. She tried to lift her hand, but damned if she could manage it. Her swollen fingers ached and the other arm felt like it was... tied down? Why couldn't she lift her uninjured arm?

"Oh," the beast muttered. "That's right. You wouldn't be able to. Here." It leaned forward and slid a clawed hand underneath her back. Gently, it lifted her up and pressed the tankard against her mouth.

Amicia gulped mouthfuls of the cool liquid like it was some magic potion to heal all her wounds. And perhaps it could. As the water slid down into her stomach, she felt a burst of relief and life pour into her body.

The Dread helped her back down, but even that movement exhausted her. She tried to still her ragged breathing, so it didn't disturb her lungs too much, then looked around the room.

She was in the kitchen, the one where the beast had fed her the first time. The golden table was a dead giveaway, although she didn't know *why* she was here. Of all places, they'd taken her to the kitchens? Were they going to eat her?

The Dread dragged a stool over to her side. The movement was awkward to watch. Its wings impeded its movements, flopping at its back, catching on the table and underneath the stool until they settled at its sides.

Heaving a breath, it stared at her with slitted eyes before saying, "You must have questions."

"Several."

"You are allowed to ask them." It blinked at her, the eyes too large for its face and the candlelight glinting against its large teeth.

Amicia wanted to snap a sarcastic response. She could ask as many as she wanted. They didn't have to answer them.

But this creature had shown her kindness when none of the others had. It deserved a little more of her respect than those who had tried to see her killed.

The first question that slipped off her tongue was, perhaps, a foolish one. However, she still asked, "Why did you help me?"

The Dread's mouth dropped open for a moment before it cleared its throat. "You are just a girl."

Amicia waited for the rest of the explanation, but it became clear the beast would not continue. That was all it planned on saying, as if the words were enough of a reason to feed her. "You wanted to help me because of my sex?"

"No, because you seem like little more than a child. I don't enjoy scaring children."

Amicia was hardly a child. She should have been married with children by now, but her father had needed her help in the workshop. The beast was kind to think she had aged well, but she wasn't young by any means. "Thank you... I think."

The Dread inclined its head in respect, then glanced up. Was it waiting for more questions?

"How did I get here?" Amicia asked.

"We think you came from the nearest town. I don't know the name, but that is what they assumed."

All right. She would need to ask much more specific questions. "How did I come to the kitchens after I was thrown off the roof?" she clarified.

The beast shifted its wings in clear excitement. Leathery appendages snapped out, high above its head, drawing its back straight and firm. "The Master brought you here to me."

"The master."

"Yes, he is a good master. Loyal to his people. And he

entrusted me to keep you alive." The beast was obviously proud of such a task, but it did little to explain why she wasn't dead.

"He what?"

The words made little sense. The King of the Dread had tossed her from the roof of the chateau. A decision that was undeniable. He wanted her dead; otherwise he would have dragged her through the broken windows and done whatever he'd wanted to do with her.

Amicia turned her head on the pillow beneath her, pressing her left cheek against the scratchy fabric. She winced. There had to be some explanation, but she couldn't think of one. She wanted to prod at the Dread more, to get her questions answered more thoroughly.

Her gaze fell on the doorway to the kitchens where the shadows parted like a curtain to reveal a much darker form lurking there. The King of the Dread, it had to be. None of the other creatures had eyes like that. Candlelight reflected in them, making them glow a deep red.

He stared at her with such hunger she worried he would stalk into the room and finish what he'd started. The beast inside him wanted to kill her, that much she knew. He wanted to plunge his claws into her chest and pull out her beating heart just so she could see him devour it before she died.

She swallowed hard, trying to push the fear down in her chest. Fear would only fuel the rage inside him, and she refused to let him think she was weak. Even wounded, she would meet his gaze without flinching.

He did not enter the room. Instead, the King of the Dread remained standing in the shadows. Watching her but never moving.

The Dread beside her continued speaking about what an honor it was to heal her body, but Amicia only caught the end of its words.

"You have broken many bones in your body, but I have

splinted them as best I could. Your leg may not heal naturally, but that is to be expected. I'm afraid doctoring was never one of my talents, but we will get you walking again, mademoiselle. I'm certain of it."

"Thank you," she whispered, still staring at the King. "But why did you let me live?"

Her question wasn't for the Dread beside her, but for the creature who lurked in the darkness.

Why hadn't he finished the job? If he had found her still breathing in the snow, he might have crushed her skull with his foot and been done with it. He could have turned her into one of his own, which he had wanted to do only moments before.

Instead, he'd carried her in from the storm and given her to the only Dread who didn't seem to hunger for her blood.

"Why?" she repeated once more.

The King of the Dread turned away from her. His thudding footsteps echoed in the halls beyond, melding with the sound of his wings touching the walls and scraping the delicate wallpaper. His tail lashed behind him, the wicked tip glinting.

The other Dread didn't appear to react or even know that its master had been standing and listening to them speak. "I'm not sure, but that is a question you might ask him. I'm certain he'd like to see you. It's all rather odd, if you ask me, but there's nothing I can do. I'm just a lowly servant."

Amicia had more questions to ask, but her body was tired. Exhaustion played across her vision in sparks of light and dark. "Perhaps we will both get our answers. I must rest."

"Yes, you should. The best way to heal, after all, is to sleep."

Amicia didn't know if she could ever sleep again. Every time she closed her eyes, she saw the glowing red gaze throwing her off a roof. But she wanted answers.

So she would heal, and she would force him to explain his actions.

CHAPTER 13

"*Y*ou are, without a doubt, the most difficult patient I have ever treated."

Amicia grinned and situated the makeshift crutches underneath her arms. "What luck you must have then! I'm the only patient you've ever treated."

The Dread harrumphed and jolted forward when Amicia listed to the side. It let out a long sigh before grumbling, "It wasn't luck which sent you to me."

"No, it wasn't. It was a demon straight out of Hell, and yet you still call him master."

One week of feverish ramblings had turned her voice raspy and her throat sore, but at least she could think clearly now. That was a start and the first step toward healing. Amicia was just grateful she felt like herself again.

The shadows weren't moving anymore. The fire didn't burn her body from the toes up. These were a step in the right direction, and a direction she hadn't thought would be possible.

The Dread had hovered around her for the entirety of each day. Its master had seemed to relinquish their cook to take care of her. Another strange thing Amicia didn't understand in the slightest.

She was certain the creature who looked over her was male. When he helped her to change out of her dirt-smudged dress, he would blush a darker gray. In addition, he was likely a lot younger than he looked.

Perhaps her own age, or maybe even younger. Although she had seen no children in the Dread's ranks. It made sense they would want to procreate, but wouldn't their young be small?

Amicia allowed the Dread to steady her, blew a strand of dark hair out of her eyes, and grinned at the beast. "See? No problem at all."

"You're going to re-break your leg."

Maybe, but she couldn't lay on that bed a moment longer. Now that the Dread weren't chasing her through the chateau intending to devour her whole, she would get clean. Even if it meant re-breaking her damn leg.

She tested out the first step and hopped on the second so she wouldn't jostle her left leg. Her left broken arm made this a rather ungainly movement and one that hurt no matter how hard she tried to favor the side. But she moved, step by step without falling over, which meant she could make it to the bathing house the Dread claimed was outside.

"See?" she announced, triumphant in her new movement. "I didn't fall over."

"You will."

Amicia glanced over her shoulder at the glowering beast. Even now, her heart skipped a beat at the angry expression. She felt the blood drain from her face and her knees grow weak. Was this when the beast decided it didn't want to put up with her anymore? Was it going to lunge at her?

The grooves on the Dread's face deepened, and it let out an angry huff. "Stop it. Whatever that thought was, enough of that. You'll fall over, and then I must pick you up."

"Sorry," she muttered.

"What were you thinking, anyway?"

Amicia didn't want to admit it had been fear turning her stomach. The beast had been nothing but kind to her. Admitting such a thing felt like she was letting the King of the Dread win. Not all the Dread were slavering beasts.

She hoped.

Shaking her head, she took another lumbering step toward the door and focused on the pain in her bicep. The bone had snapped clean underneath her when she fell, according to the Dread who watched over her. It hadn't broken through skin, so a simple splint had been easy enough to affix.

Her leg had not suffered a similar fate. The bone of her thigh had been sticking out past her hip, while the other end had somehow stuck out in the other direction. They'd wrestled both back into place, but the scars would be nasty, and she might never walk normally again.

The Dread had given her herbs, although she didn't know their name. It tasted like peppermint and wine. Too many flavors to count which had made her gag. "Dread medicine," the creature had called it.

Amicia tried hard not to think about the consequences of this. She would heal; that was the first step. And if she didn't walk the same way, then…

She shoved the thought away from the forefront of her mind once again. Dark thoughts would swallow her whole if she let them. Whispers claiming she would forever be useless. That her life would never be the same. That the Dread had ruined her even in her human form, whether they'd changed her or not.

And then, if she let her mind wander down that road too far, she would hate the creature who had saved her life. It wasn't his fault that his master had thrown her from the roof. It wasn't his fault she had come here. Nor was it his fault the Dread had attacked her home.

It wasn't *his* fault.

Amicia hadn't thought of the beast who had helped her as anything other than an "it" until this moment. But now, she realized he had a sex. And he might have a name.

She paused. "What's your name?"

He had been walking right behind her, stepping on her heel as he hovered to catch her if she fell. At her question, he froze. No breath moved his bare chest, nor did he appear to blink for the long heartbeats as he thought about her question.

"I don't know," he replied. "I don't think I have a name."

"You must have a name." Amicia gestured with her uninjured arm, pointing up and down his body. "This wasn't always your form, if I understand your kind well enough. I saw one of my own change into one of you. So you must have been like me at some point."

He swallowed hard, eyes widening until she could see their whites. He started breathing again, this time hyperventilating with each word. "I don't know my name. I don't have a name. I didn't have a life before becoming one of the Dread."

She'd said something wrong. Something had caused the poor thing to go into shock.

Amicia leaned over and placed her hand against his arm. They both stared down in shock at the contact where she had been trying to comfort him.

His skin was gritty. Like sandpaper. She'd felt nothing like it before. Even a lizard was smooth in some places. But touching him was like touching rough granite.

"I don't enjoy being touched," he murmured, still staring at their contact point like she had shoved a knife in between his ribs.

Oh, no. She hadn't meant to make him even more uncomfortable. She'd just been trying to make him feel better about not remembering his name. Which, in her opinion, was a rather important part of being a person. Knowing your name was knowing who you were and where you came from.

She dropped her hand from his side. "I'm sorry."

He still stared at the now vacant space where her fingertips had brushed his skin. "I didn't know, either."

He didn't know he didn't like to be touched? Amicia couldn't imagine why he wouldn't remember that, but then again it appeared he remembered little.

Every piece of knowledge she learned about him and his kind tugged at her heartstrings. Though she was still terrified of what he could do to her, he seemed more human than any of the others. He wanted to remember. She could feel that deep in her soul somehow.

"Bernard," she murmured, watching him for any kind of reaction. She wanted to snap him out of the odd mood he'd lost himself in.

The Dread looked up at her, his eyes wide once more. "What did you say?"

"You look like a Bernard to me."

"I look like nothing," he replied. "I look like one of the Dread, and we all look the same. We are meant to look the same so none might discern a difference when we attack. We are an army of beasts and nothing more."

"You are different, though." Amicia gripped the crutches and made her way to the door again. "Besides, you're the only one who talks to me. I'll say that's a Bernard if anyone could be."

He repeated the name behind her as he followed, the quiet word said repeatedly until she heard him snort. "It's a silly name."

"Why would you say that? It means the bear, brave and hardy."

"That's why it's a silly name." The Dread now called Bernard strode ahead of her so he could lead her toward the baths. "I'm nothing like a bear. I'm just a weakling who couldn't even fight with the other Dread."

"Strength means not only physical prowess," she replied. "Strength can be a person's ability to withstand great hardship. It can be a person's ability to seek flaws in their own soul and fix them."

They made their way through the halls of the chateau. Now that she could see the building in the sunlight, Amicia realized this place was far more beautiful. Rays of sunshine danced on the gilded edgings, turning the entire hall into a beam of light. The statues glowed, the white marble pristine despite all the time that had passed since a servant dusted their faces.

Her eyes hurt staring at such perfection, so Amicia watched her feet instead of all the surrounding things. But even the floor was lovely. Fissures of dark marble split through the white like veins of a living being. With each step, she followed the dark flow toward something she couldn't imagine.

"Breathe," Bernard said. "You've stopped breathing, human."

"My name is Amicia," she replied. "And such splendor was not created for eyes such as mine."

"But it was created for mine?" He snorted. "Mademoiselle, it is not for any of us here."

He had a point, and one she couldn't quite deny. Blowing out a breath, she focused on keeping herself upright and moving.

In the three weeks of her healing, her arm had gone from white hot agony to an ache that never disappeared. It wasn't as bad as her leg, as though her body wanted to focus on one injury at a time. Her leg was no better. The ragged, red wounds on either side of her thigh were worrisome.

She didn't want to lose the leg. Amicia didn't know if she would survive the loss. She wasn't some noblewoman who had servants who might help her. At least then she would only be looking at the life of a spinster. But as a peasant? She wouldn't be able to work. Wouldn't be able to make her way, and in the end, would be a beggarwoman on the streets where she would die in the matter of one winter. Disappearing into the forgotten areas of people's minds.

"Where did the beggar woman go?" someone might ask in a few years after her passing. "She used to fix my watch whenever it broke."

Amicia forced her thoughts away from morbid subjects. For now, she was here, and she would need to keep her mind here.

Bernard led her away from the areas of the chateau where she had already explored and toward a door she'd never seen before. Glass window panes had once been inserted in the frame. Now, the glass was little more than jagged edges.

Through the door, she could see out into the labyrinth of an old hedge maze. The backyard, she realized. This was the place where she had likely fallen.

"Here," Bernard said, reaching out and wrapping an arm around her waist. He took in a deep inhale at the contact and a muscle jumped in his jaw. "Let me help you down the stairs."

"I can manage on my own."

"We both know that's a lie."

It was, but she wasn't happy to admit it. She wanted to do things on her own and rush the healing process. Amicia knew it might result in some kind of injury that she'd regret. However, that didn't mean she wouldn't stubbornly push her body.

Together, they stepped down from the chateau and out into the fields beyond.

Amicia made the mistake of looking back at the chateau and saw a small indent in the snow just next to the door. A hollow with snow faded to pale pink.

"Is that—"

"Yes," Bernard interrupted her. He swept the snow out of her way with his wings, making her process through the snow almost easy. "There is no other way to get to the baths. I'm sorry you have to see the place again."

"I don't remember it," she whispered. "I only dream about falling, but I don't remember hitting the ground."

"Hopefully it never comes back to you." Bernard shuddered, his great wings flopping on his back before he returned to sweeping the snow out of the way. "It made a horrid sound."

She didn't need to know what it sounded like when his master thrust her off the rooftop to her death. And she had no question the King of the Dread had intended to kill her. His last words still played in her head.

You should never have come here.

What had he meant? To this chateau with long picks of ice dripping from the rooftop? To the home of the Dread who would hunt her down until she couldn't run any farther? She didn't know which one he'd meant, but it didn't matter.

He'd tried to kill her. And for that, she could never forgive him.

Bernard led her around the edge of the chateau. She looked for a building where the bathing house would be. In her small town, it was little more than a shack with separate doors for males and females. The men were always sectioned away from the women, but there was a flimsy divider between the two areas. Some couples had been daring enough to remove the divider when no one was looking.

Sneaking a peek of each other's bodies was just part of the flirting game. A game she had never indulged in when there was work to help her father with. Sometimes, she wished there had been a man willing to court her. A man who had wanted to see her in the bathing houses.

Now, the likelihood of that happening had disappeared. Her city was gone. Her body mangled and likely ruined for the rest of her life.

Amicia let out a small breath and forced her tense shoulders to relax. At least now she knew there wasn't a reason other than her own unfortunate circumstances. Her mind wasn't the threat or the discouragement to men. It was something out of her control.

"Here we are!" Bernard said, his voice a chirp of happiness. "Let me get the ice out of the way for you."

"Ice?" Amicia looked around for a bathing house with warm water and steaming comfort. There was none.

Instead, Bernard leaned down to what looked like a watering trough and punched his fist through the ice at the top. Water underneath splashed up against his fist.

Chunks floated at the surface still. Cold enough that all the gooseflesh on her arms popped to life without even touching it. Amicia gulped. "This is the bathing house?"

"House? There's no bathing *house*, per se. But we bathe here when we need to."

"Oh," she said with a quiet breath. "This is too cold for me to bathe in, Bernard. I'll catch my death out here."

He looked up at the bright sun and cloudless sky, then wordlessly handed her a cloth to clean with. "I think it's warm enough for you. I'll be just around the chateau. Yell if you fall down." He started to move away, but then hesitated. "Please don't fall. I've already seen you naked enough times. It's even more uncomfortable now that you're awake."

She might have retorted with something sarcastic, but Amicia was too busy staring at the icy trough. She waved him off and then shuffled close enough to lean against its edge without falling down.

Icy waters for a bath. Broken body and an army of creatures who wanted her dead. What had happened to her quaint little life?

Every inch of her body rebelled at the thought of touching that water to her skin at all. She would catch a cold and her death. Bernard wasn't a healer; he didn't know what would happen if she got sick.

And yet she was the one who had claimed she was strong

enough to do this. Her pride would never recover if she limped back to that room, covered in blood, dirt, and who knew what else.

Angrily, she reached up and stripped off the makeshift top the Dread and herself had constructed. It wrapped around her well enough to cover all the bits that needed to be covered, but unraveling it took time. Eventually, she bared herself to the waist.

Dipping the washcloth into the water numbed her fingers. She bounced on her foot, shifting her balance to prepare for the cold.

"Damn it," she muttered and then rubbed the cloth over her torso and arms.

Amicia made it a point to never swear. She didn't like such dirty words slipping off her tongue, but the cold made her say things she'd only heard outside of taverns. Over and over she cleaned the dirt from her body, soiling the water and making her entire body shiver and quake.

But the longer she did it, the more it felt good. She was once again the woman she knew. Though broken and tired, she was no longer the runaway covered in grime, but the woman who had lived in a tinker's home and knew how to save herself.

Hands shaking but mind clear, she felt gooseflesh raise on her back. Not from the cold, but from eyes staring down at her.

She stiffened, pressed the icy cloth against her breasts, and glanced over her shoulder up at the windows of the chateau. There, in the farthest windows where the sun reflected off the still intact glass, was a shadow.

She couldn't see who dared to watch her bathe. Her gut, however, knew who it was. The King of the Dread. The only person who made her skin crawl and heat at the same time. It had to be him. She would know the feeling of his stare even from all the way down here.

Every ounce of her hard-won strength drained out of her

body. White faced, dizzy, she stared up at the chateau and waited for him to burst out of the windows. She waited for him to order her to her death once again.

When he did nothing, she turned away from the fearsome creature. Staring up at him did nothing. She couldn't change the path he sent her down anymore than she could change her own broken and battered body.

Amicia woodenly dipped the cloth back into the water and continued with her washing. She finished her top half, then found she couldn't take off her pants. Not with him watching.

Instead, she dipped the cloth into the water and shoved it down the borrowed pants, wiping what she could before leaving the washcloth behind. She wrapped herself up in the makeshift shirt. It didn't cover her all the way this time, but it covered what it had to cover.

She turned to stare defiantly back up at the chateau, only to see the shadow had disappeared.

CHAPTER 14

*T*he King of the Dread set aside the tome in his hand, staring at the door upon which someone dared to knock against its surface and interrupt him. Had he not requested silence? For at least the rest of the evening?

He ground his teeth. Anger bubbled in his chest, impossible to control, and yet he wrestled it back into the recesses of his mind. His people knew how to take orders. He'd drilled it into their heads from the moment they became one of his. If they dared knocking on the door, that meant there was something wrong or something that needed his attention.

There was a time when he wouldn't have cared. When he hadn't tried to control the rage burning in his chest like a living being. Now, he knew to take a few breaths and give his own people the benefit of the doubt.

When had he learned how to do that?

"Enter," he barked.

The door creaked open, so slowly he wondered if it was a stiff breeze blowing against it rather than the hand of one of his army. And yet, a gray foot entered the room followed by a body he recognized.

The King pinched his nose, inhaling to calm the instinct to kill before he listened. "What is it?"

The Dread was the one who looked after the human woman. The one who had completely and utterly shifted the way things were done in this chateau. A human was alive, walking the halls and the Dread had to control themselves. They never controlled their urges. She did not understand the impact she had, and he couldn't think straight.

He'd even gone to the library, again, to clear his mind. To lose himself in the pages of a book where he could think of only fiction and not reality.

Even in his sanctuary, she was there. Just outside the window and undressing as if she didn't have a care in the world. As if the Dread were just animals who didn't look at human bodies in the same way.

He wasn't a damned horse or dog. And her body was exquisite in the way of a working woman. She wasn't some noble lady who had spent her life indoors. Her back was a map of adventures, scars, and sunburns that had left strange, lacing patterns. He could see it all, even from three stories up.

Suddenly, his sanctuary was invaded with thoughts of soft skin and memories that he shouldn't have. The King of the Dread was a monster. He'd never touched a human woman other than to turn her into one of his army.

But, he remembered the velvet softness of a woman's thigh. The graceful dip of her waist rising to her hip as she rested in a bed beside him. The way her ribs expanded with each breath, revealing the delicate bones that caged her heart.

These memories couldn't possibly be his. He didn't know *whose* they were, but the King had always been a king. Nothing more and nothing less.

The Dread shifted forward, clearing its throat.

Had he been stuck in his mind again? "What is it?" he repeated.

"As I was saying, the girl is healing well."

"Woman," the King snarled. "Don't try to paint her as a child to garner my sympathy." The idea of her as a child made him uncomfortable.

Besides, he'd seen the way her body looked, or at least half of it. The woman was no child, although she might want the others to think of her that way. If her game was to get them to pity her, then she would have a much more difficult time doing so than she realized. His army was unkind to a fault. They were selfish beasts.

He'd designed them that way.

The King closed his eyes and tilted his head to the side, trying to chase the thought like a popped bubble in his mind. He'd made them that way? He hadn't created the Dread any more than they had created him. They were a product of his species. Weren't they?

"Master, she's rather... genius." The Dread twisted its fingers together, a nervous tick the creature had always had. "She created crutches for herself out of broken table legs. I've never met a woman like her before."

"Creating crutches isn't difficult."

"But a woman doing so? She has these ideas and things she says—"

That wouldn't do. The woman couldn't be putting thoughts into the heads of his people. They were already too fragile. They listened to him and him alone, but they had never really been exposed to the outside world. Once they were his, they forfeited their memories.

He couldn't have her twisting their thoughts away from him. The King leaned forward and interrupted the Dread's ramblings. "Do not listen to the words of one who does not understand us. She is human. Weak and therefore, flawed. Never forget that."

The Dread gulped. "Understood, Master."

The King leaned back in his chair, tapped a claw to his lips, and stared out the window of his personal study. He wanted to dismiss the Dread back to the hole from which it had crawled out, but this subject of the woman... It intrigued him. The anger that usually distracted him was silent.

So he continued the conversation, though it made him uncomfortable. "What has she been doing?"

"Not much, sire. Healing has been her main goal, or so she tells me. But she has asked for a few books."

"Books?" He opened and closed his wings, restless at the thought of her in his library. His sanctuary. "What would she want with books? She's nothing more than a peasant woman."

"Apparently, she can read." The Dread stood a little straighter when he said the words. As if he were... proud of the woman?

Not in the King's chateau. He wouldn't have any of his people falling in love with the little slip of a female he should have changed when he'd had the chance.

He stood to his full height, towering over the Dread who cowered. Rounding the desk he sat behind, the King approached the small creature with a snarl on his lips and sadistic intent in his steps. He wanted to hurt the Dread. He wanted to tear it limb from limb for stealing her attentions and for somehow garnering her trust when *he* was the one who had spared her life—

The King grabbed the Dread by the throat and lifted it up. He stared deep into the creature's eyes, trying to see what made this one different from all the others. What was it about this Dread that made her talk to him?

"Master," the beast croaked. "Please."

"Silence," he growled.

He continued to stare at the beast, turning it side to side as if there was maybe something in the set of its horns that was different. Perhaps it was the softened tips. Maybe this one was less terrifying than the rest of his army.

Certainly, she wasn't intimidated by this one, and that was why she felt comfortable speaking with it. Maybe she had decided there was no threat from this one.

It was what he would have done. The King regularly surveyed the others to know who would be the one to challenge him, which ones of the Dread could defeat him.

There were none. He made certain no Dread lived that could someday rise and overthrow him.

He tossed the Dread back onto the floor and cared little that the beast crumpled. The Dread were hardy monsters. If they couldn't withstand a little manhandling from him, then they didn't deserve to be in his army.

He strode back to his desk, having discovered nothing in his attempt to understand the woman. For a moment, he'd felt that if he stared deep into this Dread's eyes, he might peer into her mind.

Clearly, that wasn't the case. A fool's task, nothing more. And besides, he didn't care what she was thinking or why she did the things she did.

He slumped back into his chair, sullen and angry once again. "Go back to her then," he grumbled. "Do what you can to heal her."

The Dread got up from the floor and rubbed its neck. "Understood, Master. Shall I feed her, then?"

The King sat up straight. He bared his teeth in a sudden flare of frustration and panic he'd never felt before. He pronounced his words carefully so the beast would not mishear him. "You haven't been feeding her?"

"I've been feeding her. I just wanted to know if I should continue." A sly grin spread across the Dread's face. "It seems you want to keep her, Master. Should I plan on bringing the human food for a long time?"

Tricks and more tricks. He didn't answer to the Dread; they answered to him. He should have killed the beast for daring to say such things, but he didn't trust any of the others to not gnaw on her bones and ask for forgiveness later.

The King slumped back in his chair and waved a hand. "Do what you must to keep her alive. I haven't decided what I wish to do with her just yet."

"Understood, Master."

"Dismissed, Dread."

The beast turned toward the door but paused in the doorway. The King didn't know what to think of the sudden confidence in the being's shoulders or the way it suddenly held itself like a man, not a hunched monster.

It turned to look back at him. "Bernard."

"Excuse me?"

"The woman has named me." The Dread lifted its chin. "I am not a soldier in your army, and I see no reason why I might not have a name. She gave it to me, and I should like to keep it."

The King felt his brows draw down in a terrifying expression with bared teeth and eyes that glowed red. But the Dread did not show any sign of fear. If anything, it straightened further and seemed to prepare itself for a fight.

She was naming his creature's now? How dare she?

She had no right to come into his chateau and *change* things. She should be terrified. Cowering in a corner in fear his army would devour her limb from limb while he watched.

He let out a growl from deep in his chest. If the woman wanted to play games, then two could do so. "Advise her I would like her company at dinner tonight."

"Master? She's not healed enough to eat with the army—"

"I didn't ask for your opinion," he interrupted. "It's not a choice for her, but an order. She will join us for dinner."

The Dread, Bernard, swallowed hard. "As dinner, sire?"

The King leaned back and let a slow grin spread across his face. "That remains to be seen. We'll see how well she behaves."

CHAPTER 15

*A*micia stared at the dress Bernard held out to her with mouth agape and eyes wide. "You want me to… what?"

"Put on the dress and go to dinner with the King."

"Just the King?"

Bernard hesitated, then shook his head. "Not exactly."

"He wants me to have dinner with the Dread, I assume his most trusted members, wearing *that*." She pointed at the ugly thing Bernard held out to her and wanted to disappear into the floor.

The mere thought of eating while in the presence of the other Dread made her want to vomit. She wouldn't keep a bite of that food in her stomach, and she'd be lucky if she didn't throw it up all over the dinner table. They frightened her to no end. Not to mention she thought of them as monsters who went bump in the night. She couldn't eat with the damned beings!

And the dress would make her look even worse than she already did. The yellowish pink color made her think of more vomit, so at least she'd be wearing the same color that she was tossing out of her stomach. It was also covered with a plethora of ribbons from the shoulders down the bodice and around the waist. It looked like a little girls' dress, just adult-sized.

Bernard shook the dress out a bit and held it back out to her. "It's a rather pretty dress. I found it myself."

The puppy-dog look in his eyes was not playing fair. She couldn't tell him no when he was so proud of the item he'd found. Maybe this was in fashion back when the chateau hadn't been overrun by monsters.

Amicia relented and reached for the dress. She held it up to her body for his inspection. "How will it look?"

The happy expression on his face melted into one of utter disappointment. "Well, that's not your color I suppose."

Of course, it didn't look good. She could have told him that just moments ago. But he was disappointed, and she didn't want him to look like that. He'd worked hard to find the dress in a ruined palace like this. "Oh, it'll be fine. We'll just snip a few of these ribbons off, toss them into my hair, and I'll be ready for dinner with a king."

A dinner where she threw up on said king, but that was all right. Such was the only fate she thought he deserved. The beast could wallow in vomit for the rest of his life, and she still wouldn't be happy.

"Help me get it over my head?" she asked. "At least it doesn't have sleeves, Bernard. I'll be able to fit my cast through it. See? You were thinking in the right direction."

He helped her get it over her head and then smoothed it down her sides, pulling her arm through the hole even though she let out a whimper. The leg was easier to deal with. She didn't have to use it that much now that she had the crutches. But the arm ached.

At least her ribs weren't pulling as much. They were still broken, but the tight binding helped. She could breathe again.

Once Bernard had gotten her into the dress, he took a step back and stuck out his tongue. "No, that's terrible."

She was certain it was. Probably the worst thing he'd ever seen in his life, and that was saying something.

"Well…" Amicia glanced down at the dress. "It's a good thing I'm not looking for a husband then. In fact, I'd rather be unimpressive to the rest of your kind. Maybe they'll leave me alone."

"I doubt that," he muttered. Stepping forward, Bernard started to snip off some ribbons and the bows at her shoulders. "They're all fascinated with you."

"With me?" Amicia couldn't understand why. They had hunted her, she'd survived, and now she hid in the kitchens with the Dread who seemed like the only servant in the entire place. "That seems rather silly. Don't they have kingdoms to bring to their knees?"

"Little Marsh was the last. There are no other towns for us to focus upon. The King is at rest."

"The last?" Amicia knew that couldn't be true. There were plenty of other places who had never even heard of the Dread. Her father used to tell her stories from his travels where people knew nothing about the beasts who plagued them. And those stories were from a short time ago. "But there are other kingdoms."

Perhaps she shouldn't have mentioned it. Maybe the Dread didn't know there was a world out there who hadn't heard of them.

Had she doomed another kingdom to the same fate?

Bernard hung one ribbon over his right bottom fang, apparently to keep for later in her hair. "There are plenty of other kingdoms, mademoiselle. But they are not ours to condemn. We are here for this kingdom, and this kingdom alone."

"That makes little sense. If you're pillaging and plundering, why wouldn't you continue when your own kingdom has finally been brought to its knees?" Again, she warned herself to stay silent. These creatures might not have thought far ahead and she should keep her mouth shut giving them ideas.

"The King decides these things," Bernard replied with a shrug. "It's not for me or the others to say. Now, they are focused upon you and the questions that come with you. We do not know why the Master has allowed you to live, and yet, here you are. Alive and well with me as your manservant."

Amicia snorted. "Manservant? Unlikely. I'd call you a strange new friend, nothing less."

He paused in his snippings to stare at her with wide eyes. The ribbon started slipping off his fang, which she reached up to catch with her good hand.

Bernard barely reacted to the movement. Instead, he asked, "You consider me a friend?"

"Well, you saved my life."

He shook his head. "I didn't save your life. The master did. He bid me to take care of you, but he is the one who carried you here."

"Taking someone to a healer doesn't make them a savior." She refused to think of the terrible beast as the man who had saved her life. He'd tried to take it.

"But he was the one who—"

"I don't want to hear it, Bernard. Besides, dinner is about to be served, is it not? I need you to finish fixing my new dress."

Perhaps her words were a little desperate, but she couldn't listen to him sing the praises of the monster who had tried to kill her. She was just finding herself comfortable around *this* Dread. The last thing she wanted was for him to paint himself as a beast along with his master.

Bernard kept his mouth shut and finished snipping off the ugly ribbons, although some remained stitched into the shoulders and at the bodice. The dress was ugly, but perhaps that was better.

She didn't want them to think she was pretty. She didn't want to be the lovely tinker's daughter who made people smile when she walked by. Amicia had left that girl behind.

Now, she wanted to be a woman who made people look away. A ghost, a shadow who remained in the corners of the world, not having to worry about others seeing her.

She wanted to be invisible. If an ugly appearance could accomplish that, then she would cover herself in mud and disappear forever.

Bernard stepped back and touched a claw to his chin. "You'll do, I suppose. Although, the dress is..."

"Terrible?"

"That's a decent enough word for it."

Amicia reached for her crutches and tucked them underneath her armpits. "These will only make it worse."

"I can't say I've ever seen someone arrive at a noble dinner with those." Bernard cleared his throat. "But you have caused a stir already. I suppose it's no surprise you'll continue doing so."

Amicia didn't want to garner any more attention with her presence, however, she couldn't move without her crutches. Letting out a frustrated huff, she made her slow way to the door. "Where is this dinner?"

"The formal dining room."

She waited for more direction, then sighed when he remained stock still in her room. "Which is?"

The scraping of nails on the floor sounded as Bernard raced after her to show her the way. He might play the role of a lady's maid, but he had clearly never been in this role. Even Amicia knew a lady would be shown where the dining room was, not just told.

He stepped ahead of her and they made their arduous journey to the dining room where she hoped she wouldn't be feasted upon. Her palms grew slick on the rungs of the crutches, making movement a little more difficult than usual. Somehow, the pain in her body seemed to worsen with every step toward the beast who had done this to her.

The monster who had taken away her graceful walk. The

beast who had wanted to see her dead. The nightmare whose red eyes still plagued her dreams.

Bernard stopped in front of twin doors stretching higher than two men. They were solid gold, smooth like a mirror, and reflected her terrified expression. Staring into her own wide eyes, Amicia forced her face to relax.

"Are you ready?" Bernard asked, his hands placed against the surface of the gold.

She wanted to tell him he would leave fingerprints on such glorious doors, but couldn't seem to open her mouth. Her teeth chattered as she nodded.

Would this be her last moment alive? What waited for her behind that door?

Bernard shoved it open and revealed the golden dining room beyond. Three glass chandeliers hung from the ceiling. Thousands of candles decorated the walls and the ceiling, some so high she couldn't imagine how they had ever been lit. A long mahogany table took up the entire room. A white silk runner covered the wood, and golden plates sat at each padded seat.

One of the Dread sat upon each silken cushion in uncomfortable looking chairs that were solid gold. They looked ridiculous seated like people. Their wings folded over the back of the chairs, most wearing torn shirts that stretched over their muscular, deformed bodies.

As one, they all turned to stare at her in silence. The nearest one fiddled with something underneath the table, then let out a slow hiss. Its eyes flared with bright light, and its wings twitched the moment it saw her.

Amicia's stomach clenched even though none moved. Oh, they wanted to. They would always want to continue the hunt.

Bernard whispered behind her, "Don't just stand there. You're the guest of honor."

She swallowed hard. She might be the guest, but where was she meant to go? She was a peasant woman. Fancy dinners back home had been in someone's root cellar with cards thrown about, mead flowing a plenty, and laughter so loud the neighbors would bang on the door to complain.

Dinners weren't anything like this. No one stared in silence, nor did they sit with their backs as straight as the chair they sat upon.

Amicia's gaze trailed up the table until she saw *him*. The beast who deserved a dagger plunged into his breast. The monster who had tried to take everything from her.

The King of the Dread stared back at her with an apathetic gaze. He slouched in his chair as if he were bored, the only person at the table with poor posture.

A single chair was vacant beside him.

She took a deep breath and flexed her hands on the rungs of the crutches. She had to sit next to him. That was the expectation. What little bread she'd eaten this morning pushed against the back of her throat, threatening to come back up in an explosive rejection of this dinner.

Nostrils flaring with her inhale, she started down toward the chair. Each click of her crutches hitting the white marble floor sounded like the cracking of bones. Perhaps her own, once she sat down next to their king.

Amicia tried not to slow as she approached him, and yet, she did. It was a slow crawl until she made it to his side and stared down at the chair. She'd have to balance on her good leg to pull the chair out, which meant she would be off kilter. Perhaps that was when they would take advantage of her, flip her onto the table, and tear into her belly. Or would they turn her into one of them?

The chair shifted out from underneath the table, pushed by a gray foot with claws at the tip.

The choice to run removed, Amicia put her crutches aside and lowered herself with a thud into the chair. It hurt her leg, but the spike of pain helped clear her mind from the terror freezing the blood in her veins.

Her father would have been disappointed in her. He hadn't raised a woman to flinch away from monsters. He'd tried to raise her to see beyond the fear and understand why she didn't feel like she belonged. Or why they wanted to hurt her.

She'd been the first child to take a feral dog in, to not be afraid of snapping jaws and ferocious snarls. She could tame those beasts, so why did these terrify her so?

Amicia knew the answer to the question the moment she thought it. These weren't monsters. These were people in the bodies of animals. They had feelings like any other person. They knew what they were doing, and they still hunted, killed, destroyed.

Somehow, such knowledge made their actions all the worse.

The King of the Dread said nothing to her. Instead, he lifted a hand. Suddenly, the walls opened up, revealing hidden doors that led into the kitchens she had yet to see. So many rooms, so many kitchens, so many places in this chateau that stretched on forever.

Food had been set upon the tables. Four roast turkeys, plates full of carrots, potatoes, and bread. So much food she couldn't imagine where they had gotten it all in the middle of winter.

Her expression must have played her thoughts like a book. The Dread on the other side of the King snorted. "We got it from your village, girl," he snarled. "You don't recognize it?"

Amicia straightened her back and croaked, "No. I don't recognize stolen food."

Only then did the King speak. He grunted out a low growl, then said, "Food is food, whether or not it's stolen. You'll eat it."

Her sudden bravery disappeared the moment she heard his voice. Amicia didn't hear the words he'd said. All she heard was, *You should never have come here.*

The King stared at her, watching her expression with red eyes.

Amicia held his gaze and her own breath. What would he do now? Grab her by the throat again and toss her down the table for the feast?

A servant leaned in front of her and set down a bowl of green soup. Pea soup? She had expected raw meat from these creatures, not something that looked so civilized.

"Meek is not what I expected from you," he said, spooning soup into his mouth.

Amicia was fascinated he even knew how to use a spoon. He held it between his claws with almost grace, although she hated to pair the word with him. "You threw me off the roof of the chateau. You broke my body, and yet you expect me to be... what? Forceful in my demands?"

"Did I break your spirit as well?" He lifted a dark brow. "'Tis a shame."

"You destroyed my home, killed my people, and what few were left you turned into monsters like yourself. You and your people hunted me for days while I tried to hide and wait out the storm. Then you broke my arm, my leg, my ribs. I have no fight left in me." She licked her lips, voice shaking with emotion. "Whatever you plan on doing with me, do it now. I'm done being toyed with."

Her ragged speech rang through the air and settled into the sudden silence of Dread who stared at her in shock. Perhaps she still had a little fight left, after all. A meek woman, a scared woman, would never have taken such a tone with the King of the Dread.

Amicia held her chin high and stared down the table at them all. She would not look at their king, who likely was already gnashing his teeth in her direction. She would observe his people, some who might have been once *her* people. They would remember her bravery first, and not that she had given up.

Instead of snapping jaws, all she heard from the creature beside her was the soft clink of a spoon hitting a bowl.

When she couldn't take the slurping sounds any longer, Amicia broke and looked over at him. He was waiting for her. A grin flashed across his face, revealing sharp teeth.

"Quite a speech," he replied. "But I'm afraid I haven't decided what to do with you yet. You'll have to wait a little longer."

"I don't enjoy being the mouse to your cat."

"Ah, but I like your spirit." He pointed at her bowl with his spoon. "Eat. Gather your strength so you might heal the wounds I inflicted."

She waited for him to say more, something, anything. But he didn't. Instead, he continued to eat as though her outburst had never happened.

What madness was this? He was evil. She knew that in her very soul. No good person, nor one with gray morals, would allow someone to kill another. But evil people didn't heal those they had harmed.

She picked up her spoon and tasted the food. Were they poisoning her? She had seen none of the others with upset stomachs. Yet. There was always the chance they ate something different from her, or the food would kill a human.

The soup tasted like pea soup. Rather good, albeit a little bland.

Her stomach rolled underneath her ribs, and the food stuck in her throat. Amicia set her spoon down after a few sips. Throwing up the food that the Dread had worked hard on would only be seen as another insult. For the time being, it appeared she was on friendly terms with the beasts.

The Dread seated to her right was smaller than the others. Similar to Bernard in build, it struggled to use the utensils. All the Dread were struggling through this dinner, she noted.

Amicia tapped the table, garnering the attention of the Dread to her right. "You don't usually eat like this, do you?"

It flicked its eyes to the King, then remained silent.

She looked over at the creature to her left who acted as

though nothing had happened. "Am I not allowed to ask questions of your people?"

He shrugged. "You may ask as many questions as you wish."

"But will they answer?"

Once again, he shrugged. He reached forward for a loaf of bread, split it in half, and used one piece to mop up the remaining soup in his bowl. All this, and he did not answer her question.

"Am I a prisoner?" she asked.

"This is a chateau, not a prison."

"But am I a prisoner?" Amicia's sharpened her voice into the crack of a whip.

He popped the bread in his mouth, chewing almost silently while meeting her gaze head on. "That remains to be seen."

"Are there rules to this? Some engagement I might entertain to sway your opinion of prisoner rather than guest?" Amicia glanced down the table when a few of the Dread snickered.

The King of the Dread chuckled along with them. "There are engagements you could consider, but I highly doubt you would be interested in such... entertainment."

Breathing hard and trying to keep herself in the seat so she didn't wrap her own hands around his throat, she took a long, deep breath and replied, "Then I *am* a prisoner."

"Perhaps. Time will tell, little human."

"Please don't call me that."

The King of the Dread set the bread down on the table, hooked an arm over the back of his chair, and turned toward her. He was too close, too big, sucking up all the air in the room. He was too intense, too broad, too... everything.

"What else would I call you?" he asked.

"Mademoiselle," she snarled.

"You have no name?"

"Not one you are allowed to call me." Amicia fisted her hands in her lap. "If this is a game for you, know it is not for me.

You killed my family, took everything away from me, and now you toy with me as a cat does a mouse. I am not a mouse, monsieur."

He leaned closer, inhaling her scent as an animal might. "And yet, you hid in my walls. Scratching behind the wallpaper just as a mouse might. Perhaps I shall call you *petite souris*, little mouse."

Amicia stood abruptly, the legs of her chair squealing against the marble. Her leg screamed at the movement, bone shifting against broken bone, but she hardly felt the pain.

All the Dread stared at her then, some with eyes wide in shock, others with a hunger she felt deep in her belly. They *were* toying with her. Playing some game she didn't know the rules for.

No more. She would no longer endure this madness.

"Sit down," the King ordered.

Amicia straightened her shoulders, reached for her crutches, and replied, "No."

The King's eyes widened, and a muscle on his jaw jumped. "What did you say to me?"

"I said no. I will not endure a moment more of this charade. I avail myself of this evening, monsieur. I have never, and will never, suffer the company of a cruel-hearted man. Good evening." She tucked the crutches under her arms and made her way back toward the door.

He called out after her, "Then you are a prisoner, *petite souris*."

"Not for long," she snarled. "Be certain of that, *grand imbécile*."

Amicia left with the raucous laughter of the Dread ringing in her ears. Whether they were laughing at her or her words, she would never know.

CHAPTER 16

*A*micia couldn't remain in the kitchens for any longer. She'd been here yet another week with none other than her unwilling manservant. And she couldn't stand a single second more, or she would shred Bernard's wings.

He sang when he cooked, a new development compared to a week ago. And he sang horribly. Off key. In the worst ways she had never heard someone wail before. Because Amicia could hardly think of it as singing, and to save her own sanity, she couldn't listen a moment longer.

Amicia tucked the crutches underneath her arms and started toward the door.

"Where are you going?" Bernard asked, stopping mid verse.

"To the library."

"You aren't supposed to wander the castle without me." He wiped his hands on his apron, staring at the unfinished loaf of bread with a sad sigh before starting after her.

"I don't need a guard all the time," she grumbled.

"But the master said—"

"And I don't care what your master said. I'm going to the library, you're staying here to finish your work, and neither of us will get into trouble." Amicia glanced over her shoulder to cast a withering stare in his direction. "No more, Bernard. I will return in one piece."

He wrung his hands, struggling with the order. He had much to finish, as his job here was more than just looking after her. "Fine. Just stay out of trouble, please. Otherwise it'll be my head on the chopping block."

"Somehow, I doubt anyone else would want to deal with me. The King needs you until he decides to put me out of my misery." Amicia made her way out the door and down the immaculate halls to the library.

She would find some book to keep her mind off the terrible caterwauling of the Dread who never left her side. The King of the Dread must have given her this manservant because he knew how annoying Bernard could be. He thought to drive her mad rather than kill her.

Two could play at that game. She would steal books from the library, specifically on torture, and someday she would drive nails underneath the King of the Dread's fingers.

Amicia turned a corner, twisting her broken leg a little too far. It ached, as it always did when she moved too fast. Two weeks, and it still wasn't any better than the moment he had thrown her off the top of the chateau. She thought by now she would at least see some kind of improvement. Instead, she would hazard to say it was worse. Growing more and more difficult to walk on her own.

The library doors loomed in front of her. Their dark wood so different from the rest of the chateau. Why was this place different from the rest? Perhaps she would have asked the King if she didn't want to tear him limb from limb.

Stepping into the library, however, was like taking a fresh breath of air after living inside for years. The smell of parchment relaxed all the tense muscles in her body. She had forgotten how being surrounded by books could make her so blissful.

Hundreds of novels filled the room. Amicia didn't know which one she wanted but any of them would do. She wanted to disappear for a few hours into a world unlike this one. It didn't matter what world that was.

Books had a way of transporting the reader into a place better than the one they struggled through.

She hobbled over to a shelf and snagged the first book her fingers brushed against, then made her way to the twin chairs near the windows. The sun shone on the snow outside the glass, so bright it lit up the entire library with its glimmering reflection.

"If only you had come out when I was trying to escape," she muttered. She slumped into the chair on the right and leaned her crutches against the window. "I could have used the sun that day."

Now, there was so much snow outside she couldn't have managed with two good legs. Let alone the broken body she'd now been handed. And none of the snow appeared to be melting. It was as if the chateau was enclosed in its own glass snow globe. Stuck in winter for all eternity.

Considering what the Dread looked like, Amicia wouldn't be surprised if it was always winter here. She allowed her gaze to linger on the frozen lake beyond, covered by snow so no one would even know the dangers beneath their feet, then she turned to the book.

This one wasn't like the first she'd picked up on Little Marsh. Instead, the pages were filled with the adventures of a man named Padraig from a far-off land. He traveled across the seas into lands long forgotten that held great beasts, whom he did not kill, but tamed.

She was so engrossed in the story and the fantasy she didn't hear the library door open. Amicia was holding her breath at the climax of the story when two feet stepped into her line of vision just above the spine of the book. Gray feet, clawed, with long backward knees that warped the figure in front of her.

She thought to herself, please be anyone but him.

Luck had never been on her side. Lifting her gaze from the book, she looked up at the King of the Dread who stared down at her with a curious expression on his face. It was almost as though she had confused him just by sitting in this chair.

When he said nothing, just glowered at her, she cleared her throat. "Can I help you, grand imbécile?"

Her voice seemed to snap him out of whatever trance he was in. The King shook himself, rather like a dog getting out of the water, and replied, "What are you doing here?"

She lifted the book in her hands. "Reading."

"I can see that, but why are you here?"

She could answer a question like that a hundred different ways, but Amicia settled on the truth. "To read."

His nostrils flared wide in a deep inhale she assumed was in frustration but could very well have just been pure anger. His eyes flared brighter, and his strange cat-eye slits narrowed until there was barely any pupil left staring at her. Then, he turned on his heel and stalked away from her.

Good riddance. The last person she wanted in this library with her when she was finding a bit of peace in such a cursed place was the King who had started it all.

Amicia turned back to her book, diving into the story of Padraig and the three-headed dragon who had plagued a town. Padraig would not kill the beast; he would tame it with an offering of gold he'd stolen from a local witch.

She could only imagine how he would tame a dragon. She'd heard of their sort before. They were terrifying beasts with a hunger that could not be satisfied. Gold was their weakness. But was it enough to save an entire town when the beast was starving?

A loud thump interrupted her reading, followed by a cloud of dust bursting into the air and filling her nose. She sneezed, accidently jerking her broken arm too hard. The sneeze merged into a moan of pain even as she turned to glare at the creature seated beside her.

The King acted like nothing had happened. He held a tiny book in his hands, not quite a novel and more like a journal. A pale blue cover with gold caps on the corners suggested it was once owned by a very important person.

"Now, what are you doing?" she grumbled.

"Reading."

"Why?"

He held up the book and then placed a finger against his lips. "Libraries are supposed to be quiet places."

Was he shushing her? How dare he even consider such a thing when he was nothing more than an animal who had taken over this place? He couldn't know what a library was.

But... how else would he know people were meant to be quiet in libraries?

She turned back to her story and allowed him to read. The question could wait. He had made it clear she might live a little longer. Which gave her a small moment to breathe.

Now, the only thing she wanted was to heal and then perhaps escape. She needed to find out more secrets about the castle, ask those who lived here ways to leave. With the storm no longer raging outside, the snow would eventually melt. Then, she could make it if her leg was better.

The question of how he knew of libraries burned, however. It ached inside her, digging at her ribs and spine until she could barely handle it any longer. He said the words as though he'd been in a library. Not just a room which held a collection of books in his own home, but a real library, as there were in the cities.

How could a creature like him ever walk into a normal building? Let alone such a sacred place?

Amicia leaned back in her chair, curious about the creature next to her but not wanting to appear as if she cared at all about him. "When was the last time you were in a library?"

"A few hundred years ago I imagine," he murmured, thumbing open his story and slumping into his own chair. "The great Library of Omra, the largest city on the continent and the greatest collection of stories."

She'd heard of Omra, but only in passing. It was too far away for anyone to travel in a lifetime, and yet he claimed he'd been there? And that he was hundreds of years old?

Amicia looked back at her own pages, but the words blurred before her eyes. Questions welled up inside her until she felt near to bursting. "Hundreds of years ago? Omra must be a very different place now."

"I'd imagine it is. But I am a very different man."

"What was it like?"

His shoulders stiffened at the question. She watched the strangest occurrence fold over him like a shadow. The relaxed stature of his body suddenly disappeared. His fists closed over the edges of the book so tightly she worried he would rip the pages. The aggressive expression and huffing breaths she associated with him returned tenfold.

A snarl ripped between his lips, pushed through the fangs in his mouth. She didn't know if the sound was a word or merely an expression of anger.

"I don't remember," he growled.

Amicia shrank back in her chair, pressing her novel against her chest. She turned away from him, staring out the window until the bright snow burned her vision away. "I apologize. I should not have asked."

He stood, pushing the chair back so violently it screeched back several feet. "Such curiosity is dangerous, petite souris."

A vision of the man in the catacombs, beautiful in a bed of white feathers, flashed in her mind's eye. "In a place such as this, I agree."

She could feel his eyes on her. Searching for something? Or perhaps arguing with himself on whether he should kill her now. The King stalked away and slammed the library door behind him.

Amicia didn't realize she had been holding her breath until she blew it out in a great rush. She hadn't wanted to anger him. For a moment, she'd forgotten that she was afraid of him. They could sit and read together in silence. Perhaps that might have been… all right. At least she hadn't been afraid when they had sat together.

Hands shaking, she set aside her book. She'd put it back where she found it and head back to the kitchen where she didn't have to worry about a king who would find her. She would tuck herself back into the place where she belonged.

A peasant woman in the kitchens. People like her didn't belong in the libraries of rich, noble men.

Crutches firmly under her arms, she turned toward the door only to see the King had left the tiny journal on the chair where he'd sat. The pale blue cover and golden edges called out to her, making her fingers itch.

"Curiosity has no place here," she reminded herself. "You'll get yourself killed if you keep pushing, Amicia."

And yet, it was right there. So easy for her to lean down, smooth her palm over the supple cover, and to pick up.

She held it up to the light, reading the golden pressed words. "The Celestials," she murmured.

The word was unfamiliar. She'd never heard of such beings, not in her life and nor had she heard the word whispered in the city. Celestials. What did that mean?

As they had in the catacombs, a strange phantom hand

touched her back. "Read the book," it whispered in her ear. "Discover all you wish to know."

The last time she'd listened to this voice, the entire chateau had almost come down around her ears. The Dread had hunted her, she'd been thrown off the roof of the building, and found herself trapped here for the length of her healing process.

Her hand moved of its own accord, tucking the book into the waistband of her borrowed pants and shifting the wrapping of her shirt so it was hidden. Apparently, her mind would struggle while her body decided for her. She would keep the book and read it later on.

Somehow, it felt important.

The doors to the library slammed open once again, shaking the bookshelves beside it. Amicia gasped, snapping her attention back to the doors as if the King had stalked in to tear her to pieces.

Instead, it was Bernard who ran toward her, wings spread wide behind him and flapping to give him the extra speed. Out of breath, he skidded to a stop in front of her. "You need to get back to the kitchens."

"What?" She took a step back, shaking her head. "Why? What's the matter?"

"The alchemists are here." Bernard reached for her. His hand slid underneath her back and swept her legs up into his other arm, ignoring her gasp of pain and the crutches that fell to the floor. "We have to hide you."

"Who are the alchemists?"

He stared down at her, yellow eyes wide in what she had to assume was fear. "They gave him the ability to make monsters, mademoiselle. They started all this."

CHAPTER 17

*T*he King of the Dread lounged upon his throne, projecting for all intents and purposes that he was at ease. And why shouldn't he be? He was in his own home, surrounded by his army of monsters, and no one would ever unseat him.

Yet, the beings who walked through the door and stalked toward him were the few creatures who could destroy him if they wished.

The alchemists were clad in red robes; the hoods pulled over their heads. When he'd first seen them, he'd been struck by how little the fabric shifted with their movements. Unaffected by the wind, their robes appeared to glisten in the light, like blood pouring over their bodies rather than velvet.

The only part of the alchemists bodies that could be seen were their hands. Demurely folded in front of them as they walked, the robes were so stiff nothing past their wrists were ever bared.

Each hand held different markings tattooed on their fingertips and knuckles. Marks that indicated what they studied and what they should be feared for.

A single alchemist walked in front of the others. This was the one the King knew far better than any of the others. The one who could cause unimaginable pain with just a flick of his fingers.

The King tapped his claws against the arm of the throne, impatiently waiting for them to reach him. They liked to make a display of their arrival the few times when they did come to his chateau.

He didn't like it when they were here. Sometimes they stayed for weeks, leaving a slick oil on the floor wherever they walked. Their shadows remained in his halls for too long, and the King always felt as though their eyes remained. Then, sometimes, they stayed only for a few hours.

He hoped this time would be the latter.

The leader of the alchemists bowed before his throne, hood touching the ground before he straightened. "Great King of the Dread. Thank you for welcoming us into your home."

The King inclined his head. "You are always welcome in these walls, my trusted advisors."

"It has been a long journey, but we cannot stay long."

Relief eased the tension at the base of the King's spine. He shifted forward, leaning his elbows onto his knees and staring down at the alchemist. "May I ask why you are here? It has been a long time since I have needed your council."

"It is about the curse, great king."

When was it not? The first time they had waltzed through those doors, he had tried to kill them. This alchemist was the one who had put him on his knees, tattooed hand raised to make the King's blood boil within his body.

They had told him that he was cursed. But there was a way to break it, although it was not a good way for the people of this land. He must turn all the humans into beasts like him. He would bring about a new age for the kingdom, and in doing so, break the curse upon himself.

They had never told him what curse was laid upon him. He did not know if this form was the curse, his anger, or the ever present desire to kill. But he did know they hadn't given him much of a choice. Try to break his own curse, or die.

He had chosen to live.

"I have completed the tasks you set," he replied. "What else could you tell me?"

"That you have been careless in your tasks and missed many opportunities." The alchemists voice was chiding, like a father whose son hadn't realized life was so much harder than he thought. "We are here to help you rectify that."

The King didn't know what they meant. There was only one human left, the girl, and he had her in the chateau. He could turn her whenever he wanted.

He leaned back in the throne, staring at the alchemists as if one of them would give him a clue. Instead, they all stood silent. Their red robes undulated and, for a moment, he thought he saw a dark red stain eking out from underneath the edges. Spreading out over the cracked marble floor, turning the stone from white to blood red.

He blinked, and the vision disappeared. Magic had always been a talent of these creatures. He didn't know what they were or who they had sold their souls to for such power. Nor did he wish to know.

A memory whispered to life in his mind. A memory of a woman walking through the doors in a blood red dress.

"I seek sanctuary," she had begged, the words dripping from ruby lips. "Please, help me."

He had refused, and then her dress had slid from her body like a river pouring from her veins. She hadn't been a woman after all, but an alchemist who had desired something from him.

Something... but he couldn't remember what.

The alchemist before him was speaking, and the King had no idea what the other man had said. He snapped his jaws, adjusted his wings, and interrupted the creature. "Repeat it all again."

"What?" The alchemist asked. "Your majesty—"

"Again, alchemist."

The long and sudden silence did not bode well for the King, but he knew better than to agree to anything the alchemists asked without knowing the details. These creatures were tricksters at heart. They would try to bind him to a fate worse than death if they could.

The alchemist began again. "The conditions of your curse were that you change the entirety of this kingdom into the same beast as yourself. In doing so, you would change the course of the kingdom. Remaking it in your own image."

"I remember."

"You have sent your army instead of yourself, and as such, have received sloppy results. Do you believe you've changed all the humans?"

He thought of the girl with her big brown eyes staring at him with so much hatred and fear. The chocolate color had reminded him of something he'd once... not loved, but thought of with fondness. He wanted to know what more secrets she could pull out of his mind.

"I have found all the humans," he replied. "I've completed your task."

Movement in the back corner of the room caught his eye. None of the Dread would dare to budge an inch. The last time one of them had caught the attention of an alchemist, their blood had splattered the wall.

The Dread who watched the woman, Bernard, would know better than to go against his orders. He was to keep the woman hidden away from sight until their unwelcome guests had departed. The alchemists would kill her and be done with the whole situation. He knew they grew tired of his anger and dealing with the King of the Dread.

He trusted his army to do what was right. He trusted them to not make foolish mistakes because they knew what his wrath tasted like.

And yet, he saw a subtle flash of dark hair behind a marble statue of a woman pouring water, only to see her disappear back into her hiding place once again.

He would kill Bernard for putting his king in a position like this. The woman wasn't important in the long run. She would die. But he wanted to know what other memories she revealed in his mind, and he couldn't do that if she was killed before he had the chance to learn what she could show him.

Snarling, he leaned forward to catch the attention of the alchemists completely and utterly. "All the humans," he repeated, giving them no opportunity to look to the corner where the King could hear the distinct sound of a crutch creaking.

The leader of the alchemists tsked. "Not all of them. We've gathered them up to assist you, however. We left them outside the chateau with a few of your monsters watching them. I'm certain you know what to do."

They'd found more humans? But the King had been so thorough, his army had been... He waved a dismissive hand. "Yes, yes, I know what to do. And then?"

"We'll return when we feel the magic and curse has been fulfilled." The alchemists turned to leave as one. The leader tossed one parting shot over his shoulder as his people filtered out of the Great Hall. "Do not disappoint us again, King of the Dread. I'm certain you remember what it feels like to know my touch."

A phantom pain raked down the King's back. He arched away from it, certain the alchemist had sent a spike of power his way.

He remembered the pain. How could he forget the feeling of blood boiling in his veins?

The alchemists left the Great Hall, but he didn't move until he felt them exit the front door. All the darkness seemed to seep out of the room through the floor. The wet stains on the marble disappeared as though they evaporated.

Only then did he look toward the corner where the girl was hiding. She had no right to sneak through his castle like some stowaway. The secrets he kept were his own. Hadn't she already tried to discover too much? The last time had been in the catacombs, a secret even he hadn't mustered the courage to look upon.

And now, she wanted to see what the alchemists were. He vowed to frighten her out of her wits so she wouldn't push anymore. Never again would this girl seek answers when she answered his questions.

The King pushed himself out of the throne and strode across the floor to the statue she'd snuck behind. The statue had always been his favorite. Every inch of it had been lovingly crafted by a master artisan who knew how to create such subtle folds in the fabric he often wondered if the wind could blow it.

Clearing his throat, he stood in front of it for a few minutes before leaning around the corner when she didn't reveal herself. Tongue ready to provide the lashing she deserved, the King froze when he saw nothing at all behind the marble.

Had he imagined it? Was he seeing her in every corner of his chateau when she wasn't even there?

He was losing his mind.

"Master?" a voice interrupted his thoughts.

"Bernard," he snarled. "I thought I told you to watch the woman."

"You did, master." Clicking nails approached, followed by the awkward rustling of wings. "I lost her in the confusion. She said she would rest a few moments, and when I turned, she was gone."

"She's an injured woman on crutches, Bernard. You are one

of the Dread. How did you lose her?" He turned around to cast a glare that threatened death upon the creature. Soon.

Bernard met his gaze with worry and not fear. A strange thing, considering the beast would have cowered before him only a few days before. "I will gladly have this conversation with you soon enough, master. But I think we both have a larger problem."

"Which is?"

"Did—did the alchemists mention where the new prisoners were waiting your judgement?" Bernard nervously glanced toward the door. "And do the other Dread know what she looks like if she attempts to—ahem—free said prisoners?"

The beast had a point. Sudden anxiety rose over the King's head and broke down like a crashing wave that sent his heart beating rapidly.

He didn't answer the Dread. Instead, he opened his wings wide and sent himself careening toward the front door with a burst of air.

The woman was in grave danger.

CHAPTER 18

*A*micia pulled herself on her belly through the snow, one arm over the other as her useless leg dragged behind her. The ache of the broken bone grew worse with each movement, but she could survive this.

There were other humans here. Those creatures had brought them, whatever the strange robed figures were. They had taken humans from their homes, just like her. They had brought them here to be sacrificed to the beasts, and she couldn't let that happen.

But she needed to be careful. The Dread watching the humans would recognize her. The moment they saw her, they would know what she was trying to do.

She had strapped her crutches onto her back, laid down in the frozen drifts, and crawled her way to the humans. It had taken longer than she thought there was time for, but no one had come to take the humans away.

There were no guards but the two Dread who stood with their backs to the group huddled at the rear entrance to the chateau. An entrance that was very near the servants' kitchens, an exit the humans could escape through.

Three men and two women huddled together for warmth. They wore furs that had seen better days, and their hair was all a matching set of muddy brown. Amicia could hardly tell what they looked like under the grime.

Had she looked like that when she arrived? No wonder the Dread had hunted her like an animal. She must have looked like nothing less than one.

Finally, she made it near the door. She waited for the Dread to turn the other way one last time before she rolled her body up and over the snow drift nearest to the humans and down into the gulley where they awaited their fate.

One of the men pulled a wicked blade from his waistband. He lunged toward her only to pause at the last second to stare down at her in shock.

He had blue eyes. Eyes like ice and a chiseled jaw that had been chipped from a glacier. He was lovely. Far more handsome than any of the men she'd ever seen in Little Marsh. But he wasn't from Little Marsh.

"Who are you?" he asked.

"Amicia."

"What are you doing here?"

She cleared her throat, leaning into the knife pressed against her neck to remind him he still held a blade to her. "I'm here to save you," she whispered.

"You?" he asked, his voice a little too loud.

"Shh," Amicia scolded. She rolled once more, ignoring the pain in her leg to confirm the Dread were still looking in the other direction. They appeared to be conversing, something she couldn't remember any of them ever doing.

One of them she recognized. It had come into the kitchens to bother Bernard, refusing to talk when she was in the room. There was a tear in its wing that appeared to prevent it from flying. She hadn't been able to tell if it was male or female then, and still couldn't.

Sliding back into the gulley with the other humans, she gestured for them to come closer to her. "Through the door behind you is the servants' quarters. If you take a right and then another right, you'll be back outside without the guards to stop you. Once there, run across the lake into the forest. As fast you can."

The two women turned toward the door with one of the men. All three had round faces and dark eyes. Perhaps they were siblings?

The two remaining men hesitated. The man with the knife reached out a hand for her to take. "My name is Ivan. I'll not leave you."

Amicia pointed to her leg and arm bound to her chest. "I'm broken. I won't be able to keep up with you, and I'll only slow you down. You have this one chance for freedom. Please. Leave me. Knowing you are free is enough."

"It's not." He bent down and tucked his shoulder into her good armpit. Hoisting her in the air, he grinned down at her. "Together. That's the only way we'll best these beasts."

Amicia felt no guilt in leaving. She nodded once and together they hobbled toward the door. The other man held it open for them, checking to make sure none of the beasts were following them before they raced through the halls.

It felt like years ago when she had burst into this forgotten kitchen. When she had seen the molding fruits and vegetables and assumed this place was abandoned. The door still stood open. Had she left it like that? Or had the women in their escape?

Their footprints stood out in the snow like stains. The Dread would follow them, but at least they stood some kind of chance. They weren't delivered like cattle for the beasts to feast upon. To change into their own image with no memory of who or what they were.

She'd done the right thing. Amicia couldn't save them in any way other than to give them a few more moments of freedom.

Her feet touched the snow once more, and all she could think was the bitter wind beyond was the most beautiful thing she'd ever felt in her life. Ivan's hand at her waist was real. No claws marred his fingertips pressed into her ribs. The hand of a man had never felt as good as in this moment.

The pots and pans hanging on the wall behind them rattled, and a great roar echoed through the chateau. She'd heard it before. It was the sound of a king ordering a hunt.

Amicia met Ivan's horrified gaze and whispered, "Run."

She used her good leg to push forward, hopping with him although he carried most of her weight. Her broken arm was squished against his side. Spots of black and white danced in front of her vision as the pain caught her breath. But she wouldn't make him stop. This was their chance. She could see the forest. She could see the trees that would give her cover, and they were closer than they had seemed from within the walls.

Ivan tossed his knife to the other man. The blade arced through the air, glinting in the dying sunlight. "Die well!" he shouted.

"Go!" the other man replied, turning to stand his ground against the Dread who raced after them.

Amicia focused on keeping her breathing even. She watched the sky in horror as a wave of Dread flew above them. Ten, no, fifteen, monsters tracked the three women who had barely made it to the edge of the lake.

They swooped down in one movement. Vultures. They all reached for the women with claws as long as their forearms, slashing down upon their backs and faces. Their shrieks echoed through the air just as the man behind them started swearing.

"Left," Ivan snarled. They pivoted around the fifteen Dread and started in a different direction toward the lake.

He moved like lightning, slicing through the snow as if it

didn't bother him at all. Muscles bunched against her side. He moved them forward with a speed that should have been impossible for a human. Maybe he wasn't.

For a second, she believed they would make it. The moment their feet touched the frozen lake, she believed they could get to the forest. If anyone could, it was this strange man with icy eyes and a determined set to his jaw.

Ivan tossed her forward into the snow as something struck them from behind. She soared through the air, turning just in time to take the impact on her good shoulder before skidding a few feet away.

The King of the Dread crouched above her would-be savior. His wings spread wide, he lifted his clawed hands above Ivan's head. Straddling the human, there was no chance for Ivan to survive. But he wasn't looking at the man.

He was looking at her.

Her chest heaved as she stared back at him. Red eyes, inhuman and so unfeeling. She hadn't been able to escape them every time she closed her own. Those nightmarish orbs that glowed from within the sockets of his skull had plagued her every dream.

The King could have turned Ivan into a Dread like the others. She could hear the women's screams turning from pain into victory as they joined the ranks of monsters.

But the King of the Dread didn't turn Ivan into a creature like himself. No. Instead, he brought his claws down and sliced the man's throat open.

Rivers of blood poured out of Ivan as he gargled his last angry words. "A curse upon you."

What he didn't know was that they all suffered a curse already. A curse she had somehow managed to entangle herself in as well.

Blood mixed with snow, oozing toward her like veins.

Amicia couldn't stand to stay here a moment longer with these beasts. She would rather die than watch this repeatedly.

Gasping, she pulled the crutches from her back, scrambled onto her feet, and raced across the frozen lake.

"Stay where you are!" The order cracked through the air like thunder.

But she didn't want to listen to him anymore. She couldn't listen to someone like that. A beast should never masquerade as a man.

Her feet pounded the snow-covered ice and it let loose a grumble. The sound was like that of a giant in the fairytales. Like a water monster hid underneath the surface, just waiting for an unsuspecting traveler to set foot upon the surface so it could launch itself through the ice.

But Amicia was light, and she had already made it across the frozen lake once before. She didn't pause or hesitate as she fled the chateau. Her leg screamed in agony, deadened and dragging behind her. The crutches pressing against her broken ribs refused to allow her to draw in a deep breath.

She wouldn't let it stop her. She was so close to freedom as the sun set on the horizon and darkness blanketed the land.

"Woman!" the King of the Dread screamed behind her.

She would not stop. She didn't have to listen to him or any other who was so heartless.

The ice cracked. The sound was that of bone snapping, porcelain shattering, glass breaking. Amicia froze, waiting for the breath-stealing water to rise over her head. She wouldn't be able to swim with a matching broken arm and leg. She'd try her best, but the icy waters would win.

Her breath remained in her lungs and her clothes remained dry. He had not caught her, when all logic said he would.

"What?" she whispered, turning to see the King of the Dread had fallen through the ice.

The King held onto the edge of the ice, but the water

dragged down his wings that kept getting stuck underneath the ice shelf. He dug his claws into the snow, losing purchase now and then, sending him deeper and deeper into the water. Shaking his horns, he scrabbled harder. The muscles on his arms bulged as he tried desperately to save himself.

The others remained on the shore, screaming out their anger, but none moved to help their king. She stood in the center of the lake, watching them.

Not a single one followed him. Some took to the air, flying circles around their fallen leader and diving close, but never close enough for him to catch their outstretched hands. Why weren't they helping him?

It was a losing battle.

She could stand here and watch him die. It wouldn't take long. The frigid waters would slow down his heartbeat, and soon he would slide into the lake. Likely to join many souls who had died in its waters.

Or she could turn around and not know what happened. Maybe one of the Dread would save him. She didn't understand why they weren't crossing the ice to get their king already, but it wasn't her problem.

This was the monster who had thrown her off the roof of his chateau. He could drown for all she cared. She'd flee to one of the other kingdoms. Maybe even Omra which he seemed so fond of. Let him track her all the way there.

Amicia turned away from him, staring at the edge of the dark forest. It was right there. Just a few more rambling steps and then she could run again.

But she couldn't do it. All she could see was her father. Trapped, blood pooling around his body and she had done *nothing*. Something bone deep inside her refused to walk away again. This time she would at least try to save someone.

Snarling, she spun and shuffled through the snow toward

him. Her crutches pierced down to the ice, crunching as she went.

Amicia dropped onto her knees a body's length away, not wanting to test the ice any further. "You couldn't have just let me run?" she huffed.

The King sank his claws deeper into the ice, snapping his fangs together. "After all the trouble I went through to keep you?"

"What trouble? You threw me from the roof of your chateau!" She situated herself onto her bottom, digging her good heel into the snow until she had enough purchase to hold herself. Reaching out one of her crutches, she grumbled, "Grab onto this."

"I was trying to save you," he replied, not moving to grab onto the offered crutch. He stared back at her with those red eyes, something flickering in his gaze that she couldn't name. That same, soft expression he'd had just moments before he'd thrown her to her death.

"Save me?" She scoffed and waved the end of the crutch in his face. "Allow me to show you how to save someone, King of the Dread. Take it."

"I don't need saving, petite souris."

"You are a grand imbecile! You will freeze to death in that water if you don't get out soon. I can help you."

"Why would you help me?"

He raised a good point. Amicia struggled to find the words before she blew out a ragged breath. "Maybe because I want to redeem myself, and not let anyone else die because of me. Even a monster who just killed a man without remorse."

The King of the Dread relaxed his hold on the ice, claws slipping as he drifted deeper into the waters. Waves crested his shoulders and his teeth chattered together. "Maybe I was saving him, too."

"Oh, don't you dare," she snarled as he slid into the water.

Amicia lunged forward and snagged a hand on one of his horns. The texture abraded her palms, but she refused to let him go. She would not live with the guilt of his passing for the rest of her life just because he was a coward.

His weight pulled her forward into the water with him. Amicia tried to hold herself in the snow, but she couldn't hold onto him as well.

Together, they slipped into a silvery, moonlit world. They hovered, suspended in the waters, staring at each other in shock.

Here in this otherworldly place, he looked almost handsome. Like a demon who had risen out of Hell itself to find her. Floating wings spread wide, horns stretching up from his skull, he painted a picture of sheer darkness against the beams of moonlight. A few air bubbles escaped from his loincloth. They traced a path up the broad planes of his chest, then decorated his horns like pearls.

A chunk of ice slid by her, and Amicia's lungs squeezed. She hadn't taken a deep breath and even if she had, the cold would have stolen it. Looking up, all she could see was a sheet of ice above them.

Where was the hole? Where had they fallen through?

Panic tightened her chest, but she still tried to kick up toward the surface. Her broken leg refused to move. Her pants helped her to swim with her good leg, but the muscles soon froze. Lungs screaming, she looked to the King with wide eyes.

She didn't want to die with him. She'd wanted him to disappear from her life, certainly. But she'd always thought someone good and kind would be with her in her last moments. Not a monster who had been born out of her nightmares.

The King of the Dread flapped his wings and swam toward her with the speed of a shooting star. He struck her hard, gathered her against his chest, and broke through the ice with his horns. Together, they rose into the air, raining shards of ice and frigid water in their wake.

Gulping air, she shivered against his icy chest as he flew them back to the chateau.

"You should not have tried to save me," he said, barely affected by the cold now that they were in the air once more.

"Watching you die like that isn't defeating you," she said through her teeth. "And I want to defeat you, King of the Dread. In more ways than one."

He chuckled. "Feisty as ever, petite souris. Shall we get you warm?"

"If only to live another day, my captor."

"You are no more a prisoner than I am." His words were quiet, though, and she wondered if there was another meaning in them.

Was he a prisoner? Was that why he'd been content sinking into the lake?

Amicia stared up at his granite hard face and wondered at how little she knew this creature who had tried to take her life only to save her. Twice now. Perhaps there was more to him than she had thought.

CHAPTER 19

*A*micia hobbled after Bernard, her crutches clicking on the floor and her breathing already ragged. The race across the frozen lake had re-broken a few of her ribs, which made it difficult for her to use the supports.

Bernard had re-wrapped them the best he could when he didn't know what he was doing. The bindings were much tighter than before. They constricted her breathing and made her lungs feel heavy. She could do nothing other than lay in her cot, staring at the dried herbs hanging from the ceiling.

Two days had passed since the frozen lake. Two days spent in silence as her unwilling keeper had been so livid at her he'd barely been able to speak. And now, he was taking her somewhere in the chateau with an angry clip to his step. His claws left scratch marks on the marble floor everywhere he passed.

"Bernard?" she tried again. "Can you at least tell me where we're going?"

He grunted and turned a corner, taking her in a direction she'd never been before.

At least, she didn't think she'd been this way. Traveling

through the walls differed significantly from making her way through the chateau as one should walk through a building.

"Bernard?"

He flared his wings wide and glanced over his shoulder. "You'll see soon enough. Still afraid we're going to kill you?"

The insult stung, but he wasn't wrong. Amicia was slowly letting go of the concern. After all, their king had saved her from certain death twice now. He'd caused both, but that didn't mean he hadn't saved her. Something in him had changed from the monster desiring nothing but death.

The fear remained buried deep in her chest, however much she tried to banish it away from her thoughts. She wondered when they would stop being so kind. When they would finally give it up, and her fate would be nothing more than the rest of the humans.

He still hadn't explained what made her different. Even Bernard didn't know the answer. And she liked to think her manservant was at least a little happy she was still around.

The others, she wasn't so certain about.

They passed by one of the Dread, a new one. The features were familiar, a little more delicate than the other Dread she'd seen. Female? Her chest was as flat as the others, her body muscular and her legs still strangely bent. But there was something feminine the way she walked that set her apart.

As they passed, Amicia made eye contact with the creature in hopes it would give her some kind of reaction. If it were one of the women she'd attempted to save, then it should at least be mad at her. She'd been the one who had them run. Maybe they had another plan to save themselves. Maybe...

She walked by the Dread female and saw nothing in her gaze. There was no flare of the wings, no set of the jaw, nothing more than a morbid curiosity.

This one didn't remember Amicia at all. This one only

remembered the last few days since it had been born. That was all.

Her heart throbbed in sadness. Even if this wasn't one of the women she tried to save, this Dread female didn't know who she was. Who she used to be.

None of them did.

Bernard stopped in front of a door that might have once been beautiful. Chips of gold paint had flecked from the surface long ago. Tiny remnants of the paint glittered on the floor. Pale blue wallpaper had once decorated the hall, only a few strips remained fluttering in the slight breeze. The others hung like wilting flowers, drooping toward the floor and tattered from neglect.

He reached out and flicked off a piece of paint flaking from the wooden door. "This will be your room, mademoiselle."

"My room?" she repeated, wrinkling her brow in confusion. "I don't have a room. I stay in the kitchens with you."

"The master would no longer like you living in the servants' quarters. He said it's long past time for you to have a room of your own."

She didn't want a room of her own. Had the master of the chateau thought of that? Amicia enjoyed being around Bernard, the herbs, the smell of cooking. It reminded her of the home she'd left behind and the one that still made her chest ache at the mere thought.

Her heart skipped a beat at the possibility of being... alone. Eyes wide, fists clenched on the rungs of her crutches, she stared at Bernard like he could help her, or at least change her fate. "My room?" she repeated.

Perhaps there was pity in his gaze this time, although she wasn't confident. It was still difficult to read the expression on their stony faces. "Mademoiselle, please."

So there would be no arguing on this. Only the order

existed, and she would stay in this room whether she wanted to or not.

A part of her planned to stalk right back down the hall and scream for the master of the castle. King of the Dread. The title was not one he had earned, nor one she respected. He needed to know she was angry, and she wasn't going to do whatever he ordered her to do.

The logical side of her brain reminded her she was still broken. Still healing and trying to make her place here because there was nowhere else to go.

The Dread had fed her. They had clothed her. Now, they were giving her a safe place to call her own, and she was ungratefully still frightened of them. And why? Because they were monsters out of the storybooks who killed her kind?

But they hadn't killed her.

She blew out a long breath, nodded her head, and opened the door. She could stand in the hall and argue until she was blue in the face, but that was a waste of time for both of them. Bernard had more work to do, and this would free his time.

The door swung open on rusty hinges, creaking like the gate to a haunted graveyard. But the room beyond was... pretty. Once upon a time.

The floor was a lovely white marble like the rest of the chateau. The wallpaper had once been lavender, although it had faded to a pale gray. Tiny flowers climbed up the walls, some painted, others stretching from the floorboards and blooming on their vines.

A fainting couch was covered by a white sheet in the corner, along with what she assumed was a dresser and vanity set. A large fourposter bed sat in the center, gauzy fabric blowing in a wind rushing through a broken window framed in gilded edges.

She looked up at the ceiling and tried to keep her mouth closed as she marveled at the lovely paintings of women and angels lounging in a garden. Hand painted, the mural was the only thing in the entire room as pristine as the day it had been painted.

This was the room of a noblewoman. Not a peasant who had entered the chateau without permission.

"Why would he give this room to me?" she asked. "This is too nice for someone like me."

Bernard snorted. "It's too nice for one of our kind. We'd destroy it in a heartbeat."

"Destroy it?" Apparently she'd turned into a parrot, but Amicia couldn't stop repeating all the words he said.

"The Dread are more comfortable in nests," Bernard replied. "This is too... put together. We'd rather have all the furniture in pieces on the floor so we can arrange it better."

That explained why so much of the chateau was shattered pieces of what might have once been here. The Dread preferred nests? Like birds? She'd never seen one asleep, so she couldn't imagine what that looked like.

She knew so little about these creatures. They frightened her, yes, but there was an air of mystery and undiscovered knowledge about them she found so intriguing. If only she had the time to study their habits without them knowing. Then she could write all her findings down and put it in a library somewhere.

Bernard gestured to the wardrobe hidden by the large sheet. "There should still be clothing in there. The master said some of it might fit you, and would be more appropriate than the clothing you've been wearing."

Amicia looked down at the pants and strips of bindings on her chest. The master was right, but there were no humans here. What did the Dread care about dressing appropriately? Almost all wore nothing more than loincloths.

"I—um—" she stammered, trying to find her tongue and finding it tied in knots instead. Finally, Amicia cleared her throat. "I'm confused."

Bernard grumbled something under his breath that sounded like, "We all are," but before she could clarify, he left the room and closed the door behind him with a sudden crack.

She was left alone. For the first time since she had been running from the Dread.

Amicia didn't know what to do with the sudden silence. It loomed around her like a physical presence, a specter grinning from the shadows, waiting for when she would let her guard down so the nightmares could creep out from underneath the bed.

Her father would have loved this adventure. Every bit would have called out to the inventor within him. He'd have wondered if there were hidden secrets in this room like the rest. And if there weren't, then he would have made them just in case the Dread decided he wasn't a valuable addition to the army.

Tears pricked her eyes, turning her vision blurry until she couldn't see anything but blurry shapes. She missed him. So much that it was hard to focus sometimes when his ghost appeared in her mind and whispered truths in her ear.

"I'm trying to be brave, father," she whispered. "Just like I know you would want me to be."

But it was hard here. Even harder when there were no distractions. Just herself, her thoughts, and the stinging nettles of memories.

Sniffing hard, she clacked through the room to the wardrobe. Grasping the white sheet, she ripped it off and stared at the white and gold masterpiece beneath. Even a wardrobe in this chateau was covered in gold leaf and perfectly created with tiny vines carved into each shelf.

She slid one drawer open. It had been sealed shut by moisture for a long time, and when the drawer wouldn't give, she put her entire weight into yanking it open.

The King of the Dread had been right. Silken dresses filled

the drawer, although she was certain these hadn't been worn in a few hundred years. She'd never seen this style in Little Marsh.

Pulling one out, she shook it hard until the long skirt fell onto the ground. Real silk. The fabric shimmered in the dimming light like the moon on water.

"This is too good to be on the likes of me," she whispered. But it was lovely...

One of the ladies, Miss Abernathy, who used to live next door to her had a nightgown like this. Or at least, similar. Amicia had only seen it once when she went over to borrow a bit of milk. Miss Abernathy hadn't changed out of her nightgown yet for the day, and Amicia remembered thinking she had been so beautiful in it. Like an angel or a fairy who had drifted out of the garden.

She wondered what had happened to her neighbors. She hadn't thought of them at all, just the collective of Little Marsh as if all the people were one being. But had Miss Abernathy, the angelic pixie of a woman, been turned into one of the Dread? Or had she died in the fires Amicia had set ablaze?

The breath in her lungs felt cold, sticking in her throat and sending shards of ice through her veins. She needed a distraction, or the guilt would come bubbling up again.

She had done what her father bid, though perhaps he was aware her soul would be damned forever. No matter. The city would fall one way or another. They would have been turned into monsters who no longer knew who they were. Instead, they had burned.

What a horrible way to die.

Amicia snapped the silken gown once more, bringing her thoughts back to the present and forcing her attention away from such thoughts. She could try the gown on. That wouldn't hurt. She could feel the silken fabric on her healing body and pretend to be a lady of the manor for a few moments.

Anything to distract her. Anything to take her mind away from those terrifying moments.

She leaned her crutches against the wardrobe and stripped. The pants were difficult to take off when her leg already screamed in pain, but she managed on her own. The bindings she left on her chest so her ribs might heal a little longer.

Slowly, she put the nightgown on. Up and over her head, then sliding down her torso like water. The long skirt fell to the floor on one side, the other catching on the brace that held her leg together. She could only imagine what that looked like.

"The lady of the manor with her skirts hiked up to the high heavens," she said with a snort. "That is the lady this place deserves."

Amicia hobbled to the vanity, still covered by a white sheet. She had to see what sort of picture she made, even though she was certain it was a laughable sight.

With a quick jerk, she yanked the sheet away from the mirror. The fabric snapped in her hand like a whip, falling away from the mirror to reveal her own image in the cracked glass. But Amicia didn't look upon her own visage. Instead, she stared at a dark shadow the mirror revealed in fractured portions.

A demon stood in her doorway.

He held his wings close to his sides like a cape, like a noble gentleman who called upon a noblewoman. Yet, he was still shirtless with his broad chest too strong for a man with royal blood. He wore the same torn loincloth since the moment she'd first seen him. His tail lashed behind him, perhaps a sign of discomfort, although she didn't know why he would be.

Amicia didn't turn. She stared at him through the mirror, frozen in place. "You gave me a room."

"I did."

"Why?"

The claws at the bend of his wings shifted a little, as if he was trying hard not to open his wings. "You shouldn't be in the servants' quarters with Bernard."

"Why?" she asked again. The answer seemed far more important than any of the other questions burning in her chest. Why was he doing all this for her when there was no logical explanation? She had to know, or it would eat her alive.

He shook his head, horns scraping the hallway ceiling. "I suspect you have many questions."

"More than I can count."

The King of the Dread stepped into her room. He had to duck low and tilt his shoulders just to fit, and once he was inside, he took up more space than he deserved. All the air disappeared in the wake of his aggressive size. Heat radiated from his body, even though it should have been cold since he appeared to be made of stone.

She sucked in a deep breath. "What are you doing?"

"Come with me, and I will answer all that I can."

She didn't know what to say. Amicia didn't want to be alone with him. He'd tried many times to end her life, and every broken bone screamed that he was…

A monster? She asked herself if she believed the thought and realized she didn't anymore. He wasn't just a monster, he was a creature who had thoughts, feelings, a history she didn't yet know, but wanted to know. A creature who made mistakes, who killed, but who always claimed he was saving his victims.

She stared at his reflection in the mirror, a reflection he appeared to avoid. The King of the Dread stepped closer, reached forward, and hooked a claw on the fabric caught upon her leg brace. Carefully, he pulled the silk just enough for it to slip down over her hip and thigh.

"Come," he murmured, his voice deep and gravely. "There is much we must speak about."

The only words which came to mind fell from her lips like a

river of sound. "I'm not appropriately dressed. Isn't that what you wanted?"

His red eyes flared brighter for a moment before he turned away. "You'll do."

Amicia followed him out of the room and deep into the heart of the chateau, chasing the answers to all her questions.

CHAPTER 20

*S*he followed him far away from the side of the chateau she was most used to. Past the kitchens, the library, even the living quarters she had seen through the walls. Eventually, she lost track of where they were.

With his guidance, the chateau seemed larger. Following the dark silhouette of the beast was little more than something out of a storybook. A devil leading her toward hell, or perhaps, redemption.

Amicia tried to minimize the sound of clacking every time she moved with her crutches, but eventually that grew tiring. She couldn't continue on the way she was, and he wasn't slowing down. So she let the sound thud through the halls, echoing around them like a heartbeat.

Was he going to answer all her questions? Why then did they need to travel somewhere else in the chateau?

Doubt clawed through her mind, leaving trails of fear and horror. Maybe now was the time he would turn her into a beast like him. Maybe now he would finally do what his people were supposed to do. Turn her into one of their own, a Dread, a monster who came out of the night and stole the souls of humans.

She wouldn't blame him. It had been a long time coming. But that didn't mean she was ready for it.

Amicia tried to think about what her father would do, even though it stung her heart to think of him. He believed there was good in everyone, but that the good sometimes had to be teased out like he used to have to untangle the long snarls in her hair.

"Amicia," he would have said, disappointment staining the warm tones of his voice. "You haven't given them a chance, not yet. It's time to let the beast come clean and see what this is all about. Maybe, you can help."

His voice was so clear in her mind, it was almost as though he'd remained by her side, not burned to a crisp in the city she had destroyed.

The King of the Dread paused in front of a stairwell leading up, higher than she thought the chateau had gone. They were already on the fourth story. Even outside she'd counted only three levels.

He cast a severe look up and down her figure. "You can manage the stairs?"

"I have been ever since you broke my leg."

He grunted. "Make your way on your own then."

As he started up the spiral stairwell, she wondered if that was his way of asking if she needed help. Did he want to assist her as she followed him? That was far too kind for someone like him. Monsters didn't care if other people were comfortable... did they?

Step by step, she followed him up the narrow stairwell. By the time she reached the top, her leg and arm were on fire. But Amicia was bound and determined to make it on her own, even if it was just to send a message to him. He might have broken her, but she was not dead.

The stairwell led to the roof, not to another ghostly level of the chateau she couldn't see. Flat and expansive across the entire chateau, it was covered in a thick layer of snow. Blank. Pristine. Amicia was almost disappointed there wasn't yet another secret for her to learn.

Perhaps it was better this way. Her own curiosity had gotten the better of her lately. Broken bones as proof.

She hesitated to step out onto the same area where he had thrown her all that time ago. It felt like forever, and yet, just a heartbeat since she had been suspended above the snow.

He turned toward her, horns outlined by stars. "This is not a night for death."

"The last time we were here, you threw me from the roof."

"And you survived." The moonlight caught in his eyes, reflecting like that of an animal. Glowing in the darkness. "I was not myself, that night. I haven't been for a long time."

The moon was out, but the stars shone brighter than the orb controlling the tides. Great swaths of stars spread across the sky, a river of pinprick lights setting the entire world aglow. Each one had a story. Her father used to tell her their tales before her bedtime, pointing out every constellation.

Amicia was so engrossed with the stars she didn't notice the strange chapel in the middle of the roof until the King of the Dread started toward it.

The building was smaller than she would have expected, perhaps inspired by another country. Four twisted spires of marble rose to tangle with each other and create a roof. An artist had carved runes into each. The strange symbols seemed to glow, but then she'd turn her head just so, and the brilliance disappeared.

The King of the Dread created a dark silhouette that blotted out the eerie light. None of it touched the darkened figure striding toward the chapel.

Swallowing hard, she tried to spread moisture through her suddenly dry mouth.

She reached the chapel long after he did. Amicia reached out and placed a hand on one spire to balance herself. "What is this place?"

"It was once a house of worship," he replied. The King of the Dread made his way to the center of the strange building where a single statue stood and knelt before her.

The marble might have once been carved into the figure of a woman, but Amicia couldn't know for certain. The face had been shattered long ago. Chunks of marble chipped away from the chest, hip, and feet. It was little more than a relic of a day long past.

Strangely enough, it made Amicia very sad to stare at the statue. She licked her lips. What did one say when someone else grieved? The King of the Dread's wings drooped around his shoulders, tucked into his sides. He lowered his head in reverence, holding up his hand and hovering it just before the statue.

A few whispers of a prayer reached her ears. The language was one she didn't understand, but the sentiment was one she'd heard before.

He was begging for forgiveness.

She remained silent, standing sentry for the King who had done all he could to destroy her. In this moment, they were not the captor and the woman who destroyed a kingdom. They were simply two people who knew what it meant to seek forgiveness from a higher power.

When the whispers slowed, then stopped, Amicia clicked forward on her crutches. "You said you would answer my questions."

"I suspect you have many."

"More than I can count," she replied. "But I think first I wish to know what you are and how you came to be."

The King lifted his head, staring beyond the statue and out into the night. He did not look at her when he replied. "I don't remember that, sadly. I'm afraid many of your questions will remain unanswered because my memory is... lost. Sometimes I think I know something and other times I don't even know who I am."

"When are the times when you know something?" Amicia's pulse seemed to stop, her breath freezing in her lungs, everything hesitating as she waited for his reply. The moment felt important. Like a great secret was about to be released.

The King turned his head, staring into her eyes with a red, cat-eyed gaze. "I only remember who I am when I look at you."

Amicia's tongue tied itself into a knot, and her palms grew sweaty. She didn't know if there were words in her language to respond. The few that slipped off her tongue were, "I don't understand."

If she wasn't mistaken, his face wrinkled with disappointment before he rose from his kneeling position. The King of the Dread towered over her, horns stretching toward the sky, wings spread wide. "Neither do I. And yet, you are the only thing which has made me remember some memories I have lost."

So her thoughts were correct—none of the Dread remembered who they were, only what they had become.

But if he could remember some things he had forgotten, then perhaps so, too, could the others.

Immediately, tears burned in her eyes so hot she knew they would tumble down her cheeks before she could catch them. Twin droplets burned, gathering at her chin and searing her flesh.

"What is this?" The King of the Dread reached out, a single claw catching the droplets. "Tears for me?"

"No," she said, choking on the words. "If what you say is true, then I killed my father for no reason. No matter what choices I made, my fate brought me here. You will never change me into one of the Dread because I remind you of what you once were. My father might have been one of your kind, but I could have worked to cure him. Instead..." She swallowed hard, pushing back the anguish that threatened to overwhelm and destroy her. "Instead, I killed him."

The King stepped away from her then, turning his gaze back to the statue. "You cannot know that to be the truth."

"If I hadn't set the city on fire, would the Dread have captured me?"

"Yes."

"And if they had brought me here, would I still have reminded you of something? Would your memories still have returned?"

The King ground his teeth, a muscle on his jaw jumping. "Most likely."

"Then my father is dead because of my own decisions, not because of you." The pain in her chest swelled, pressing against her heart and lungs, forcing its way through her ribs like fingers pushing them apart. Amicia pressed a hand against the ache. "I can't blame you for that, any longer. I can only blame myself. I could have saved him."

"Believing such things can only end in regret," the King hissed. "The more I remember, the more choices I hate myself for. Bury those memories, petite souris. Until they disappear."

She couldn't imagine forgetting this. She couldn't imagine ever forgiving herself for all the things she had done. And yet, staring at the pointed horns on his head, the bulging muscles and claws that opened and closed, she wondered if redemption would ever be possible for either of them.

All the hurt he had caused, all the pain and the anguish... And yet, he was still trying to remember.

"What have you remembered?" she asked. Perhaps his memories would distract her in this moment when she couldn't breathe or think of anything but her own mistakes.

He moved as though wounded, or exhausted beyond measure. The King lowered his body down to the edge of the broken statue. Seated like that, he almost looked human if it weren't for the wings, horns, and clawed feet.

Amicia corrected herself. He didn't look human at all in form, but his expression was one she recognized.

Sadness.

"I told you some," he replied. "Omra and the places I have traveled. But since then, they've started flooding my mind. I wasn't always like this. I was the first, and I was the one who infected the world with my mistakes."

"Infected?"

He tilted his head to look up at her. "I assume you read the book I was reading, the little blue one."

Amicia lifted a shoulder. "You shouldn't have left a book in a library if you didn't want others to read it."

"Have you?"

"Read it?" At his nod, she shook her head. "No."

"It's about my people, although I've never been able to read it. The words jumble together, as though I'm not the one meant to read its contents." The King shifted his wings, spreading them wide and letting them fold down until they rested upon the ground. Wings of a broken angel, one who had fallen from the Heavens only to find the world was not as pleasant as he'd thought. "You should read it. Perhaps it will explain a few things more clearly than I can. My memory of the Fall is hazy."

Questions bubbled to life, popping inside her skull repeatedly. What was the Fall? What had he been before this? Was he human or something else?

She needed all these questions to be answered, but the only thing she blurted out was, "What else do you remember?"

The question surprised her. So many other questions were more important. And yet, the one she wanted to know was only to know more. It didn't matter what he knew of his history; she had the book. She could find the answers out for her own.

But she wanted to know what she reminded him of. Was it

good things? Had she inspired memories of light or memories of war?

The King cleared his throat. "I remember white and gold, images flashing in my mind of carvings, gilded swords, and hair white as snow."

"The chateau in its prime?"

He shook his head. "No, I believe it to be something else. I don't remember what, however."

"Is that all?"

The King froze, hesitating for the briefest of moments before he let out a long, slow breath. "I believe I remembered my name."

His name?

The Dread had no names, that's what Bernard said. Not a single one of them. She'd even gifted one to her manservant, so he had something to remind him of his humanity.

But the King of the Dread had remembered the most precious thing a human had. The one thing that set them apart from the masses.

He had a name.

She felt as though she needed to sit down as well. The realization that he had been something, someone, before all of this made her knees weak. Amicia leaned hard against her crutches, thankful she had something to hold her up. "You have a name?"

"I believe so."

"What is it?"

He met her gaze, red eyes glowing in the darkness. "Alexandre."

Lord, knowing his name somehow made all of this real. He was a person now. Not just a monster who had tried to kill her. A person with a name, a history he couldn't remember, and one who needed help.

She tried to still the shaking of her hands at the crutch

rungs, but couldn't. Mouth dry, she coughed out her own name. "Amicia."

The King of the Dread, no, Alexandre, drew his wings in to his sides once more. "Amicia, it's a pleasure to meet you."

"And I, you."

She didn't know where to look, now that he had become something more than a storybook horror. He was... Alexandre. A cursed man, one who had been turned into a monster, perhaps even against his will.

"If I..." Amicia hesitated, then plunged forward with a plan she'd never once thought she would voice. "If I find out what happened to you, and if there is a way to mend what was broken... will you let me go?"

Alexandre stood, his height still intimidating and far too tall, but less fearsome than before. He stooped so he could look her in the eye, horns pointed forward and wings spread wide. "Yes, petite souris. I will let you go if you discover what happened here. But I fear if this is a deal you wish to make, then you will remain in this cursed place forever."

Amicia had other plans. She would find the answer to this curse, and her own freedom. "It's a deal."

CHAPTER 21

*A*micia tossed the little blue book aside, a headache blooming between her eyes so powerful it made her nauseous. She'd tried to read the damned thing, but it refused to be read. Three days she'd wasted trying to decipher the words. Three days trying to catch the wiggling lines that shifted and warped until her eyes ached.

He hadn't been joking when he said the book didn't want to be read by him. But it didn't want to be read by her either.

She couldn't understand what the book was. The moving lines were clearly handwritten. The swirling letters were elaborate, leading her to believe this was more likely a journal than it was an official document.

Most of the books in the library seemed to be accounts of townships, with a few storybooks along the way. Very few were journals or diaries.

Amicia glared at the book. Maybe if she just figured out how to intimidate it, then it would reveal the secrets held between its covers...

Nothing happened.

She snarled, then reached for her crutches. "Damned book,"

she muttered, shoving the padded ends underneath her arms. "I can't stand looking at it one more minute when it's just mocking me at this point."

Her skirts tangled in her legs, forcing her to stop and jerk them aside. Her usual cotton pants had disappeared suspiciously from her room a few nights ago. Until that point, she had decided upon wearing her own clothes.

Now, she was forced to wear the silken gowns provided by the Dread and their leader. Alexandre made it clear she was lucky to wear such finery. That most women would have been pleased.

Amicia was uncomfortable in the watery fabrics. They made it difficult to walk when she was used to her skirts rigidly staying in place when she moved. Silk and velvet adhered to her body like she'd touched sap on a tree. The dresses clung to her and made movement difficult. She had to walk slower, more delicately, when all she wanted to do was charge forward.

"Damned skirts," she growled, tempted to rip them apart and walk around in nothing more than her shift. "Damned creature making me wear god knows what kind of dresses. My mother is rolling in her grave at the indignities."

Amicia didn't know where she was going, only that she couldn't stay in her little room any longer. The pretty wallpaper, the gilded edges, all the delicate glass, it was swallowing her until she couldn't think or even breathe.

She didn't belong here. She wanted to go back to the kitchens where it was warm and smelled of earth. The herbs hanging over her head had grounded her. The heat of ovens warmed her bones. The scent of bread cooking and dough rising only reminded her to be thankful for the food on her table.

Here, she was lost. A block of dirt staining marble, silk, and glass. This wasn't where she was meant to be, and yet, she was chained to this glamorous place as if it were a prison.

To her, it was.

Walking helped. Movement centered her thoughts and drew them away from suffocating fabrics and frustrating books. At least she could focus on something other than what happened to the Dread.

She was no closer than she had been that night Alexandre had brought her to the rooftop chapel. She could still see him standing there with sadness in his eyes and the defeated droop of his wings.

A creature such as he should never look so weak. It was unnerving to know even the great King of the Dread was decidedly human. She wanted to think of him as some storybook monster who didn't know the difference between wrong and right.

Instead, she had discovered he was eerily similar to a man. A voice in her head whispered that might be the answer to all of this. He might be a man after all. A cursed one whom she could save.

But that answer was far too simple. The secrets hidden in this chateau couldn't be so easy.

Could they?

Clacking through the halls, she found her feet leading her deeper into the shadows. Back into the belly of the chateau where all her troubles had begun.

Back to the crypt where the strange and beautiful body lay.

Since that night, Amicia had dreamt of the man who waited there. He was a figment of her imagination, conjured by lack of water and food. No corpse could have been so pristine unless...

Unless he had just died.

She wondered whether he was a human, like her. She'd seen the Dread change people into one of their own. There was no reason for a man such as him to be laid out on display.

Alexandre didn't seem the type to keep trophies either. She had seen nothing from other towns or worlds here. If he had wanted to take memories from the people and townships he had destroyed, then he would have at least a few souvenirs lying around.

So who was the man? Was he some lost, forgotten soul who should have long since died? Was he cursed like the rest of them?

"Good idea, feet," she whispered, making her way carefully down the dark stairwell that led into the crypt. "Perhaps if we find out who the man is, then we will know more about the curse. At the very least, he must be connected somehow."

The stairs were much more difficult to traverse when she only had one good leg and one good arm to balance the crutches upon. Her ribs were much better, and she'd even removed the bindings now that she could take a deep inhale without it hurting. The arm and the leg were another story. Bones were slow to knit themselves back together.

Clicking down, she paused to lean against the wall to balance herself. She tried catching her breath. The heaving of her lungs refused to calm. So she continued to wind down the stairwell into darkness. Finally, she saw the crypt, still lit from her last time here.

She assumed. Every torch affixed to the wall shook with fire that made the gilded room glow. Could fires last so long?

A shiver traveled down her spine at the mere thought someone else might be in this haunted place with her. Someone, or something, staring back at her from the shadows.

"Pull yourself together, Amicia," she snapped. "No one is here but dead things."

And yet, she remembered all too well the voices whispering in her ears. She could still feel the press of spirits from where they rested within the carved walls of the crypt. Each tomb marked by a sigil of the sun.

She didn't want to hear the voices of the dead again. Their cold touch along her arms was well and good once. Amicia had been reminded and assured that life after death was coming for her. But once was enough.

The long hobble toward the sarcophagus seemed unending. As though she had to struggle through time itself to make it to the edge where she could peer down once more.

She wondered if the body would still be there. Whether he would still be as beautiful as she remembered, or if she had conjured his image.

Reaching the edge of the sarcophagus, she took in a deep breath before looking down. "Please don't be a rotten body," she murmured.

It took all her bravery to look down over the edge at the man who laid out in the small space as though he had fallen asleep. She hadn't imagined him. Worse, she hadn't remembered him as glorious as he was.

A curled lock of golden hair had drifted down over his forehead. She longed to reach out and readjust the errant strand, too pretty for a man and yet somehow perfect on his flawless face. Not a single scar nor mark of acne made him anything other than a marble statue.

But he wasn't marble. He was breathing.

Amicia stared at his chest in horror as it lifted up and down. It wasn't possible the man was alive. Was it?

A gust of wind shoved hard at her back, pushing her forward. She dropped the crutches onto the floor with an echoing clang and caught herself on the edge of the sarcophagus, suddenly much closer to the man who was everything she'd always dreamt of, and more.

He was a golden hero. A man who stepped out of a storybook and told a woman he would take care of her forever. The hero everyone knew could save the city. Just one look from him was enough to reassure he could fight a dragon if he wanted.

Amicia was so caught up staring down at his perfect features she almost missed the leathery sound of wings rubbing against stone walls. The gust of wind hadn't been some kind of ghostly intervention.

One of the Dread was in the tomb with her.

Swallowing hard, Amicia looked over her shoulder, but she already knew who it was. She could feel him the moment her mind turned away from beauty.

Dark shadows clung to his shoulders and horns. They dripped like ink off him as he stepped forward into the light. For a moment, the shadows clung to the top of his head, creating what looked like a crown. He was a monster. A beast.

A king.

"What are you doing down here?" she asked, although she had no right to the question.

"Seeking answers."

Her hand slipped, falling deeper into the sarcophagus but never touching the strange, sleeping man. "Did you find any?"

"Not until you arrived."

Amicia wasn't made of answers. She'd spent the last three days trying to read a book that fought back. She feared there were a hundred different ways to find the answers he sought, and she could have left long ago.

No matter what she did here, she felt very much as though she wasn't good enough. Not for the clothes they had dressed her in. Not for the room they bid her sleep in. And certainly not for this strange quest that could only end in heartbreak.

She gulped, then asked the question burning on her tongue. "What answers did my arrival give you?"

"Uncomfortable ones." He strode forward and stood beside her, staring down into the sarcophagus with a disgusted look on his face. "What do you make of this?"

"The body?" She looked with him at the strange dead man who wasn't dead at all. "He doesn't appear human."

"Why do you say that?"

"He's too perfect," she whispered in response.

The man appeared to be able to open his eyes at any moment. He was breathing, therefore it wasn't such a stretch to think perhaps he was resting. That this poor man would awaken with a strange, broken woman and a terrifying monster staring down at him.

A long sleep sounded lovely to her when it was all she could do to get through a single night without nightmares banging at her skull.

"He's not human," Alexandre confirmed. "He's one of the Celestials."

"I've heard that name." She wracked her memory. The spirits of those who had lived here were the first to whisper the name, she remembered. But what else… Amicia yanked her hand out of the sarcophagus and snapped her fingers. "The book! The blue book you were reading, the one neither of us can decipher. That book was titled The Celestials."

Alexandre turned a narrowed gaze upon her. "You can't read the book?"

She shouldn't have admitted that. The book was her only way of finding out what was going on, or at least, he was convinced of that fact.

Amicia cleared her throat. "I'm working on it and making progress. It's just not as easy as I thought."

Namely because the book didn't want her to read it. She was unsure if maybe it didn't want anyone to read it at all, or if there was something wrong with her. Maybe she wasn't the one meant to read its pages.

That was almost worse than being captured by the Dread. Being deemed unworthy to read a book was the ultimate condemnation.

When Alexandre continued to stare at her with a disgruntled expression, she turned back to the man in the sarcophagus. Amicia furrowed her brows. "Did he move?"

That snapped Alexandre out of his grumpy mood. He leaned

far over the sarcophagus, wings spread wide. "That's impossible."

"But you're looking."

"What moved?"

She hadn't thought far ahead when she'd exclaimed the words. Mostly, she just wanted him to not stare at her like he would tear her arms off if she didn't figure out what was happening. "His hand."

Alexandre leaned closer, inspecting the appendage as if he could make it move again just by staring at it intensely. "I don't think it did."

"Perhaps I was mistaken." She observed the body, surveying him for a few more moments before she asked, "Why did you say it was impossible for him to move? He's breathing."

"Breathing doesn't mean life."

"Of course, it does. How else would we define life? If a person isn't breathing, then they're dead."

Alexandre shook his head. "Not in this case."

The words made even less sense than he'd made thus far. It sounded like he already knew the answers she sought. If he knew what was happening here, then why wouldn't he just tell her? Why make her run around trying to find out the story?

She let out an angry huff of breath. "How do you know he's a Celestial? What is a Celestial?"

"These are questions I cannot answer." When he leaned away from the sarcophagus, a flicker of darkness crept over his shoulders. For a moment, they looked like skeletal hands, sinking into the flesh of his arms and neck, squeezing hard. "You will need to find the answers yourself."

She didn't understand that logic. He knew what was going on. Or at least, enough that he knew this creature before them wasn't human.

"Can you at least tell me what the Celestials are?" she asked again. "I know they aren't human."

"They are not." He did not continue, but he had answered her question.

Amicia thought hard about her next words. "Are they like you?"

He shook his head, albeit slowly. Almost as though he wasn't confident in his answer. "No, they were not like me."

"But could they be like you?"

The spark in his eyes made her breath catch in her lungs. He stared at her as though she was the most intelligent woman he'd ever met. Stepping much closer, Alexandre reached forward and tucked a strand of hair behind her ear. His hand lingered at the nape of her neck. "Yes, petite souris. Yes, they could be like me."

She couldn't breathe. He was too big, too close, too dangerous. If he wanted to attack her, he could do so with very little effort. All he had to do was lower that hand, wrap it around her throat, and...

Her heart raced at the thought of his hand around her throat. Only this time, fear was a secondary emotion to that of a strange thrill she'd never had before. Why did her heart race at the thought of him touching her? Why did her palms itch to reach out and smooth the gooseflesh she could see decorating his granite-like chest?

The shuddering breath that shook through her ribcage sent an answering warble through her voice. "How? How could they be like you?"

The spark in his eyes disappeared. "That I cannot tell you."

Amicia didn't have time at the moment to wonder why she wasn't afraid of him. Not even a single fiber of her body or a whisper of her soul said he would hurt her. Instead, all she felt was a confidence that she could trust him.

Because he was trusting her.

"There are rules, aren't there?" she asked. "Rules that say you cannot tell me everything you know."

"I do not know if there are rules," he replied. He leaned

closer, the torchlight making his horns gleam red. "But I know I don't want to risk anyone finding out I helped you."

"I've been trying to read the book. The words keep moving, like someone is writing over them in another hand."

He nodded, then stared at her expectantly. There was another question he wanted her to ask. Another thing that might help her, and yet...

Amicia took a deep breath. "Is there another book that might help me stop the words from moving?"

And again, a glow of pride illuminated his gaze until his eyes were twin fires set within his skull. "The alchemists were the ones who created the book. There are more of their works here in the crypt."

"Where can I get them?"

"Reach inside the sarcophagus. Underneath his right arm is a book written by the alchemists. Basic alchemy, but it should help you read the book on the Celestials."

Amicia moved without thinking. She plunged her hand into the sarcophagus once more, this time brushing her finger over the man's arm as she reached beneath him.

When she pressed against the golden man's arm, she saw an answering indent in the arm of Alexandre. She couldn't be certain, for the moment was fleeting, and it passed in a blink of her eye. But it was enough she was certain he was tied to this man who slept in the crypt.

Her fingers closed on the worn edge of a book. She pulled it out into the light and stared down at the blood red cover.

She turned it over in her hands. "No title?"

"There's no need for titles on books of alchemy. The inside is already filled with darkness. Once you open it, there is no turning back."

"I thought alchemy was science and magic combined?" She glanced up at him. "How could that be bad?"

"You'll find out, I'm certain of that." Alexandre backed away from her. "Be careful with that book. The abilities within are dangerous. Choose carefully which you enact in your life, petite souris."

"Then why give it to me?"

His throat worked. He opened and closed his fists, then spread his wings wide in a shrug. "I do not know."

Alexandre left her alone in the crypt, and Amicia felt the book grow heavy in her hands. What had he given her? What madness could this create?

CHAPTER 22

*A*micia bit into an apple, chewing as she read the last bit of the thirteenth spell in the book of alchemy. Tiny flecks of apple juice fell onto the book. Somehow, it always seemed to absorb whatever she spilled onto it. Amicia had given up trying to keep the book clean. If it wanted to eat, let it eat.

"They use a lot of gunpowder," she remarked, turning the page over. "I don't know why. It doesn't seem to make sense."

Bernard snorted from the other side of the table. He worked on creating the perfect loaf of bread while she read her book. Amicia kept her elbows on the table while she poured over the pages even though she knew it drove him mad.

"If you read less of that book and spent more time helping, I might be done with my work for the evening."

She turned another page over. "Your job is to feed the masses. My job is to figure out what happened to all of you."

"We were turned into the Dread. We are now part of the Dread. There is no going back. There is no going forward. We are what we are, and that is something we all must understand." He blew out a frustrated breath. "What has convinced you otherwise?"

Amicia took another bite of the apple. "Well, there were strange men in bloody hoods walking through the halls. There's a dead man who isn't dead in the basement. None of you remember who you are, but some of you are remembering at least a bit of who you might have been. None of this is ringing any warning bells?"

"I only remembered a few things," Bernard grumbled. "That doesn't make you the savior."

He'd remembered something? The apple fell from her numb fingers, rolled across the table, and bumped into the perfect loaf of bread he was struggling to create.

"Amicia," Bernard groaned. "How many times do I have to tell you? The bread won't rise if you insist on putting strange things in it. An apple touching the side will make that side fall!"

"You remembered something?" she whispered, still frozen in her seat.

Bernard stiffened. He snapped his wings close to his body and shook his head in denial. "No. I said nothing of the sort."

"You said you remembered a few things. What did you remember?"

"Nothing."

"Bernard!"

He sighed in defeat. "Just a little, and it was nothing more than a dream. A farmhouse on the edge of a city. A cow that used to kick over the milk bucket just when I finished milking her. That's all."

"That's not nothing," she exclaimed, hopping down from her stool and grabbing for her crutches. "Bernard, that's something significant! You remembered who you were!"

She clacked around the table, and he went in the other direction.

"Amicia, go away," he snapped.

Amicia continued to chase him in circles around the table

until he finally relented and let her catch him. She latched on and squeezed his waist hard. "You remembered!"

He struggled in her arms, twisting this way and that. "Okay, enough, get off me. I don't like this."

"But we should celebrate!"

"We will celebrate nothing. You were supposed to return to your room hours ago. I'll already be in trouble if anyone finds out."

She wasn't aware she was under curfew, but apparently she was meant to be places at certain times these days. Amicia released her unwilling captive and wrinkled her nose. "I don't have to be in my room if I don't want to."

"Do you remember the last time you did that?"

"Yes. I went to the crypt and had a lovely conversation with your King."

Bernard pointed at the book on his table as though it were cursed. "And you came back with that. I don't want to hear any more of that haunted mumbling. As above, so below yourself back to your bedroom, woman!"

"Don't you think that's a little dramatic?"

"I think you're a bad influence."

Amicia leaned down and picked up her crutches. She tucked them under her arms with a grin. "But if it weren't for me, you wouldn't have remembered that cow."

"Ah, what a life I must have had led if the first and most important thing I remember is jerking on some disgusting animals teats." Bernard waved a hand at her. "Off with you. To bed. Tomorrow you can continue reading that terrible book and playing at fantasy heroine in your head."

Amicia didn't know what she would have done without the unusual Dread. He made her laugh as she couldn't remember laughing. In all the darkness and sadness of her life, he was the light at the end of the tunnel that distracted her.

Even if she was a prisoner in the Dread's chateau, even if she had lost her father and all her friends, he had somehow still made her laugh.

"Good night, Bernard," she said, gathering the blood red book and tucking it into the waistband of her borrowed dress.

"Good night, mademoiselle. Sweet dreams."

As Amicia made her way back to the bedroom, she wondered if tonight would be the first night she would have good dreams. Dreams without people reaching out of the shadows or family members on fire asking why she had killed them. She tried her best not to think of the nightmares when the lights were on. But it was getting harder.

She couldn't help but wonder if they were a message. Were some spirits, maybe not the ones who were here, but the ones from her past, trying to tell her something important? Something she might have missed?

A howl rolled through the halls like a wave that blasted by her and shook the chateau on its foundation. She'd only felt something like this once before, when she first opened the crypt.

This wasn't a scream of rage, though. It sounded as though an animal were wounded.

Or a man being attacked by nightmares.

She reached the door to her room. Pretty and simplistic, the room beyond would offer a haven. The door even nudged open. It swung on silent hinges, offering her an escape from the sound and the terror now given life in the darkness.

And yet...

Another howl rocked through the chateau. Amicia caught herself on the wall and knew she couldn't leave him to this pain on his own. Alexandre had relented to a fragile partnership. And even if he had tried to kill her, they were turning over a new leaf.

She thought of him as a strange acquaintance. Someone who could become something like a friend.

Friends shouldn't suffer on their own. She would be a terrible person if she ducked into her room and ignored the screams of a man who needed help.

Amicia nudged her door open more with her foot, tossed the alchemy book into the darkness beyond, and then turned back to the hallway.

She didn't know where Alexandre's room was, but she didn't need a map. All she had to do was follow the anguished cries. Shockingly, it didn't take long to find the room where he resided.

He had put her very close to him. Only three turns down a hall and then she was before a door trying to hold in the sound of his pain. Three gashes marked it, like someone had tried to claw their way in multiple times.

Strange, she would have thought he would try to claw his way out. Not in.

Amicia frowned and then tried to figure out how she should enter. Should she knock? Perhaps not. That didn't sound like the approach would work. He'd tell her to go away, and then she would be at a standstill, making the same decision as she was now.

Did she push the door open and waltz in like she owned the place? It was the riskiest. He might not like her to see him. What if he had injured himself?

Another moan, softer this time, convinced her he wasn't feasting on some poor soul beyond that door. He was in pain, suffering, agony running through his body with such strength it came out in those sounds that tore her heart asunder.

Rather than bursting through the door like a woman hunting him, she nudged it and stepped inside.

The room beyond would have been splendorous in its day. Red fabric had once hung in beautiful tapestries from the wall, now torn and hanging by threads. A second level housed a four poster bed, equally crimson but broken in two. The ceiling was white marble, angels carved into it and reaching down for the people who stood within the four walls.

A great fireplace roared to her right. The stone carefully placed once, now crumbled on the left side, threatening the entire room with flames.

And before its great hearth, the King of the Dread slumped. His wings askew, chest heaving, he glimmered in the firelight from sweat slicking his skin. Dark hair tangled back from his face, hanging on his horns like spiderwebs.

He arched into himself, arms clawing at his ribs as something shifted inside him. Some darkness that expanded the bones in his body, making even his spine move in a wave until he groaned in pain.

It appeared as though something were trying to crawl its way out of his body.

Amicia stepped closer, trying to maneuver herself through the fragments of old furniture and broken bits of marble that had rained down from the chipped ceiling. "Alexandre?" she asked.

He fell forward onto his forearms, chest still heaving and breath racing through his lungs in great gusts. "You should not be here."

"You've ordered me around the entire time I've been here. And I'm always where I'm not supposed to be." Amicia leaned her crutches against the wall beside the fireplace, then slid down beside them. She stretched her leg out straight, the ache burning up to her ribs. "Can you tell me what's happening?"

He shook his head.

From this angle, she could see him better. The sweat dripping down his brow, the fangs bared in pain. One of his wings was askew at a different angle than the other, the position painful to look upon.

She'd never pitied him before. Not once. Amicia told herself she would never pity the monster, but he wasn't a monster anymore. And he was in immense pain.

Just like her.

She cleared her throat and asked, "You can't tell me what's happening to you, can you?"

He shook his head again, staring down at the floor. His claws flexed on the marble, which she now realized was raked with old furrows. He'd done this before.

How many nights had he spent alone like this? How many nights had he suffered with no one to commiserate?

A pile of pillows had been tossed haphazardly near her, most of the cushioning ripped out, but some were good enough. Amicia leaned over, grabbed a handful of them, and shoved them underneath her knee. At least her leg could be comfortable while she waited through the night with him.

Alexandre growled under his breath, "What are you doing, fool woman?"

"I'm keeping you company. I take it there's nothing I can do to heal you? To make this easier?"

Another wave shifted through him, his bones undulating underneath his skin. He wheezed out a long, low breath before he shook his head once more. His words ripped out of him on the end of a long moan straight from his core, "You should not be here. Not when I'm like this."

"Why not?" She told herself not to be insulted by a man in pain. He didn't want her here for his own reasons, not because he thought she was a bad person or...

She didn't want to entertain the darker thoughts whispering in her mind. The thoughts that told her she wasn't good enough, and never would be.

He sucked in a deep breath, riding the pain as it moved down his body. She could see his ribs shifting and swore he was growing larger.

"I tried to kill you," Alexandre choked out. "I threw you off the top of the chateau, and I intended to kill you then. I have frightened you. Convinced you I was nothing more than a monster, and I am. I will be nothing other than what you see now."

Amicia observed him. Every aching movement and pain-filled wince. When the wave of whatever plagued him finally passed, she shifted onto her side, laying down with the fire at her back. She reached out her good arm and laid her hand, palm up, on the floor near him.

"I think you want to be a monster," she whispered. "I think all this is so much easier if you believe you deserve it."

His red gaze met hers, cat-eye slits so narrow they almost disappeared. "I broke your bones. I pierced your skin. Death flirted with your soul because of me. You should not be here, petite souris."

"Perhaps not," she whispered. "But I am learning how to forgive."

Eyes flicking side to side, searching her gaze for something, he gave in. Alexandre leaned down, mimicking her posture, and reached out his own hand. Gently, he placed his clawed hand on top of hers.

His hand dwarfed her own. The claws scraped the delicate skin of her inner wrist, but she was not afraid.

"If only I could learn to do what you are doing," he whispered.

"Then we'll learn together, King of the Dread."

Amicia did not know if forgiveness was something that could be taught, or something that must be earned. Either way, she knew he had her trust now.

CHAPTER 23

*A*lexandre shouldn't be here. He should leave her alone in the library where she was seeking solace and privacy from the hordes of his people.

He had known she would be here. Where else would he find her? The woman was relentless in her quest to find out what happened to him and his people. He didn't have the heart to tell her many of his memories were returning. Every moment in her presence revealed more and more about their situation.

And that her quest was hopeless.

The door to the library was the only barrier between them. He could hear her on the other side, rustling through pages of a book in the shelf nearest to the door. The heat of her body almost permeated through the wood, like her scent.

The damned woman smelled like lemons and fresh air. How was a man meant to keep his head when all he wanted to do was lean close and see if it were her hair or her skin that smelled so delectable?

He placed a hand against the door. Told himself he should leave and give her the privacy she desired. She was researching.

He remembered what it was like to research a topic and be interrupted.

Without permission, his hand shifted the door and his feet carried him into the library. Already, he cursed himself. Amicia deserved a place where she didn't feel hunted by him and his own people.

They were always hunting her. Even he, the one who had remembered the most of who he was, could feel the rage bubbling at the surface. The beast inside him slathered at the mere thought of her blood coating its tongue. It wanted to feast, to devour.

The man in him wanted to as well, just not in the same way.

She stood next to a bookshelf in the plainest of gowns he'd sent to her room. A pale yellow chiffon, the bodice was tight around her tiny waist. The arms were long and wide, while the skirt was loose and flowing around her body. Somehow, it still clung to her strong thighs and backside.

Amicia was a temptation any man would have to be insane not to adore. Alexandre did not know how to manage these emotions with the ones he already fought every single day.

She reached up for a book too high for her to grab. He lunged forward, leaning above her head and grabbing the vellum before she realized he was even in the room.

He expected her to make some sound of surprise or fear. Nor would he have blamed her for being afraid when a winged, horned beast appeared out of nowhere and leaned over her. What was he thinking?

Instead, she didn't react in fear at all. She tilted her head back against his chest and stared up at him with a smile. "Thank you," she said, her voice melodic and so sweet. "I was looking for that one."

Alexandre found himself frozen, staring down at her as she looked up at him without a single spark of fear in her gaze. It was almost as if she were looking at a friend, rather than the monster who had tried to kill her multiple times.

Of course, he wasn't that monster anymore. Not really. He remembered who he was and where he had come from.

He just couldn't tell her any of the details. He had wanted to tell her the secrets of the man in the sarcophagus, what the crypt held and all the magic that lay within these walls. But she needed to discover these details for herself.

Such were the "rules," as she liked to call them. Rules he had no part in building, nor had he ever wanted to follow. Yet, here he was. Following the rules and staring down at her like a fool.

Clearing his throat, he stepped away with the book in hand, turning it over in his grasp for some kind of distraction. "The History of Soleil?"

Why did the name sound so familiar? He'd never heard of a kingdom named that. Omra, yes. Little Marsh, certainly. Soleil was not a place he had ever heard of before.

"I think it's where we are," she said, reaching for the book in his hand. "At least, that's what it looks like on the map I found."

"Map?" There were no maps in the chateau. He had searched for them himself, in the early days when he couldn't remember anything other than hunger and hate.

Amicia pointed to the table where he usually sat. Only now, there were no stacks of tomes for him to read. The table was covered with unrolled parchment paper that looked like a map.

Where had she found that?

He walked to the table in a daze. The entire kingdom was laid out before him with the title Ember at the top. He'd forgotten this place was all in the Empire of Ember, and each kingdom was ruled by someone who had reported to…

He couldn't remember that last detail, although it felt very important. Before a splitting headache had time to arc through his skull, Amicia leaned around him and pointed to a particular spot on the map. A lake, it appeared.

"I think this is where we are," she said. "I don't see any other large lakes that are worth putting on a map, so it stands to reason we're in Soleil. I just don't know how I got here so quickly since Little Marsh is all the way over here. Next to Hollow Hill." She slid her hand over a considerable amount.

Alexandre could have explained, once. Now, he could only nod his head and try to unstick his dry tongue. "That appears to be where we are."

She was too silent in response. He feared her silences, as they meant she was thinking, and Amicia thinking could only result in something that caused him trouble.

Alexandre flicked his gaze to her, finding Amicia staring at him so intently it almost burned. "Yes?" he asked.

"You know how it's possible I traveled that far, don't you?"

The curse upon him bound his tongue, but it didn't stop his head from nodding.

"And it's another thing you cannot tell me?"

Again, he nodded his head.

She heaved a great sigh. "This is getting a little frustrating."

A chuffing sound erupted from his chest, though he tried to cover it up with a cough afterward. "For you and me both."

She peered up at him with a questioning look. "Was that a laugh?"

"I doubt it."

"I think it might have been." Her brows furrowed, and he couldn't tell if that was a good or bad thing. She tsked. "Whatever are you going to do, King of the Dread? No one will find you frightening anymore if you laugh."

"I shall remove you from the room should I desire to be frightening."

"And a compliment?" She arched a brow before turning to head back to her chair. "What has gotten into you, this morning? I don't know what to do with this kind version of you."

He wanted to tell her this was how he had always used to be.

He remembered teasing his brothers and sisters and the local women who had giggled whenever he looked at them. Once upon a time, Alexandre had been a good man. The man whom many women had wanted to be with.

One of his wings scraped the floor. He'd forgotten to hold them up, their weight dragging down on his spine until the muscles between his shoulder blades ached.

He was a monster now. His body reminded him of the fact, one he could not forget.

Alexandre grabbed the nearest book and followed her to the cushioned chairs where they had first spoken as equals. Perhaps even friends.

He sank into the chair beside her and tried to think of a conversation to start. He wanted to know more about her, but any topic along those lines seemed to open doors to harmful memories. The attack he had ordered resulted in the death of her family. He couldn't ask about her home; it no longer existed. There were so many things he couldn't ask and, eventually, he didn't know what to say at all.

Amicia cleared her throat. "Can I ask you a question?"

He hadn't expected her to start the conversation, but he would tell her anything he could just to hear her voice. "Yes."

"Did you get bigger?"

He twitched, claws digging into the book in his grasp. Before he answered, Alexandre forced his hands to relax. "Why do you ask?"

"Because you look bigger. And when I joined you in your room, it looked as though the muscles and bones in your body were moving on their own."

She'd noticed? How bad had the attack been?

He didn't want her to know that, yes, he was bigger. That one night every month, he grew even larger, even more monstrous. Eventually, he would be nothing more than a beast, hardly recognizable as human at all.

This time, strangely enough, his feet had taken most of the changes. Although the pain had centered on his torso. He slid them underneath the chair so she wouldn't look, but he no longer had feet like a human. Instead, he had padded paws.

"I don't think I'm any larger than I was before that night," he lied.

"Hm," she grumbled, then looked back at the book in her hands.

Thank all the gods she'd given up. Now he didn't have to explain what that meant, even though he couldn't. His tongue would stick to the roof of his mouth, chains locking the words inside his body.

She didn't stay silent for long. "It's not like you can hide the fact that you're bigger, you know."

"I'm not."

"You are. A lot bigger, actually. Your chest, your shoulders, everything. And you can tuck your toes underneath the furniture all you want, but I can see you don't have the same feet as before."

The woman was too observant for her own good. Where had this sudden bravado come from? She was supposed to be frightened of him, damn it. The beast inside him wanted to remind her she had a place in this chateau, and that place was beneath him.

The man inside him, the one who had awoken the moment she touched the body in the tomb, agreed wholeheartedly. She would be lovely to have under him.

He didn't know how to manage these emotions. Alexandre was simultaneously angry and aroused. He couldn't stay in this room with her any longer, or he'd do something foolish he would regret.

Abruptly standing, he opened his mouth to make up some excuse that would allow him to leave her side without having her question him further. But before he could speak, he noticed a small dark spot on the horizon. One that careened toward the windows of the library so quickly, he hardly had time to lunge forward.

He scooped her up into his arms, turning them both and spreading his wings wide. Whatever had bolted toward the windows of the library crashed through the glass. Shards sliced through his wings, the pinpricks of pain nothing compared to the fear surging through his veins.

Was she all right? Had he caught her quick enough? The glass rained down upon them, and that could hurt her so easily. She was too delicate to survive such an attack.

"Amicia?" he snarled, pulling back just enough to stare down at her.

She blinked up at him, glass decorating her hair like starlight. "I'm fine."

His knees grew weak with relief. Not because he wouldn't have any more memories without her, but because she was all right.

That wouldn't do. He couldn't have feelings for the woman.

Alexandre dropped his arms from around her and helped her sit back down. Only then did he turn to look at the Dread who had shattered his most precious window and ruined the space where he could be alone with Amicia.

The female Dread stood with a lithe movement that belayed her status. She wasn't just one of the Dread, but the greatest of his warriors. A female who had disappeared some time ago and should have remained long gone.

"Vivienne," he snarled.

She tilted her head to the side, oddly bird-like in her movements with flared wings and gnashing teeth. "So you remembered my name after all this time."

"Why are you here?"

"I have news, King."

"Of what?" He didn't want her here. He didn't want her so close to the human woman who was his only link to his old life.

Vivienne's eyes turned from him then, casting her gaze to the human. Yellow burned there, and the hunting instinct flared to life.

Alexandre stepped between the two women. "You shall report to me in my own quarters."

"There is a human behind you, King."

"And she will remain human, by my orders."

Vivienne snapped her jaws. "Much has changed since I've been gone," she replied with a growl.

"Much." He didn't look over his shoulder at Amicia, couldn't for fear of what he might see. Instead, he beckoned his greatest warrior out of the library and prayed the little human was all right.

CHAPTER 24

*A*micia picked the glass out of her hair. Every breath slowed the frantic beating of her heart, but she didn't know what to think. Who was that Dread? She had seen none that looked so... female.

Maybe all the Dread here were male then. That creature had breasts. Full breasts, on display and bared for the world to see. Amicia had never seen such confidence or disregard to any kind of decorum.

Seconds after the door closed behind the King and the female Dread, the door opened again and Bernard burst through.

"Amicia?" he called out frantically.

"Here," she replied, waving a hand with a smile. "I'm fine. Nothing happened."

Bernard raced to her side and ran his hand up and down her body to knock glass shards out of the way. "Did she touch you?" he asked. "Did she do anything other than come in that window and immediately leave with the King?"

"She didn't touch me." Although Amicia didn't understand why he was asking. She hadn't seen the Dread woman before.

Maybe the others had been told to not hurt her, but this one hadn't. It was the only explanation she could think of.

"Thank the gods." Bernard blew out a long breath, his wings drooping in relief. "Stay away from her, Amicia. I don't care what it takes. That one is not for you to be alone with."

"Why?"

"She's dangerous." Bernard shook his head. "No, not dangerous. That isn't the right word. She is the woman who will tear your head off just for having the favor of the King."

That made little sense. She didn't have the favor of the King, to start. Alexandre had made it very clear she was here only as a prisoner. He'd even locked her away with a curfew to make sure she was in her room so he could control where she was at all times. That didn't sound like him favoring her.

And who was this woman after all? Bernard seemed afraid of her, and though he was afraid of many things, she didn't understand the correlation to this Dread who was smaller in stature than him.

"Who is she?" Amicia asked. "I haven't seen her before."

"They had a disagreement before we were all sent to Little Marsh. She wanted to kill everyone and get this all over with. The King wished to turn everyone, and Vivienne said there were enough mouths to feed. When it was clear the King wouldn't give in, she…" Bernard lifted a hand to the back of his neck and scratched. "Well, no one knows where she went, but she went somewhere."

"None of that explains who she is."

Bernard hesitated long enough for her to grow nervous. Who was this woman? What had she done that made everyone so afraid?

Finally, Bernard blew out a breath and replied, "I shouldn't remember this. I shouldn't remember anything at all but… Vivienne was once meant to be the King's betrothed. She was destined to be his queen, and then the memory gets all foggy. I remember her, but not her, and then I don't remember what stopped the wedding. As it is, she's his best general and the only one who has his ear. Until—" Bernard stopped speaking.

"Until what?" Amicia pressed.

"Until you."

"Oh." Until she had walked into the chateau and everything had changed. The problem was that she didn't know why everything had changed or what she had done to start it all. "Well then."

Bernard snapped his wings close to his back and crossed his arms over his chest. "I didn't tell you those things so you could feel sorry for yourself. This isn't the end of the world, nor should it change your plans."

"I don't know what you're talking about."

"The man has an intended. You know now, and it's time to move on."

Amicia lifted her hands in the air. "I don't know what you're talking about, Bernard. The King has been kind lately, that is true. But we are nothing more than friends. Him having an intended changes nothing about the relationship we currently have. We're... partners."

"Partners?"

"Yes! We want to know the answer to the same question, thus we are working together." Even she didn't believe herself.

Amicia could see how suspicious Bernard was, and if she had been in his position, perhaps she would have been. The lie she told was thin.

She didn't know how she felt about the strange King of the Dread. He had become a partner, as she stated, but he also had become more than just a king to her. His memories were as intriguing as the rest of this place.

The longer she stayed here, the less afraid she was. His size wasn't as intimidating as she remembered. Nor were his odd looks as important as before. He was just Alexandre, the King of the Dread who needed her help.

That was all it was, she decided. A king wanted her help. Plain Amicia from Little Marsh, the daughter of a great tinker who couldn't walk in her father's footsteps once she grew up and wanted a family.

She was the one who now helped a king.

Squaring her shoulders, she met Bernard's suspicious gaze head on. "Partners," she repeated. "Nothing more and nothing less."

"Well, then. Perhaps you would be pleased to know as his partner he took Vivienne back to his private chambers."

The words shouldn't have stung, but they did. She hated to think of that creature running her clawed hands all over…

No. She couldn't think about that. It wasn't what a friend or partner would think. So instead of allowing the thoughts to run rampant in her mind, she shrugged her shoulders. "Good for him. He can do whatever he wants in his spare time as long as it doesn't interfere with the research we're conducting."

"What he does in his spare time," Bernard said with a scoff. "You mean who he does in his spare time."

He wasn't playing fair, and she could see that from a mile away. Still, her feathers ruffled more than she wanted to admit.

"Go away, Bernard," she scolded. "I'll find myself a blanket and continue reading."

"There is glass all over your chair."

"Then I will find a different chair." The words might have sounded more like a snarl than human words. "You're distracting me."

"Of course, mademoiselle." He bowed mockingly, then left the library with a jaunty walk.

Was he trying to drive her mad? It didn't matter the King had someone else in his life. Good for Alexandre.

She limped over to another chair, much farther away from

the windows where cold air now streamed into the room. She would stay as long as she could survive the shivers before she finally gave up. Her father hadn't raised her as a weakling who was afraid of a little chill in the air.

Amicia opened the book in her hands a little too hard. The spine cracked with a satisfying creak that made her want to snap open the others as well. It was easy to imagine the book as Alexandre's spine, snapping underneath her hand, because he would clearly become distracted now that the woman had arrived.

No one could blame a man for being distracted by a woman's beauty. Not that the female Dread was beautiful by any standards.

That thought was a little too black, even for Amicia. She grumbled under her breath, "I suppose she was pretty in the way of the Dread."

Muscles had hardened the female's body, strong and capable where Amicia was not. The Dread all were far stronger than a human, and her wings had been rather impressive. They were more delicate than her male counterparts, though still adequate.

Amicia sighed. The Dread would find their own kind attractive. Just as she didn't find Alexandre attractive, although his red eyes were more expressive than before and his arms and chest were more reassuring than frightening.

She closed the book with a harsh thump and set it aside. Thoughts like this would get her nowhere and lingering on images of his body would only frustrate her more.

She hadn't lied when she told Bernard they were merely partners. That was the truth of her reality and she couldn't let that change. Not for anything or anyone.

The wind rushed from the windows, bending around her and slipping past the bookshelf at her back. It whistled down a long hall she couldn't see, yet another of the servant passages lacing throughout the chateau.

This was where she had first seen him, saw the King of the Dread when he had stepped into the library and when she'd realized he read books. Perhaps as much as she did in her spare time.

If she had stopped to think about her next actions, Amicia would have picked up the book and started reading again. She would have forgotten all about broken windows, intimidating Dread females, and what the King did in his spare time.

But she didn't think. Not even a little.

Her feet carried her away from the chair, back to the bookshelf where a small lever opened up into the servants' passages. They were big enough for her to move through, even with the crutches hindering her pace.

She shouldn't even try to do this. She should turn right back around, go back to the library, and bury herself in a book. Distractions were necessary when temptation called.

But her feet wouldn't stop moving.

Amicia argued with herself all the way to the sharp right turn that would take her to the King's chambers. She knew this only because she'd seen where his room was, and…

There were no excuses. She shouldn't know anything about his personal life at all. They were acquaintances, slowly becoming friends.

Yet, she was curious about his life. She was curious about the way he lived, how he felt, what his memories were. She wanted to know his history and all the stories he could tell her. Curiosity burned in her chest, questions a thousand-fold she needed answers for.

Amicia tried to think of a single reason for her to spy on him. To find herself in the walls once again, when he was trying to find some privacy with this… woman. Not a monster. She couldn't call Vivienne a monster without also calling Alexandre a monster.

And she didn't think of him as a beast anymore.

She reached the hidden wall behind his room all too soon. Amicia stared at the hole in the wall, the one that would allow her to see what they were doing, and told herself to go back to the library. She had made the journey to his room. She'd done what her heart wanted, but she could still turn away.

Her feet took her forward, and her back bent so she could stare through the small sliver into the room beyond. The hole pointed at the large, crumbling fireplace, still lit, where she had slept beside him. Amicia could still feel the heat of his great hand resting atop hers.

Alexandre stood before the fireplace, his silhouette larger than life and impossibly strong. The smaller Dread, Vivienne, circled him like a hunting beast.

"A human, Alexandre?" the female Dread asked. "You know the decree of the Alchemists."

"I do."

"All humans must die or become one of the Dread. That is what they charged us with. Are you going back on your word? Against the greatest of all living beings?"

Alexandre's wings flexed, stretching so wide she could see the fire glimmering through the webbing. "I am not planning on breaking my vow."

"Then why are you keeping her?" Vivienne snarled.

Amicia could see the other woman's face now. A twisted expression marred her beauty, teeth bared, brows furrowed, and a feral look in her eyes made Amicia wonder what had angered the woman. Amicia wasn't a threat. The Dread must know the truth. A little human couldn't compete with someone like her.

Could she?

With a low rumble deep in his chest, Alexandre turned toward Vivienne. His face was cast in profile, fire playing across the harsh, stone-like features. "I don't have to explain myself to you."

Vivienne's entire demeanor changed the moment he showed

frustration. Her expression softened, her shoulders slumped forward, and she reached out with delicate hands to touch his face. "Mon cherie," she murmured, her voice a soothing rasp. "You may keep a pet if you wish, you know I will not judge you for such a thing, but you must tell me."

"A pet?" Alexandre repeated.

"Yes, of course." Vivienne tugged his face down and ghosted her lips over his. "That is all humans are, wouldn't you agree? Animals compared to us."

Amicia felt her throat closing up, tightening with anxiety and fear. What would he say? He couldn't agree when they had come so far. Together, they would find out what was happening here. He had shown her so much of himself, his own insecurity, his fear, his history.

He wouldn't think of her as an animal, would he?

The darkened silhouette of his body curved around Vivienne. He wrapped his arms around the female Dread, and she heard his answer groaned, "You are right, my general. They are little more than animals."

Amicia's heart thudded hard against her ribcage. Her breathing grew erratic, and shame made her shake. She turned too quickly, the tip of her crutch clacking against the wall.

"What was that?" she heard Vivienne ask, but Amicia didn't slow.

She wasn't here to make friends. She wasn't here to be kind to the King of the Dread who had destroyed her city, her home, her family. Pity was a weakness she had succumbed to for a few moments.

Now, all she had was the desire for freedom. And she would do whatever it took to free herself from the clutches of the Dread.

CHAPTER 25

*S*he avoided them all for days afterward. They couldn't help her seek answers, and thus, talking to them was a waste of time.

Amicia had poured over the tiny book for hours until her eyes crossed and her head felt as though it would split open. She might have stopped if last night there hadn't been the faintest glimmer of hope. For a fraction of a second, the lines on the blue book had stopped wiggling, and she'd seen a single word.

Celestials.

Crutches clacking on the floor, she made her way through the empty kitchen. Most of the Dread were likely in the Great Hall, feasting upon their breakfast, unaware their human pet was working already.

She reached for an apple with her bad arm, pleased that the ache was barely there now that she had stretched it out. Last night was the first day she'd taken it out of the bandages and wiggled her fingers, lifted the appendage up and over her head.

The injury didn't bother her anymore. The leg, of course, was another story. That particular ache still plagued her, but nowhere near as bad as before. It appeared she healed faster in this place, though it had still taken a long time. She was almost ready to be back in fighting shape.

She palmed the bright pink apple and lifted it to the candlelight. No fruit should grow this time of year. Dried apples she might have expected, but an apple such as this? With flesh perfectly formed, the roundness crisp and firm?

This place was different from the rest of the world, even the food reminding her of that. And she needed to get out of here as quickly as possible.

Amicia left the kitchens with a blanket around her shoulders, apple in hand, and a book in the pockets of her thick woolen dress. It was the plainest piece she could find in all the outfits she had been given. The wool had been dyed a lovely, pale pink. The skirts were cut like rose petals, laying out around her body and swishing with her movements.

Somehow, it still kept her warm. She stepped outside, her momentum swinging open the door and pushing her toward the gardens of the chateau. There she might find a little solitude among the frozen trees, and the hidden statues.

Her feet crunched through the top layer of snow, the snapping sounds echoing in the near silent courtyard. No birds sang, no wings fluttered, nothing but the sound of her own movement.

"Strange," she muttered as she made her way to a bench that had seen better days. One corner had been demolished. The other side was suitable for her to sit upon as it balanced diagonally on the rubble.

She propped one foot up on a stone and stretched out her bad leg, then leaned back against the bench supporting her back. It would do for reading.

Amicia set the little blue book in her lap and took a big bite out of the apple in her hand. "Well," she began, "we meet again."

If she had believed in magic more than science, she might have thought the book scoffed at her. It certainly sounded like it when she turned the pages to the part where she had seen the word.

"Tell me your secrets today," she breathed. "What could you be holding onto so desperately?"

In the frigid air, the book came alive. The lines that had moved, squiggled like someone was writing over them again and again, froze. Words appeared in a handwriting that was both elegant and aggressive. Words in a language she understood.

Amicia leaned forward and read the words aloud, "The Celestials were sent from the sky. Legends say a great beam of light sent their people from high above the clouds. One for each of the Kingdoms of Ember. One for each King.

"They were sent to guide the humans into a new life, a better one. Though the Celestials were all different and came from different constellations, they all were similar in size and build.

"Beautiful is the word all used to describe them. Gilded as though they were dipped in gold themselves. Some darker than others, some so pale they were almost diamond in appearance.

"Humans did not know how to accept them at first. Winged beings had walked into our kingdoms with abilities beyond our reckoning. Some Kingdoms accepted them. Others tried to chase them from the borders and into the wilds. None left.

"Eventually, the Celestials were understood to be what they were. Kind. Here to assist. Their only purpose to ensure that humanity did what we were meant to do. Build a better place for all."

Amicia turned the page to see a diagram, a crude sketch perhaps, but one that startled her. The charcoal man was stunning. Even in the artist's limited ability, he had captured the painful glory of the Celestials.

Four wings stretched from the man's back, feathered and pale. His face was magnificent, haunting even. But it was the gold-dipped pieces the artist had layered over the portrait that captivated her. He had drawn along the edges of the wings, as if each feather had been plunged in molten splendor.

These Celestials must have been marvelous. If they were so unusual, she understood why the humans would have feared them. But it made little sense to shun them if they were here to help.

Of course, she didn't understand why they had come. The passage she'd read hadn't explained that. Beings falling from the clouds to help humanity? Why?

She turned the page again, only to find the words moving once more.

"Come on," she muttered, closing the book and then opening it again. "You have more to say!"

Apparently, the book was done with her reading today. The words didn't stop moving other than the ones she'd already read. The diagram was still painful to look upon, and the explanation only brought about a hundred more questions.

She reached for the apple and finished it quickly. "Did you want me to eat? Fine, I'm done. Let me read more."

Amicia chucked the apple over her shoulder and heard it hit the snow with a soft thud. If the book wanted to take care of her, then she would eat a hundred apples. But the blue vellum revealed nothing more than the three pages it had already showed her.

"Playing hard to get," she snarled. "Fine then, I will reread every word a hundred times if that's what it takes. I understand the message. I'll memorize everything you've shown me, and then you will tell me even more."

The day passed slowly. Over and over, she read the words, murmuring them under her breath, trying to figure out what the book wanted her to understand. But there was nothing to understand.

The Celestials were beings who came from the clouds. They

were sent to help humans. She understood that part, and yet, the book showed her nothing else.

Was she supposed to have some kind of epiphany before it could show her more?

She reached beside her, picked up the apple, and bit into the crisp, pink side and chewed thoughtfully. The book had to have some kind of hidden meaning. Or there was some secret she didn't understand.

Magic wasn't real. This wasn't some cursed book that knew what she was thinking and how much she understood of what it wanted to tell. Which meant there might be a latch on the side or some kind of switch so small she didn't know where it was.

Her father had known a clockworker who could create things like this. Tiny objects with the smallest of switches that looked like the hands of a clock, or a sword that could be removed from a nutcracker's hand. That's what she should look for.

"More and more secrets," she muttered as she turned the book over and over in her hand. "More and more..."

Amicia paused and looked at the apple in her hand. She'd only brought one apple with her. One was hard enough to carry, let alone juggling two when she already had her hands full with a book and crutches.

She stared long and hard at the red surface before she finished with one more bite and set it down. This one she wouldn't throw away. This one, she kept right beside her. Just in case.

"I don't believe in magic," she repeated, looking at the book. "But..."

Another apple rolled through the snow and landed at her side. A few bits of crusty snow stuck to the stem.

"I know you're there," she called out. "What I don't understand is why you're throwing fruit at me."

Snow crunched as someone approached, but Amicia refused

to look around. There were only two people here who would roll food at her. Only two people who would even consider that she wasn't eating enough.

Bernard was unlikely to be outside. He claimed to have an aversion to all the things in areas not controlled by his own cleaning method. Amicia couldn't blame him for that. He didn't like any flecks of dirt on his table, let alone his clothing.

Which could only leave one other Dread, and the one she had been trying very hard to not think about today.

"If you're working this hard, I thought you might need more than a single apple." The grumbled words sent gooseflesh dancing across her arms.

How was it that his voice could make her shiver far more than the icy air? She could handle the harshest of environments but the mere timbre of his voice made her weak. It was shameful.

It made her heart race.

Amicia stared down at the book a little harder, resolving to not look at him. "I'll eat later, thank you."

"And yet, it appears that you are not reading that much after all." Alexandre sank down into the snow beside her. He crouched on his haunches, looking very much like the gargoyles on top of Little Marsh's greatest mansion.

"I'm reading," she snapped in response. "The book showed me its secrets."

"Has it?" He lifted a brow. "And what secrets are those?"

"That the Celestials were sent here to help humanity. At least, that's what they believe. I know what the Celestials looked like. They were gilded, winged creatures who many thought were dangerous in the beginning." She didn't know much more, but she trailed off her words like she might.

He nodded, his gaze drifting through her as though he were brooding over the subject. "Yes, I believe that is correct. The Celestials were sent to... help."

"Why did you hesitate?"

"Because I'm uncertain that is correct."

"How could it not be?" Amicia waved the book in the air. "You gave me this because you said it had the answers."

"I thought it had the answers. I haven't been able to read it myself." He grinned. The large fangs in his mouth poked past his lips, looking all the more terrifying and strange. "You're the only one who's done so."

"What an honor." Amicia couldn't stop the sarcastic tone of her voice.

She had thought being around him would be easy. She'd already decided there wasn't anything she could do about the female Dread. Vivienne was just another obstacle between her goal, and as such, Amicia shouldn't be upset because she wasn't interested in him as anything other than a partner.

She couldn't be interested. Amicia stared at him hard, reminding herself of all the oddities and differences. He had wings. Gray skin. Leathery appendages that flexed when he was angry. Not to mention the claws at the tips of his fingers, the strange feet and odd angle of his legs. He wasn't human, and these reasons were more than enough to dislike him.

Softer thoughts trailed after she angrily picked apart his monstrous differences, however. He needed her to help him. His expression softened when he looked at her now. He wanted to know what happened in the past and had shown remorse for trying to kill her.

Amicia ground her teeth together and looked away. "I was reading another book in the library. It had an interesting passage on the relationship between the captor and captive."

"Did it?" Alexandre shifted his wings until they draped around his shoulders like a cape. "Enlighten me."

"Apparently it's rather normal for a captive to feel some... fondness for their captor. After a while, the brain tries to convince the captive the person who is harming them psychologically is doing it because they care for the captive. Compassion soon follows."

"Are you trying to tell me something?" Alexandre asked dryly.

She was trying to put a little distance between them and force herself to realize these feelings weren't natural. Amicia should hate him. She had hated him, only a month ago.

Amicia cleared her throat. "I'm telling you it's survival, a way for the brain to explain the dependency upon someone who is trying to hurt me."

"Are you trying to tell me you feel a certain sense of fondness for me, Amicia?"

He didn't understand what she was saying at all if that's what he took from this conversation. The last thing she wanted was for him to think she enjoyed his company. She didn't. This entire ordeal was nothing more than a trial of her life. She would figure out his curse, leave, and then never think of this place again.

"No," she replied, but her voice shook. "I am not telling you I'm fond of you or any of the other Dread here."

"Bernard would be saddened to hear that. He has a fondness for you."

"Stop saying that word," she whispered. Her heart ached at the mere thought of hurting Bernard. That Dread had a heart of gold, and he cared whether or not she was comfortable. Now, all she could do was pray Alexandre would never tell the others about this.

"What word?" Alexandre leaned forward into her line of vision. Pieces of icy snow clung to his horns, glimmering in the early morning light. "Fondness?"

"It sounds unnatural coming from your lips."

"This doesn't have to do with Vivienne returning, does it?"

Amicia snorted, the sound ugly and cold coming from her lips. "No. It doesn't. I don't care at all who you consort with."

"I know you were in the wall," he replied, a calculating expression on his face. "You heard what we said, but I don't know why you believed it."

"Believed what?" Amicia's jaw hurt she was grinding her teeth so hard. "That you and all the others here value humans as nothing more than animals? That you think so lowly of me, I am nothing more than a pet?"

"You know I didn't mean it like that."

"That's exactly how you meant it, and I now know where I stand." Speaking of, Amicia wouldn't sit here any longer arguing with him and the little blue book he'd given her. She struggled to her feet and shoved the crutch underneath her armpit. "I have work to do."

"You live here with all your desires at your fingertips," Alexandre remarked. "What work calls you?"

"The only thing I have to pass the time," she snarled. "Finding out what happened to you and your people so I can leave."

Her heart ached. She didn't want to tease him about the woman who had returned. She didn't want to know why her stomach twisted at the thought of them together, or why he hadn't denied consorting with Vivienne. He claimed he didn't view her as a pet, but he hadn't denied he thought of her as an animal.

"And where will you go when you leave?" he called after her. "There is nothing left out there, Amicia."

"And whose fault is that?" She crunched through the snow, jerking her feet out of the holes she made even though it made her leg ache.

"I think you're jealous!"

"Jealous?" She whipped around, nearly toppling over when her crutch stuck in the ground. "Jealous of what?"

He remained crouched where he had been, eerily still. For a moment, he looked as if he were the stone his people's skin resembled. "I think you know," he mumbled, his words drifting over the snow like wind. "Return to your library and safe places in the walls, petite souris. But I think you'll always return to antagonize the cat who hunts you."

She ground her teeth, and she turned away again. "Don't think I like you, grande imbecile."

"How could I ever think that?"

Amicia stalked back to the chateau, rounding the corner until she couldn't feel his eyes on her back any longer. Beside the door, a rose bush bloomed where it hadn't before. She was certain of it.

She stared at the frozen droplets of water suspended on each perfect petal. A rose bush in winter? Impossible. And yet, many things appeared impossible here.

CHAPTER 26

*T*he Dread descended upon the table in the center of the Great Hall. The food piled high might have been delicious if Alexandre didn't have to watch them devour the meat and vegetables like… animals.

Gods, he couldn't get the conversation with Amicia out of his head. She hadn't wanted to be viewed as a pet, and he didn't think he had been viewing her as such.

But had he?

He watched as Vivienne, sat to his right, yanked an entire roasted chicken off a plate and bit into the side. In comparison, Amicia, down the table to his left, gently pulled a leg off one and then took the time to use her utensils. She sliced off a single piece, speared it with her fork, and placed it on her tongue.

Every bite was delicately taken. Every slice assured no food splattered or sprayed onto the table next to her counterparts who sat beside her and created a mess.

He sat at the head of the table, as always, but barely touched any of his food. Not tonight. He had too many thoughts in his head to consider eating like this.

Bernard walked by with another plate laden with food. He

juggled so much, every night, and not once had he heard the other Dread complain. But now, he could see how much his manservant did.

"Bernard?" he called out, reaching out a hand and snagging the Dread's apron sleeve. "Where does this food come from?"

The Dread shrugged. "The kitchens."

"Yes, but where? Do we have a farm somewhere? Animals to slaughter when we desire it?"

Bernard's gaze went foggy, staring right through Alexandre. "I don't know, master. When we need food, it's there."

"So you haven't been killing these animals yourself?"

"Should I?" He shifted the plate of food to his other hand. "I can try to send out some Dread for a hunt, but it would take time, and the others would starve before they come back."

Alexandre released the other man with a quick shake of his head. "No, there's no need for that. It's just... I hadn't ever wondered where the food came from, and I don't understand how we have so much. Fresh food even in winter is bound to raise questions."

"It's always winter here, Master."

Bernard wandered off, leaving Alexandre with even more questions. Had it always been winter around his chateau? He thought there had to be summer at some point. They ate food that was always in peak season. There must be a garden and one of the other Dread delivered the food to Bernard to cook.

Leaning back in his chair, he stared at the vegetables as if they would grow legs and walk off the table. Impossible meals, so it seemed.

Alexandre leaned an elbow against the arm of his chair, chin on his fist. There had to be some explanation for all the strange traits of this place. He could almost feel the answer in the corner of his mind. He knew why things were like this in the chateau. But he couldn't quite remember.

"My King," Vivienne inquired, "are you not eating?"

He waved her off, dismissing her with ease. "I shall eat when I'm ready, General."

"I am more than your general," she replied with a chuckle. Some of the other Dread who had been eavesdropping also laughed. "Or have you forgotten so much?"

"I'm remembering more and more." He remembered her before all this, or so he thought. It had to be her in his memories but... not.

The tangled snarl of black hair on her head had once shone in the sunlight like oil. He remembered brushing it, or perhaps just sliding his hand through the long locks reaching her hips. Yet, the hips he remembered weren't gray as granite. They had been warm, caramel, and... He couldn't remember anything else. It was as if someone had built a wall in his mind.

He remembered human skin. Which would make sense when he thought about it. All the Dread had been human once. Hadn't he changed many of them himself?

And yet, in his mind, none of them had histories. They had always been Dread just as they remembered.

Why didn't he remember their history if he was the one who had turned them?

A soft clink of utensils striking plate brought his attention back to the little human seated between monsters. Amicia's gaze was on him, though her gaze flicked away the moment she saw him watching her.

They'd made so much progress, and all it took for him to lose momentum was the return of another female. Vivienne couldn't hold a candle to the human woman. His mind returned repeatedly to Amicia's sunburnt skin, the freckles dotting across her nose, or the mop of dark hair that curled so tightly he wondered how long it actually was.

Such a curl had fallen out of her thick braid. It swung next to her face, and he wanted to tug on it. His claw might slice it off, however. And as much as he wanted to have a keepsake from her, he couldn't bear to separate something so beautiful from a woman such as her.

Snap out of it, he told himself. Humans weren't obsessive over the Dread for any reason other than fear. And she had every right to fear him. Just as he had no right to think of her as anything other than his captive.

Feeling the burn of his general's eyes on him, Alexandre looked back to the woman at his side. Vivienne stared at him with so much anger and hatred he wondered that he hadn't burst into flame.

"Yes?" he asked. "Do you require my attention?"

"You stare at the human girl?"

He leaned closer with a hiss. "Your voice carries, General. I advise you to keep your temper and your tone on a tighter leash."

"Why should I? Does it matter what one little human thinks?" Her eyes flashed bright yellow, and she clutched the arms of her own chair until he heard the scrape of her claws digging into wood.

"I care what the Dread think of me. Your little rumors will only go so far. You may have once been betrothed to me, Vivienne, but do not think I will allow you to test my good name. If necessary, I will do to you as I have done to so many others."

"You would have me sent away?" She scoffed. "Unlikely."

"I would tear you limb from limb and set you outside for the crows to feast upon. I will not lose this throne for a woman."

Vivienne looked pointedly down the table at Amicia. "Are you so certain of that, my king?"

He stared with her, unable to keep his gaze from the human. A flash of something burned behind his eyes. It felt as if someone had stuck a needle through his socket, deep into his brain, but then a flash of memory appeared before him.

He was flying. High in the sky with misty clouds all around him, their peaks circular and fluffy. It looked for all the world as if he could walk upon the clouds themselves. And just out of the corner of his eye, a single gilded feather floated down from above.

"My king?" Vivienne asked again.

Through a tense jaw, he muttered, "What?"

"You're cracking the table."

Alexandre realized the chatter and loud noises from the table had ceased. Instead, all the Dread stared at him. His claws were dug deep into the wooden table, his wings spread wide and flared out behind him, each two men long.

Carefully, he drew his wings tight to his sides and tried not to shake his head. Even his horns ached, but it was his mouth that hurt the most. Had he bitten through his lip in his rush of memory?

"Alexandre?" Her light voice trailed down the table like a butterfly dancing toward him. "Might I fetch you something?"

"Ah, the human understands her place after all," Vivienne replied. The female Dread leaned against the table, nearly climbing atop its surface in her sudden desire to hunt. "I had wondered why the servants were eating with us."

Amicia's back stiffened. Alexandre almost reached out and sank his claws through Vivienne's back. She had no right to say a word to his little human, let alone insult her. He could end his general's life; there were many who had fought for her position. They would do just as well as the female had.

But he had forgotten Amicia was no shrinking woman, nor a noble who needed a man to step in and save her. She was made of harder stuff.

His human charge tilted her head to the side and smiled. "When I am given the job of a servant, I will happily eat with them."

"That can be arranged," his general snarled.

"I await the order." Amicia reached into her lap and set a folded napkin back on the table. Slowly, she pushed her chair away from the table and reached for her crutch. "I'm not so spoiled that hard labor frightens me. Nor do I view people who serve others as lesser, simply because they were not born into better circumstances."

Vivienne dug her claws into the table, leaving gauges as deep as Alexandre had. "Are you suggesting I was born with a silver spoon in my mouth?"

"I am suggesting you look down upon servants because you think their occupation makes them less than you." Amicia tucked her crutch underneath her arm. "That is the sign of someone who doesn't understand there are very few of your kind, and very many of mine."

"Look how she squirms. See how uncomfortable she is in the presence of the Dread who were once nobility? Should the curse break, she would be eaten alive standing amongst beauty when she is nothing more than a dandelion. A weed growing in a rose garden," Vivienne growled. "You are far outnumbered here."

"I don't believe I am." She reached out and patted the shoulder of the Dread nearest to her.

Alexandre hadn't realized she wasn't wearing her sling until that moment. She reached with her bad arm, the one he had remembered snapping like a twig when he'd thrown her. The arm moved correctly now, and she didn't favor it, although he was certain she had only a few days ago.

The Dread shifted underneath her touch, the granite texture of his cheeks turning darker. Amicia smiled first at the Dread, then at Vivienne. "Louis was a mason. The lovely man next to him was a farrier. Bernard was a farmer."

He was stunned, and it appeared so was Vivienne. She shifted back into her seat with a solid thud that rocked the table.

The Dread were remembering who they were? They were remembering their names?

Alexandre stared at her in equal parts shock and horror.

Who was this woman who had wandered into his chateau uninvited, but somehow had changed so much?

Amicia continued, "Perhaps I was once outnumbered by the Dread, but now I'm proud to call them friends. Men and women whom I have met, who have introduced themselves and their history at this very dinner. You should do the same, Lady Vivienne. But never make the mistake to think I am alone or outnumbered here. I should hate to prove you wrong."

With that, Amicia made her way out of the room. The echo of her crutch clicking against the marble floor was the only sound in the Great Hall. Not a single one of the Dread made a move, sound, nor reached for any more food.

Alexandre shifted back in his throne, propping his chin upon his clenched fist once more. The woman was an enigma, that was for certain. He did not understand what else she could change, but he looked forward to the possibilities.

"Are you going to let her speak to me like that?" Vivienne barked. "My King, I am the general of your army!"

"And she is the one who is researching how to break our curse."

"You know the curse is sanctioned by the alchemists, and not a single person can know how to break it if they themselves claim it to be permanent."

He watched the door that Amicia had exited, his eyes searching for the slightest of movements. Perhaps she would return. Perhaps being in her presence would give him another memory, another clue to who he was.

"If anyone could find the truth to what is happening here, it's her," he replied. "And I intend to give her every opportunity to try."

CHAPTER 27

*A*micia blew the hair out of her face, her armless linen dress tangling in her legs, and the box in her arms straining her healed arm. She shifted the weight. The wooden crate was from the kitchens, although Bernard would be distraught when he saw she had stolen it. Still, how else was she supposed to move all her things?

The Dread didn't want her to move. Already, two of them had stopped in her bedroom door and cleared their throats. Apparently more and more of them were finding their voices with her.

She was less than interested in talking with them.

They had all stayed silent throughout the nightmare of a dinner party, which only meant they agreed with that monstrous woman. If she was little more than a pet to them, then she would live like a pet.

Her research required more attentions, anyway. She could waste time by making her way back to her room, crutch in hand, and only a few books in her arms to read for the night. Or she could stay in the place where the research took place.

She'd already found the perfect spot for her to build a nest.

Though she hadn't been able to drag the mattress down with her, and she'd tried, the pile of blankets and pillows she'd mounded in the library's corner proved surprisingly comfortable. Amicia had tried it out just before coming up for the last couple boxes of things.

The mere idea she had things here was ridiculous. At first, she thought she would just be able to move the blankets and pillows. But then she missed the little books she'd brought up that were adventure stories. The candlestick Bernard had given her so she could see in the night. The box of sweet treats she had swiped from him.

Her list grew longer and longer until she'd finally snuck into the kitchens, gotten herself a crate, and started filling it with all the items she knew she wouldn't be able to live without.

Hairbrush, mirror, even a few of the warming rods she could stick in the fire and run underneath her blankets to keep her toes warm in the colder nights. More and more things piled up until she realized this place had become a home to her.

Only homes had stuff like this. There were memories here that were dear to her, comfort items that made certain she was happy and relaxed.

When had that happened?

Shifting the box in her arms, she hunched down to turn the knob of her door. There were only two more boxes worth of stuff, although she could fill a third if she didn't make these so heavy.

Her arm ached already, but it felt good to stretch out the muscle. The injury wouldn't stop her, especially now that she could use it without a sling.

"Damn it," she muttered, the curse flying from her lips as the box slid sideways. Amicia sidestepped away from the door, only to find herself back in the same position. Locked in her own room with a box in her arms.

Logically, she could have put the box down, opened the

door, and then picked the box back up. But it was heavy. And her arm was already shaking.

Trying one more time, she let curses fly through the air until the door opened on its own accord.

Pausing mid-curse, she looked up at the wall of gray chest now blocking her way. Well, at least she'd gotten most of the room moved before the King of the Dread decided he needed to be involved.

"Alexandre," she said, shifting the box so she could dart past him.

He stepped in her way. "Amicia. What are you doing?"

"I'm moving to the library."

His cat-eye pupils expanded. "Why are you moving to the library when you have a good room here?"

"I think it will be easier to finish my research in the library where I am surrounded by books. I'll be able to research for much longer without having to bring books up and down the stairs." She stuck out her splinted leg and wiggled it. "This makes things a little more difficult."

"Yes, I understand it may be hard for you to manage the stairs." He crossed his arms over his chest and didn't move at all. "However, you may ask any of the Dread to procure a volume for you while you're upstairs."

"So I needn't move at all?" She blew another strand of hair out of her face. "I think the Dread have made it very clear everyone has the same opinion of their little pet human. I can manage on my own."

"That's what this is about?" Alexandre shifted again when she tried to move, pushing her farther back into the room with just his bulk.

She had difficulty walking without the crutch, a new improvement on her condition, but with him bumping her backward, her leg nearly gave out. "This is about me having more time to research."

"This is about jealousy, again. Amicia, whatever Vivienne said was nothing more than fabrication."

"It's the truth." Though the words hurt to say, she knew they would strike him where he was weakest.

Alexandre flinched, his head tilting to the side as though he were dodging a blow. "What do you mean, it's the truth? What she said—"

"Was what she believed," Amicia interrupted. "And what others believe as well. And she's not wrong, Alexandre. I am a weed in a garden of roses. I don't belong in a room like this, and I certainly need not wear these lovely dresses. I'm happier in wool and linen than silk and velvet. I belong in the servants quarters or the library, and that's where I'm happiest."

He opened and closed his mouth, struggling to find words before he finally straightened his shoulders and set his jaw. "I won't allow it."

"You don't have a choice in the matter." Amicia tried to scoot past him again, setting her shoulder against his chest and shoving hard.

They both froze the moment her bare shoulder touched his bare chest. Heat bloomed through the contact, a strange heat that made the back of her neck warm.

He wasn't rough like the others. The few Dread she'd touched before always felt as though callouses covered their entire body. The abrasive texture made her dislike them even more. But him? The King of the Dread was smooth as the velvet she said she didn't need.

A ragged breath escaped her lips. "Please move."

"I'd feel better if you remained in this room."

"Move Vivienne in. She used to be a noblewoman and deserves such lavish quarters."

"Amicia—"

She couldn't listen to this anymore. She couldn't stand here and talk about that woman as though it didn't make her stomach churn at the mere thought. She still pressed her shoulder against his chest and it was so warm, so comforting, so…

No. This was nothing more than her brain trying to make her like her captor. This was just an excuse, so she didn't feel like she was trapped any longer. She needed to be smarter than this. Better.

Her father had been the smartest man in Little Marsh, and she needed to uphold that intelligence. She would not fall prey to her own mind wanting to seek the easiest route.

Although, it felt good to lean on him for a few moments. And he wasn't trying to convince her to do anything. He just stood there, letting her lean against his chest and draw whatever strength she could from his broad shoulders.

Taking a deep breath, she forced herself to move away and limp past him. The leg he had broken ached. The arm he had snapped suffered under the weight of the items he had given her.

Everything was all twisted up in her head. She needed space. Time away from him so she could untangle the thoughts in her mind.

"Amicia!" he called out.

She didn't stop her slow progress down the hall. Alexandre could try to distract her all he wanted, but she would make it to the library and put her box down with all the others.

She would empty it out when she got there like she had the past four times. If he wanted to hover while she worked, then he could. But she would not stop just because he ordered her to.

A low snarl rumbled through the hallway and the telltale sound of wind rushing through wings meant he had flown the last few steps so he was beside her once more. "Amicia, this is ridiculous. If you want to argue with me, then would you just argue?"

"I don't want to argue with you." She eyed the stairs that had nearly bested her three times now. Thankfully, the library was only one floor below her bedroom.

"Then why are you moving?"

"I've answered this question a hundred times, Alexandre. I'll not answer it again."

"You've answered it once," he growled. He reached out and cupped a hand at her elbow, helped her down the stairs. "And it wasn't a satisfactory answer."

Amicia wanted to shrug him off, but having someone help her balance proved to make the journey easier. Her arm was already trembling with the pain. "A satisfactory answer isn't always agreeing with you, Alexandre. Sometimes, it's just the truth."

"I disagree."

"That's because you've lived as a prince your entire life, and everyone has to agree with you."

"I have not!" He hesitated, then cleared his throat. "That I remember."

The stairs would have been easier to manage if the carpet wasn't torn up in pieces. She tripped on the edge of one before he steadied her. "I don't need to tell you that not remembering who you were only makes my point more logical than yours."

"I disagree."

"I'm basing my assumptions on your behavior. You're basing your assumptions on not wanting me to be right." They reached the end of the stairwell and Amicia shrugged his touch off her arm that still tingled with heat. "You were most likely a prince, or some other nobleman if you were engaged to Vivienne. Which you were. More people than just Vivienne remember that bit of memory."

Alexandre rolled his eyes, staring up at the ceiling as if it could give him the patience to deal with her. "And we're back to the jealousy."

"I'm not jealous!" Her voice rang out and clear through the

hallway. The words bounced back to them over and over again, warping the lie. "She can have you if she wishes. All I want is to get out of this place. I want to stay in the library so I can research longer."

"You already have the only book that could give you any insight on what is going on here. And it is not revealing its secrets just yet." Alexandre stepped closer until she could feel his belly expand with each inhalation. "We live in the same chateau, petite souris. You cannot run from me just by changing rooms."

"I'm not running."

"Aren't you?"

She was. Running as far as she could just so she could breathe a little more. His presence overwhelmed her. Maybe if she was in the library, she wouldn't hear his tormented shouts in the middle of the night. She wouldn't want to return to his room just to hold his hand so he could get at least one restful sleep.

All these feelings were just her natural desire to help. Her soft touch, the part of her that bled for people who were hurting. That was what drew her to him. Nothing more, nothing less.

"My arm is hurting," she muttered, moving past him and into the open door of the library.

Amicia slammed the box onto the nearest table, dragging items out of it and placing them wherever she could think to put them. It didn't matter if they were haphazardly thrown around the place. This was to be her new room, and no one came into the library except...

Him.

Had she put herself in the only place in the entire chateau where she knew they would have some time alone together?

Shock had her freezing long enough for Alexandre to saunter into the library. He stared at the broken windows thoughtfully. "Well, if you plan on staying here, then perhaps I should have the windows boarded up."

"No thank you."

"It's cold."

"I don't mind the cold," she snapped, whirling upon him with a sudden burst of anger. "How many times do I have to tell you I'm not some delicate little noble who needs you to take care of her? I've survived worse than this frigid air. You threw me from the roof and I survived. A little cold will not take me. Now get out of the library."

"It is my chateau, you know?" He crossed his arms over his chest and glared at her. "I can go anywhere I want."

"Yes, you can, but now that I'm in the library permanently, I'd very much appreciate you asking if you can come in. Wouldn't want to have an awkward meeting when I'm changing, now would we?" She nodded toward the door. "You can go now."

Remarkably, he stalked to the exit and began to leave. As if he understood she needed privacy and was comfortable to give up his most sacred place in the entire chateau.

She hadn't thought her speech would work, and yet, it had.

Amicia trailed along behind him, putting her hand on the door, ready to snap it shut in his face. Expect, when he turned around, she noticed something rather odd about his mouth. His lips weren't pushed out as much. They were... well, flatter.

Furrowing her brow, she leaned a little closer as he began to talk. "I wish you would reconsider, Amicia. This chateau still isn't all that safe for you—"

"Yes, yes. Dangerous, poor little human can't take care of herself, and you wish she would listen. I've heard it before, and I'll be fine." She leaned back, distracted by the proof of change she had just seen for herself. "By the way, your fangs are gone."

He blinked at her, his jaw falling open for a second before he snapped it shut. "What is that supposed to mean?"

"I mean it quite literally." Amicia reached up and tapped her own mouth. "Gone."

Then she slammed the door shut in his face. What in the world was going on in this chateau? Blooming roses and missing fangs?

CHAPTER 28

*A*lexandre buried his nose in the book a little further, holding it up as a shield so he could watch her buzzing around the library like some kind of demented bee. What woman cleaned this much? She had claimed moving into this space was just so she could research more, but he hadn't seen her research at all this morning.

He'd come here intending to force her back into the privacy of her room. He'd even ordered a few of the Dread to pop in and meander around the shelves. They couldn't read, although he wasn't sure why, but they could make it difficult for her to research.

But she wasn't researching. Instead, she gave up on reading and started cleaning. Of all things!

When she'd left the library, he'd felt a thrill of accomplishment. Then she had returned with a bucket, mop, and broom.

Damned woman always seemed to be one step ahead of him. He slouched in his chair, staring at her over the pages of the book as she precariously balanced on a ladder and reached with the broom to wipe away some spiderwebs.

"Stop staring at me," she said, her voice ringing through the rafters.

"I'm not staring," he grumbled. "And the library isn't dirty."

"It is dirty. It looks as though no one has even attempted to clean the place in years, and I believe there's a hundred spiders up here making their little families and nests."

Alexandre snapped his book shut. "Then perhaps you should let them live their lives, woman."

"Woman?" She held onto a rung and swung a bit to stare at him. The mere movement gave him a heart attack. Did she want to fall?

"Would you prefer it if I returned to calling you petite souris?"

"I have a name," she snarled.

She was so pretty when she was angry. Heat turned her cheeks a lovely shade of pink and made her freckles stand out all the more. The dark waves of her hair were far too pretty for him to focus on anything else. The light reflected off the strands in blues and purples the color was so dark.

A voice in his head said to keep quiet and let her work. He was bothering her when she had finally chosen a place in his chateau to call her own. It was progress, and any progress was good.

But another voice said to poke and to prod. To tease until she couldn't stand it anymore and she hopped down off the ladder. The red on her cheeks would reach the tips of her ears, and the sway of her hips when she stalked toward him to scold would only capture his attentions even more. He'd reach out with his clawed hands and place them on the dip of her waist and—

He needed to focus, damn it. She was his prisoner, he was her captor, and he couldn't be thinking like this.

Clearing his throat, he stood from the worn chair. "Give me one good reason I should allow you to continue cleaning."

She lifted a delicate brow. "Because it's dirty."

His tongue stuck to the roof of his mouth. There wasn't an argument to that. He knew the library needed cleaning, just like the rest of the chateau.

And he couldn't lie and say the difference she'd already created wasn't visible. The bookshelves looked more like they used to. Back when the entire room gleamed in gold, the chandelier on the ceiling lit with hundreds of candles, and scholars finding the exact volume to help in their research.

He could almost see them wandering through the shelves, hanging onto the ladders, standing in front of the window silhouetted by the sun.

A memory? Again?

All because this little mouse of a woman had cleaned the library. He could feel more memories bubbling in the corners of his mind, tiny flickers of life as it once had been. Details of who he had been and what his life had once been like.

Alexandre licked his lips, then set his book on the table beside the chair. He made his way toward Amicia. "What can I help clean, then?"

"You?" She hooked her elbow through the rung and stared at him as if he'd grown two heads. "Help clean?"

"Is that so surprising?"

"Do you even know how?"

He didn't, not in the slightest. But it couldn't be that hard. He ground his teeth and replied, "Just tell me what you want me to do, petite souris."

She stared at him for a few more moments before shrugging her shoulders. "Far be it from me to look a gift horse in the mouth. The curtains on the windows are too high for me to remove, but if you could get those down, that would be a good start."

"Why are we taking down the curtains? They help keep the heat in."

"Because they are filthy. We need to take them outside and beat them."

He flared his wings and gave her a feral grin. "What did they do to deserve a beating?"

"They got dirty." She flashed him her own mocking smile before returning to her work. She ignored him better than he thought would be possible considering his size.

Damnable woman thought she could best him just by ignoring him? Well, two could play at that game. And he wasn't about to make it easy for her to pretend he wasn't in the room. She wasn't used to the Dread just yet, even though she thought she was.

Flexing his powerful wings, he burst up into the air with a single flap. Great gusts of wind pounded down on her as he made his way to the curtains, ripped them from the rod with a single pull, and sent them down to the floor with a great, echoing thud.

Her task had been simple, at best. Easy at worst. He crossed his arms over his chest and turned in the air to hover.

Amicia held onto the ladder with both arms now, completely covered in dust and spiderwebs the wind must have pushed down from the tops of the bookcases. She looked like she was covered in snow there was so much of it.

A single cough puffed out her mouth. She blinked up at him. "Was that necessary?"

"Absolutely." At least she couldn't ignore him now.

Amicia sneezed once, twice, three times before her hold on the rungs slipped. He watched her as if in slow motion, each finger sliding from their secure hold and sending her backward, tumbling toward the floor.

He didn't think; he reacted. Alexandre shot down from the air with a burst of speed that surprised even himself.

Instead of hitting the floor, she tumbled into his arms. He caught her just at the knee and behind her back, careful he didn't jostle her broken limbs. But there was no way to be certain of that. He let himself fall onto his knees. They skidded a few feet before settling onto the floor with her cradled in his arms.

One of his wings had folded in front of them, a shield in case they struck a bookcase. The thin membrane created a strange cocoon for them once they stopped on the floor.

A cobweb stretched over the top of her head, a single strand of it stuck to her eyelashes. Dust decorated the dark locks of her hair like starlight. Amicia blinked up at him, and even covered in dirt, he marveled at her beauty.

Staring into her dark eyes was like staring up into the heavens at night. Darkness, vast and nebulous, but with tiny pins of light that promised so much more than emptiness. Her eyes were full of life, vivid and painful to behold, yet far more captivating than gazing upon the stars.

She reached up and placed her palm against his cheek. "You caught me."

Words pressed against his lips. I will always catch you. I made the mistake of letting you fall once, and it is my infinite regret. The thought of you hurt again leaves my soul raw and bleeding.

These were not the words he said. Instead, he whispered, "You've been hurt enough in this place."

"I suppose I have."

A memory burned through his mind, searing in its intensity. A woman with dark hair in his arms, just as he held Amicia. But there was blood trailing out of her mouth in a thin trickle, her eyes vacant and body growing cold.

He'd killed more people than he could count, but this one felt different. He hadn't killed this woman. The crimson blood stained his fingers, but it wasn't him who had caused her death, and he was so angry. The rage burned in his chest, up through his throat in a primal scream, the heat traveling up to his eyes until they ached like someone had thrown sand in them.

She shouldn't have died. He remembered thinking that. And he didn't know her name, who she was, but that he was supposed to protect her and he... he had failed.

"Alexandre?" Amicia's voice broke through the memory, and the cool touch of her palm slid up his cheek, her thumb tracing just below his eye. "What's happening?"

"I remembered something, that's all."

"Something important?"

He shook his head, clearing the lingering vision from his mind so he could stare down at her eyes. Her dark, star-filled eyes met his gaze with more worry than he deserved. "Nothing you need to know."

"Your eyes have changed," she whispered. "They aren't red anymore."

His hands started to shake. "What color are they?"

"Gold," she replied, her thumb stroking again. "Gilded like the finest of coins."

Everything was changing, and yet it couldn't. He was the King of the Dread. The one who had sent his armies to destroy her homeland and her people.

Yet she stared at him with something more in her eyes. Something that looked like she wanted him as well, or at the very least, that she saw him as more than just a monster. More than a beast at her doorstep.

Her lips were berry red, stained like she'd eaten raspberries this morning. Bee stung and perfect, oh so perfect. Alexandre stared at them and wondered whether he would taste starlight if he kissed her.

Her hand flexed on his cheek, her eyes widened, but the pressure on his face was not to push him away. No, she drew him closer to those lips beckoning him.

And once again, he marveled at the purity of her soul. For

only a woman filled with infinite light would dare to kiss the damned.

"Master?"

Alexandre froze, his lips close enough to hers so that her sudden exhale fanned over his mouth. She smelled like lemons and mint.

He swallowed hard, ground his teeth, and called out, "Yes?"

"You are needed in the Great Hall. A fight broke out between a few of the Dread, and they have summoned you to make a decision for them."

Amicia's eyes widened even further, and he knew the moment between them had passed. She was afraid of him once again. Though she did not struggle to free herself from his arms, she might as well have shouted for help.

"I'll be there in a moment," he replied to whoever stood in the doorway to the library. "Leave me."

He waited until the claws echoed down the corridor before he unfurled his wing. It wouldn't do to reveal her in his arms; the gossip throughout the chateau would catch like a wildfire.

The moment he released her, Amicia scrambled to her feet. She tugged on her woolen dress, ensuring it was in place before clearing her throat. "Thank you for the help. I can manage the cleaning from here."

"I have work to do," he said over her words.

They both kept their gazes on the floor. He couldn't stand the silence when he had almost kissed her. And she wouldn't want to kiss a monster like him.

This was a mistake.

He snapped his wings close to his sides, gave her a curt bow, and exited the library without another word. The Dread could distract him from the embarrassment for a little while. But he knew later tonight, this would prove to be a memory he wished he could forget.

CHAPTER 29

*A*micia pulled the last bits of splint off her leg and flexed the limb. For the first time in longer than she could remember, it didn't hurt. Of course, the muscle was rather tender but the ache of the broken bone was gone.

She pulled on the brown boots she'd found in one of the abandoned rooms. Her foot had been so swollen, all she could wear was slippers for the past few months. But now, she could finally put on leather and explore outside.

Brightly colored socks stretched up her legs, each stripe a different color. She'd hiked up the layers of pale woolen skirts up to her knees and tucked them into her belt for the time being. Two scarves over her shoulders, one blue and one purple, would keep her warm if the wind kicked up.

For now, she would enjoy herself and explore.

Amicia grabbed the cane she'd found in another room and twirled it in her hand. It had been painted black once, but time had peeled the paint off in places, revealing ashen wood beneath.

She stood, testing the leg, making certain it wouldn't

collapse underneath her weight. Amicia took a few shaky steps. She held her breath through the whole process but the leg held.

"Healed," she whispered. "Already."

With a sudden burst of energy, she spun on her heel and snagged the blue book from the table where it had stayed since she moved into the library. It had revealed no more secrets, but that didn't matter to her. She would conquer the beast today whether or not it wanted her to.

She tucked the book into her waistband and patted it. "You and I are going on an adventure," she said. "Let's go explore the grounds a little more, shall we?"

As she strode out the door, Amicia snagged a leather thong dangling beside the door and twisted her hair into a thick pony-tail at the base of her neck. For the first time in a very long time, she felt like herself. As though she could conquer the world if she wanted.

No Dread would stop her today. She straightened her shoulders and marched through the chateau as though she owned it. And in a sense, she did. What human could say they walked through the home of the Dread without a single one bothering them?

The sun shone bright and heavy outside. She crunched through the snow and tucked the tails of her scarves into her waistband beside the book. Heat beat down upon her from the rays of light.

"Perhaps winter has broken," she mused.

Amicia took her time picking a direction. The lake was straight ahead, although it was everywhere if she was honest. She'd done a few laps around the chateau before, but never had she gone through the hedge maze, laden with snow.

"Shall we?" she asked, stroking the leather binding of the blue book. "Do you think there's a secret at the center? Perhaps we'll find something remarkable. Maybe I can write it down in your pages."

The book seemed to quake underneath her touch. But she didn't believe in magic. A woman of science, she dismissed it as her mind putting too much stock in a fairytale.

Amicia strode into the hedge maze with confidence but stopped for a moment as the glimmering beauty stole her breath away. Chunks of snow and ice hung from the tops of the emerald green hedges, sparkling in the sunlight like a thousand diamonds. Birds sang at the top of their lungs here. Their trills filled her soul with something like... happiness. She hadn't felt the emotion in so long she'd almost forgotten what it felt like.

She patted the book one more time. "Father used to talk about mazes. Did you know they're all the same in some sense? To solve it, put your hand on one wall and never take your hand off. Eventually, you'll get to the center and then out."

She stretched out a hand as her father had taught her. Something in her soul clicked in place. Something soft and quiet, not stinging and aching like it usually felt when she spoke of her family.

Today was a day for healing, it seemed.

A smile stretched across her face, unbidden and so wonderful. Amicia made her way through the labyrinth of greenery. The journey gave her leg time to stretch and get used to having weight upon it, while giving her heart time to enjoy being here in this chateau.

Her thoughts slowed, then stilled. She allowed herself to be in the moment, not a captive, not a human pet. Just Amicia.

And she soon realized she had missed herself.

All too quickly, she moved through a part in the hedges and out into the center. A large fountain stood in the center with a winged man crouched above it. She caught her breath, ducking behind the hedge and listening for sound.

The man had been far too perfect to be one of the Dread. His wings were feathered, decorated with golden tips and... a Celestial? They were all gone, weren't they?

When she heard no movement, Amicia leaned around the hedge to stare at the man. Stone. He was a carving, nothing more, nothing less. But beautiful and so incredibly lifelike that she had been convinced he was real.

"Goodness," she said with a chuckle. "Did you think he was real, book? I certainly did."

But there was a loaf of bread beside the fountain. Someone must have been here, and recently, although it wasn't the hidden Celestial as she had thought.

"Hello?" Amicia called out, her voice ringing clear and strong through the crisp spring air. "Is anyone there?"

No one responded.

She thought it strange, but the whole place was rather strange. She'd gotten used to the intricacies of the chateau and how the entire kingdom seemed enchanted. Straight out of a fairytale, if one believed in that.

The waters in the fountain weren't frozen like the rest of the chateau. She assumed it was connected to a hot spring. Glancing over the rolled marble edge, Amicia was shocked to see golden fish swimming in the depths.

"How are you still alive?" she asked. "You couldn't possibly survive winter in a frozen fountain."

And yet, they were alive. The sun danced along the scales on their back. Shimmering like they were rays of the sun, they danced before her. The gossamer flutter of their tails caught her eye.

She glanced over at the bread then looked around once more. No one would notice if she snagged a couple crumbs. The poor fish had survived the entire winter. They deserved a snack.

Amicia didn't hesitate. She tore off a bit of the bread, crumbled it into pieces, and then tossed it in the water. The fish splashed as they fought for a few bits of food. Amicia glanced up at the Celestial statue and narrowed her eyes.

"Were you always smiling?" she asked him.

The statue didn't respond. However, she was more careful as she fed the fish, then pulled off her scarf to place on the ground. Amicia settled herself with her back against the fountain and pulled the little blue book from her waistband.

She turned it in her hands, admiring the sunlight playing across the pale blue surface before she tapped on it with a single finger. "I've taken you on an adventure, we've fed the fish together, survived a labyrinth, and met a Celestial. Certainly, now, you are satisfied enough to reveal a few more of your secrets."

Holding her breath, she flipped the pages open to the same diagram that had haunted her thoughts for days. The Celestial on the page had a different face than the one behind her, but he was still intriguing enough to catch her eye.

Maybe she would flip the page and be disappointed again. But something seemed to hang in the surrounding air. A sense of the entire world holding its breath with her. As if the maze, the fountain, and the statue all knew something would happen. Something wondrous.

Amicia licked her thumb and turned the page.

Swirling handwriting undulated before her eyes, slowing down until finally she could see there was at least five more pages of the book for her to read. Ready and waiting to reveal all the secrets she needed to know.

"Thank you," she whispered, frozen in place as if moving might make the handwriting disappear. "If it's adventures you want, then I will give you an adventure every day if you will reveal a little more to me."

She leaned over the book and devoured the writing. The passage appeared to be written by a different person, for the handwriting was less structured and seemed more like thoughts taken in shorthand. But she knew what each word meant and how much information it gave her.

The Celestials became the rulers of the kingdoms. They

were both king and watchman, protecting the lands from whatever might befall them. All of Ember became prosperous, the kind of prosperous that was only spoken about in legends—until something happened.

The arrival of a new people who came across the sea. The blue book didn't name them, but only said they had a crimson banner dripping blood. Some of the Celestials spoke with them; others banished the newcomers from their kingdoms.

The passage ended by stating the new people would create a problem that none of the Celestials had anticipated, and that the kingdoms would fall under the malice of these new arrivals.

Amicia closed the book and leaned her head against the fountain. "Crimson, bleeding banners?"

She'd seen that before while hidden behind the curtain in the Great Hall. The alchemists? They were the ones who had ended the prosperity in the kingdoms?

They were the only creatures she'd seen with crimson banners, and they didn't appear all that trustworthy. But, they were supposed to be Alexandre's advisors. She tucked the book into her waistband once more. "I think I'll keep this to myself until I find out more," she murmured.

It wouldn't do to tell him there was something about the alchemists tied to the curse when she didn't know what tied them. What if she was wrong? She didn't know all the details; the book had only laid the groundwork for mistrust.

The Celestial statue stared down at her, and this time she knew the expression had changed. It looked as though the being was crying. A single droplet of water trailed down its cheek. Melted by the sun, perhaps, but it appeared as though it were filled with sorrow.

Wings beat at the air, gusts raining snow down upon her as a creature fell from the sky and landed in a crouch before her. When Alexandre shook his wings, even more snow blasted toward her.

Amicia raised her arms up, and laughter burst from her chest. "What are you doing? Stop it!"

He shook himself like a dog once more before he finally let his wings still. "No one knew where you were."

Amicia lowered her arms back to her sides and shrugged. The Dread rarely needed her. They weren't all that interested in where she was most of the time, other than this one. "I rarely tell people where I'm going."

"If I need you, then I should know where you are."

"You don't usually need me."

The severe expression on his face changed, softening into something impossible to guess at. And yet, her stomach twisted and her heart raced at the sight.

She should have been frightened of the beast crouched in front of her like a monster out of a nightmare. But all the fear in her had disappeared in the wake of a bright light blooming deep in her soul. A golden light that saw him for what he was. A good man, trying to change himself and succeeding no matter how much he had to fight.

Alexandre cleared his throat. "What are you doing?"

Quickly, Amicia scrambled to pull the book from her waist and brandish it at him like a shield. "Reading."

"Find anything interesting?"

She hesitated before answering. They hadn't lied to each other, ever, but it felt important he didn't know the truth. He shouldn't know his alchemists might not be trustworthy when she couldn't give him a reason other than a hunch. Something more than a journal written in the hand of someone they didn't know.

So instead of telling the truth, she bit her lip and shook her head. "No, nothing all that interesting."

He stood, his clawed feet shifting in the snow and his wings spreading wide to keep himself balanced. She followed his gaze to the statue behind her, the one whose wings were feathered and delicate rather than leathery and heavy.

"I don't remember this being here," he muttered.

Amicia didn't know what to say. Did she explain she thought the statue could move on its own? She said none of the thoughts that ran through her mind. "What did you need me for?"

"Hm?" He murmured the sound, still staring at the statue as though he might remember something.

It gave her the opportunity to stare at him, and the changes in his body. His eyes were no longer red, but a warm gold that drew her attention. His teeth looked more human and... were his claws shorter? They didn't look so sharp.

She tried not to think of their almost kiss. The heat that had radiated from his body still lingered underneath her skin. Bursting back into full force whenever she thought of the look in his eyes and the way he had leaned closer and closer, as if he would do what she knew they shouldn't.

A kiss with a monster? Amicia had never thought she would find herself in that position and yet, she had wanted him to kiss her. Even now she wanted to see what it would be like to kiss such a dangerous thing.

But that would change everything. They wouldn't be able to be partners in research, and he had tried to kill her. Had killed her family and her friends. Perhaps not with his own hands for the latter, but his order had done so. She couldn't be interested in him in any way other than as a beast who held her captive.

Then he turned to look at her, and all those thoughts fled from her mind. He didn't appear as the King of the Dread any longer. He was Alexandre, curious about the details she might have found and the world around him. Desperately seeking more memories and attaching himself to her side because she reminded him of a different time.

She lost all the air in her lungs when he looked at her with that soft expression. His features changed from fearsome to kind.

"You're shivering," he said.

"I'm fine." She couldn't admit she shivered from the memory of their almost kiss.

"Amicia, you're allowed to feel the cold. It's not a weakness. It's admitting you can feel something."

"I can feel!" It was just the scarf around her shoulders making her cheeks red, not the frigid air. Besides, the fish were alive behind her. Surely, he could see life continued through the winter. "I'm not some delicate little thing, Alexandre. I'm fine."

"Seated in the snow?" He arched a brow. "You'll come back with frostbite."

"Stop trying to baby me, please. I'm not your dear, precious Vivienne with her noblewoman sensibilities. I'm happier sitting in the mud than I am at the dinner table." Well, that just made her sound like a pig, and that wasn't what she'd planned on him envisioning her as.

Flustered, she remained frozen while he marched toward her. She didn't say a word until he knelt beside her and slid his arms underneath her legs and back. "What are you doing?"

"Stop talking, petite souris."

"Alexandre, put me down!"

He chuckled, his breath brushing through the strands of her hair. "Can you breathe without arguing on the exhalation?"

"Not with you." But she let him shift her until he was seated on the scarf she'd laid out on the ground.

His hands on her body left scorch marks that only she could feel. Every imprint of his fingers left her breathless and confused. She needed to move. She couldn't think when he moved her body as though he owned it. What was he doing, anyway?

He settled, then seated her between his legs. Two powerful thighs bracketed her, caging her in between the bulging muscles. He placed a hand low on her belly and tugged her backward. Then she was pressed against his chest, feeling the heat of him warming her entire body with every breath.

His fingers spread wide for a moment, pressed against her softness before he slid them away. When he spoke, his voice was deep and rough. "What are you reading?"

She held up the blue book, although he had known what she was reading. Apparently, they were both thrown off by the sudden position he had thought was a good idea.

Only one thing bothered her, however, and the words slipped out unbidden. "What about Vivienne?"

Alexandre stiffened for the fraction of a second before sighing. "Continue reading, petite souris. I'll keep you warm."

He flexed his wings, spreading them out to create a canopy trapping all the heat. She was infinitely warmer, even her fingertips found it easier to turn the pages. Blowing out a low breath, she stared down at the book and began to memorize each passage as she had the others.

To his credit, Alexandre didn't look over her shoulder. Instead, he tilted his head back and closed his eyes. She thought maybe he was listening to the songs of the birds, the burble of water, and the drip of melting snow.

His hands were braced on his knees beside her. She didn't know what made her look at them, perhaps a sound or perhaps instinct. But as she stared at his claws, they grew shorter until they were nothing more than rounded tips.

She glanced over her shoulder at his closed eyes once more and decided not to mention a word of anything. He would see the changes, eventually. But for now, she would merely absorb his warmth for a little longer.

CHAPTER 30

*A*lexandre sat before the broken remains of a mirror in his room. He'd kept it covered with a sheet for many years, but now he wanted to see the damage to his body. He wanted to see what he looked like and how much he had changed.

He stared down at his hands as he had for the past ten minutes. Turning them slowly, he tilted the appendages that looked so unfamiliar suddenly. No nails curved out from them like a cat, sharp claws that could rend flesh from bone. Instead, these were the hands of a man.

They were still gray. Still stone-like in texture with calloused palms. But he could see the individual tendons of his fingers, the half moons of nail beds. Even lines across his palms he remembered having read once by a woman with wild hair and dark eyes.

He flexed his fingers, curled them into fists, then stared at his reflection in the shards of the mirror. A monster stared back at him. Horned, winged, and with cat-like eyes. But he had human hands.

Leaning closer, he pushed up his lip and stared at teeth he

remembered poking from his lips in a near constant snarl. The teeth behind his lips were human now. Blunted and weak, they were... perfect.

Fear sparked in his chest like someone had sunk a dagger into his chest. If someone challenged him now, he would be at a severe disadvantage. He was still larger than any of the other Dread, some things hadn't changed. And if Amicia's observations were correct, he had grown even larger since she'd been here.

At first, he'd thought the curse was worsening. That her presence, him keeping her alive as the only human left in Little Marsh, had meant he would pay the price.

Now, he wondered whether she was his salvation.

The door to his room swung open, the offending Dread not knocking or even asking permission to enter. Only one Dread had such confidence.

He watched her approach in the mirror. One of the few female Dread, although he still couldn't remember why there were no women here in his chateau. He couldn't remember a lot of things. Vivienne might have the answers, however. She certainly appeared to remember more than he did.

"My king," she said, her hips swaying with sultry purpose. "You've been hiding from me."

He most certainly had. Once upon a time, he had found her irresistible. They had found pleasure in each other at night. Claws scratching, teeth biting, horns locked in battle until one of them had finally bested the other.

The memories only made him uncomfortable now. Her touch wasn't soft, but abrasive. Her words always had a bitter bite to them as she tried to make him think less of himself. And still, he couldn't send her away.

Not when she was promised to him. Not when they had so many memories they shared. She was as much a part of him as the curse. No matter how badly he wanted to free himself from them both.

Vivienne reached out and stroked a rough hand down his cheek. "You're not yourself these days."

He made certain his lips covered his teeth as he spoke. "Many of us are changing, so it seems."

"The curse?"

"I can feel it is close to breaking. I cannot explain it, nor do I wish to disturb such a gift. It is long past time our people ended their suffering."

He caught the shift in her expression, the way her mask slipped. Her brow furrowed, her jaw clenched, and rage appeared in her eyes for a moment before it disappeared. "Our people do not appear to suffer in the slightest. We've been given power and strength, my king. Have you forgotten already?"

"I've forgotten much in the many years we've fought."

And he found himself tired. So exhausted of having to fight, to battle, to plan. Instead, Alexandre wanted a few years of peace. These months with Amicia in the chateau had been the best he could remember in forever.

"Alexandre," Vivienne said, seating herself upon his knee. She brushed her hands over his horns, stroking down to his ears which she gave a soft tug. "The alchemists have called upon us once more. They will arrive soon and have requested we host a ball. Something splendid and wondrous in their honor. I replied since you were nowhere to be found."

His gut twisted in something that felt eerily like fear. "You said we were in no place to host something so grand as a ball."

"I said no such thing. The alchemists called. We are the Dread. We answer them." She frowned. "I'm having the ball-room cleaned now. I thought you would be happy."

"We haven't had a ball since..." He tried to remember, but this wasn't like sitting with Amicia. Being with Vivienne made his mind foggy and searching for memories was like trudging through quicksand.

"Since long ago." She finished the sentence for him unbidden. Vivienne leaned closer, her breath whispering over his lips. "Come, my king. Shall we entertain ourselves while the servants work?"

He almost leaned in. He almost fell under her spell as he had a million times. But a single word stuck out, and his spine stiffened in response. "Servants?"

"We have servants," she replied with a chuckle. Then she tugged his head down closer to hers. "Alexandre, I have missed you."

He shook his head, dislodging her hands from his horns. "Would one of those servants be the human woman?"

"Of course." Vivienne leaned away from him then, and rage turned her features ugly and cruel. "She is a servant. She even said so herself at the dinner table."

"Amicia is not to be treated like a servant, regardless of what foolishness she claims." He stood abruptly, dumping Vivienne from his lap to the floor. "She was injured and should not be working."

"The girl seemed fine to me," Vivienne snarled from the floor. "You have forgotten your place as king, Alexandre. Worrying about servants does not befit your station."

He strode away. "It does, in fact, befit the station of a king, Vivienne. I am not king of the privileged. I am king of all. You'd do well to remember that."

Alexandre stalked from the room before he said something else. Something far more aggressive and something he might very well regret. If anyone could challenge him, it was Vivienne. The only thing holding her back was her ridiculous and fanatic trust in him.

Once she lost that trust, he knew she would try to take the throne. And he had no doubt she could.

Frustrated, he made his way through the halls to the ballroom that had remained closed the entirety of his rule. He didn't even remember what it looked like, only that there was a balcony upon which he could see the proceedings of servants.

As if Amicia was a servant. How dare Vivienne suggest such? Though Amicia wanted to be seen as one, it was merely because she felt out of place. The Dread were not her people. Well, they had been once, he corrected himself, but they were no longer. Which meant she would feel as though she was lesser. She was certainly smaller. One could assume a smaller stature meant she wasn't equal to them, no matter how much he'd tried to prove she was just as important.

When he pushed the door open to the ballroom balcony, his rambling thoughts halted. Had the ballroom always been so grand?

The walls had once been wallpapered a lovely pale blue, the windows outlined by gold filigree and the in-between space of the walls decorated with more golden carvings. The ceiling was one giant frame painting of angels and humans consorting. Such a blue sky had somehow survived the years of neglect and was as vivid as the sky outside.

The Dread had hardly touched this room. Instead, it was as pristine as it had been long ago. He wished he could remember what it looked like when this place had flourished.

One of the Dread flew to the highest of the windows and brushed it with a—he leaned over the edge of the balcony—yes, the Dread was using a feather duster to clean. He didn't have to look to guess who had given one of his army that particular weapon.

But look he did. Alexandre searched the throngs of servants to find Amicia. She threaded her way through the crowd, a gray gown hiked up to her knees and a cane supporting her movements. She limped by, a broom in her other hand and a grin on her face as she ordered the Dread around.

Had he ever seen her look so happy? He didn't want to ruin the moment by shouting at her to get back to her room to continue with her research. Though he didn't want her to be in the servants quarters or feel as though she must work for her room and board... she appeared to be enjoying herself.

One of the Dread nearest to her said something he couldn't hear, but her laughter was loud enough to feel in his bones. She spun with the broom, as though she were dancing with a partner.

That was all it took. A simple movement and memory burst behind his eyes. He'd stood on this balcony before with hundreds of people spread out before him, each more glamorous than the last. Silk and velvet skirts twirled in shades of cream and gold. Masks covered their faces, but he knew each one as well as he knew himself.

He had stood above them, breathing in the smoke of burning candles and the perfume of so many women his head ached. They were all dear to him. And he was proud of what they had created together.

For him? The ball had been in celebration of him. Why had the humans been celebrating a monster?

The memory cleared from his vision, and he saw what the people had become. The vision of jewel encrusted dresses faded into granite skin and bat wings as the Dread balanced themselves to clean. All the people who had once thought so highly of him, he'd destroyed.

Each and every one.

Alexandre almost turned and left. The sorrow building in his chest threatened to swallow him whole, and he was not a strong enough man to suffer it in silence. Yet, his gaze caught on the little human woman who pulled a sheet off a pianoforte and ran her fingers down the keys.

All the Dread in the room froze and then turned as one

toward the music chiming like bells. One of them called out, "Do you play, mademoiselle?"

Amicia smiled and shook her head. "No. I never learned. My father was more interested in science than the arts."

Alexandre watched with rapt attention as one of the smaller Dread, a creature Alexandre had denied going out on raids with the others, approached Amicia's side. It reached out with a clawed hand and touched a finger to the keys.

What was happening? The Dread shouldn't remember who they were, as far as he knew.

But this Dread, who had not been around Amicia more than the time in which they had been cleaning, pulled the bench out and sat down at the pianoforte. It laid its fingers on the keys and began to play.

The song was familiar and yet not, though it swirled through his mind like a music box. A haunting tune which, some winter long ago, he may once have danced to.

His gaze turned toward the Dread in the room and saw everyone had paused. Some of their eyes drifted shut, others swayed on their feet. Almost as if they, too, remembered this song. Remembered that once, long ago, there were words they all knew. Words they understood.

A small voice sang the words, quiet and yet pure. "Aimer c'est voler le temps…" To love is to steal time. She hummed the rest, but he remembered the lyrics.

To love is to steal time. To love is to live.

The sound of her voice and the song died, and the rest of the room held their breath in anticipation.

The Dread seated at the pianoforte looked up at Amicia and asked, "Will you be going to the ball, mademoiselle?"

She shook her head and placed a hand on his shoulder. "I don't believe so. I'd stick out like a sore thumb in all this wool and old dresses."

Alexandre leaned over the balcony, wings spread wide behind him. "Find her a gown."

The sound of his voice broke the spell of music like shattering glass. The Dread rushed to finish their work other than the few nearest to him. One ran from the ballroom to find the perfect gown, he assumed. The one at the pianoforte bowed his head to his king. But his brave Amicia stared up at him with fire in her eyes.

"I'm not going. Peasants don't go to balls."

He grinned down at her. "Ah, but you aren't a peasant now are you, Amicia? You are the woman who tamed the Dread. You're more like a knight, and knights go to balls."

Her cheeks flushed bright red. Alexandre pushed himself away from the edge of the balcony and turned to leave, his chest puffed out with pride.

She would come to the ball, and he had made her blush. Perhaps today wasn't so bad.

CHAPTER 31

For the hundredth and final time, Amicia smoothed a hand down the bodice of her borrowed dress and shook her head. "It's too fine for the likes of me, Bernard. I couldn't. I can't!"

He pressed his fingers against his lips, eyes wide and wings tight against himself. "No, my dear. You most certainly can."

Amicia stared at herself in the mirror. The woman looking back at her wasn't the daughter of a tinker.

The golden dress looked as though they had taken it right from the walls dripping wealth in the chateau. The heart-shaped bodice accentuated the lines of her collarbone, making them appear delicate and fragile. It was sleeveless, with a strip of fabric draped over her biceps.

Threads hung from the top of the bodice, glimmering with diamonds and jewels. They made her entire body shine every time she shifted and moved. Sparkling lights drew the eyes down to the point of the bodice at her belly and then the great mass of golden brocade that spread out wide around her.

Actual gold had been woven into the fabric in patterns of roses stretching up from the ground. She was a gilded garden who would walk amongst the Dread as if she hadn't just been called a weed.

Her heart lodged in her throat. Amicia pressed a hand against her stomach and took a deep breath, or as much of a breath as the corset would let her.

The ties of the corset weren't as bad as she had always thought they would be. Or perhaps Bernard hadn't tied them tight. Whatever it was, the bodice tucked in her waist, giving her a bell shape far too lovely and even more strange.

"This doesn't look like me," she whispered.

"My dear, this looks exactly like you were supposed to look. I've never seen a lovelier image in my life."

There were tears in Bernard's eyes. Amicia tried hard not to let her own grow weepy. This was just a ball. No meaning, just a night of revelry she shouldn't let go to her head. She was just a woman.

Besides, if they were holding a ball for the alchemists, this was a chance for her to understand what the book wanted her to know. If the alchemists would really be here, then she had to ask them questions. She had to understand why they weren't trustworthy.

She wasn't going to outright ask them if they were lying. No accomplished liar would ever admit to such a thing. Still, Amicia was certain she could figure out the truth given the chance.

All she had to do was see if she could corner one.

"What are we going to do with your hair?" Bernard quipped, his voice finally changing into something a little less sad and a little more aggressive. He'd fallen back into his old habits rather quickly. "It will not do as it is."

"Can you braid it?"

He pressed a hand against his chest as if insulted. "Do I look as though women raised me?"

She arched a brow in response.

"Stop it. I don't know how to do hair in the slightest, mademoiselle."

Neither did she. She'd always thrown the dark locks on top of her head whenever she was working. And if she could lift her arms, she might have braided the mass, but she couldn't in this dress.

Which left only one way to wear it that would have shocked the sensible nobles of this chateau. Likely their spirits would roll over in the graves deep below her.

Amicia sat down at the mirror, reached for the silver handled brush, and held it out to Bernard. "Brush it for me, then? Just a few strokes. I'll leave it down."

"Down?" If his cheeks could turn even more ashen, they did. "Is that… done?"

"No. But neither is allowing a peasant to attend a ball. Might as well remind them of who I am."

He took the brush from her, his claws curving around the handle with utmost care. "Who we are, mon cherie."

Amicia let her eyes drift shut and enjoyed the feeling of the brush massaging her scalp and smoothing out any knots that might remain in her hair. She didn't want to look upon the strange visage staring back at her. She didn't know who the woman in gold was, nor was she interested in finding out.

That wasn't Amicia. Underneath all the heavy layers of brocade and silk lay a peasant woman who wanted to feel dirt under her nails once more.

"There," Bernard said after a few moments. "Now it shines as it should."

Amicia let her eyes drift back open. Her dark hair smoothed back from her face, falling down her shoulders in gentle waves of darkness gleaming in the candlelight. It was beautiful. She was beautiful.

She couldn't remember another time in her life when she

had thought that. Amicia truly believed in this moment every inch of her was breathtaking.

"Up with you." Bernard helped her stand. He shook out her skirts with a few tsking sounds then finally grunted his approval. "You'll do. Yes, you'll do marvelously."

"What am I doing?"

Again, his cheeks turned dusty before he shrugged. "Oh, just enjoying yourself, mademoiselle."

"Hardly. I intend on getting there early, tucking myself into a corner, and watching the revelries alone. This ball isn't for me, I'm perfectly happy to stay out of the way and observe."

His eyes had widened even larger as she'd talked until finally she ran out of breath. What bad news could he possibly have to tell her?

He cleared his throat. "Early?"

"Yes, early. I don't want to make a grand entrance when the alchemists will be there. They want me either dead or one of the Dread. They weren't exactly shy about such facts the last time they were here."

"I didn't think you knew." Bernard twisted his fingers together.

"What did you do?"

"Nothing, mademoiselle just... the ball has already begun."

Her heart jumped in her chest. How had he let her be late? Now she couldn't sneak into the ballroom, and everyone would stare. They would all know where she was, that she wasn't one of the Dread nor one of the alchemists. It boiled down to her being terrified they would all look upon the lamb wearing the clothes of a lioness.

She hiked up her skirts and raced from the room. Bare feet slapping against the marble stone.

"Mademoiselle, your shoes!"

No one would know if she wasn't wearing shoes, and she wasn't about to stop. Not when the ball was already going. They would stare at her, she would faint, and her heart was already racing.

She thundered down the stairs, blasted through the halls until she reached the ballroom where two Dread sentries stood. Amicia might have ran past them too if she wasn't so stunned.

They were wearing clothes. Brocade vests, pants with rips for their tails to slide through. Their muscles distorted the seams but... they were wearing clothing. Real, actual clothing they might have worn in their previous lives.

She skidded to a stop before them, breathing hard and hair in disarray. "Good evening, monsieurs."

Both Dread bowed at the same time, but one looked up at the last second and winked at her. "Good evening, mademoiselle."

"Has the ball already begun?"

"Indeed."

Every inch of her body shook in fear and, suddenly, she knew without a doubt she couldn't do this. She couldn't walk into that room full of monsters who wanted to kill her and alchemists who were questionably aligned.

She was a brave woman, but she wasn't that brave. Amicia shook her head and gulped. "Then I shall go. My sincerest apologies, monsieurs for missing such a special occasion."

The Dread who had winked at her caught her elbow while the other opened the doors wide. "Mademoiselle Amicia!" he called out.

Beyond the doors, the Dread had created something stunning. The chandeliers were filled with hundreds of candles. Their flames caught on the dangling crystals and fractured glass, sending rainbows dancing across the room. All the Dread had packed into the room, each dressed in their finest doublets and hose. A few female Dread were even there, although some of them she hadn't realized were even female.

No one seemed to care while they danced. Males partnered

with males, moving through the steps they shouldn't have been able to remember.

Two of the Dread were in the back of the room, one on the pianoforte and the other with a violin in his hands. It wasn't a full band, but the music they played was hauntingly beautiful.

Those who weren't dancing held food or drink in their clawed hands. Amicia was surprised they could hold the crystal goblets without crushing them.

Throughout the crowd were alchemists in their dripping-red robes. A few of them turned toward her when the announcement was made, then the Dread turned until everyone in the room stared at her.

She leaned harder against the Dread holding her elbow. She was the oddity here. The strange little pet who no one understood.

Inhale through your nose, she told herself, and exhale through your mouth. Over and over, she did this until she finally got her rapid heartbeats under control. And still, they were staring at her. Everyone in the room.

Amicia leaned over and whispered to the Dread beside her, "Why are they all staring?"

"Perhaps because you are so beautiful, mademoiselle."

She felt her cheeks heat in a blush. "Somehow I doubt that's why they're all looking rather angry."

"Not angry." The Dread released her elbow with another wink. "Not in the slightest. But you are supposed to curtsey."

"Oh." She dropped into what was perhaps the worst curtsey ever attempted in a splendorous place like this. If anyone in the room didn't know she was a peasant yet, they certainly did now.

When she straightened, shaking on wobbly knees, she looked out over the crowd. There, far in the back of the dance nearest to the musicians, Alexandre stood still as a statue.

Their gazes met as the violin struck a magnificent chord. Her heart clenched, hard. It didn't matter Alexandre had been dancing with Vivienne. It didn't matter the alchemists were all turned toward her as though they might attack at any moment.

Her eyes took in the finery of their king who, for the first time in a very long time, looked like a man. The silver doublet he wore fit him perfectly, even with his wings splitting open the back. Strange, for none of the clothing the other Dread wore fit them. Black buttons ran in matching lines down the center, accentuating the strength of his broad chest.

She'd seen that chest bare every day she'd been here, but somehow he was more with clothing covering him. The pants on his legs were too tight even for peasants. But she wouldn't complain when the hard muscles of his legs were on display.

When he took a step toward her, she took an answering step back. Amicia locked her muscles until they were frozen, then reminded herself he was the King of these people. She couldn't run from him even though her heart screamed to run.

She hadn't been able to breathe when he was before her in his true form. As a monster. But this? This was too much. He was a man with hunger in his yellow eyes and a purpose in his steps as he approached her faster and faster until he fairly flew to her side.

Alexandre was breathing hard when he stopped before her and his chest expanded in a great inhalation. He held it, staring down at her with wide eyes.

"Words cannot express," he finally said, his voice little more than a rumble. "You rival the sun itself, petite souris."

"Surely not." Her voice wavered.

"You need not believe it for it to be true." He reached forward as if to brush a strand of her hair behind her ear, only to hesitate and let the hand fall. "Would you dance with me?"

"I don't know how."

"You'll stand on my feet then. I used to dance as such with the children."

Amicia arched a brow and couldn't stop herself from teasing him. "Am I like a child to you then?"

The heat behind his yellow eyes flared even brighter. "Oh, no. *Tu es la plus belle fille que j'ai jamais vue.*" You are the most beautiful woman I have ever seen.

Her breath caught in her throat and, this time, she reached for his hand when he offered it. How could she not when he spoke such pretty words? Words that filled her soul and spoke to the peasant girl in her who was terrified she would never be enough for these people.

Amicia feared she would always be the weed. Always the one with dirt smudged on her cheek and the outcast who dirtied the pristine linens.

But he made her feel like more than that. He watched her movements with appreciation, grinning down at her with a feral smile when the Dread parted like a wave before them. He didn't even look at Vivienne who glared at them from the corner with the alchemists whose undulating cloaks appeared to move ever faster.

Not once did his eyes stray from her. To him, they were the only couple in the entire room.

He stretched out her arm, placing it high on his shoulder. "Rest the other on my arm."

She gently placed her hand on his bulging bicep. Her heart stuttered at the contact, then stopped altogether when he placed a hand on her waist and tugged her closer. They were nearly pressed against each other, shoulder to hip.

How was she supposed to think when his heat seeped through the thick brocade of her dress? She could feel him as though they wore nothing at all.

Breathless, she murmured, "Everyone is staring."

"Let them."

"It doesn't unnerve you?"

His hand tightened at her waist, and then they were spinning. The violin and pianoforte grew to a crescendo they danced upon. Every step was coordinated with the music in a way she hadn't known possible. Their bodies became the song.

Alexandre leaned down and pressed his lips against her ear. "Nothing unnerves me when you are in my arms, mademoiselle. No one but you exists in this moment. Enjoy it."

Amicia tilted her head back and let out a bark of laughter bursting forth from her belly. "Does that work with the ladies, King of the Dread? What a horrible way to convince a woman to pay attention to only you!"

"It usually works," he replied with a frown. "Or, at least, it used to."

"I'm not a noblewoman. Pretty words won't convince me of anything other than your insincerity."

He leaned away from her, spinning her slower so he could stare into her eyes. "Then what would convince you?"

"Of what?"

"That I find you beautiful. That everyone should stare at us because you are the most beautiful woman in the room."

"There are hardly many women here."

"Amicia," he chided. "You know it's more than that."

She didn't know that for certain. Perhaps the female Dread had been spectacular specimens in their day. Everyone here might have looked down their noses at her had they not been turned into monsters.

"Amicia," Alexandre said. He released her hand to touch her chin, forcing her to look up at him. "You belong here just as much as they do. You are not some peasant woman or lesser than they are. That is not the kingdom I have any intent on ruling."

"Then what kind of kingdom do you want to rule?" she asked. The words slipped out before she realized how rude they were, and yet... she wanted to know. The answer to that question was more important than any puzzle she'd ever solved.

He frowned. The gears were turning in his head, she could see that like reading a book, but she didn't know what he had planned until they were dancing away from the others. Farther and farther away until they were right next to a door she hadn't noticed before.

"Shall we, mademoiselle?" He stopped their dancing, bowed low, and stretched an arm toward the door.

"Where are we going?"

"A place I just remembered existed." He straightened and then pushed the door open. "Come with me, Amicia. There's something I would like to show you."

Beyond the door was a set of stairs. It seemed for a breathless moment as though the entire thing had appeared out of thin air merely because he remembered it.

She stepped past him and began ascending. Her skirts were almost too big to fit in the winding stairwell, but she managed well enough. The marble stone chilled her bare feet, in a way that felt good. That felt alive.

The longer it took for them to reach their destination, the more she wondered where they were going. Her heart raced. Her palms grew slick with sweat. And yet, Alexandre said nothing as they continued their journey high into the peak of the chateau until the stairwell opened up into the most beautiful room she'd seen yet.

The floor, walls, and ceiling were all plated with gold. A single candle illuminated the room from a small stand in the center with mirrors that bounced the light around and around until it appeared they were standing in the center of the sun. Tiny punctures in the gold allowed more light to filter through from all angles, even the floor, pinpricks of starlight unlike anything she'd ever seen before.

"It's beautiful," she whispered. "What is it?"

"I don't remember. But I know I spent a lot of time here." He strode past her into the room, touching fingers to the holes and blocking out the light. "I can't remember why, but I know most of my days were in this room. Researching, learning, understanding your people."

Not for the first time, she wondered where the Dread had come from. Where he had come from. Surely, the Celestials wouldn't have allowed something like him to exist. Had he killed them? Was he the reason the Celestial in the tomb below their feet lay dormant?

Or perhaps was there something more?

"Alexandre..." She didn't know what to say. Was there anything she could say? He remembered fragments of who he was long ago, but that didn't answer any of the questions he had. His past had been stolen, and she was no closer to discovering who he was.

"You asked me what kind of king I want to be." He paused in the center of the room with his back to her. Music filtered up through the holes in the floor like the candlelight below them. "If you had asked me the same question mere weeks ago, I would have said the king I already am. But now, I'm not so certain."

She opened her mouth to reply but found no words. He needed to speak, and she shouldn't alter the way the words would come out. So instead, Amicia remained silent.

"Before you came here, I was content with the way we lived our lives. We fed, we hunted, we survived in this wilderness of darkness and snow. Then you opened my eyes to all my people could be." He stared into her eyes, yellow gaze finding hers from across the room so easily. "To what we once were."

"It's my pleasure to have awakened whatever I could."

"That's the strangest thing of all this. No one else reminds me of who I was. What I might have been before all this darkness descended upon my throne. I want to be a king who people remember and revere, not one whom they fear."

Alexandre approached her then, his feet blocking out the

light as he strode forward. Tiny stars disappeared in the wake of his darkness then burst into light as he left. He reached for her hands and clasped them close to his heart. He squeezed her fingertips then murmured, "You changed everything."

His hands were so warm around hers. Calloused with use but dear to her now. So dear, and yet she didn't know how he'd slipped underneath the walls around her heart. "I didn't mean to do so much. It was unintentional, if that helps."

Alexandre chuckled. "Take a compliment for once in your life, petite souris. You are a marvelous being. I'm only sorry it took me this long to realize just how much you have done."

He drew her closer and, this time, she felt the breath leave her lungs far before his eyes drifted to her lips. He inhaled, somehow bringing her even closer. Or had she stepped closer herself?

"I haven't given up on finding out what happened to you and your people," Amicia said, licking her lips and trying to still the thunderous beating of her heart.

"Oh Amicia, I already know what happened." His deep growl echoed through her chest. "Someday, I'll tell you all the secrets I remembered."

"Why not now?"

"Tonight, let me savor the feeling of you in my arms. Let us not be the captor and captive, but Alexandre and Amicia. Together, in the dying light of the sun."

Her entire body tensed, waiting for him to finally break the barrier between them. She stepped closer so she could inhale all that he exhaled. So she could finally understand what it felt like to kiss a man as close to a god as one could get.

Perhaps, in the future, he would say she moved first. When his lips brushed hers, it felt as though they had kissed a thousand times before. Velvety soft, he caressed her mouth with his own, tender and quiet. Not the kiss she had expected from a monster.

She'd thought he would try to devour her, but instead, he consumed her very soul. Alexandre tunneled his hand underneath her hair, holding the back of her head while stroking her cheek with his thumb. His other hand curved around her waist, holding her in place, but so tenderly it made her feel fragile.

With a simple movement, he pulled her into his arms while he continued to kiss her. He shifted their bodies into a slow waltz, his arms holding her, his lips captivating her, and she knew what it meant to have her heart sing.

The symphony inside her head rivaled that of the noble musicians. She knew now what it meant to have a devil steal her soul. And to never want it back.

After what felt like hours and yet must have been only mere moments, he drew back enough to stare down at her with a soft smile. He stroked the highest peak of her cheekbone with the pad of his thumb. "I would go to the ends of the world for you, mon coeur."

Her tongue stuck to the roof of her mouth. She turned her face then, pressing her cheek against his shoulder and holding him close to her thundering heart.

Mon coeur, my heart.

Just before she closed her eyes again, to savor the gift of this moment, he flexed his wings to balance them in a grand spin. Before her eyes, leathery wings turned white as snow and a single feather fell to the floor.

CHAPTER 32

*T*hey returned to the ballroom, and Alexandre was immediately swept away by the Dread and alchemists. Amicia was nothing more than the human girl who didn't fit in. But for the first time, he looked over his shoulder and winked as he left.

She wasn't alone, anymore. Even when she stood in the center of the ballroom with a crowd of people ignoring her.

His wings had returned to normal. For a moment, she wondered whether she had imagined the moment. The white wings. The feathers falling like snow. Such gilded beauty was burned into her eyes, however. She could see them when she let her lids fall shut.

Perhaps now the book would have something else to tell her. No one would miss her presence if she slipped away for a few moments. There must be something new on the pages. It would tell her what was happening.

Telling no one where she went, Amicia slipped out the ballroom doors and raced toward the library. She'd only be gone for a few moments.

The library doors slid open silently. She hiked up her skirts and ran to the place where she'd left the little blue book. Right next to the nest of blankets that made up her bed, far more comfortable than the mattress she had left in her old room.

Skidding to a halt, she stopped and stared at the table where the blue book had rested.

"Gone?" she whispered.

Certainly not. She was careful where she'd placed it. The pages held the secret to her release, and she wouldn't have misplaced the volume. It held everything between its covers. All the important things that had led her to this moment. To this explanation, this proof, why she had seen gilded feathers when she held Alexandre in her arms.

"Looking for this?" The voice was raspy, as though years of smoke and sacrifice had turned the bearer's throat into dust.

Amicia fisted her hands in the voluminous fabric of her skirts and turned to stare at the man standing behind her.

The red robe revealed nothing of the face in the shadows of its folds. Oozing liquid dripped from the top of his head, the wet plops echoing in the library. But the alchemist reached out a skeletal hand, white and tattooed in unreadable marks. Her book was clutched by bony fingers, a single smear of blood across the cover.

She swallowed hard and tried to hide the shaking of her hands in the folds of her skirts. "I was, thank you."

"This book is a magical book," the man said, his voice little more than a whisper. "Did you know that?"

"There's no such thing as magic."

"Oh there is, you innocent little thing. A tinker's daughter, isn't it? Florin and Amicia of Little Marsh, the family who knew so much about the world. And yet, your father never taught you magic and science go hand in hand?"

He knew too much. So much more than she'd ever told the Dread.

She took a single step back. Somehow, the movement

brought with it the metallic scent that wafted off him. "Do I know you?"

"No."

"How do you know all that, then?"

The alchemist shrugged, the book still held out for her to take. "I know many things, as do all the alchemists who protect this place. But do you protect the chateau? Or have you come to destroy all we have wrought?"

She remembered what the book had said. That the alchemists were not to be trusted, and they only did things for themselves. They were the ones who had started another war with their crimson banners.

Amicia ground her teeth, straightened her shoulders, and refused to cower before this man. This creature who was the real monster within the walls of the chateau. "I do not intend to destroy, but to heal. I wish to know what happened here, so I can leave."

"You want to return home? Your home is gone. Your people are the Dread. They do not wait for you in that haunted, abandoned place. Little Marsh is nothing compared to the chateau."

"Little Marsh will always be my home."

"You would do well to remain here, mon cherie."

Gooseflesh danced up her arms at the sound of such an endearment on the tongue of the alchemist. She reached out and snatched the book from his hand. The sight of him touching her only hope at freedom, her only hope to leave... it gutted her.

"Thank you, but I would like to return all the same." She held the book away from her dress, ensuring the blood didn't smudge the beautiful fabric. "I don't trust you."

"Nor should you. The end of this story is near, and I don't intend for you to ruin all we've worked for." Slowly, the alchemist bowed his head. For the briefest of moments, she saw what was underneath the robe. The soaked fabric had fallen to the side. Beneath, the alchemist was nothing more than a scarred ruin of what a body should be. Black marks, like scorched bits of flesh, covered a bald head that was mottled and pockmarked from years of abuse. But it was his eyes that frightened her most of all.

Eyes sunken into a skull that shouldn't have been alive. Flat eyes, blind but somehow seeing. He grinned when he caught her staring. There were no teeth left in his mouth, just an open maw of darkness threatening to swallow her whole.

"The secrets you wish to discover are hidden within those pages," he said. His voice was warped by the missing teeth and the scars traveling throughout the length of his destroyed body. "But you will not like them."

"The book hasn't led me wrong yet."

"Perhaps you should give up now." The alchemist straightened and adjusted his hood. Monstrous form hidden once more. "Such a beautiful thing you are. I'd hate to see you break."

"I'm stronger than I look."

"I hope so, for what that book will beckon you to do will shatter even the strongest of resolves." The alchemist turned and left the library. But a smear of blood showed his trail.

The moment he left, Amicia frantically opened the book. "Please, please," she whispered as she thumbed through the pages, though she knew not for what she begged.

New pages burst into life. She skimmed them, but they weren't what she wanted. Just information, the history about the Celestials she would read later. None of this answered her questions.

Until she landed on the last page of the book, suddenly full of information it had never wanted her to read. And there, on the last page, were the words that made her heart hesitate to beat.

Amicia read the words out loud, her voice choking in her throat. "The curse of the Dread is brought about by greed. Only the Celestials who have lost their way will turn to the path of darkness. They are the ones who will lead the others into destruction and ruin.

"The Dread will spread like wildfire. Throughout all those the Celestial loves, and to those whom deserve no darkness in their lives. It will take their memories until there is nothing left of the Celestial. The plague will spread throughout the land.

"To end the suffering, a pure soul must plunge a knife into the heart of what remains. The heart of the Celestial who vowed to protect his people with his life, but who betrayed them. Immortality is gifted only to the good and the just.

"The knife will be created by a lost people, forged in the fires of a burning city. And held by…" Amicia choked on the last word but something compelled her to finish reading it aloud. "Held by a loving hand."

The book slipped from her fingers and hit the ground with a loud crack. The sound might as well been thunder for all it made her flinch. She stepped away from the blue book only to trip on the fabric of her makeshift bed.

Amicia fell onto her bottom hard. The skirts of her beautiful dress pooled around her, suddenly less beautiful and more binding. Her corset dug into her ribs. The boning felt like a cage stealing her breath.

A shuddering sob slipped from her mouth. The floodgates opened, and tears streamed from her eyes. Kill him? She couldn't. She couldn't suffer through knowing that she must kill yet another person she loved.

Hands shaking, she pressed them to her mouth and stared at the book. "I love him," she mumbled through her fingers. "I don't know why or how, but I love him, and you can't make me do this. Not to someone else. Not again."

The pages flipped on their own. She knew the words had been the last page in the book, and yet, there was another. Amicia crawled on hands and knees to see it was an illustration of a knife. A gem encrusted handle, a wicked looking blade, and a shimmering outline that made her eyes sting.

The outline grew brighter and brighter until she had to lift an arm to cover her eyes, else she might go blind. When the light disappeared, she dropped her arm to see the book had closed, and the knife lay atop it.

It was a beautiful blade. Made by the most talented of black-smiths. She didn't want to touch it, but again, it felt as though a hand slipped underneath her arm and forced her to reach forward. Forced her to pick up the blade that felt as though it had been made for her hand.

In a way, she supposed it had been.

The handle curved into her palm, and the silver blade winked in the candlelight. Such a deadly weapon shouldn't look so beautiful.

A hand pounded on the door to the library, then paused, and a quieter knocking followed. "Amicia?" Alexandre called through the door. "You left in a hurry. I wanted to be sure everything was all right."

She slowly stood. The knife seemed to vibrate in her hand as she approached the door. Almost as though it knew it was close to the one it had to kill. The only one who could stop all the suffering.

"I'm fine," she called back, but her voice wavered and her throat closed up in fear. "I'm fine, Alexandre."

"You don't sound it."

She didn't know how to respond to his kindness when she stood with a knife in her hand. "I needed a break, that's all. The alchemists frighten me."

The door creaked, not opening but as though he leaned against the solid wood. "They are not comfortable for anyone to be around, but I thought you didn't have it in you to be afraid. Not anymore."

"I'm afraid right now." Not for reasons he might think. The

knife sang in her hand, whispering dark thoughts of opening the door and sliding its length between his ribs.

She already knew what it would be like. His slick lifeblood pooling over her fingers, dripping down her hands as he stared at her in shock. Then sadness.

What a fitting end to their story. He had tried to kill her when they first met. Now, she must kill him to end everything.

Amicia ground her teeth against another sob pushing against her lips. He couldn't hear her crying because then he would push his way through the door and would see everything. He would know everything, and she couldn't do it, not now.

"You shouldn't be afraid here. You've survived the Dread, turned monsters into allies. How many people can claim such a thing? You went from victim to hero in your own story and convinced a king who wanted only to conquer that there was more to this world than pain and sadness."

She shakily inhaled. Her breath caught in her throat. When she could muster her words, she buried the emotions deep inside herself and replied, "You give me more credit than I've ever asked for, Alexandre."

"Amicia—" Something scraped the door, a claw perhaps? No, he didn't have them anymore. Perhaps just a granite-rough palm pressed against it. "Will you let me in?"

She reached out and pressed her own hand against the door. Almost as though she could feel him through its heavy weight, the warmth and solace his touch might give her. "Not tonight, Alexandre. I'm tired."

"Sleep well, petite souris."

Amicia waited until she heard his heavy steps down the hall before she dropped the knife. It clattered on the marble floor, but it was still there. She could feel the weight of its responsibility on her shoulders.

She was the woman who had killed her entire kingdom. She had killed her father and now she must kill her only love.

This was bigger than her. There were hundreds of the Dread here who deserved to remember who they were. Who deserved to go back to their home as humans, not as beasts. A tear slid down her cheek again, though she resolved it would be her last.

Tomorrow, she would kill the King.

Tonight, she would mourn his death.

CHAPTER 33

*A*micia stayed in the library for longer than she should have. The Dread began to ask questions, knocking on her door and asking to enter. She denied them every time.

Eventually, she knew they would force their way through the doors and drag her back out. Not because they desired to kill her as she had thought for so long, but because they cared about her wellbeing. They wanted her to be happy.

She couldn't be happy when she knew the answer to saving them, all of them, still lay on the floor where she had dropped it. And she couldn't pick it up. She couldn't lift the blade that would end all of this, for if she did, then she lost something so important to her.

All night she had tried to convince herself she didn't love him, she couldn't care less if he were dead.

And yet, every time she looked at the blade, she saw something else. The first moment recognition had flickered through his eyes at a memory. The first time he sat across from her in the library and chuckled at a joke. The laughter in his eyes when she didn't want him to help keep her warm as she memorized the pages of the little blue book that had betrayed her.

Hundreds of memories, both good and bad. Memories that had created her belief in him. Alexandre had proven, though he might have been under the curse of this place, he could change. He could grow into a man who desired to be good and to help those who were under his command.

Surely, that counted for something. Killing him would free her people from this sickness, but there had to be another way. Why did death have to be the only answer?

Over and over, she fought with herself. The incredible pain and misfortune of losing another person who meant the world would ruin her.

Death followed in her footsteps. Every time she thought she was happy, content, it took and took until there was nothing left. Until she was, yet again, alone and lost in the woods, hoping someone would find her. Hoping someone would look upon her with mercy.

Morning came and went in the library. Amicia remained in the seat staring out the broken windows at the melting snow beyond.

Almost all of it was gone now. Spring had come to the chateau. Though winter had arrived with a storm to change the landscape, spring came with a whisper. Just the drops of water hitting the ground and the bright colors of flowers blooming already.

The door behind her opened and closed. "Leave me," she said, exhausted and numb. "I have no wish to entertain."

"Then it's good I have no desire to be entertained."

Him. Again.

Amicia couldn't be near him, not now. She had too many thoughts to sift through. Too many possibilities she hadn't weighed. He would force her into a decision she hadn't planned on making just yet.

"Amicia," Alexandre begged. "Would you at least look at me?"

She didn't want to. Looking at him would only make him

even more human, and she couldn't stand to think of him like that. Not when she had to kill him.

But she looked, because her heart could deny him nothing.

Tears in her eyes, she stared at him where he stood. Leathery wings, yellow eyes, but lacking all the things that had made him so frightening. Dark circles ringed his eyes. Perhaps he hadn't slept either.

Her chin quivered as she held in more tears. "Why do you think you've changed so much?"

"What?"

"I need you to answer the question, Alexandre. No more secrets or veiled words. Where are your fangs? Your claws? Why do you look so much like a man?"

He took another step closer, though still hesitating to approach her. "The moment you snuck into this chateau, I knew I was found. I had lost myself in this curse, this sickness which destroyed your home and your people. They are mine as well, and I had forgotten. But you? You never lost sight of what we needed. Of who we are."

Sweat gathered at her brow. "Please don't say that," she whispered. "Please don't make me think of them in a time like this."

"I don't understand why you are upset. Was it the kiss?" He fisted a hand and pressed it against his heart. "If I misjudged you so, I will not touch you again."

"No, it's not that."

"Then what?" He stepped closer again. His foot caught the knife on the floor, sending it rattling toward her. It settled between them, and she saw his gaze lock upon the handle.

And so it was revealed. The knife was a symbol of everything she didn't want to say. All the lies, the pain, the torment. She had gone through so many emotions this night. All she could feel now was numb.

"Amicia?" he asked, still staring at the knife.

He didn't need to ask the question. She knew what he

wanted to know. Why did she have a knife? Was she so afraid of them again?

The answer to the latter was yes, but she didn't know how to say it when the words stuck in her throat and made tears gather in her eyes. She couldn't admit she knew how to end all this, but she must admit it. All of their lives depended on it. On them.

"I returned here because I saw something when we were in the Sun Room. Your wings turned white for a moment, just the briefest of glimpses, but I saw it." She caught her breath, swallowing down the emotions that threatened to bubble up again. "An alchemist waited here for me. He had the book and claimed it had all I needed to know on how to break the curse."

Alexandre nodded. "The alchemists have always been an ally to the Dread. We listen to their wisdom when they impart such things."

"I cannot."

"Why?" He stepped closer, stopping just at the knife. "Why would you not be able to listen to them? We knew the book held the secret."

"Because I cannot."

"Amicia." His voice sharpened, as deadly as the blade of the knife between them. "Tell me."

"A knife created by a lost people, forged in the fires of a burning city." She spoke through choking tears. "Held by a loving hand."

"What are you saying? What did the alchemist tell you?"

"To dispel the curse, I must kill the king." Tears slid down her cheeks. "And I don't think I can do it, Alexandre. I don't think I can kill you."

His eyes ripped from hers to stare down at the handle of the blade. What must he think of her? She had all but agreed to kill him; that's what it looked like. The knife was already there. They were close enough she could lunge forward, and it would all be over. She wasn't stronger than him, but she was quick and small.

He leaned down and picked the dagger up off the floor. In his hand, it looked ridiculously small. Far too little for her to ever think it might hurt him, and yet, she knew such a thought was foolish. It could hurt him. All it would take was a small thrust and twist.

Six steps, and he was in front of her. A heartbeat of time passed, and then he knelt before her with the dagger offered to her from his own hand. "If this is the way to end the curse, then this is what we must do."

"I will not kill you," she whispered, muscles locked tight against any movement. "I can't do it, Alexandre."

He stared at her with wide eyes, and she watched as the slits in his pupils dilated then changed shape. He looked at her with the golden eyes of a man.

Alexandre lifted a shaking hand and brushed a strand of hair behind her ear. "Did you read the book?"

"I did."

"And what did it say?"

"It said to kill the king was the only way to cure the people of Little Marsh and any affected by the Dread."

He smiled, eerily human and monster at the same time. "And what else did it say?"

She didn't want to voice her suspicions. Not after everything she had learned about the Celestials and how they were sent to this place to help the people. They were like gods, and she was nothing more than a mortal. Amicia shook her head, praying he wouldn't make her say the words.

"Now you know," he murmured, his fingers tracing her jaw. "The body you saw in the crypt is me. I was the one who betrayed your people. I was meant to protect you, and I forgot what that meant. My purpose grew muddled with pleasure and greed. For all I have done to your people, to you, to the history of Little Marsh, this is the least of the punishment I deserve."

"Please don't say that."

"It's the truth, and you know it as much as I." He trailed his hand down her neck, shoulder, and arm. Alexandre tangled their fingers for a few moments, then drew her hand to his mouth where he pressed his lips against the back of her hand. "I am a lucky man to have spent my final days with you. My soul takes flight when you are here, and I would have it no other way."

Amicia choked on a sob. "I can't do it."

"Then allow me to help, mon amour."

He drew her hand to the handle of the blade, curled her fingers around it, and drew her close to his chest. She rocked forward on a gasping sob. Her eyes locked on the glint of the blade pressed against his bare chest.

"Look at me, Amicia."

She stared at the droplet of dark blood beading already at the tip. She shook her head. Looking at him would only make this even more real. She was hurting him. Choosing to hurt him of her own accord, and she couldn't be that much of a monster.

"Please."

Slowly, she moved her gaze up the strong column of his throat to eyes that stared at her with so much love.

"You are doing the right thing," he said. "There is no guilt here."

"You called me the sun," she choked out. "But it is you who will take the sun with you when you go. I cannot end your life without also taking away all the light from mine."

"Perhaps that is your payment and your sacrifice." He pulled her hand, forcing the blade to sink deeper into his chest. Alexandre gasped in pain, but he still stared at her with a softness in his expression.

"I don't deserve to sacrifice any more than what I already

have," she whispered. Amicia slipped from the chair to kneel before him on the floor. "I know you want me to be selfless, to right all the wrongs you have done. But I choose to no longer suffer in a world that has taken everything from me. I would rather burn for all eternity than lose a single moment with you."

Amicia tore the blade from between their fingers and threw it toward the window. It wouldn't go far, but maybe she could convince him or run away fast enough that he couldn't make her kill him. He couldn't make them save her people if she didn't want to.

The dagger hit the window and shattered it, falling into the snow with a soft thud. Shards of the remaining glass pane fell with it in a sparkling shower of pain and memories of a dying winter.

Alexandre stiffened underneath her hand laid against the wound, pressing the blood back to his skin. He stared at the window, and a frown wrinkled his brow. "You choose to let our people suffer?"

"I choose to see that sometimes forgetting who you were doesn't mean you forget who you are."

He swallowed hard, his throat working to release the words that tore her heart out of her chest. "Then you have found your cure, and you may go home."

"I have no wish to go home. My people are here." She pressed her hand harder against his chest. "You are here."

"But you did not choose us in our hour of need." He looked at her then, and she saw all the light had drained from his eyes. "Go home to your barren city. Perhaps the ghosts there will find more mercy at your hands than the Dread."

"You don't mean that." How could he be saying these words? She thought he had felt the same and yet...

"You have no place here, Amicia. Not if you are unwilling to do what our people need you to do."

Her stomach rolled and her heart clenched, but Amicia

stood on shaking legs. If he wished her to leave, then she would. For at least now she knew he was alive. And that was better than wandering through this world knowing he was dead.

She stumbled toward the library door, the golden gown swirling around her with every movement. She paused at the doorway for a moment. Should she tell him? Should she admit all the things in her heart? That she loved him more than life itself?

Amicia looked over her shoulder and saw white wings, permanent now, draped around him where he knelt on the floor. Blood smeared the ivory feathers whose tips were dipped in gold.

He was a fallen angel too far out of her reach.

Amicia turned and raced away from the chateau. She fled across the lingering ice on the lake that surrounded the place she now considered home. And with each step, the ice cracked behind her, then gave way.

CHAPTER 34

*A*micia had remembered the painful grasp of the forest as it clutched at her body and clothing. But she hadn't remembered how violent it could be. Branches snapped, flying back into her face and scratching at her cheeks and neck. Twigs caught in her hair, ripped at her dress until she left bits of gold fluttering in the wind behind her.

Mud splattered the hem of her dress and squished between her toes as she ran, barefoot and sobbing, from the chateau. She didn't care if she caught a cold. She was strong, but she didn't care if she got sick when Alexandre's words echoed in her head.

Not once had Amicia ever belonged there. The chateau was the home of the Dread, not of a human who wanted to change the way they saw the world.

How could she have been so foolish as to think he wanted her? The kiss had been little more than a man enjoying a woman he thought was attractive. Alexandre was King of the Dread, he was one of the Celestials, and he would have far better women at his beck and call than the lowly daughter of a tinker.

She swiped at the tears on her cheeks. She had already given him enough space in her mind. No more tears for a man who didn't care about her.

The forest fell away from her feet, sending her tumbling down a gully. Amicia rolled over and over, mud splattering along her arms and legs. She ended up at the bottom almost as quickly as it started. One of her legs rested in the burbling stream, her dress soaked and frigid in the icy water. Sharp stones poked into her torso, digging into her ribs, stealing her breath.

Perhaps this was only more of the same bad luck she would suffer for the rest of her life. She sat up with a moan, slicking back her hair, now more mud than anything else.

For once in her life, she had been beautiful. Wearing a gown made of gold and dancing in a glorious ballroom full of dreams.

Life was having a laugh with her now. Destroying all the things that could remind her she was beautiful, even if she was just a peasant.

She lifted the edge of the gown, heavy and drenched with water and dirt. Amicia let it fall back into the stream with a wet slap.

"Now what?" she whispered. "Where am I supposed to go?"

Little Marsh was nothing more than ruins; the alchemist was right. Even if the Dread had stolen the people from the city, it would have been difficult for the city to remain functional. But she had burned the entire city to the ground. There was nothing left there for her.

Omra was always an option, but she would have to walk for at least a month to get there. No travelers would stop and offer her a ride because there were no travelers coming out of Little Marsh any longer.

She was stuck in the mud both literally and figuratively.

"What would father say?" she asked herself. "He would have some kind of plan that wouldn't end with me becoming a bog witch and scaring any Dread who came my way with the threat of more curses."

Although, the idea had merit. She wouldn't mind making them afraid of her for once.

No matter what she did with her life, Amicia couldn't stay on the ground. She'd catch a chill, and no one was around to help her through an illness.

So she rolled onto her feet, groaning at the new bruises and scrapes decorating her body. The stream had to lead somewhere. Perhaps even to the ocean she'd never seen before. Then she could try to find somewhere to end up. A place to rest her head for a few moments.

Loose stones shifted underneath her feet. The stream hadn't been disturbed in a long time. Not even animals could find their way down here unless they fell.

She walked by a particularly large skeleton and grimaced. Eerily human, she stared into the empty eye sockets until gooseflesh popped on her arms. She didn't want to think of what the creature might have done to her if it had been alive.

Amicia had forgotten there were more practical things to be afraid of in the woods than the Dread.

She walked for hours, perhaps even days, before she realized there was a light in front of her. The small, bouncing light might have been a will-o'-the-wisp if she had believed in them. Instead, she realized she was weaving in her steps, not the light.

Like a beacon in the middle of the ocean, it led her from the darkness and dim light of the gully to a small hut standing at the edge of a river. It stood in the dim light with a tiny dock stretching out into the river. A single lantern hung from the end of the dock, the light guiding her.

"So," she muttered to the stream, "you get bigger."

Much, much bigger it appeared. The river roared with so much violence and thundering water she wouldn't ever be able to get across. Even a boat would have a difficult time managing those rapids.

The hut, in comparison, was small. Its thatch roof was well taken care of, the windows still intact, and a small candle beside the door lit the way for visitors. Amicia couldn't see anyone moving behind the windows, but she supposed it was late.

She climbed up the two stairs to the small porch and knocked on the door. "Hello?"

Instead of an answering call, the door swung open on its own. Hinges creaked as it shifted to reveal a single dark room beyond. A small cot rested at the back, next to a fireplace stacked with wood. A table with glass containers was underneath the only window. Amicia couldn't see what substances were in the smudged and foggy vials. Spiderwebs covered the space, dust fluttered from the ceiling at a breeze pushing through the hut. No one had been here for a very long time.

"But..." Amicia looked at the lit candle, the small flame flickering in the wind.

How was it possible there was light if no one was here?

She was so tired of strange occurrences like this. Amicia was her father's daughter. She didn't believe in magic, yet it appeared magic wanted her to believe in it.

Giving up, she strode into the hut and flinched when the door closed on its own behind her. Shoulders slumped forward with exhaustion, she relented to the world or whatever curse wanted her to listen.

"I'm here," she said. "What do you want to show me?"

Another gust of wind, impossible in its strength, blew over the table. Two candles at either end burst to life and one of the books shifted toward her. Enough that she knew it was the one she was meant to read.

Her hands shook as she reached forward, touched a single finger to the book, and nudged it onto its side.

"Book of Spells?" she read aloud. "Surely, you jest."

Amicia didn't know who she was speaking to, but there was someone in this house with her. Books didn't move on their own. Wind didn't burst into life from nothing. There were always scientific explanations for something like this, but she couldn't find a single one in this moment.

A hand touched her shoulder. She looked to the side, seeing nothing but still feeling each individual finger pressed against her skin.

"Are you a ghost?" she asked.

The fingers squeezed tighter, then released.

"A ghost then." Amicia nodded and turned back to the book. "Of all the strange things that have happened to me, I suppose this is the least of the oddities."

She stepped closer to the table and opened the book. The strange wind blew again, pushing the pages until they settled on a particular page. Another unseen hand, or perhaps the same one, moved her hand forward and touched a line.

The book was handwritten, small scribbles in the corners amending the spells that had been written many years ago. The pages were stained by tea and time, although she swore she could still smell peppermint on the paper.

"A spell for clarity," she read aloud. "Why do I need something for clarity? I remember what he said. He didn't want me to stay. That's why I left. I need not understand what happened. I need to know what to do moving forward."

The hand nudged her hard in the middle of the back. It apparently wanted her to perform a spell which felt rather strange.

But what did she have to lose? After everything, the Dread, her family, even running across the frozen lake that had cracked in the middle of winter but not spring... All these details were things she couldn't logically explain.

Besides, she was too tired to argue with someone who was

already dead. She'd rather try a little magic and see how it changed her life.

"Rosemary, ginseng, and turmeric," she read. "Ground in a mortar and pestle, then boil above an open flame. Drink until memory returns."

She shifted the vials around on the table until she found what she needed, although she didn't know what ginseng was. A mortar and pestle rested on the table as though it were waiting for her. Only moments ago it had been filled with dust, but when she turned back to it, the dust was gone and it appeared almost as new.

"Thank you for the help," she murmured, then started grinding her ingredients. "This is just a tea, you know. It's not magic."

This time, she didn't feel a hand, but she heard a strange voice, one she had heard before, reply, "It's magic if you believe it is."

Well, now she was talking to the dead. Amicia had led a strange life, but even her father wouldn't have believed this if he was still alive to hear her story.

The question now was whether or not she believed in magic. Amicia didn't think she did, and yet, the past few months had proven her wrong. Even the Dread were not an infection. No human could grow wings, and she had just been denying herself the truth this entire time.

Maybe magic was real. Maybe she had denied it her entire life because she didn't want to believe in it. Because it was different, and different was scary.

She carried the mortar and pestle to the fireplace, a hearty flame now burning in its depths. She hadn't lit the fire, had she? Every movement seemed a little slower in this place, as though she were running through water.

Lighting a fire was a rather strange thing to forget. Perhaps the ghosts had done it. Could they do something like that? Something so powerful when they were already dead?

She poured the powder of herbs into the pot hanging over the fire. Boiling water enveloped what she'd created.

Was magic real? It could be if she wanted it to be. What would her father have said?

As if she had conjured him up, she saw his image seated beside the fire on the cot. He stretched one of his legs out, the other bent at the knee. He'd injured it when he was younger, and the bone had never been quite the same.

"Ami," he said. She hadn't remembered the wrinkles at his eyes being so prominent, but perhaps he aged in the afterlife as well. "You've done well, daughter of mine."

"Apparently, I've forgotten something." She took the small stool from the worktable and dragged it in front of the fire. Amicia stretched her hands out, her fingers icy. "And I am to believe magic is real."

"How else would I be here?"

She glanced up in surprise. The laugh lines on his face deepened, and he grinned at her with so much mirth, she almost believed he wasn't dead. "You're just a figment of my imagination."

"Am I? What are spirits then? Magic or mud?"

Amicia touched a hesitant hand to her head. The mud was drying, cracking where she touched it and raining down upon her shoulders. "I suppose the right answer is a little of both."

"I never left, you know." He leaned forward and grasped her hands. She could feel his fingers, strong and confident in hers. "I've always been here, helping to guide you, and I always will be."

Tears burned her eyes and blurred her vision. "I killed you, Papa. Why would you ever stay with someone who did that?"

"Because you're my little girl, and you always will be. I love you more than life itself, mon cherie. You are not alone, even in the darkest of times."

Letting out a long, low breath, she nodded. "I suppose I've always known it was you."

"Drink your tea, darling."

Amicia hardly realized her movements were slow and wooden. She poured the water from the kettle over the flames into a mug at her elbow, although she didn't know where it came from. She sipped. Hot water burned the roof of her mouth, and flavors burst on her tongue.

Her father leaned forward. "When you were speaking with the King of the Dread, what did he say?"

She swallowed. "He said I didn't belong there. That I couldn't make the right choice for our people, and I must leave for forsaking them."

"Think harder. The alchemists are tricksters. There must have been something they used to warp your mind."

"I don't think so." Amicia had to make him understand. She didn't know why it was so important her father saw the world the way she did, but it was. "The book Alexandre gave me has all the secrets. The book was the one that gave me the blade."

"Was it?"

Heat bloomed again. She'd sipped the tea without realizing it, and with the second swallow, her memory shifted. The book hadn't given her the blade at all. The alchemist hadn't left yet, and he was the one who set the blade atop the book. His sunken, flat eyes had stared at her in the mockery of a smile before he left.

"No," Amicia gasped. "The blade was left by the alchemist."

"Take another sip, daughter. Focus on the words the King of the Dread told you. What did he say?"

She drank deeply, two, three more sips until the cup was empty in her palms. She forced herself to remember those hated words, the ones that still stung her soul to think of.

"He said..." The world spun, as if something inside her was fighting against the tea. She swallowed hard, forcing the gorge in her throat back to her stomach. "He said, 'You have no place here, Amicia.' And then told me to go back to my barren city."

"Good, Amicia. Now remember what he really said."

Suddenly, she was seated in the chateau's library once more. Alexandre was on his knees before her, grasping her hands within his.

She could hear the same words she remembered, but his mouth moved differently. His lips didn't say that she had no place.

What was he saying?

Amicia leaned closer, focusing so hard a headache nearly split her head in two. The memory, warped and wrong, finally gave way until she could hear what Alexandre had really said.

"Please," he begged. "Don't leave. No matter how hard it is, or what we will become, stay. I need you, Amicia. All I have ever needed was you."

Amicia pulled out of the memory with a gasp of pain and anguish. Breathing hard, she dropped the cup that shattered on the floor.

The ghost of her father leaned back, the outline of his body becoming foggy and transparent once more. "And now you know."

"I remember."

"What shall you do now, daughter of mine?"

Amicia met his gaze as it faded away and felt resolve settle hard on her shoulders. She straightened her spine, squared her shoulders, and set her jaw. "I'm going back."

CHAPTER 35

*A*lexandre didn't know what had happened in the moments between the kiss and the library meeting. He had been trying to do the right thing. To put his own concerns and desires aside.

And then, when she couldn't kill him, he had felt the most uplifting hope. Maybe she loved him. Maybe, just maybe, she wanted to stay here with him.

He knew what he looked like. There had been some pleasing changes. He was looking more and more like the man he used to be, but his hope could only stretch so far. Amicia must have known he would never be the Celestial he was before. A curse was a curse. And if she couldn't break it, then he would return to the monster she had once feared.

For a moment, he had hoped she could overlook his ugly visage. She had seen the man underneath the horrific skin and had kissed him. Then she wouldn't kill him. That had to mean something.

And yet, when he had asked her to stay, she had left. Fled from the chateau.

He couldn't stop her this time when she knew what he was.

A monster. Real and true, the kind that she had always feared he would be.

Alexandre wandered through the halls in a daze after she had left. Unsure of where or what to do. She had been the light at the end of the tunnel for so long, the beacon in the darkness drawing him out of the shadows and fog of his own mind.

He remembered everything.

Days after she had left, he found his feet carrying him toward the crypt where his old body awaited. It was nothing more than a corpse now. He couldn't return to that gilded form when he knew she wouldn't break the curse.

He reached out a clawed hand and placed it on the wall to guide him deep into the belly of the chateau. Claws. He scraped the walls as he walked, digging into the soft stone because he was changing back into the monster. The longer she was gone, the farther he fell into despair.

The lights never went out in the crypt. At least, that's what he remembered from the old times. This was supposed to be a place where he honored the most beloved of his people. It didn't matter if they were noble or not. He had laid them to rest here because their hearts had deserved the greatest of honors.

Each slot in the wall held someone who had changed him. The first man who had stopped on the road when he had arrived with the other Celestials was in the grave to his right. The man had offered him water, said Alexandre had looked thirsty. It was the last bit of water the old man had, but he was happy to share.

Above that tomb was the woman who had named Alexandre. She had said he looked so handsome; he deserved a name just as beautiful as he was.

Countless people. Each more kind than the last, the ones who had been the real heroes of the kingdom and who had taught him so much about love.

And yet, he still couldn't remember what had brought him to

this moment. The moment where he stared at his own body laid out in a sarcophagus before him.

Alexandre stopped beside the body, staring down at it with a mixture of horror and sadness. "Who were you?" he murmured. "And why was I ever fool enough to think I could return to you?"

The corpse didn't respond; of course, he didn't. This was the husk of a Celestial, the last remaining piece of the man he should have been. Though it breathed, it was only because the body waited for the soul to return. And Alexandre feared he could never return to that state. No matter if the curse was broken.

She had changed him. Fundamentally, deep in his soul. The Celestials were supposed to help all humans, force them to see reason and punish them if it was required. They were not supposed to fall in love with them.

And yet, his soul was not his own any longer.

"And so the King falls," a voice said from behind him. Considering it oozed from the shadows, Alexandre already knew to whom it belonged.

Sighing, he turned to stare at the alchemist who had followed him. This was the leader of their dark troops, the one man who had forced Alexandre to his knees and who could do it again.

Dark tattoos spread across the alchemists knuckles. Their black shapes warped as he pushed the hood back and revealed the mess of his face. Alexandre had forgotten how ugly the alchemists were.

"What do you want?" Alexandre growled, turning away from the disgusting sight of the alchemist's face.

"We told you the girl should die or you should turn her into one of the Dread."

"I could do neither."

"And now, here you are. All we wanted was to prevent your

suffering, King of the Dread. But you have never been talented at listening. Have you?"

Alexandre wasn't here to be scolded. He rounded the other end of the tomb, staring up at the numbered graves where all the people he had once loved were put to rest. "I see no reason for you or your people to remain here. You gave her the knife to kill me. She refused. Now, you may return to whatever darkened hole you crawled out of."

"No, Alexandre." It was the first time the alchemist had ever used his name. "If the curse will not be broken, then you must uphold your end of the bargain."

"What bargain?" He remembered nothing of what the alchemist was talking about. Alexandre turned back to his own grave and clutched the edges of the coffin. His nails made the stone screech as he shifted. "There was no bargain between us."

"Of course, there was. We allowed for one attempt to break the curse, but if it failed, you were to become the King we always wanted for this land." The alchemist stepped forward, blood oozing from his robes. "Now, you will fulfill that position."

"I will not."

"You have no choice, King of the Dread. You signed a bargain with us a long time ago, and now your little shield is gone. Forever."

Alexandre didn't remember this. With all the memories swirling around in his head, he had thought this would be something that would appear once he focused. However, he could remember nothing. "What does this bargain entail?"

"Forsaking all from whence you came and accepting your place as King of the Dread." The alchemist spread his hands wide. "That is all."

It didn't sound like a small feat, and yet, Alexandre saw no reason why he shouldn't. Amicia was gone. His people were already the Dread.

Becoming King for all eternity didn't sound like a change of his fate in the slightest.

Bowing his head, he nodded. "If that was the bargain, then I will uphold what I said all those years ago."

A cold blast of wind rocked through the chateau. His breath fogged before him as the winter returned in full force to his land. Pain skittered along his spine, and he felt his wings moving of their own accord. Felt his body changing once more.

Alexandre looked up and saw the alchemist's wide grin. A pit formed in his stomach and he had a mere moment to think, "What have I done?" before all the lights went out.

CHAPTER 36

*A*micia burst out of the hut, only one thing on her mind. She would save the Dread and the man she loved, no matter what the cost.

The door slammed against the wooden side, rocking the structure behind her. She paused only for the briefest of moments to stare in shock around her. She was no longer in the deep gully. Instead, she was right back at the edge of the frozen lake, staring at the chateau encased in ice.

"Okay," she whispered. "I believe in magic now."

The echo of a chuckle ghosted through the surrounding air, then a hand pushed against her back. She was supposed to be running, after all. Or had she forgotten?

Amicia burst into movement once more. She slogged through the knee deep snow that clung to her ankles and threatened to pull her deep and deeper. She wouldn't let it, however. She would make it to the chateau. No one, not even the alchemists' magic, would stop her.

The lake had broken, shattered the last time she had seen it. And yet, now it was frozen solid, the ice so thick it felt like a marble floor underneath her feet. She had never seen it like this before.

Even more concerning was the layer of ice coating the chateau. The entire building looked as though it had been blown out of glass, or perhaps as though someone had draped a sheet of glass over the top and let it melt down upon it.

Why was it covered in ice? Amicia shook her head and continued on, focusing on the first task before she let herself worry over another.

The snow gave way and allowed her to stumble onto land at the foot of the chateau. She paused for a moment, her breathing ragged and her body aching. The dress provided little warmth, but she felt strangely fine. Even her fingertips were not aching with the bitter cold.

Amicia stood and stared up at the chateau as though it were another enemy for her to destroy. And destroy she would. Nothing would stop her, not in this moment and never again.

She stalked to the front door of the chateau. Ice covered it in a thick shield. She wouldn't be able to reach the door through the thick mass of glittering ice.

"That will not stop me," she growled. "You must do better than that."

The statue next to the door had once been a man holding a shield. The other side was a man holding a spear. Both had been destroyed by the Dread, but there were shards of stone on the ground.

Amicia bent and picked up the largest one she could lift. She was stronger than she ever had been, hard work and labor had turned her into a woman of means. She hefted the marble over her head and, with a great cry, sent it flying toward the ice.

Though it didn't break immediately, she had left a chunk in the chateau's icy armor. A large chip spider-webbed away from the door and gave her the only thing she needed to continue.

Hope.

She picked up the stone again and lifted it above her head.

"This is for my father," she snarled, heaving it against the ice again. "This is for my family and friends." Another crack fissured out from the others, and the ice groaned. "And this for Alexandre."

The final strike shattered the glass just enough for her to slip through. Amicia dropped the stone. Her lungs ached from gasping in the cold air, but she couldn't stop to rest now. Not when there was so much more to do.

She reached through the hole in the ice, turned the knob of the front door, and pushed it open. It swung on silent hinges and revealed a silent hall beyond.

The hall had never been hushed before. There were always the Dread watching each entrance. At least a few of them milling around, on their way to another room or to start their watch.

Where had everyone gone?

Amicia crawled through the ice and landed on hands and knees in the entrance hall. Her hands sank into the sticky carpet soaked with... She lifted a hand. Blood stained her fingers, thick and oozing. Not normal blood. But that of the alchemists.

She curled her lips in a snarl, baring her teeth. The monsters were still within the walls.

The golden dress was already ruined, so she didn't feel bad wiping the blood on the silken fabric. She stood and marched toward the Great Hall where she had seen everything begin. The Great Hall where she had lost the first of her people and watched him turn into a beast. The Great Hall where she had first seen the King of the Dread and felt frightened.

But it was also the place where she had first realized he wasn't as much of a monster as she thought—the dinner where he had shielded her from Vivienne's hatred.

As if her thoughts had summoned a dark spirit, a shadow passed over the wall in front of her. Amicia froze, her hands curling into fists. Slowly, she turned around and saw one of the Dread standing in a doorway behind her.

Not just one of the Dread, but the general of Alexandre's armies. The one who would have seen Amicia killed.

"Vivienne," Amicia growled.

"You're supposed to be gone," Vivienne replied, stepping into the weak light filtering through the ice. "And yet, here you are. Once again ruining everything."

"I have no intention of ruining a single thing. I'm going to save him."

"Save him?" Vivienne chuckled. She flexed her clawed fingers and opened her wings wide, clearly trying to intimidate. "He doesn't need saving. He's accepted his place as King of the Dread for all eternity, which means we shall become even more powerful. This land is ours, human."

"No." Amicia shook her head. "It's not yours, and it never will be. This land is cursed, and I intend to see that curse ended."

"Won't you need this?" With a flourish, Vivienne reached behind her and pulled out the jeweled blade that was meant to kill Alexandre. "I was the one who found this blade, you know. The alchemists requested I find it, and I did. Even though I would never have seen you break the curse. I was the one who helped them in the first place, all those years ago."

"You wanted our people to be cursed?"

"I wanted power." Vivienne closed her hand around the blade. Blood welled up from the Dread's palm, dripping down her forearm and landing on the floor in wet plops. "The alchemists are the only ones in this realm with real power, and if you don't believe that as truth, then you are more foolish than I thought."

"The alchemists are monsters." Amicia took a step toward the Great Hall where Alexandre must be. "They want to ruin this land and its people. I won't let you or them destroy all that I love."

"How adorable. You think you have a choice."

Vivienne launched herself at Amicia. Her great wings spread wide and her claws outstretched to rend and tear. This was what Amicia had wanted to avoid every time she was near one of the Dread. They were so much larger than she was. So much faster.

She dove to the side, rolling on the ground to get away from the great battering ram of Vivienne's body. The other woman's wings spread wide to slow her down, and she skidded along the marble. Her claws made a horrid screeching sound as she dug them into the floor.

Amicia glanced over her shoulder. Vivienne stared at her with glowing yellow eyes, her teeth bared in a grin that meant the hunt was on. But Amicia had survived this before. She had been hunted by the Dread, and they hadn't found her then. This one wouldn't either.

Hauling herself to her feet, she sprinted down the hall. Windows flashed by at the sides of her vision, chandeliers clanked above her as the wind from her pursuer pushed them into motion. But Amicia just needed to get to the statue. The one she had first hidden behind. The one she now knew stood on wobbly feet.

A claw hooked at the back of her dress, and the fabric tore. Amicia spun, her hands just catching the statue and tugging it forward. It crashed not into Vivienne's skull as she had hoped, but against the Dread's shoulder and right wing.

The force was enough to make Vivienne stumble. The dagger fell from her hand and skittered across the floor. Landing at Amicia's feet.

She snatched it, holding the blade out in defense.

Vivienne saw her clutching the tiny metal piece and laughed.

"Do you think you can kill me with that? It's nothing more than a letter opener."

"I think it was made to kill the Dread, and it can certainly kill you."

Vivienne's eyes flashed brighter. "Then come here, human. Let's see if you are killer after all."

Amicia turned to run, but Vivienne had anticipated her movements. The Dread flew over her head and landed in her way. She couldn't slow her sprint and ran directly into the Dread's arms.

Breathing ragged, Amicia squeezed her eyes shut and waited for the inevitable crush of death. When no pain came, she blinked her eyes open and met Vivienne's horrified stare.

She felt it, then. The wet warmth dripping down her hands from where the blade had sank into Vivienne's chest.

Amicia gasped, releasing the handle. She stepped back and shook her head. "I'm sorry. I didn't mean to... I'm sorry."

Vivienne released a wet gurgle and then fell onto her knees, then onto her side. Blood dripped from between her lips, and a pool of it grew around her body like a lake had been released.

Blood slicked Amicia's hands again. This time, warm and new instead of the old blood that dripped from the alchemists. Amicia wiped this blood on her once-golden dress. She had never thought of herself as a killer, and yet...

These were thoughts she would deal with later. When the night had passed and she could mourn the life she had taken. The darkness had spread in her soul and taken root in her mind, but it could be banished. Later. Until then, she had work to do.

She pushed the fear and guilt away, shoving it into a corner of her mind to rest until the right time came.

Running again, she sprinted toward the man she needed to save. The only one who had set her soul free and made her feel as though she were something more than a tinker's daughter. That she could be anything.

Amicia slid to a stop just outside the Great Hall doors. She stared up at the imposing carvings. This was the moment where she could save them all, or she could fail them again. The moment when she could finally prove herself to him, to everyone, that she would do anything for her people.

That she belonged. Even if those words hadn't been his, they haunted her still.

She placed her hands against the doors and shoved them open.

The Great Hall was covered in ice. Coated from top to bottom with the strange slickness. Alchemists lined the walls and the balcony, their dark cloaks undulating and streaking the ice with blood. The Dread filled the room, each more terrifying than the last. But they appeared to be in a line leading up to the throne where Alexandre sat. He was larger than she'd ever seen him. His horns stretching back from his skull with a dark crown lodged between them.

One of the Dread strode up to him, the first in the line, and knelt before the king. Alexandre reached out as if he would place his hand against the Dread's shoulder, only he didn't. Instead, he slit the throat of the Dread and watched as the dark blood pooled on the ground.

The lifeblood traveled up the throne and seemed to sink into Alexandre's body. As she watched, another set of horns appeared to the side of the first two.

Amicia gasped. The alchemists were turning him into even more of a monster and forcing him to sacrifice those he loved. Two birds with one stone.

They were getting the dark king they so desired and killing all the people who could convince him otherwise.

"Stop!" Her voice rang clear and true through the room. The word bounced off the icy structures and rained down upon all those in the room like snow.

Everyone paused as if time itself had stopped. She stared at the man she loved, the one who should have remembered her, and saw no recognition in his gaze. Instead, a low growl was her only response.

One of the alchemists stepped forward, only to be halted by one of the Dread. Her people wanted to see what she would do.

She planned to save them. Even if that meant sacrificing herself.

Alexandre stared her down, blood soaking his feet where he sat on the throne. The body of the Dread before him shook in death throes. Her heart stuttered at the mere thought it might be Bernard, but when she grew closer, she did not recognize the Dread's face.

No one stopped her as she knelt before the throne. Not a single alchemist approached when a wall of Dread prevented them from moving. She had the distinct feeling the entire room was holding their breath, waiting to hear what she would say.

"You don't have to do this," she said, staring up at the man she loved and seeing no one other than her Alexandre. It didn't matter he looked more monstrous than ever before. He was still hers. "Take me if you must kill someone, but leave our people alone."

He glanced at the man dying beside her. "What care do you have for them?"

"All the care I had for them when they were human. All the love I shared for every individual who is the Dread now. None of that has changed."

"And yet, you abandoned them."

"No," she replied fiercely. Amicia reached out and touched a hand to his knee, holding onto him as she would never have dared before. "No, I did not abandon you. Trickery warped my mind, but you were never far from my heart."

The red glow of his eyes died down to orange. "They were never far from your heart."

"You were never far from my heart, mon amour."

Alexandre shook his head as if clearing dark thoughts from his mind. He shook himself like a dog and leaned forward, closer to her. "A being of light such as you could never love a monster."

"A beast is no longer a monster when he is loved," she whispered. Amicia shifted closer to him, still kneeling, but both elbows braced on his knees. "Come back to me, Alexandre. I don't care what they've done to you."

A voice interrupted them, cruel and harsh from the balcony above. "You are too late, human. He has accepted the deal and will become the true King of the Dread."

She stared up at the dark waves of red. Blood dripped from the balcony in sheets of liquid, as if they knew just by her being here that their very intent was threatened.

"I'm not too late," she replied. "I would never be too late."

"Then kill the King if you must," the leader of the alchemist called out. "Try your best. But we have made him far stronger than the blade."

She turned back to Alexandre. His eyes had died down to the molten gold she knew so well. She reached out and cupped his cheeks in both her hands.

The words on her tongue became a whisper, although they rang through the room as if they were a shout. "Then it's good I've never been talented with a blade."

Amicia drew his face toward her and kissed him. She lingered on the mouth warped by fangs. She kissed away the sharp points and dulled them back to the teeth she knew and loved so dearly. Without thought, she ran her hands up his arms to the horns on his head and pressed down upon them. They shrank under her touch, flattening against a head full of curly locks.

She drew back and stared at a face kissed by the sun. No more horns, nor claws. He was a gilded, golden man staring at her with so much love in his eyes it hurt to look upon him.

Curly blond hair cascaded down his broad shoulders. Great, white wings spread out behind him.

"I love you," he said. Alexandre reached up and tucked a strand of her dark hair behind her ear. "Why are you always arriving at my chateau covered in mud?"

"I'll answer that question in a moment." She grinned at him, then leaned close for another quick kiss. "But first, I love you, too. More than I could ever express in words."

"Then let's finish what you set out to do, petite souris."

Alexandre stood, holding out his hand for her to take. Amicia let him lift her up then turned to stare at the Dread who held back the alchemists. The blood red figures were trying hard to push through their ranks, but they had created monsters stronger than themselves.

Alexandre pointed toward the beings in red, his voice thunderous and shaking the chateau. "Begone from this place, cursed creatures. You are no longer welcome here."

The leader of the alchemists stepped forward, his words a crack of lightning against the thunder. "We are not yet finished, King of the Dread!"

The knife appeared in Amicia's hand once more. The same knife she remembered leaving in Vivienne's breast. She stared down at it in shock, only to hear a voice whispering in her ear.

"You don't know what the Celestials can do. You don't know what they're capable of. He fell into temptation once, and you are nothing more than the daughter of a tinker, a peasant girl. Do you think you can hold him at bay when all his powers return?"

She knew it was the voice of the alchemist, although it sounded like her father. Amicia swallowed and tried to release her hold on the knife. The handle burned against her fingers, fusing into the flesh.

"Kill him now, or all will be lost."

The room warped. Twisting to the side like she was looking

through a broken mirror. Alexandre stood before her, all the other Dread as well. But the figures in red... she was meant to be looking for figures in red.

Her head swum as though she had drank too much wine. She couldn't quite see straight, or maybe it was that everyone in the room wasn't formed correctly anymore. Why couldn't she see?

"Kill him, Amicia. Do it now." The voice whispered in her ear, but this time she knew what to do.

She turned on her heel, lifted the blade, and struck out blindly.

The thick blade sank into flesh, digging deep into the heart of the alchemist standing behind her. Her world settled, and she stared into the vacant, flat eyes.

He let out a soft burbled word, perhaps a half hearted curse he couldn't give life. He reached up and wrapped his fingers around hers. The blood covering both their hands was too slick, however, and he dropped to the side in death throes.

She had no time to apologize or realize she had killed a man. Instead, Alexandre stepped forward and wrapped her hands in his.

The blood disappeared underneath his gilded fingers. Amicia stared up into his livid gaze and watched as he turned to glare at the remaining alchemists.

"I said, begone."

A gust of wind punctuated his words, then thunder rocked through the Great Hall. The marble beneath her feet cracked and split, fissures racing toward the alchemists. Some did not move in time and were swallowed by the sudden gaping wound in the middle of the chateau.

Her jaw fell open. How was he doing this? She glanced up at him to see a grin on his face.

He winked. "We're not done yet. Look."

Amicia turned back to their people and saw a gold, glittering light pass over the nearest Dread. The monstrous visage fell away to reveal a man she'd seen once before. The baker in Little Marsh, with a smudge of flour on his nose.

The light chased down each of the Dread, turning them back into weavers, farmers, fishermen. Over and over again, it revealed more of her people until she could only see hundreds of humans. People she loved and had never forgotten.

The cracked floor surrounded their people, and the alchemists fled in the wake of a Celestial's power.

"Alexandre," she said. "You've saved them."

"No, petite souris, mon amour." He drew her into his arms, tucking her against his heart and squeezing her tight. "We did this together."

"Now what?"

He reached between them and tilted her chin up so she could look at him. "I want to show you something. One more surprise."

"Should we leave them so soon?"

His gaze swept over their people before he nodded. "They know the way. And we will not be long. But first, I have much to explain."

Amicia only had a moment to nod before he spread his wings and, together, they flew out one of the broken windows into the frigid air outside.

CHAPTER 37

*A*micia stared at the golden plates of his wings, the individual feathers as they worked together to keep them aloft. She'd never thought metal could fly. It must have been too heavy and yet... here they were. Aloft.

His wings flexed with each movement. His strong arms were wrapped around her, holding her against his heart as though she were the most precious thing in the world. And, for the time being, she felt very much as though she were.

Amicia rested her head on his shoulder, breathing in the clean scent of him. Before, he'd always smelled like earth and metal. But now, he smelled like a fresh spring in the mountains. Clean. Welcoming. Comforting.

"We're almost there," he said, the base of his voice rumbling against her chest.

"I'm not afraid."

He chuckled. "Of course, you aren't. When are you ever afraid, petite souris?"

She could list a hundred times when he and his people had made her afraid. When she'd cowered in the walls of the chateau because she didn't know what they might do to her.

Things had changed so much since she had come here. Now, she had a people. Now, she had a man she loved more than life itself. Fear wasn't an option when she was no longer alone.

Alexandre shifted her in his arms, and then she felt him settle onto something solid. But that wasn't possible. They were so far in the air, there wasn't any way for them to be standing on anything. Even the mountains didn't reach this far.

She opened her eyes and glanced around them, staring at wispy mist of clouds. The rolling columns appeared as though they were solid, but she knew it was impossible to stand upon them. However, much of what she believed to be true of science she had found she needed to let go.

"We're here," Alexandre said. His arms tightened around her before releasing her from his arms.

Amicia let out a squeaking sound of fear, one she'd never heard come out of her mouth, and one she hoped to never hear again. She frantically grasped onto his neck and held herself tight against him. "Don't drop me! Are you mad?"

Again, that ridiculous chuckle rumbled against her ear before he set about unlatching her arms from around his neck. "Have you not seen enough to trust me, Amicia?"

She'd seen enough from Alexandre the Dread, the beast who looked into her eyes so soulfully. But she felt as though she didn't know this strange, golden man who had carried her into the skies.

Amicia released her hold from around his neck and let her feet fall to the clouds. She winced before they touched. She would fall right through and then what would he say? Believe a little harder?

The soles of her feet touched the clouds and held. In fact, there was a strange solidity just underneath her feet. Almost as though there were a floor holding her up.

She stomped first one, then the other foot, before looking up at Alexandre with a raised brow. "Where are we?"

He had stopped looking at her. Instead, he gazed past her toward something behind Amicia. "Home," he replied with reverence in his voice.

Swallowing hard, she turned around and didn't know what to expect. Nothing in her human brain could have cooked up what magnificence she stared upon.

It was a city made of the sun. Golden columns like the pipes of an organ stretched high into the sky. Gleaming glass reflected the sun in her eyes until she could barely stand to look upon the metallic structure that was nothing like any castle she'd seen before.

Amicia waited for Celestials to burst out of the windows and glide toward them on gilded wings. When she would finally see the city for what it was, but nothing happened.

She held her breath for what felt like ages until she finally released it on a sad sigh. "Where is everyone?" she asked.

Alexandre's gold eyes had turned sad. His wings were held tight against his body as he had when he was one of the Dread. He took a step forward, then another.

The clothing he once wore as the King of the Dread looked out of place on him now. Moth-eaten clothing too drab to cover the body of one who was so wondrous. So immaculate. And yet, he wore it well.

The smooth planes of his chest gleamed in the sunlight just like the city that had once been his home. His biceps were flexed, the tight muscles of his stomach solid with every movement. He was so much like her version of the man she had known, and yet, so different at the same time.

Perhaps she would always miss the horns that had once graced his head, or the long tangled matts of hair swept back from his face.

"Alexandre?" she asked again. "Where is everyone?"

"Your little book could only tell you so much," he murmured.

"We were sent to help the humans. All of us. Every single one. Some fell in the war when we tried to convince the humans we could benefit them. You were scared of us, at first."

Staring at him now, with wings dipped in gold and a body so much larger than any human man she'd ever seen, Amicia could understand their fear. She gulped and inquired, "There was a war?"

"Still is in some parts of this world. A war you and I cannot stop no matter how hard we try." He turned to her and reached out a hand. "Come with me, Amicia. Let me show you who I am."

She wasn't certain it was such a good idea. Her footprints would dirty the steps of the castle and she would be little more than a mouse once more. And yet, she still took his hand. If Alexandre had taught her anything, it was that he would never let her be anything less than herself.

His hand was warm in her grip. No claws scratched at her wrists, and yet, the callouses felt familiar. She stared down at the human-like hand with gold nails and smiled. "We were scared of you at first?"

"Very much so." He squeezed her hand in his and drew her toward the city. The clouds drifted away from their feet, revealing a gold pathway that led them. Straight and narrow. "But we were rather persistent. Hence the war."

"Who won?"

He shook his head sadly, staring at the abandoned city in the sky. "Neither side. The humans accepted the Celestials could help them. But we lost many of our people."

"I can't imagine anyone capable of killing someone like you or your kind." Amicia could only imagine the battles, the way the Celestials had swooped down from the sky like the Dread, only infinitely more powerful. She shivered. "It must have been a massacre."

"It was," Alexandre agreed. "But there were many more humans. No matter how many we fought, there were always more to take their place. There are so few of us left the humans were perfectly happy to leave us alone after that. And we helped their lands prosper. To grow."

Amicia could understand that. She had only seen Little Marsh as an idyllic life, when the history books accounted for famines and disease. Those stories had always confused her. How could any city have disease when people so rarely got sick?

More questions needed to be answered, however. "How were you cursed?" she asked, pausing in their walk to the city. "If everything was so well, then... how?"

Alexandre licked his lips and narrowed his eyes, as though he were trying to think hard about her question. As if he still couldn't quite remember it. "I... I don't remember. I know it was the alchemists. The moment you said you loved me, that I wasn't a monster, I remembered so much in that instant. It was as if you had cleared my mind of fog I hadn't even realized was there. But there is still much I've lost."

"The book said the alchemists were the ones who did it."

"I wouldn't be surprised. They were controlling me as no one else has ever done. They followed us, you see. When we first came here, they are all that is evil to our good. They would destroy this world and then leave it for another if they could. I suspect that is what they planned to use me for."

Amicia pulled her hands from his and tucked them behind her back. She began to pace a large circle around him. Her father used to do this when he was thinking, and now she understood why. It helped.

Clearing her throat, she thought aloud, "The alchemists didn't put up much of a fight when you banished them. That's concerning me."

"I agree."

"Why didn't they fight? If they were controlling you so thoroughly, why wouldn't they have at least attempted to sway us a little more? Why wouldn't they have attempted to silence me?"

Alexandre snapped his fingers and spread his wings wide. "There are more kingdoms."

"And?"

"And there are more Celestials there. If this curse wasn't limited to only me, then losing one Dread isn't the end. They could flee to another one of those kingdoms and continue on with their plan."

"But what is their plan?"

Alexandre turned on his heel and strode away from her, toward the city. She chased after him. Gold passed by her with every step, clouds disappearing to give way to intricate sculptures of winged beings guarding every pathway toward smaller castles where others must have lived.

Finally, they made it to the city center where Alexandre gestured for her to sit with him on a bench made of solid gold.

She gingerly sat down beside him. They faced what looked like a cliff, and yet it was simply the end of the city. The clouds parted and revealed all of Little Marsh below her. The city where small puffs of smoke could be seen even this high up. Not from embers or ash, but from people returning to their homes and beginning to pick up the pieces.

"They wanted me to accept my position as King of all the Dread," he murmured. "At the time, I thought they meant only those who I had turned. But I think it meant more."

"What would be more?"

"The Celestials as well. As King, I could force them together once more. I could turn them all into monsters equally powerful like myself. The alchemists want to summon the end of the world so they can remake it in their own name."

Amicia swallowed. "That sounds bad."

EMMA HAMM

"It would be the end of all we know."

She reached out and placed a hand atop his on his knee. "Then we must stop it. We'll reach out to your brethren, tell them what's happening."

"We cannot. It was part of our pact long ago. To rule the humans, we swore an oath we would never speak to each other again."

Amicia let out a frustrated huff. "Oaths can be broken."

"Not this one." Alexandre turned to her and lifted both their hands. He cupped her cheek, so gentle and kind. He stroked a thumb along her jaw. "You are so giving. So kind in everything you do, I aspire to be like you someday, mon amour."

"My love," she whispered. "I could get used to you saying that."

"As could I." He tugged her closer and pressed their lips together in a kiss. A promise. "I love you, Amicia. We will weather this storm together and pray my brothers and sisters will do the same."

"Perhaps we'll check on them?"

"Oui, that we can do." He pulled back to smile down at her, eyes crinkled at the edges and golden hair drifting in front of his gaze. "Until then, I say we live."

"Shall we rebuild the city?"

"Yes, that."

She grinned. "Shall we adventure through the kingdom?"

"Together, we may do whatever you wish."

There was only one more thing to ask him then, and just the asking of it made her quake. "Do you promise to love me forever, then?"

"Oh, much longer than forever," he murmured. Alexandre dug his hand into the hair at the nape of her neck, drawing her head closer to him until she could taste his wild breath on her tongue. "You are my sun, moon, and stars. My reason for life, until death do we part."

She kissed him then and felt every fiber of her being fill with a light that took seed deep in her chest. In that moment, Amicia was not just a woman.

She was every atom of a falling star who had raced an entire lifetime to be reunited with the light she had lost.

THE STORY CONTINUES...

*T*urn the page for a sneak peak of Emerald Rose! Preorder now!

* * *

"Parry."

Danielle shifted her weight, lifting the heavy sword across her body as though she were trying to stop someone from attacking her. She paused for a moment, closing her eyes to imagine the person attacking her.

Armor covered his body. Heavy, silver, it would impede his movements more than her own supple leather. Although his strikes would be stronger, she was faster.

"Lunge."

She twisted the sword in her hands then bolted forward. The sword tip struck her imaginary foe, but slid off his breastplate. She'd have to do better than that if she wanted to ensure he was dead by the time she left.

"Counter."

Her feet tangled together as she tried to sidestep the imagined attack. Danielle tried to correct, but couldn't stop herself from falling onto her bottom in the dirt.

"Damn it," she muttered, remaining seated for a moment and staring up at the clouds which passed by overhead.

Fighting looked so much easier when the soldiers did it in the yard. They all fought with each other, not even imagined opponents, and their feet rarely tripped them up. Some of them ended up in the dirt. But it was usually because they were put on their ass by someone else.

Not by themselves.

Groaning, she rolled back onto her feet and lifted the sword in her hands once more. She continued through the movements she had observed from her room in the palace.

All this would be much easier if she had someone else teaching her. Danielle couldn't see what she looked like as she parried, let alone thrusted the sword. Her form was probably atrocious, and that was why she kept falling down.

She could only sneak into the mirrored ballroom so many times before one of the servants would see her. They would inevitably tell her father, and then this would all be over. He didn't want her to learn how to fight. He wanted her to be the little princess everyone thought she should be.

As she practiced the movements, she grunted out the words that haunted her sleep. "Danielle, fix your skirts. Sit up straighter. Smile, the people will think you're mean."

If one more person told her to smile, she would run away into the forests and never return. She could survive on her own!

The imaginary attacker shifted in her vision. Danielle countered, her feet following the path they were supposed to this time. With a shout, she struck out with her blade in an arc that would have beheaded any man who stood before her.

Deep in a lunge, she paused. Her thighs shook with exertion but she felt *good*. She had used her body as most people did every single day. Sitting on a plush cushion only made her feel ill. She wanted to be outside in the sun but sunlight made freckles appear on her nose and no foreign prince wanted a princess with spots.

At least, everyone claimed princes hated freckles.

"Find a prince, Danielle, and you'll be happy for the rest of your life." She sang the words then crossed her eyes and let the sword fall into the grass around her legs.

Finding a prince wouldn't make her happy. Finding a prince would make everything worse. They'd have opinions, tell her what to do with the country which was her god given right to rule alone.

Even her father agreed. She would become the maiden ruler of Hollow Hill. But only when she had a husband to "help".

Marriage wouldn't help. It would distract because eventually she would need to procreate. The mere idea made her stomach clench and gorge rise in her throat. She wasn't old enough for children, and she didn't want to go through the pain. Not yet. Maybe never.

Sweat dripped down her brow and stung the corners of her eyes. She rubbed them then stared back at the sky, tracking the sun so she wouldn't be late to return.

This was meant to be a trip gathering herbs for the local herbalists. She was certain they wouldn't tell her father she hadn't delivered anything. And hadn't for the past five times she'd used the excuse.

Eventually, that one would dry up.

But she loved coming here alone. To this field in the middle of the forest which surrounded Hollow Hill. Green grass filled a small circle where none of the trees had grown. Stones encircled the small area, and a brook babbled at the other side.

She made her way to the running water, sunlight sparkling across its surface and making spots dance in her vision. The water was crystal clear and tasted like perfumed air. Danielle had drunk from its waters so many times she could hardly count them.

Her mother used to bring her here. She sank down in the plush moss at the edge of the water and dunked her hands into the stream. Icy water made her fingers sting.

She lifted a handful to her mouth and sipped at it, drinking deeply and trying to banish thoughts of the court. That's what her mother had always done here, after all. They would come to this field together, pick flowers, laugh at all the things the courtesans had done.

Now, her mother didn't laugh at all.

Frowning, Danielle stared down at her reflection in the water and sighed. She'd pulled her long, blonde hair back from her face severely. A pretty face, although one which looked better smiling than it did frowning. Her father said she looked too aggressive when she wasn't smiling.

He was probably right. Danielle's lips were a little too thin, and when she pressed them together, they looked downright shrewish. Her brows arched too much, making her look as though she were judging everyone who stood before her. Her jaw was too square, her cheekbones too high.

For all her looks, she was made to be a warrior. She should have been fighting at the forefront of battle.

But they couldn't afford to lose the princess of Hollow Hill. So instead of being where she wanted to be, learning how to fight with the other soldiers, Danielle was here. Hiding in the forest, hoping no one found out she'd stolen a sword from the barracks.

She didn't hear the bushes rustling until it was far too late. Perhaps if she'd kept her sword, she might have been more prepared. Just having the weapon made her aware of her surroundings.

As it was, Danielle didn't notice something was even approaching her until she heard a branch snapping. A dark shape emerged behind her.

Her mind couldn't quite process what it looked like, even as the stream warped its reflection. Large wings stretched from its back, horns reached above his head like a demon from the storybooks.

She didn't react. She froze in place because there couldn't be a monster looming above her like some kind of horrific nightmare come to life. Her mind must have conjured her worries into reality.

It wasn't possible the creature behind her was reaching for her. She couldn't believe it.

A clawed hand grasped the back of her neck. She had a moment to gasp in a lungful of air before it pushed her down and dunked her head into the stream.

Cold water washed over her face and up to her neck. She burst into action, wrapping her hands around the strong fingers which only clasped harder. Claws dug at the soft skin of her neck and she saw blood bloom in the water from her forehead. A rock had scratched it, although she couldn't feel the pain.

She scrabbled at the creature's hand, trying hard to draw blood of her own. But it did not release its hold upon the column of her throat. If anything, it only squeezed harder until stars sparked in her vision and she couldn't think of anything but death.

Was this how the princess of Hollow Hill died? Killed by a monster in the forest no one would ever know existed?

She wouldn't allow it. Danielle forced her body to relax and at the moment when it thought she had drowned, she kicked out with her legs. One foot connected hard with its knee. The creature let out a grunt she heard even underwater and released its hold just long enough for her to wiggle free from its grasp.

Dragging herself across the stream, she scrambled to the other side and rolled onto her back.

It didn't give her time to escape. The creature gave one heavy beat of its wings and then it was on top of her again. This time, it wrapped both hands around her throat and squeezed hard, pushing her into the ground with its weight.

Danielle held onto its hands, but she couldn't force it to release her. It sat upon her, straddling her waist and effectively pinning her down.

She couldn't move.

She couldn't free herself from its grasp.

Wide eyed and terrified of the death which awaited her, she stared up at the pale creature. The wings she'd seen in the reflection of the stream were even more formidable this close.

Pale, almost ghostly, its wings were ragged with holes and faint white scars creating a lace pattern over the thin, violet membrane. One of its horns had been broken at some point. The jagged edges had long since healed, yet the rough, half horn still looked painful.

The most eerie thing was that its face still looked very

human. A man's face, though grey in tone and wrong, stared down at her. His expression was twisted with aggression and hatred, yet familiar.

He might have been a man she would see in the street if not for his colored skin and fangs which poked out from his bottom jaw. How strange to be killed by a creature she never knew existed. That no one knew existed.

With the same suddenness as he attacked, the creature loosened his grip on her throat. He stared at the forest with a frown.

Danielle gasped in as much air as possible, certain he would squeeze again. His claws still grazed her neck with clear intent. If she made a sound, he could rip out her throat with those claws.

The ringing in her ears stopped, replaced by the sound of thundering hooves approaching through the forest. *Guards.* Likely sent to search for her by her father, which meant this creature recognized the sound.

How did he know what horse hooves sounded like?

And it was certainly male. The creature leaned away from her, hands still placed at her neck, but she could now see its torso. Broad shoulders, bare of even a stitch of clothing. The flat planes of his chest rippled with muscle. He was stronger than any soldier she'd seen in the yard. His muscles weren't puffy like the human men she'd seen. Instead, they were wiry and strong.

She swallowed hard through the pain of her throat. A dribble of spit slid down her cheek but she didn't dare move. He stared intensely at the forest.

Perhaps he knew if the guards found her dead body, they would kill him. It didn't matter who he was or why he was there. Ten guards must be able to take on a creature such as this. Although, with wings, he must be able to fly.

The quietest whimpers escaped her lips. The creature flicked his gaze to her, a censoring expression clearly meant to warn her.

"Please," she whispered. "I don't want to die."

Danielle didn't know the reason the creature had attacked her. If he knew guards were dangerous, then he couldn't be some kind of forest creature they'd never seen before. And he wore clothing, she could feel fabric pressed against her belly where her shirt had ridden up. Animals didn't wear clothing.

The hooves were approaching, and the creature had to make a choice. He leaned close to her, his lips twisted in a snarl, staring into her eyes with so much hatred it made her heart hurt.

He dragged his claws down her throat, the fine points pricking her skin. She didn't feel warm blood, but she knew if he hadn't broken skin, he had left welts.

His hot breath fanned over her mouth. Great puffs of air as he snarled, then released her neck to slap his hands onto the ground at either side of her head. She flinched, closing her eyes and accepting her end.

But death did not greet her on this day.

She was buffeted by a wind stronger than any she'd felt before. When she opened her eyes, the creature was gone.

Danielle sucked in a deeper breath, terrified, her thoughts racing. Why had it left her? It had attacked her, it meant to kill her, and yet the sound of hooves made it leave her alone?

She scrambled toward the forest as the hoofbeats grew ever closer. They couldn't see her like this. Soaking wet, clothing askew, bruises around her throat. What would they think?

Likely that she needed to be dragged back to her father and married off to avoid a scandal. No one would believe her if she said a monster crawled its way out of the forest. Hollow Hill was the safest place in the Kingdom of Ember, now that Little Marsh had fallen. She'd be dubbed a liar and married to the oldest prince they could find.

So, instead of begging the guards for help as she wanted to, Danielle hid herself in the bushes at the edge of the forest. She watched the guards ride by with their golden saddles and plumed armor.

She pressed her hands to her lips to still the sobs shaking her shoulders as the anxiety and fear pressed down upon her. But the creature had let her live.

Now, she just had to make it back to the palace without it trying to kill her again.

ACKNOWLEDGMENTS

There are too many people to thank for this book. An author's nightmare is having a preorder up and then an editing mishap that causes either a cancellation, or putting on your big girl panties and finding a way to make a book happen.

When I realized this book might need to be delayed, I almost had a breakdown.

But then... You happened.

Readers, just like you, reached out in DROVES to make sure that this book was exactly how it should be.

Authors like J.M. Butler, Nicolette Andrews, and Miranda Honfleur helped edit.

Over 50 beta readers assisted in catching errors.

My heart is overflowing with appreciation. Love. Adoration. Too many words to count.

So this book is for you.

All of you.

ABOUT THE AUTHOR

USAToday Bestselling Author Emma Hamm grew up in a small town surrounded by trees and animals. She writes strong, confident, powerful women who aren't afraid to grow and make mistakes. Her books will always be a little bit feminist, and are geared towards empowering both men and women to be comfortable in their own skin.

CPSIA information can be obtained
at www.ICGtesting.com
Printed in the USA
BVHW082236150820
586526BV00003B/135